P9-CDW-679

KGB agents who were responsible for initiating the B-2 hijacking.

Irina Rykhov, a strikingly beautiful young woman with sensuous hazel eyes, and Aleksey Pankyev, a dashing and experienced agent, had spent the previous six months systematically organizing the operation. They were both distinguished graduates in military intelligence from the prestigious Bukharin Academy, and had worked as a team for more than three years. They had been directly responsible for obtaining the classified Trident D-5 missile specifications.

Now, Levchenko thought as he adjusted the radio volume, Rykhov can execute the final step to carry the hijacking to completion. The Motherland would have an American B-2 Stealth bomber in a matter of weeks.

PROLOGUE

EDWARDS AIR FORCE BASE, CALIFORNIA
6:50 A.M.

Gennadi Levchenko leaned against the side of his Lincoln
town car, braced his elbows, then stared at the B-2 through
his binoculars. The senior KGB officer, dressed in khaki-
colored slacks, brown loafers, and a green windbreaker,
blended in with the throngs of spectators watching the Stealth
bomber accelerate down the runway on one of its routine test
flights.

Levchenko, shivering slightly in the brisk morning air,
followed the takeoff and initial climb. He lowered the binoculars, zipped his jacket, and got back inside the warm,
idling automobile. The KGB Stealth project officer was feeling more confident by the minute. After waiting eight months
and enduring many arduous trips to Moscow, Levchenko had
received permission straight from Golodnikov, chief of the
KGB, to commandeer a Stealth bomber.

The crowd returned to their vehicles, and as the cars in
front of him began to move, Levchenko placed the Lincoln
in gear. He had a meeting in San Bernardino with the two

to absolute power, decided to implement a bold plan of his own. The first step was to get his hands on the Americans' B-2 bomber. The ambitious operation, worked out in secret by the chief during November 1989, was an intricate plan to acquire the radar-evading aircraft, reverse engineer the B-2, then manufacture clones when the military regained power.

Golodnikov was confident that he had thought of a political escape route for every contingency. If the plan succeeded, the chief would would be held in high esteem by the leaders of the revived Communist party. If it failed, he would deny all knowledge of the operation.

The KGB Directorate, proceeding cautiously, had closely monitored the B-2 budget reductions. The Russian contingent in Washington, D.C., had lobbied tenaciously to either cancel the B-2 program or limit the number of aircraft produced each year. When production of the Stealth bomber was curtailed sharply, the KGB chief decided to take advantage of the situation. Golodnikov could now count on the American Stealth program to remain stagnant, and a vast strategic advantage would thereby be gained for the Motherland.

The 249-member committee had agreed to the president's plan to discard the Communist party's seven decades of monopoly on power. Gorbachev, arguing persuasively for a step toward democracy, had opened the door to political competition.

The astonishing shift in the dominance of power had shaken many hard-line conservatives. The idea of casting aside total power and risking their positions under a system of political pluralism frightened the party members. Insurgents within the Central Committee, who had grudgingly voted for the multiparty plan, were confident that the large core of Communist hard-liners would win control again when the new system collapsed in anarchy. The Soviet military, led by deep-rooted conservatives, had the raw power to crush any political opposition.

Gorbachev, moving swiftly, convinced the Congress of People's Deputies to grant him unprecedented broad powers to save the Soviet Union from total collapse. With the world looking on, the Communist leaders watched in humiliation as the influence of the Politburo was methodically shifted to a Cabinet style of presidential council. The key members of the council included the defense, finance, and foreign ministers, along with the head of the Komitet Gosudarstvennoi Bezopasnosti (KGB, the Committee for State Security).

The director of the KGB, feeling his power and authority slowly being eroded, had quietly aligned with hard-core critics who believed in a revolution from below. Many key hard liners, watching the riots grow more violent, had been afraid that the expanding chaos would lead to civil war in the Soviet Union.

The growing number of discontented civilian and military leaders had discussed a conservative backlash to end *demokratizatsia*. A number of expelled Politburo members, filled with rage and embarrassment, had openly supported a military coup to quickly restore stability in the Soviet Union.

The KGB chief, Vladimir Golodnikov, who was convinced that the military leaders would reinstate the Communist party

INTRODUCTION

THE SOVIET UNION

The Soviet economy had been disintegrating in the ruins of *perestroika* and *glasnost*.

Industrial growth had mired at less than 1 percent, and food production had fallen 32 percent short of the nation's needs. Absenteeism had become rampant as thousands of workers abandoned their jobs, shouting, "We pretend to work while they pretend to pay us."

National polls conducted during January 1990 had indicated that 97 percent of the Soviet citizens felt that the economic situation was critical, if not completely out of control. The nation's patience, after years of perestroika, had run short. The domestic crisis threatened both the integrity and the political stability of the state.

The president of the USSR, beset with national animosities and Kremlin challenges, had become desperate in his attempt to hold the disintegrating Communist system together. Mikhail Gorbachev, when faced with increasing pressure to revive the moribund economy, had called a plenary session of the Communist party's Central Committee during February 1990.

RCS Radar Cross Section.

RIO Radar Intercept Officer; naval flight officer in backseat of F-14 Tomcat and F-4 Phantom aircraft.

ROE Rules Of Engagement.

SAC Strategic Air Command.

SAM Surface-to-Air Missile.

SAR Search And Rescue.

Section takeoff Two aircraft taking off in formation.

Sidewinder AIM-9 heat-seeking air-to-air missile.

Sparrow AIM-7 radar-guided air-to-air missile.

SUCAP Surface Combat Air Patrol.

Tally Derivative of tallyho; target in sight.

Tomcat F-14 fighter aircraft; also called "turkey."

Trap Arrested landing on aircraft carrier.

Unload Release pressure on aircraft control stick to ease g load.

VFR Visual Flight Rules.

V/STOL Very Short Takeoff and Landing aircraft.

Viking S-3 ASW aircraft; also called Hoover.

Vulture's Row Observation deck on superstructure (island) of carrier.

IFR Instrument Flight Rules.

Intruder A-6 attack aircraft.

Knot One nautical mile per hour. A nautical mile equals 1.1 statute miles.

LAMPS Light Airborne Multipurpose System; shipborne helicopter used for antisubmarine warfare.

LCAC Air-cushioned landing aircraft.

Loose Deuce Navy and Marine Corps tactical fighter formation.

LSO Landing Signal Officer. Squadron pilot responsible for assisting other aviators onto flight deck of aircraft carrier; also called Paddles.

Mach Term, named for physicist Ernst Mach, used to describe speed of an object in relation to the speed of sound.

MAD Magnetic Anomaly Detector, used to locate submerged submarines.

Main mount Aircraft main landing gear.

Marshall Aircraft holding pattern behind aircraft carrier.

MILSTAR Advanced military satellite communications system.

NATOPS Naval Aviation Training and Operations manual. Provides rules and regulations for safe and proper operations of all Navy and Marine Corps aircraft and helicopters.

NEACP National Emergency Airborne Command Post (KNEECAP)

Nugget Rookie naval aviator.

PRI-FLY Control tower on aircraft carrier.

Phoenix AIM-54 long-range air-to-air missile.

Plane Guard Helicopter assigned to search and rescue during carrier flight operations.

Push Time Designated time for aircraft to start approach to carrier.

RAM Radar-Absorbent Material.

Ramp Aft end of flight deck; rounddown.

CAG Commander of the Air Group; oversees all squadrons embarked on a carrier.

CAP Combat Air Patrol.

CATCC Carrier Air Traffic Control Center (Cat-see).

Check Six Refers to visual observation behind an aircraft. Fighter pilots must check behind them constantly to ensure that enemy aircraft are not in an attack position.

CIC Combat Information Center—central battle management post in naval surface combat.

CINCLANT Commander In Chief of Atlantic Fleet.

CINCPAC Commander In Chief of Pacific Fleet.

CNO Chief of Naval Operations.

Dash Two Second plane in a two-aircraft section; the wingman.

Departure Refers to an aircraft departing from controlled flight.

DME Distance Measuring Equipment. Distance provided to a pilot in nautical miles from a known point.

ELINT Electronic Intelligence.

Feet Dry / Wet Pilot radio call indicating a position over land/water.

FOD Foreign Object Damage to a jet engine.

Fox One/Two/Three Pilot radio calls indicating the firing of a Sparrow, Sidewinder, or Phoenix missle.

Furball Multiaircraft fighter engagement.

G-force Force pressed on a body by changes in velocity, measured in increments of earth gravity.

G-LOC G-induced Loss of Consciousness.

Gomers Air combat adversaries.

Hawkeye E-2C early warning and control aircraft; radar eyes of the fleet.

Hornet F/A-18 fighter/attack aircraft.

Hot pump Refueling aircraft while engine is running.

ICS Intercom System in cockpits of multiseat aircraft.

IFF Military transponder used to identify aircraft (Identification Friend or Foe).

Glossary

ACM Air Combat Maneuvering; dogfighting.
ACO Air Control Officer.
ADIZ Air Defense Identification Zone.
ADVCAP Advanced Capability.
AEGIS Air Defense System on *Ticonderoga* Class Cruisers.
ALCM Air Launched Cruise Missles.
Alpha Strike All-out carrier air wing attack.
ASW Antisubmarine Warfare.
AWACS Airborne Warning And Control System.
Ball The optical landing device on an aircraft carrier. Also referred to as "meatball."
BARCAP Barrier Combat Air Patrol, used to protect vessels at sea.
Blue Water Operations Carrier flight operations beyond the range of land bases.
Bogie Unidentified or enemy aircraft.
Bolter Carrier landing attempt in which the tail hook misses the arresting wire, necessitating a go-around.
Bow Front end of ship.
Bridge Command post in a ship superstructure.

Acknowledgments

There are several special friends to whom I am grateful for their help in developing *Shadow Flight*. I would like to thank Lt. Col. John Flaherty, USAF (Ret.); Larry Hodgden; Maj. Ted Hobart, U.S. Marine Corps; Col. William Peyton Lehman, USAF (Ret.); Vern Schubarth; and former Marine fighter pilot Ray Milsap.

As always, a special thanks to Bob Kane of Presidio Press, who has guided me with friendship and wisdom.

Hats off to Presidio Press editor Adele Horwitz, who again spent endless hours providing a steady hand on the helm.

Dictators ride to and fro upon tigers which they dare not dismount. And the tigers are getting hungry.

WINSTON SPENCER CHURCHILL

Shadow Flight is dedicated to my wife, Jeannie, who has patiently supported my efforts with wit and constructive critiques; and to my grandmother, Grace Weber, for providing the inspiration to meet challenges and forge ahead in my endeavors.

This Jove Book contains the complete text of the original hardcover
edition. It has been completely reset in a typeface designed for easy
reading, and was printed from new film.

SHADOW FLIGHT

A Jove Book / published by arrangement with
Presidio Press

PRINTING HISTORY
Presidio Press edition published 1990
Jove edition / August 1991

ISBN: 0-515-10660-7

Jove Books are published by The Berkley Publishing Group,
200 Madison Avenue, New York, New York 10016.
The name "JOVE" and the "J" logo
are trademarks belonging to Jove Publications, Inc.

PRINTED IN THE UNITED STATES OF AMERICA

10 9 8 7 6 5 4 3 2 1

Joe Weber

SHADOW FLIGHT

JOVE BOOKS, NEW YORK

CHAPTER ONE

ON BOARD SHADOW 37

The Northrop B-2 banked gently to the left, then returned to level flight, as U.S. Air Force Lt. Col. Charles E. Matthews scanned the clouds below his "invisible" bomber. A tall, ruggedly handsome man of thirty-six, Matthews unzipped the top of his flight suit, stretched the underlying turtleneck, and rubbed his irritated skin.

"Shadow Three Seven, Mystic," drawled a deep voice with a southern twang.

"Three Seven," replied the Stealth's copilot, Maj. Paul Tyler Evans.

"Ghost Two Five is closing from your eight o'clock, three miles," responded the airborne controller in the orbiting Boeing E-3C AWACS. The four-engine warning and control aircraft, operating from the 552d AWAC Wing at Tinker Air Force Base, Oklahoma, was 115 miles southwest of the B-2.

Evans keyed his radio mike, heard the voice scrambler hum, then spoke. "We've got a radar lock."

The copilot, a recently qualified B-2 aircraft commander,

watched the radar display for a few seconds, then keyed his mike again. "Should have a visual shortly."

"Concur, Three Seven," the airborne warning and control officer replied. "Ghost Two Five will be up your frequency in fifteen seconds."

Chuck Matthews glanced at his copilot, then back to the civilian tech-rep occupying the cramped third seat. The new bomber, after final air force testing, would be configured for a two-man flight crew.

Shadow 37, the sixth B-2 off the Northrop assembly line, was undergoing a series of technical evaluations before final acceptance by the Strategic Air Command (SAC). For the present, the aircraft had been fitted with three crew seats.

The subcontractor-supplied electronics specialist was responsible for certification of a half-dozen electronic warfare systems. He checked the laser radar and the infrared detectors, then adjusted the covert strike radar.

"Ready, Larry?" Matthews asked the slight, bespectacled man in the aft seat.

"All set, colonel. Avionics automation up," Lawrence M. Simmons answered nervously, trying to quell his anxiety. He could feel his pulse racing as he contemplated executing his mission. The dimmed cockpit lights masked the tension on his face. Frail, prematurely gray at thirty-two, Simmons knew instinctively that after today his life would never be the same. He would finally receive the respect he deserved. He hoped that the other two crew members had not noticed his shaking hands.

Chuck Matthews, aircraft commander of the advanced technology bomber, checked the bright radar screen, then keyed his mike. "Ghost Two Five," Matthews paused, glancing over his left shoulder through the cockpit side window, "we have a radar lock at our eight o'clock, two and a half miles."

The radio scrambler hummed as a new voice, crisp and articulate, sounded in the helmets of the Stealth crew. "That's us, Shadow," responded the aircraft commander of the Rockwell B-1B strategic bomber. "Are you on top?"

"That's affirm, Ghost Two Five," Matthews answered quietly, searching visually for their teammate. "We show you out of thirty-three point two. You should break out in a couple hundred feet."

"Roger," the B-1B pilot radioed, still flying in instrument conditions.

Both air force aircraft, although different in appearance, size, and mission capability, would be operating as a team during the joint United States/Canadian forces Operation Veil. The purpose of the operation was to evaluate each bomber's ability to penetrate random radar defenses, survive the simulated bombing raid, then safely egress from the target area.

The new Stealth bomber continued to be a controversial subject on Capitol Hill, openly criticized by various law-makers. Most of the political opposition centered around the diminishing Soviet threat, along with the procurement cost of the Northrop B-2. Not lost in the controversy, and discounting cost overruns, was the undeniable fact that Soviet leaders had been frightened by the supersecret advanced technology bomber.

The outdated B-52 bomber had a large radar cross section (RCS) of approximately 1,080 square feet. Soviet air defense radar systems could locate the aging craft hundreds of miles from any intended destination.

The Rockwell B-1B, with engines mounted at the far end of long, curving inlet ducts, presented an RCS of less than 11 square feet. Advanced Soviet radar units, airborne and on the surface, could still provide a minimal amount of warning time against the B-1Bs.

As shocking as the B-1B radar cross section news had been for the Russians, the RCS report on the B-2 had been devastating. The dreaded Stealth strategic bomber had an RCS the size of a small bird. Soviet radar experts, using small drones to duplicate the radar cross section of the B-2, had confirmed that their long-wave radars were incapable of detecting the Stealth bomber. The Russian radar sites KNIFE RESTS and TALL KINGS glimpsed the intruders occasionally but could not track the aircraft at long range. When the stealth decoys closed on the long-wave sites, the radar units lost the drones completely.

The Kremlin military planners knew that the "invisible" B-2 could become their Trojan horse. An unseen, undetectable, airborne nuclear nightmare. Thwarting the Stealth bomber would be akin to sparring with an invisible opponent.

A tight cadre of top Russian scientists and technicians, along with their military counterparts, had worked feverishly to develop a similar stealth aircraft. The Soviets had discovered the basic technological ingredients—carbon fiber and composite materials—to make an aircraft invisible, but the final solution had evaded even the brightest of the distinguished academicians.

Soviet scientists and engineers had reached an impasse in the area of constructing radar-transparent and radar-absorbent materials (RAM) into airframe components strong enough to withstand high-altitude, high-speed flight. But Vladimir Golodnikov, director of the KGB, had devised a daring operation to break the deadlock and gain the stealth technology for the Rodina—the Motherland.

The setting sun forced the Stealth's pilot to squint as he watched the B-1B emerge slowly from the puffy overcast. First the tail, like the dorsal fin of a shark, then the cockpit became visible from the tops of the pea green clouds.

"Okay, Ghost," Matthews radioed, banking the B-2 into the approaching strategic bomber. "I've got a visual."

"Roger, Shadow Three Seven," the B-1B copilot replied. "We have a tally."

The B-1B pilot stared at the odd-looking aircraft for a moment, thinking that the slate gray B-2 resembled a boomerang with a saw blade attached to the trailing edge. Eleven control surfaces, comprising 15 percent of the total wing area, were mounted across the entire aft section of the irregular wing. A powerful 4,000-psi hydraulic system actuated the large flight controls.

At the outboard edge of each wing were split rudders, each having upper and lower sections that moved separately. If the split rudder on one side opened and the other remained closed, the drag would increase on the open side and the Stealth would turn in that direction. If both split rudders on each wing tip were opened at the same time, the four large sections would act as speed brakes.

Three elevons were mounted on each wing, with one adjacent to the split rudders at each tip. The six large panels, although separated mechanically for safety, worked in unison to stabilize the B-2. The elevons functioned as both elevators and flaps.

The "beaver tail" was mounted at the center of the sawtooth flying wing. The pointed tail moved up and down to help trim the Stealth bomber longitudinally. Four General Electric F-118 engines were buried deep in the flying wing, aft of the molded cockpit, to prevent radar waves from bouncing off the spinning turbine blades.

The batlike airplane did not have a conventional vertical stabilizer, necessitating the installation of a small yaw-angle sensor on top of the cockpit.

Every pilot who had flown the B-2 loved the flying characteristics and the stability. Most crew members felt that the aircraft had fighterlike control stick forces.

The B-1B pilot grinned, then checked his closure speed on the "Batmobile."

"Colonel," Evans said over the aircraft intercom system (ICS). "We're fifteen from the initial point, and we have computer alignment."

Matthews, who had been a major five days before, was still uncomfortable with his new rank. He had not had an opportunity, being on deployment, to change the gold oak leaves on his flight jacket. The new silver leaves would have to wait until he returned to Whiteman Air Force Base, Missouri, his home field.

"Okay," Matthews replied, "let's go heads up. Nav lights out." The well-built, sandy-haired pilot adjusted his helmet chin strap, then looked at Evans. "Checklist."

The copilot placed the three-position master mode switch in the go to war setting. The flight controls now operated in a "stealth" mode, the radio emitters were turned off, and the weapons systems were readied.

Larry Simmons, wearing an unadorned air force issue flight suit, looked nervously around the cockpit. He felt a constriction in his chest but dismissed the pain as psychosomatic.

Simmons finally forced himself to look forward between the helmets of the two bomber pilots. They appeared to be totally relaxed, completing their descent checklist.

"Shadow Three Seven," radioed the AWACS senior control officer. "Strangle your parrot in thirty seconds—mark!"

"Wilco," Evans responded, looking at the new digital watch his wife had given him on their tenth anniversary. "Stop squawk in thirty seconds. Three Seven."

Matthews, turning his head slightly, watched the B-1B as the dark camouflaged bomber settled into a loose formation to the left of the Stealth. The sun was descending over the Canadian horizon, turning the rugged terrain below the overcast into night.

"Ghost Two Five," the AWACS controller ordered, "turn left to three-zero-five, descend to your strike profile, and stop squawk out of flight level three-one-zero. Good hunting."

"Roger, Mystic," replied the B-1B copilot. "We're outta thirty-five, comin' left to three-oh-five."

The sinister-looking strategic bomber simultaneously rolled to the left and descended toward the black, eerie overcast. Neither bomber crew would communicate with anyone until the four-hour-fifteen-minute mission had been completed. Only an emergency would take precedence over the sortie. The order from the AWACS controller to "stop squawk" provided the bomber pilots with the opportunity to disappear—literally vanish—from any type of radar that might be tracking the aircraft. When the crews turned off their transponders, their radar signatures disappeared.

Transponders, used by most aircraft, both civilian and military, provided a means for air traffic controllers to keep aircraft separated in the crowded skies. Ground controllers assigned a different four-digit code to each aircraft. Transponders provided position and altitude information, making them invaluable in an organized and civilized environment. They were, however, a death knell in a combat arena.

The B-1B was not completely stealthy, but it would be almost impossible to distinguish the bomber from radar ground clutter during a low-level attack. The B-1B had been designed to penetrate deep into hostile territory, hugging the terrain at supersonic speeds, deploy nuclear cruise missiles, then egress the same way.

"Now," ordered the stocky, dark-haired copilot, glancing over his left shoulder at Simmons, who had access to a third transponder.

The normal transponder, with a primary and a secondary transmitter, was located on the console between the pilots' seats. A single-head backup transponder, with a separate power supply, had been installed for the testing and evaluation of each B-2. The Federal Aviation Administration (FAA) had insisted on the third transponder for safety reasons. If the normal system, primary and secondary, failed during a test flight, the backup transponder would provide a means for ground controllers to follow the Stealth.

"Number three off," Simmons answered in a pensive, quiet manner.

Paul Evans sensed that something was wrong. "You okay, Larry?" Evans asked, half turning his head.

"Yeah," the diminutive technician answered, averting his eyes. Perspiration soaked his sage green flight suit. "Must've been the burritos I ate."

"Here we go," Matthews said as he lowered the Stealth's nose and reduced power on the four General Electric engines.

"We're only four seconds off," Evans reported, writing on his knee board.

"Computer tracking?" Matthews asked his right-seater.

"You bet, boss," Evans answered, smiling under his oxygen mask. "Locked on like a poor bachelor at a rich widows' convention."

Matthews chuckled softly as Shadow 37 penetrated the dense cloud cover, rocking gently in the light turbulence. The airspeed was passing 440 knots as the covert strike radar began to see "enemy" radar emissions.

Simmons squirmed in his seat, clearly ill at ease, as he adjusted the setting in his transponder head. The tech-rep fumbled with three circuit breakers, one for each transponder, then pulled all three and placed clips over the two marked primary and secondary. He then placed the temporary transponder switch to the on position, patted his zippered thigh pocket, and wiped his forehead with the back of his flight glove.

The numeric code that Simmons had dialed into his transponder, if energized by pushing the circuit breaker back into place, would automatically trigger alarms in ground-based radar facilities. Code 7700 indicated an emergency condition.

STRATEGIC AIR COMMAND HEADQUARTERS
Offutt Air Force Base, Nebraska

General Carlton W. Donovan, SAC commander, listened intently as he watched the time/event display tracking the "expected" positions of Shadow 37 and Ghost 25. The same information was being observed in the National Military Command Post at the Pentagon in Washington, D.C.

Only General Donovan, his immediate staff, and the bomber crews knew the course that would be flown to their respective targets. The only knowns were the two simulated targets, along with the fact that the bombers would return to Ellsworth Air Force Base, South Dakota, without refueling.

The classified operation was an emergency war order exercise to test the airborne crews against alerted ground and air defenses. Canadian and U.S. teams on board two AWACS aircraft would attempt to track the elusive bombers, while ground surveillance centers focused on detecting the intruders.

The mission would evaluate the long-range, low-level capability of the new Stealth B-2 against state-of-the-art bistatic radar installations. The highly classified radar units used transmitters and receivers placed in different locations. Four separate radar sites would try to foil the Stealth's ability to deflect their radar waves. Shadow 37's smooth, flowing shape did not have sharp edges or vertical surfaces for radar waves to bounce off. The B-2 had already proved capable of absorbing other types of radar beams in the composite wings and fuselage.

Donovan, a tall, lithe, white-haired man of fifty-seven, looked at his display board, which clearly defined the route of each bomber. The two courses had been selected from a number of restricted training routes. Shadow 37 was marked in dark blue, Ghost 25 in bright orange. Both dotted lines commenced their irregular courses over the Attawapiskat River, seven miles east of Lansdowne House, the point where the two bombers separated.

Shadow flight followed a path north to Winisk Lake, Ontario Province, then northeast to the southern tip of Belcher Islands in Hudson Bay. From there, the Stealth bomber would turn west, descend to 400 feet above the bay, and traverse 255 nautical miles of open water. The simulated target was Fort Severn, Ontario.

After the strike, Shadow flight would fly a direct course south to Duluth, Minnesota, then southwest to Ellsworth Air Force Base, where the classified bomber would land. After refueling, the B-2 crew would depart immediately for their permanent home, Whiteman Air Force Base, Knob Noster, Missouri. Shadow 37 was the second Stealth bomber assigned to the base. Whiteman had been scheduled to have a complement of twelve B-2s.

Ghost flight would fly an irregular, low-level course west of the Stealth, strike a simulated target in Manitoba Province, then recover at Ellsworth. The 337th Bombardment Squadron B-1B would also refuel, then fly home to Dyess Air Force Base, Texas.

"Well, Walt," Donovan said with a pleasant smile, "we'll see if your boys are on their toes this evening."

The four-star general enjoyed working with the scrappy Canadian fighter pilot and longtime friend Maj. Gen. Stirling Walter Bothwell, Royal Canadian Air Force.

"We'll bi-god give 'er a go," Bothwell shot back, chewing on an unlit cigar. "May be a bit dicey, general."

Both officers were positioned in the rear of the SAC control center on an elevated platform. Each had a commanding view of the continuously changing tracking graphics on the brightly lighted display board.

"If Shadow flight is on time," General Donovan said with a serious look on his face, "they should be turning west over Belcher Islands. This leg will be interesting."

SHADOW 37

The Stealth flying wing, with its dull charcoal finish, rolled out of the steep left turn and started a descent toward the pitch-black waters of Hudson Bay. Shadow 37, half the size of the Rockwell International B-1B, would be difficult to spot under any conditions except broad daylight. It would be virtually impossible to locate close to the surface of the bay.

The secret bomber, only slightly longer than an F-15 Eagle fighter, measured 69 feet from nose to tail. The smoothly contoured flying wing stretched 172 feet from wing tip to wing tip. The Stealth's wingspan, almost equivalent to that of a B-52 Stratofortress, contributed to its awkward appearance.

Matthews and Evans, using their eight multipurpose displays, continually cross-checked their altimeter readouts with the radio altimeter. Both pilots felt a series of bumps as the bomber flew through a low-lying cloud deck. The soft, bluish white cockpit lights cast a faint glow on the "glass" instrument panel.

Shadow 37 had been equipped with EICAS (engine instrument and crew alerting system), the final link to the "all-glass" cockpit. The synoptic displays monitored engine, electric, hydraulic, fuel, air-conditioning, pressurization, pneumatic, and other ancillary systems. The glass tubes, when called upon, or during an anomaly, also projected aircraft systems diagrams resembling the illustrations in the flight manual. If the B-2 experienced a ground or an airborne emergency, the color-coded electronic displays would come to life with motion.

Matthews checked the operating parameters of the four powerful General Electric engines. Fuel flow, rpms, temperature. All in the green.

The four nonafterburning engines, each producing 19,000 pounds of thrust, had been designed to use a fuel additive and cold-air baffle system to eliminate contrails. The highly visible white contrails would give away the bomber's position to the human eye. The exhaust outlets, filtering through V-shaped ceramic tiles similar to those on the space shuttles, were on top of the smooth wings.

"Four thousand feet to level-off," Evans reminded the command pilot.

"Okay," Matthews replied, easing the B-2's nose up three degrees. "I'm starting the level-off. Watch our altitude."

"Roger," Evans replied, scanning the various instrument displays.

Larry Simmons watched the altimeter unwind through 3,900 feet, then removed his flying gloves and wiped his perspiring palms on his thighs. He reached over to the panel at his shoulder and pushed in the circuit breaker to the temporary transponder. He left it activated for seven seconds, then pulled it out. The tech-rep then placed a retainer around the circuit breaker, as he had the other transponder breakers, to prevent it from being shoved in accidentally.

"Thousand to go, Chuck," Evans said, following the routine descent checklist. The copilot monitored closely all phases of the flight.

"Check," Matthews replied quietly, slowly raising the nose of the B-2 as he moved the throttles forward gently. "Four hundred feet . . . we're level."

The acceleration produced from 76,000 pounds of thrust pressed the crew into their seats as the bomber accelerated to 460 knots.

"Terrain avoidance verified," Evans reported, referring to the highly sophisticated terrain anticollision radar system.

The radar screen cast a dim glow on the faces of the pilots. Evans switched the scale to three nautical miles, scanning the instrument intently, looking for any obstacle in their path of flight. Shadow 37 was now traveling over the bay at almost eight nautical miles a minute.

The strategic bomber had been designed to be subsonic to avoid detection from the supersonic "footprint." The mission of the B-2, whether flying a high-altitude profile or hugging the deck, was to penetrate the target area unnoticed.

Matthews darted a look at the electro-optical display, then concentrated intently on the terrain-avoidance system flying the speeding bomber. He did not trust the terrain-hugging system this close to the surface, especially at night.

Matthews had already experienced two failures in Shadow 37's quadruple-redundant fly-by-wire digital flight control system. One failure, at 220 feet above the Tehachapi Mountains, had almost cost him his life. His uncanny reflexes had saved three lives in less than a second.

"Paul," Matthews said, again scanning his flight instruments, "how about dimming the panel lights just a tweak?"

"Yessir," Evans responded, reaching for the interior light control switches. He gave the instrument panel knob a slight turn. The cockpit darkened as the pilots' vision adjusted to the black, overcast night.

Matthews, fighting the insidious feeling of vertigo, keyed his intercom system. "How you doin', Larry?"

Five seconds passed without a response from the weapons systems technician. Evans cocked his head to the left to look at Simmons. What he saw horrified him.

CHAPTER TWO

TORONTO AIR TRAFFIC CONTROL CENTER

Peter Dawson, journeyman traffic controller, stared at his radar-scope, mesmerized. The emergency transponder squawk—7700—was real. The code, which set off the control center alarm, had appeared instantaneously without even a primary radar return.

Dawson's supervisor, Bruce Cochrane, was already standing behind him, leaning over his shoulder. "Where the blazes did that come from?"

"You've got me," Dawson replied, looking confused. He had not been tracking any traffic twenty-five nautical miles west of the southern tip of Belcher Islands.

"Get on the land-line, Peter," the supervisor ordered, looking closer at the radarscope, "and find out what's going on out there."

Dawson nodded in response, then talked briefly with a controller in the Winnipeg sector. The young air traffic specialist listened to his associate, signed off, and turned to his supervisor. "They don't have a clue, Bruce," Dawson said, checking his pad. "That squawk popped up from an area that's temporarily restricted . . . some kind of military operation."

Cochrane shrugged his shoulders, exhaling loudly. "How long was it on the scope?"

"I'm not sure," Dawson responded, searching his mind for the answer to Cochrane's question. "Four, maybe five seconds. Long enough to trigger the alarm."

"Lad," Cochrane placed his left hand on Dawson's shoulder, "better whistle up the military boys and signal the rescue people. I think someone is shy one airplane."

SHADOW 07

Major Paul Evans, frozen in terror, stared at the business end of a bright orange flare gun. The muzzle was only four inches from his face.

Evans glanced down at the object in Simmons's lap. The technician had opened the valve of his temporary oxygen bottle. He was filling the cockpit with pure oxygen. One spark and Shadow 37 would explode in a thundering conflagration.

"What the hell are you doing?" Evans shouted as he reached over to tap Matthews on the sleeve.

The aircraft commander glanced quickly over his right shoulder. "Goddamn, Larry, wh—"

"Shut up, both of you," Simmons said in a shaky, strained voice. He was having a difficult time remembering the speech he had been taught. The hours of rehearsing had been wasted as the spiel evaporated slowly from his frightened mind.

Both pilots, remaining silent, gave each other a fearful look. Matthews raised the B-2's nose slightly, reaching for the safety of altitude. The mission had now become a matter of personal survival.

Matthews and Evans were surprised when the AWACS radioed on the emergency Guard, 243.0, frequency. The airborne controllers had also seen the emergency code flash on their radarscopes.

"Ghost Two Five and Shadow Three Seven, this is Mystic," the AWACS officer said. "Acknowledge."

Matthews attempted to speak to Simmons as Evans keyed his radio.

"Larry, you can't get—"

"Don't use the radio!" Simmons commanded, holding the quivering flare gun next to Evans's neck. "Unplug your radio cords—both of you. NOW! We're shutting down all systems emissions—everything."

Matthews and Evans again exchanged concerned looks as they complied with the order. Matthews scanned the primary flight instruments, checked the engine readouts, then spoke to his copilot. "Paul, take the controls, stay on course, and level at twelve thousand."

Simmons hesitated a second, then spoke to the aircraft commander in a steady voice. "Major . . . Colonel Matthews, I am in control of the flight."

Simmons waved the 12-gauge signal gun nervously between the pilots. "I give the orders. Turn to a course of one hundred eighty-seven, and go up to fifty-one thousand feet."

Evans paused, questioning Matthews.

"Go ahead, Paul," the pilot replied, then turned slightly to the right in order to face Simmons more fully. "Larry," Matthews said in a soothing voice, "we're going to comply— no problem—whatever you want, okay? Just relax, and listen."

"No," Simmons replied in a normal tone. "You are not going to talk me out of this. Just follow my directions, and you and Major Evans will be okay."

Matthews started to speak, then decided to let Simmons have his say.

"I am defecting to a Communist state and taking this airplane with me."

The two pilots looked at each other with blank stares. They were incredulous.

"Larry," Matthews said, shaking his head slowly, "this is insane . . . the biggest mistake you could ever make. We still have time to salvage this . . . error in judgment, if you'll give us a chance."

"Colonel," Simmons replied, pointing the flare gun in the pilot's face. "I will not hesitate to blow this airplane out of the sky if you attempt to resist."

The gun wavered slightly, prompting Simmons to use both hands to steady the weapon.

"All right, Larry," Matthews responded with a resigned look. "No problem. . . . Just don't do anything irrational, okay?"

Simmons nodded, then leaned back and wiped the perspiration from his cheeks. His chest pounded as he realized that he, Lawrence Maynard Simmons, had done it. Crossed the line. No one would ever take advantage of him again. Not his company. Not his boss, Ronald, who persistently called him "May-nerd." Not his former wife, Colleen, the bitch who had taken his home, his car, and, most importantly, his beautiful daughter.

All the miserable years of debt, humiliation, divorce proceedings, and broken promises were over. He would be a hero in his new country. A man admired by the leaders of the most efficient intelligence agency in the world. A man admired by his lover, Irina Rykhov.

Matthews pondered their options as Evans checked their rate of climb, added more power, then turned his head to glance at Simmons.

"Ah . . . Larry," Evans said in a questioning tone. "Two minor details. We're headed for Cleveland, not to any foreign country, and we don't have the fuel to make it to any other part of the world. We're only carrying enough fuel to fly the strike profile."

Simmons awkwardly unfolded a large chart and handed it to Evans. "Yes, we do," Simmons replied, watching the surprised copilot glance at the map, then hand it to Matthews.

SAC HEADQUARTERS

General Donovan noticed the absence of radio chatter from the two AWACS aircraft. The large room had suddenly become quiet. Too quiet.

Donovan was startled when his radio speaker came to life. "Veil Control, Mystic. We have an emergency. Repeat, we have an emergency."

Donovan's eyes grew larger as he keyed his communication button. He normally did not talk directly to the participating aircraft. "Mystic, this is General Donovan. Explain the nature of your emergency."

The atmosphere in the control center had changed from being relaxed, almost casual, to surprised tension.

"We just received a confirmed seventy-seven hundred squawk, sir. The IFF code came from the area we suspect the B-2 was penetrating."

Donovan and Bothwell looked at each other in agony. They had had to confront the air force chief of staff, who had been concerned about the safety factor of the mission, to have the unusual operation approved.

"Abort the mission, Mystic," Donovan ordered in an anxious, but controlled voice. "Break radio silence and call both aircraft."

"General," the AWACS controller paused, "we've called both aircraft on Guard. Ghost Two Five checked in immediately. Shadow Three Seven hasn't responded, sir."

The SAC commander grimaced, then spoke slowly to the AWACS controller. "Activate air-sea rescue on the double. I want every available piece of equipment over the area where the distress signal originated."

"Wilco, Veil," the controller replied.

The control center remained silent a moment, everyone

apparently digesting the awful thought. Had Shadow 37 crashed?

"Carl," Bothwell said in a hushed tone. "I think we should have the B-1 crew recover here. We need to debrief them personally while everything is fresh in their minds."

"You're right," Donovan replied, keying his microphone.

THE STEALTH

"Mother of God," Matthews said as the B-2 climbed through 7,000 feet. "Cuba?"

"Yes," Simmons answered nervously. "San Julian."

Matthews stared at the Jeppesen high-altitude flight planning chart. Attached to the bottom was a narrow portion of a world aeronautical chart depicting the western tip of Cuba. The aircraft commander quickly saw their destination. San Julian was a military airfield with an 8,500-foot runway.

Evans talked to Simmons without taking his eyes off the flight instruments. "We're going to have a difficult time making fifty-one thousand."

Simmons did not answer, knowing that the B-2 could climb above the advertised service ceiling of 50,000 feet. Matthews punched in the coordinates for San Julian on his touch-sensitive miligraphics terminal.

USJ N22-06.1; W084-09.4

The global positioning navigation system flashed on the screen, showing the B-2's present position, course to destination, nautical miles to San Julian, time en route, and total fuel consumption.

"I'll tell you what our real problem is going to be," Matthews said, pointing to the screen. "Even Cuba is beyond our fuel range, including reserves."

Simmons's eyes hardened. "No tricks, colonel. I mean

what I say. I'll blow us out of the air if you try to stop me.''

Matthews sighed, then spoke with anger. "Goddamnit, Larry. It won't make any difference whether you destroy us now or we wait to crash in the Gulf of Mexico. Dead is dead. We aren't carrying a full load of fuel.''

Simmons remained quiet a moment, contemplating the flight information that Irina had given him.

Evans looked at the navigation readout, then broke the silence as the powerful bomber climbed through 13,000 feet. "Larry, he isn't trying to trick you. Look at the figures. It isn't that difficult to understand.''

Simmons stared at the screen—1,820 nautical miles to San Julian; range to fuel exhaustion, counting the built-in reserve, indicated 1,790 nautical miles.

The Stealth bomber, fully fueled and loaded to its maximum takeoff weight of 390,000 pounds, had a high-altitude range of more than 6,800 nautical miles—10,800 miles with one air refueling. The low-level range subtracted more than 2,000 nautical miles.

"Major Evans," Simmons said, placing the safety pins into the pilots' ejection seats to disarm them. "I know you can step-climb to fifty-one thousand as we burn off fuel, then make an idle descent into Cuba.''

Evans spoke slowly. "That is correct, to a certain point. The higher we go, the less fuel we burn—true. But we don't know what the winds are going to be like at altitude, we don't have any current weather information, and we don't have any instrument approach plates for San Julian.''

Simmons remained quiet as he secured the supplemental oxygen system.

"Larry," Matthews said, "thirty nautical miles is a lot of space to make up between here and Cuba, especially if the weather is rotten for our approach and landing. The weather report I saw this morning showed a tropical disturbance in the Caribbean, but I didn't pay any attention to the exact location.''

Simmons struggled to extract three pieces of tightly folded paper from his left thigh pocket. ''This will help guide us in, colonel,'' Simmons said, handing the Cuban Revolutionary Air Force and Antiaircraft Defense airport diagrams to the pilot.

Matthews looked at the DAAFAR instrument approach plates with the hand-drawn lines. One prominent line began at the airfield and continued due north to the edge of the page. Matthews then looked at the Cuban aeronautical chart. The same line extended north approximately ninety nautical miles to a point just inside the Cuban air defense identification zone.

''I assume, Larry,'' Matthews paused to hand the diagrams and charts to Evans, ''that we're going to have an escort down that line to San Julian.''

''That's correct,'' Simmons responded evenly, feeling more confident. ''When we reach that point, still at our cruising altitude, we'll energize our transponder and radars so the MiGs can join up with us.''

''Great,'' Evans replied, handing the wrinkled papers back to Matthews. ''We're going to have a damned steep descent into the field.''

The cockpit remained quiet as Shadow 37, climbing rapidly through the overcast, passed 27,000 feet. The bomber was lighter than it would be after becoming operational. The Boeing-built advanced rotary weapons launchers did not contain the normal complement of sixteen nuclear cruise missiles.

Matthews checked his instrument panel, then spoke to the civilian. ''Well, Larry, you've thought of everything except one item—if we don't run out of fuel, that is.''

Simmons waited a few seconds before responding. His mind whirled, trying to comprehend what the aircraft commander was talking about. ''Yeah, colonel?'' Simmons asked, trying not to show any of the fear growing inside him. "What's the one item?"

Matthews turned to face the Stealth's hijacker. "That the commies are going to dispose of you—kill you—after they get their hands on this airplane."

WASHINGTON, D.C.

Secretary of Defense Bernard D. Kerchner, sitting at his secluded table at Twenty One Federal, lifted his aperitif glass. "Here's to you, darling. The quintessence of the perfect wife."

Kerchner touched the outstretched glass lightly, then looked into the dancing green eyes. "Happy thirty-first anniversary, Liddy."

The radiant, petite woman brushed back her chestnut hair, then squeezed her husband's left hand. "Bernie, I have always loved the irrepressible romantic in you."

Kerchner started to respond, then stopped. He had noticed the maître d' hurrying toward their table. Renoir Dutilleux, always the gentleman, apologized for intruding, then handed Kerchner a slip of paper.

"Thank you, Renoir," Kerchner said, slipping his reading glasses from the holder inside his coat.

"Again, my apologies, Mister Secretary. The general said it was most urgent."

"It always is," Kerchner replied, smiling. He waited while the maître d' bowed slightly and walked away.

"Oh, Bernie, not bad news," Liddy said softly, watching her husband's brow furrow.

"I'm afraid so," Kerchner replied, sliding back his chair. "I have to call General Parkinson at home."

The short, balding, round-faced defense secretary motioned for their waiter, then patted his wife's hand. The white-jacketed waiter crossed the elegant marble and wood floor and approached the table.

"Nicky, I have to make a phone call, so we'll order in a few minutes," Kerchner said, opening the wine list. "In the meantime, we'll sample a bottle of Côtes du Rhone Beaucastel."

"Excellent choice, Secretary Kerchner."

Elizabeth "Liddy" Kerchner, feeling cheated by the government once again, watched her husband walk to the phone near the entrance. She and Bernie seemed to have so little private time together since the shake-up at "crisis management"—Bernie's nickname for the National Security Council. The gracious, attractive woman accepted the glass of red wine the waiter had poured, then watched her husband place the phone receiver down and remove his glasses. She could see the anguish in his eyes.

Kerchner walked to the table, pulled back his chair, slid into his seat, and took both of his wife's hands in his. "Sorry, honey," Kerchner said, massaging the top of Liddy's hands gently with his thumbs. "I've got to rush over to the Pentagon. Why don't you order, then take a cab home . . . and don't wait up. I promise we're going to do this again— until we get it right."

Liddy laughed in her warm, soft manner. "I know, Bernie . . . I know. Can you tell me what has happened?"

"Yes," Kerchner replied, lowering his voice slightly. "We've lost one of our B-2s."

Liddy Kerchner was visibly shocked. "One of the new Stealth bombers crashed?"

Kerchner glanced around the room, then spoke quietly. "They don't know what happened. The damned thing disappeared over Hudson Bay—joint exercise with the Canadians—and the speculation is that it crashed in the bay."

"Oh, God," Liddy said in a hushed voice. "How awful."

"Yes," Kerchner responded somberly, signaling for their regular waiter. "I'll call you later, as soon as I know anything."

Liddy watched, unsmiling, as her husband signed the open check, retrieved his topcoat, then walked out the door.

THE B-2

Matthews and Evans had remained quiet as the bomber struggled to 51,000 feet. Shadow 37 was now passing directly over Detroit, invisible to radar screens in the Cleveland air route traffic control center.

"Larry," Matthews said in a conversational tone. "I recommend we turn on the radios, so we can at least monitor traffic and get some weather information."

Simmons thought about the suggestion, suspicion written on his face. "Why?"

Matthews looked at Evans out of the corner of his eye in time to catch the copilot roll his eyes upward. "Because we are currently traveling through one of the highest density air traffic areas in the country. There's a lot of congestion up here, Larry, and no one knows we're overhead."

Simmons remained quiet, mulling over the reasonableness of the request.

Evans half-turned, facing Simmons. "Goddamnit, we aren't going to transmit anything."

Simmons still did not trust the pilots but reluctantly acquiesced. "Okay, but don't try anything, I warn you. One word and I'll pull the trigger."

Neither officer answered as they quickly activated the VHF and UHF radios and plugged in their radio cords. The B-2 normally used UHF, or the classified MILSTAR system, but the crew also needed the VHF frequencies used by civilians.

Matthews reached down behind the console separating the pilots, and retrieved the U.S. government IFR en route high-altitude charts. The charts would allow the pilots to orient themselves and, most importantly, identify the radio frequencies they needed to monitor each air traffic control center.

"Looks like one-thirty-two point forty-five," Matthews said, tuning the VHF channels.

The padded earphones in each crew member's helmet immediately crackled to life. "United Two Seven Four, cleared present position direct to Indianapolis."

"Direct Indianapolis, United Two Seven Four," the pleasant female voice replied.

Both pilots listened to the radio chatter, waiting for ten minutes after the top of the hour. That would be a good time to eavesdrop on the civilian flight service frequencies for a picture of the weather in the southeastern United States.

"Cleveland Center, Citation Five-Fifty-Five Tango Charlie with ya at five-one-oh."

Matthews and Evans, startled, looked at each other, then listened intently to the conversation. The business jet was cruising at their altitude.

"Five Five Tango Charlie," the center controller radioed, "we have a change in routing. Ready to copy?"

"Tango Charlie, go ahead."

"Five Five Tango Charlie is cleared via Jay sixty-four Bradford, direct Des Moines."

The Citation copilot read back the clearance. "Sixty-four Bradford, direct Des Moines, triple nickel Tango Charlie."

Matthews tapped the high-altitude chart. "Look! We're about to cross Jet sixty-four."

Evans turned down the cockpit lights to the lowest setting, then looked at the chart. "It runs east and west; he has to be closing from the left, westbound, if he hasn't already crossed in front of us."

"You're right. Let's step down," Matthews ordered.

Evans gently eased the autopilot into a descent, then turned toward Simmons. "We're going to cruise at fifty thousand— it isn't a cardinal altitude."

Simmons nodded his agreement, watching the altimeter readout.

Both pilots saw the business jet's flashing strobe lights at the same instant. "JESUS!" Matthews yelled as the B-2 was rocked violently by wing-tip turbulence from the Citation III.

Evans let out his breath slowly. "We didn't miss him twenty feet vertically."

"Yeah," Matthews replied grimly. "His wing went right over our cockpit."

Evans continued the descent as the pilots listened to the frightened Citation copilot.

"Cleveland, Five Five Tango Charlie!"

"Cleveland Center," the controller answered, alert to the change in the pilot's voice.

"Ah . . . Cleveland, we almost had a midair. You have any traffic in the vicinity at our altitude?"

"Negative, Five Five Tango Charlie," the surprised controller replied in a questioning voice. "Closest traffic is east-bound, eight miles at your eleven o'clock—a Gulfstream at four-one-zero."

"Okay, Cleveland, but we want to report a damned close call. Something, and it was definitely there, passed right under us—didn't miss us more than fifty to a hundred feet."

"I don't show anything on radar," the controller replied, disbelieving. "I'm not seeing any other returns in your area."

"Well, it wasn't our imagination," the excited copilot responded. "Something went under us."

Matthews and Evans exchanged anxious looks before the aircraft commander turned toward Simmons. The tech-rep's face was contorted in fear as he watched Evans level the Stealth at 50,000 feet.

"Fifty thousand," Matthews explained to Simmons, "is a non-used altitude. We'll be in a safer position here, unless someone is climbing or descending through our altitude."

Simmons, grim faced, nodded in return.

Matthews concentrated on his flight instruments while his brain sought a way to disarm the hijacker. In spite of the imminent danger of his position—or maybe because of it—he found his thoughts interrupted by the faces of his wife, Roxanne, and their twins, Meredith and Michelle.

He had met Roxanne Paquette during his senior year at the Air Force Academy. Six months later, the day after his graduation, the happy couple had exchanged marriage vows in the academy chapel. As a newly minted second lieutenant, who had earned his private pilot license during high school, he had taken his wife on a flying honeymoon. He had leased a Cessna 182 and they had toured the Bahamian Islands from end to end.

After returning from the islands, he and his bride had driven from Colorado Springs to Boston. His first assignment as an air force officer required that he obtain an advanced degree from the Massachusetts Institute of Technology. Fifteen months later, with a master's degree in aeronautical engineering, he and Roxy had departed Boston for undergraduate pilot training at Vance Air Force Base, Enid, Oklahoma.

A popular couple, they had rented an apartment off base. Their Friday evening steak cookout and beer bust had become a weekly ritual for friends and classmates during the long, hot Oklahoma summer.

Once a month, during a weekend, they had driven to Wellington, Kansas, to visit his parents and grandmother. Roxy had spent many Sundays helping his mother and grandmother prepare the large dinner.

Three days after he received his shining silver wings—

Matthews was jolted from his thoughts when Simmons coughed. He stole a glance at his copilot, who was glaring with open hostility at the tech-rep.

CHAPTER THREE

OFFUTT AIR FORCE BASE

General Carl Donovan, leaning against his polished mahogany desk, listened to the aircraft commander of Ghost 25. The B-1B had landed only minutes before and was met by Donovan's staff car.

Major Bud Teague, looking understandably nervous, sat in one of the two plush chairs facing the general's desk. The other wood and leather chair was occupied by General Bothwell.

"General," the saddened pilot paused, "that's all I can tell you. After we broke off from Shadow Three Seven, well ...everything was normal until we had the call on Guard. The weather was fine ...we encountered no unusual conditions, sir."

"Okay, major," Donovan said, turning to walk behind his desk. "Tell me about Chuck Matthews. I understand you went through pilot training with him."

"Yessir, I did," Teague replied, watching Donovan sit down. "We went through flight training at Vance. He graduated first in the class—a real natural and a heck of a leader.

I consider him one of the best pilots in the Air Force, sir.''

Donovan sat quietly, trying to sort out the mystery, then turned to Bothwell. ''General, do you have any questions for Major Teague?''

''No,'' the Canadian replied, turning to face the B-1B command pilot. ''Major, we appreciate your input. I know it's difficult for you.''

''Yes, it is, sir. I've known Chuck a long time.''

Donovan stood, followed by Bothwell and Teague. ''Major, we have rooms ready for you and your crew in the VIP quarters. Get some rest, and take off at your leisure tomorrow.''

''Thank you, sir,'' Teague replied. ''Have you heard any word yet about the search?''

''No, they haven't spotted a single thing,'' Donovan answered, checking his watch, ''and it's been more than three hours.''

''Get some rest, son,'' Bothwell said, patting Teague on the shoulder. ''We'll let you know if we hear anything.''

''Thank you, sir.'' Teague saluted the two senior officers, then quietly walked out of the office, closing the door behind him.

''Walt,'' the SAC commander asked, ''how could a B-2 simply vanish?''

''General, if he was spot on course, they'll find something.''

SHADOW 37

The Stealth bomber, still cruising at 50,000 feet, was eighty-five nautical miles north-northeast of Tallahassee, Florida. Matthews had elected to reduce power in order to conserve the rapidly dwindling fuel supply.

Both pilots continuously monitored the global navigation readouts showing distance to destination and time to fuel exhaustion. According to the navigation equation, Shadow

37 would flame out six minutes before they reached San Julian.

Simmons sat quietly in his cramped space and mentally reviewed his instructions. He kept his right hand on the butt of the flare gun, resting it on his lap.

"Larry," Matthews said pleasantly, turning slightly to see Simmons. "I want to ask you a question."

Simmons gripped the flare gun before replying. "Colonel Matthews, I am not going to discuss anything, except getting this aircraft to Cuba."

"Okay, Larry," the pilot continued in a conversational but persistent tone. "Just one important personal question. What happened—what caused you to even contemplate hijacking a B-2?"

Simmons remained quiet, trying to decide whether to respond. He did not need any doubts creeping into his thinking. "I don't want to discuss anything. Just do as I tell you," Simmons answered, wiping his left hand nervously on his flight suit.

"Larry," Matthews said slowly, "I can't imagine anything so bad that it would cause you to . . . to do something that you'll regret for the rest of your life."

Simmons remained quiet, clenching his teeth. His mind cried out for understanding, but no one had ever really cared. No one until Irina, his lover and future wife.

Paul Evans, monitoring the Jacksonville Center air traffic controllers, turned his head to the left, then spoke to Simmons in a friendly manner. "Larry, what Chuck is trying to say is that we'll help you no matter what the problem is. You just can't destroy your whole future. We still have time to correct this situation and help you out of whatever you're facing."

"You," Simmons said with bitterness in his voice. "You two don't know what it's like to be a . . . to be treated like I have. You live in the glory world of hotshot pilots. You live in the officer-country-club world with your perfect little families. You've never been kicked around."

The pilots looked at each other in wide-eyed astonishment.

Matthews decided to try his previous approach. "Larry, listen to me for God's sake. The Communists aren't going to have any use for you after they've gleaned all the information you can provide. You'll be a liability who might defect back to the United States. They don't trust anyone, especially someone who has been disloyal to his own country."

Matthews glanced at Evans, then continued in an even tone of voice. "They'll kill you, Larry. You're the one weak link who could expose their hijacking. You're signing our death warrants, along with yours, if we don't turn back now."

Simmons glared at Matthews, then replied emotionally but evenly. "I allowed you to express your thoughts, and you are wrong—completely wrong. The Russians I work for are my friends, and I am going to be in charge of Stealth technical evaluations. Besides, I am marrying a Russian citizen."

Both pilots again looked at each other in amazement. Matthews shook his head slowly. "Larry, you've been deceived, and it's going to cost the lives of all three of us if you can't see the picture."

Simmons clenched his jaw before responding defensively. "I know what you're thinking, but you're wrong. Irina and I fell in love after she told me who she was . . . and about the B-2 project."

Evans turned his head slightly. "Right."

OFFICIAL RESIDENCE OF THE VICE PRESIDENT

The vice president of the United States, holding a phone to his ear, motioned for Bernard Kerchner and Air Force Gen. Frank Parkinson to join him in his study. They had been summoned hurriedly from the Pentagon.

The tall, lean, impeccably groomed air force deputy chief of staff for plans and operations followed Kerchner into the richly paneled room. The two men sat down in the wingback chairs on each side of the small fireplace.

Kirklin W. Truesdell had a reputation for being a metic-

ulous and highly efficient administrator. The top of his rich
cherry wood desk was immaculate, reflecting the organiza-
tional skills he had developed as a naval officer and public
servant.

The vice president had recently assumed responsibilities
as acting chief of staff. The president's closest aide and adviser, the chief of staff had been gravely injured in a boating
accident and remained in critical but stable condition in Be-
thesda Naval Medical Center.

"Yes, sir," Truesdell replied into the phone, writing rapidly on his desk pad. "We'll keep you informed."

The vice president listened a moment longer, then hung
up. "That was the president," Truesdell said, swiveling
around in his chair. "He wants us to keep him informed of
any developments in the B-2 search. Also," he continued,
scratching through a message on his pad, "he wants us to be
at Camp David at seven in the morning."

The vice president leaned across his desk, frowning, and
addressed the defense secretary. "Bernie, how the hell did
we manage to lose a B-2? They've been searching for almost
four hours and haven't found a shred of evidence to indicate
that the Stealth crashed."

Kerchner lowered his gaze a moment, then looked at the
intense former Central Intelligence Agency Director. "Sir,
the aircraft was scheduled to land at Ellsworth approximately
fifteen minutes ago. It hasn't arrived, no one has communicated with the crew, the Canadians confirm that there was
an emergency code displayed briefly where the aircraft was
supposed to be, and . . .," Kerchner paused, forming his
thoughts, "the B-1 crew hasn't shed any light on the disappearance. That's all we know."

Parkinson, resplendent in his ribbon-bedecked blue uniform, spoke to Truesdell. "Mister Vice President, all the
information indicates that the aircraft crashed into Hudson
Bay where the emergency code flashed briefly. The flight was
following a very precise, preplanned course. We'll know for
certain where the aircraft crashed when we search in the

morning. The crews will fly the same course, spread out horizontally at half-mile intervals. If the Stealth went into the bay, sir, there will be floating debris, I can assure you.''

"Have you grounded the other B-2s?" Truesdell asked, studying a Northrop flight test synopsis.

"Yes, sir, we have," Parkinson answered, then added, "until we find out what happened to Shadow Three Seven. We intend to keep the operational B-2s standing alert, but they won't fly unless we encounter a global threat of some nature.''

"Sir," Kerchner said to the frowning vice president, "whatever happened, we believe, was catastrophic. The crew never had a chance to get off a message.''

"Okay, let's get some sleep," Truesdell said, looking at the mantel clock over the fireplace. "Plan for a five-forty-five brief here, then we'll go to the helicopter pad.''

"Yes, sir," Kerchner replied, standing with Parkinson.

Truesdell escorted the two men out, shut the door, and returned to his study. He poured a small amount of Remy Martin into a brandy glass, then sat down on the handsome leather couch. Swirling the amber cognac under his nose, he stared into the glowing embers of the dying fire. He replayed the B-2 events over and over in his mind. Something did not fit.

THE STEALTH

Evans looked at the high-altitude en route chart, then switched the VHF radio from Jacksonville Center to Miami Center. The pilots listened to the busy air traffic controllers and commercial pilots discuss the rapidly deteriorating weather. The tropical depression southeast of Jamaica had advanced to a tropical storm, then to hurricane status as it tracked northwest. Hurricane Bennett was growing in intensity.

"Larry . . . ," Matthews paused, catching a pilot report from a Delta Airlines flight, "you picked a great time of year to go to Cuba. The eye of the hurricane is passing forty miles south of San Julian."

Simmons remained quiet. He had no plan for such an eventuality. Levchenko had not discussed any bad weather alternatives during the planning sessions. Would the MiG pilots be able to rendezvous with the Stealth?

Matthews cupped his hands around his eyes and looked out of his side window. "I can't see Saint Petersburg," the pilot said quietly. "We've got a solid cloud deck below us."

Evans rubbed his eyes, then looked at the navigation plot for the thousandth time. "Cuba—San Julian has to be totally clobbered. Bennett has already engulfed the southern half of Florida."

"Larry," Matthews said, turning slightly to see Simmons. "We're flying into a hurricane without enough fuel to reach our destination. You must listen to reason."

"Colonel," Simmons responded unsteadily, "we are committed to San Julian."

"Goddamnit!" Evans spat, twisting his head to the left. "Listen to reason! This is our last chance to land while we have fuel in our tanks. We aren't bullshitting you. Look at the nav plot, for Christ's sake, and add it up."

Simmons squirmed, then looked between the two pilots. He stared straight ahead into the turbulent black night, averting the pilot's questioning eyes. "We are committed to San Julian."

"Shit!" Matthews exclaimed as he pulled the number one and four throttles to idle, then cutoff.

"What are you doing?" Simmons asked in shock.

"Shut up!" Matthews barked as the EICAS annunciator warning and emergency lights flashed on, illuminating the cockpit with a reddish amber glow. "We don't have any choice," he explained as he and Evans went through the engine shutdown checklist. "It's very simple, Larry. I have to conserve fuel, so we'll fly on two engines. It's still going to be a crapshoot."

Simmons, beginning to have doubts about the outcome of

the hijacking, felt his pulse pounding. He stared at the bright warning lights, then at the flight parameters displayed on the EICAS screen. The digital airspeed indicator was decreasing rapidly through 0.71 Mach as the autopilot fought to maintain the preset altitude.

"Here we go," Matthews warned Evans as he squeezed the autopilot disengage button on his control stick, then checked the continuity of the fly-by-wire flight controls. "Descent checklist."

Simmons clutched the flare gun in both hands. "Why are we descending?"

"Because," Matthews replied, easing the B-2's nose down, "we can't maintain fifty thousand feet on two engines. We'll have to drift down to an altitude we can hold with the power we have."

Simmons remained quiet while the two pilots completed their checklist. He could feel the turbulence and rain increasing as the bomber plunged into the thick, boiling storm clouds. "Stop!" he suddenly blurted. "The MiGs are supposed to join us at fifty-one thousand."

"Screw the MiGs!" Evans shot back. "We're trying to survive, you stupid bastard."

Simmons yanked up the flare gun, then shoved the barrel into the back of Evan's neck. His hand shook. He was not as certain as he pretended to be in the face of this unplanned turn of events. "Don't screw with me, major."

Matthews turned his head and glared at the tech-rep. "Put the gun down and hang on. This is going to be a rough ride into San Julian."

Simmons lowered the flare pistol slowly, then leaned back in his seat. He felt exhausted from the strain he had been under for the past three weeks.

"Yeah," Evans said, catching Matthews's eye before turning toward Simmons. "If we don't crater someone during the descent."

The darkened cockpit remained quiet as the bouncing, yawing bomber descended through 39,000 feet. The rough ride,

punctuated with violent updrafts and downdrafts, was ago-
nizing for Simmons.

Evans punched in a radio frequency for the Miami oceanic
control area, listened to three airline pilots request deviations
around intense rain cells, then checked the fuel exhaustion
and time to destination readout.

"Chuck, we're behind the curve."

"I know," Matthews responded without taking his eyes
off the instrument displays. "All I can do is keep it high,
clean, and fast. We've only got one shot."

Simmons, bracing against the severe turbulence, had been
watching the distance to destination wind down. Irina Rykhov
and Gennadi Levchenko had instructed him to turn on all the
Stealth's radars, along with energizing the primary transponder, at a point 135 nautical miles north of San Julian. That
would be the edge of the Cuban air defense identification
zone (ADIZ). The MiGs would be circling at 130 miles to
rendezvous with the B-2 at 51,000 feet.

Simmons watched the mileage—137 . . . 136 . . . 135.
"I'm turning on our radar and transponder," he announced,
holding the flare gun chest high. "The MiGs have to find us
to lead us to the airfield."

Matthews glanced out of his side window. His gaze met
total darkness as the intense rain pounded the bomber.
"Larry, we only have one try at this, so I have to improvise."

Simmons's neck tightened as he leaned forward between
the pilots. "I have to follow the orders specifically, or they
will not attempt to join us."

"Simmons," Evans exclaimed loudly, "you just don't get
the picture, do you? We don't have the luxury of following
your goddamned orders."

Matthews spoke before Simmons could answer. "Paul, I'm
going to pass directly over the field at four thousand, then
start a two-seventy to the right. That should give us good
terrain clearance and put us into the wind on the east-west
runway."

"Okay," Evans replied, tuning the San Julian radio beacon. "Standard altitude calls?"

"Sure," Matthews responded as he looked closely at the world aeronautical chart. "They've only got an eighty-five-hundred-foot runway, so I'll have to be right on the numbers."

Evans nodded in agreement, then half-turned to face the semiair-sick tech-rep. "Hope your comrades have the lights turned up for us."

Simmons raised the shaking flare pistol, pointing it in the copilot's face. "Keep your mouth shut, major."

"Back off, Simmons!" Matthews snarled. "We can't go anywhere, so put down the gun!"

Simmons lowered the flare pistol and leaned back, frightened about the consequences of botching the hijacking. He rechecked the covert and phased-array radar units. If the MiGs could not locate the bomber, which was likely now, Simmons would have to rely on Matthews to get them down safely.

No one said a word as the Stealth descended through the torrential rain and jarring turbulence.

Evans peered out of his side window, then flinched. "We've got company. Looks like a Foxbat."

Matthews looked out to the left. He could barely make out the Cuban MiG-25 on his side. The three planes were bouncing all over the sky, making it impossible to hold any reasonable formation. Matthews quickly flipped on his navigation and formation lights.

"Yeah," Matthews replied. "I have one on this side. He has a flashlight . . . looks like he's signaling something."

"Same here," Evans responded, pressing his face closer to the window. "Looks like he's signaling to go down. Yeah, he wants us to descend."

"It's too early," Matthews said in exasperation. "We can't afford to waste the fuel." He turned slightly to see Simmons. "Is there any provision to talk to the MiGs or the San Julian tower?"

"No, colonel," the chalky-faced tech-rep answered.

"They don't want any radio transmissions from the B-2."

Evans looked quickly at the fuel gauges and navigation readout, then back out of the side window. "Sorry, comrades, we can't let down just—"

The copilot's sentence was cut off by a burst of cannon fire from the MiG on the left side of the B-2. The bright red tracers lit up the night, slashing through the waterfall of rain.

"Ah . . . Christ," Matthews said in a resigned voice. "We're starting down."

SAN JULIAN MILITARY AIRFIELD,
Province of Pinar del Rio

Gennadi Dunayevich Levchenko, Stealth project officer and director of the renegade KGB operations at San Julian, paced nervously back and forth in the control tower. The portly, bushy-haired man was the Soviet Union's highest regarded field operative. He was a ruthless, driven agent who had fought his way politically to the top echelon of the world's largest spy and state-security machine.

Now, at age forty-six, Levchenko had been given the responsibility of stealing the American B-2 Stealth bomber. The Chief of the KGB, Vladimir Golodnikov, had withheld the fact that the Kremlin was unaware of the secret mission. Levchenko had been operating on the premise that the B-2 project was a Kremlin priority.

Levchenko had attended Syracuse University, sponsored by an international exchange scholarship, where he had graduated with a bachelor of arts degree in political science. His minor had been international relations. After receiving his diploma, the future KGB agent had returned to his homeland to complete an advanced degree in international studies. He had not been aware that his activities were monitored closely while he was in the United States.

The KGB had been very pleased with Gennadi Levchenko's academic achievements while attending the American university. They were particularly proud of his unwavering dedication to the Motherland.

Barely three months into his advanced studies, Levchenko had been approached by two persuasive recruiters from the KGB. The pair had been very friendly and had outlined an agency career with unlimited potential for an individual with his credentials. Levchenko had been euphoric but managed to quell his excitement so as not to appear too eager. He had wanted to be an officer in the KGB from the age of eleven and accepted the offer gladly.

Levchenko had distinguished himself at the KGB training academy, demonstrating many of the traits that would later propel him to the top of his profession. As a new KGB officer, he quickly developed a reputation for being ruthless in his quest for perfection and recognition.

His first assignment had been a plum. Levchenko had returned to the United States, where he had masqueraded as an assistant to the Soviet ambassador. He nurtured many friendships from his university days and courted influential politicos around the Washington beltway. Charming the power brokers in the nation's capital, he gathered every piece of classified intelligence he could grasp or buy. His career flourished for years, culminating in his present assignment.

Levchenko could barely make out the MiG-23s and -25s lined up on the tarmac directly below the San Julian tower. He silently cursed the driving rain and hurricane-force winds, then walked over to the tower chief. "How far out are they?" Levchenko asked the senior warrant officer.

Yevgeny I. Pogostyan looked at the radarscope. It was almost impossible to see the two MiG-25s in the pounding rain. The B-2, squawking the preplanned transponder code—4276—registered clearly on the brightly lighted radar screen.

"Ninety kilometers, comrade director," Pogostyan replied respectfully. "We have the runway lights at the highest intensity."

"*Balshoye spasibo*," Levchenko said, thanking the tower controller.

"Do not worry, comrade director," assured Maj. Gen. Petr V. Brotskharnov, commanding officer of the Voenno Vozdushniye Sily (VVS, the Soviet Air Force) detachment. Assured, the general stared at the radar screen, then looked into Levchenko's cold eyes. "Lieutenant Colonel Zanyathov and Major Sokolviy are the two best pilots in the VVS. They will guide the Americans down safely."

"I hope you are right, general," Levchenko replied out of the corner of his mouth, "for the sake of all of us."

Both men watched the radarscope, listening to Pogostyan converse with the lead MiG pilot.

Lieutenant Colonel Zanyathov had not disclosed that he had fired his cannon in front of the bomber. His concern was landing in the hurricane conditions. The Russian fighter pilot knew his career would be over if he failed to successfully complete the secret operation.

CHAPTER FOUR

THE B-2

Matthews, staring through the rain at the MiG-25, wrestled the controls of the bucking Stealth bomber. He constantly jockeyed the number two and three throttles to maintain formation with the agile Soviet fighter.

The MiG on the right had disappeared, but Matthews knew that it was close by, probably on the B-2's tail. "We're committed to this guy," Matthews remarked to his copilot. "I hope he knows where the runway is."

"I'm sure these two are the cream," Evans replied as he watched the fuel totalizer steadily count toward zero. "Less than twelve hundred pounds, Chuck."

"Okay," Matthews replied, showing no emotion. "Switch to Land."

Evans placed the master mode switch to the land position. The flight controls transitioned to the landing mode and the checklist appeared on the multipurpose display units.

The copilot studied the screen before speaking. "We're down to flaps and gear."

"Okay," Matthews responded, concentrating on the MiG. "Too bad we can't talk to our escorts."

"Sure is," Evans said, darting a look at Simmons. "Would have made it a lot easier."

Simmons did not respond. He was nervously watching Matthews struggle to keep behind the MiG-25's wing.

"Thousand pounds," Evans reported, locking his shoulder harness restraints. "We're making a left-hand approach, according to the mileage and heading."

"I know," Matthews replied without turning his head. "Let's pray he makes a tight approach."

Paul Evans did not answer, waiting for the commands to lower the flaps and landing gear. Ten seconds passed as Evans monitored the aircraft commander. "We're outta three thousand."

"Okay," Matthews responded. "We've got terrain up to around two thousand feet northeast of the field. These bozos better have it together."

"This is like flying through Niagara Falls," Evans said, concern edging into his voice. "Nine hundred pounds."

"He's slowing!" Matthews said, caught off guard. "Give me flaps—we'll hold the gear."

"Flaps on the way," Evans responded, straining to see through the rain-splattered windshield. "Out of fifteen hundred, showing eight hundred pounds. Airspeed one-seventy-five."

"Okay," Matthews replied, tight-lipped. "Stand by for the gear and call out my altitu—"

"Shit!" Evans interrupted. "We've lost fuel pressure on number three . . . we're losing three!"

"Give me cross-feed!" Matthews ordered, advancing the throttle on the number two engine. "Boost on!"

The EICAS screen lighted, displaying the schematic diagram for the complex fuel system. The cross-feed valves and jet pumps had been energized.

"You got it," Evans shouted, monitoring the radio altimeter. "Eight hundred feet—we're bleeding off! Power—power!"

Matthews did not reply as he advanced the number two throttle to the limit. The B-2 surged forward, yawing slightly to the right, as the single 19,000-pound-thrust engine howled at full power.

"Five hundred feet, one-forty-five on the speed," Evans cautioned, squinting through the windshield. "I don't see anything—keep it coming."

Simmons placed the flare gun in the leg pocket of his flight suit, then clutched his seat and closed his eyes. He felt a wave of nausea sweep over him when the bomber yawed to the right.

"Three hundred feet," Evans reported, breathing faster. "One-forty . . . bleeding off."

"I've got it to the stops."

Both pilots flinched when the low-altitude warning alarm sounded.

"I've lost the MiG," Matthews shouted, reverting to his primary flight instruments. The radio altimeter indicated 170 feet above the ground.

"He's going around," Evans said, feeling the B-2's rate of descent increase. "Gotta hold this heading . . . we're almost there."

"God, I hope so," Matthews answered through clenched teeth. He tried to block out the flashing warning lights on the annunciator panel.

"Airspeed—airspeed!" Evans prompted. "Two's fluctuating—we're losing it! One hundred feet. Two's flamed out—raise the nose!"

"Gear down," Matthews yelled, pulling back the control stick to its limit.

Simmons gritted his teeth and squeezed the sides of his ejection seat.

"Wind shear!" Evans warned, snapping the landing gear lever down. "Get the nose up!"

"Yeah!" Matthews replied in a tight, strained voice. "Can't control it!"

Evans, wide-eyed, stared through the windshield at the black void; Matthews's gaze remained fixed on his primary flight instruments.

"I've got runway lights," the copilot shouted, bracing himself. "Gear down and locked. Ease it right—go right!"

"I'm trying . . . the wind is too strong!"

The B-2 slammed into the runway overrun, bounced back into the air, slewed to the right, then smashed violently onto the runway.

"Emergency brakes!" Matthews ordered.

Evans pulled the yellow-and-black-striped handle, then sat paralyzed as the bomber veered toward the left side of the runway. The left main gear dug into the soft, rain-soaked turf, dragging the aircraft farther to the left. Evans gripped the glare shield with both hands. "Here we go!"

The B-2 went off the runway, right brake smoking, and plowed twenty-eight hundred feet to a shuddering stop, leaving three deep furrows in the soggy ground. Both pilots sat dazed, their hearts racing, as they watched the array of vehicle lights approaching them.

"The nose gear held," Evans sighed, letting out his breath slowly. "You did a hell of a job, Chuck."

"We were all passengers the last twenty seconds," Matthews replied, placing his hands on his shaking knees.

Simmons rubbed his bruised left leg, then slowly unstrapped his seat belt and shoulder harness. The color was rapidly returning to his face.

"Well, Simmons," Matthews said, removing his camouflage helmet and flight gloves, "you better step out and greet your associates."

Matthews and Evans unstrapped as Simmons wordlessly lowered the crew entrance hatch and stepped out of the B-2's belly.

Three Soviet GAZ field cars, each equipped with a mounted machine gun, surrounded the front of the Stealth bomber.

Three rain-soaked Cubans, clothed in camouflage khaki ponchos, manned the Russian guns.

A dark brown van roared down the wet taxiway, slowed quickly, then turned onto the muddy ground and plowed toward the B-2. The pilots watched the van slide to a stop between the field car on the left of the B-2 and the GAZ at the front of the aircraft.

"Ten to one the guy in the passenger seat is Russian," Matthews remarked as the two pilots watched a Cuban soldier jump out of the van. "Ivan must be the honcho."

The Cuban, carrying a submachine gun, gestured wildly for Simmons to get into the vehicle. The hijacker ran through the rain, splashing ankle-deep mud on his flight suit, and stepped through the van's sliding door.

"Well, Chuck," Evans said slowly, noticing the Russian motioning for them to get out, "it must be our turn."

"I'm afraid so," Matthews replied as he shut off the B-2's electrical system, ignoring the checklist. "We better keep our hands above our heads, Paul. Let's not give them an excuse to shoot us."

"Right," Evans replied, climbing out of his seat. He leaned back to allow Matthews to exit the hatch, then followed his aircraft commander out of the darkened cockpit.

Matthews waited under the B-2 until Evans joined him, then the pilots placed their hands on top of their heads and walked toward the van. The wind-driven rain drenched them as a half-dozen Cuban troops surrounded them. The leader, brandishing a revolver, gestured toward the van's open side door.

"In the car!"

Matthews nodded yes, not saying a word. In his peripheral vision he could see the beefy Russian staring at him. Both pilots stepped up into the van, hands on top of their heads, then sat down across from Simmons.

"Just do what they say," Simmons cautioned under his breath, "and you'll be okay."

Matthews and Evans did not respond, each surveying the

inside of the spartan Chevrolet conversion van. Two Cuban troops climbed into the vehicle, slid the door closed, then sat down on each side of Simmons, facing the American captives.

No one said a word as the landing light of the Russian flight leader appeared suddenly in the dense rain. The MiG-25 touched down hard in the violent wind shear, then rolled out of sight toward the end of the runway.

The number two MiG, following his leader by thirty seconds, slammed into the concrete, bounced into the air, dropped back, then hydroplaned out of sight down the runway.

"Put your hands down," the Russian ordered in moderately accented English, then turned halfway around in his seat. "We mean no harm to you, if you cooperate."

The two pilots lowered their hands to their thighs and stole a quick look at each other.

"To the hangar," the Russian commanded. He turned around, folded his burly arms, and stared straight ahead as the van bounced over the sodden ground to the taxiway. The three Americans and their guards remained quiet during the short ride to the local KGB director's office.

OFFICIAL RESIDENCE OF THE VICE PRESIDENT

The early morning sun, barely lighting the horizon, crept slowly into the haze over the nation's capital. A few cars, many with their headlights still on, were beginning to fill the arterials surrounding Washington.

Standing outside the front door of the vice president's home, PO2C Miguel Santos watched Defense Secretary Bernard Kerchner and Air Force Gen. Frank Parkinson step out of a limousine. The navy steward waited until the two men were fifteen paces away, then opened the door and saluted smartly.

Parkinson returned the salute and removed his cap as he followed Kerchner into the entranceway. Santos took the general's cap, then ushered the men into the vice president's dining room.

"Good morning, sir," Parkinson said as Truesdell rose from his chair.

"Good morning, gentlemen," the vice president responded, pointing toward the two place settings on the table. "Please have a seat."

Kerchner and Parkinson took their seats as Truesdell sat down and replaced his napkin. The three men remained quiet while another steward placed a hot urn of decaffeinated coffee on the table, then poured freshly squeezed orange juice for the two visitors.

When the stewards returned to the kitchen, the vice president addressed both men. "Any news?"

Kerchner, looking fatigued, sounded unusually glum. "Only that our morning search is getting under way. We have had a lot of help from the Canadians throughout the night. They provided four search vessels, but not a trace of debris has been located."

"Nothing?" the vice president asked, sipping his coffee.

"No, sir, not a single thing," Kerchner responded, then turned slightly to face Parkinson. "General, how long will it take to thoroughly cover the area where we think the Stealth went down?"

Parkinson set down his juice. "Three to four hours, depending on the weather. We're using seven helicopters and four fixed-wing aircraft, augmented by a couple of helos and three aircraft supplied by the Canadians. Of course, we will continue the search much longer, but we should have some idea of what happened inside of four hours."

Parkinson hesitated a moment, then turned to face the vice president. "As I stated last evening, sir, if the B-2 went into the bay, which seems most likely, there will be evidence floating on the surface."

Truesdell remained quiet, ignoring his breakfast. After a silent minute, the vice president looked at Parkinson. "Tell me about the pilots—their credentials, service records, and backgrounds.''

''Sir, I don't have all the information at the moment.'' Parkinson looked uncomfortable. ''General Donovan assured me that he would have their biographies, officer evaluation reports, and flight records available by the time we leave for Camp David. They'll be waiting for us at the helicopter pad.''

''Very well,'' Truesdell responded, looking at his watch. ''Time to go. The president is waiting for a full report.''

SAN JULIAN AIRFIELD

The Revolutionary Air Force and Antiaircraft Defense Base, guarded heavily by a combination of Soviet and Cuban soldiers, lay adjacent to the sleepy village of Mendoza. The air base, on the western tip of Cuba, near the Gulf of Mexico and Peninsula de Guanahacabibes, was 170 kilometers west-southwest of Havana.

Soviet Stealth experts, technicians, and combination soldier/construction specialists had been preparing San Julian for the B-2 hijacking for more than seven months. An underground hangar had been built below the guise of a baseball field. The camouflaged facility, wide and deep enough to conceal the bomber with four feet to spare at each wing tip, had been constructed with cement blocks. A row of offices, work spaces, sleeping quarters, a kitchen, a restroom, a sophisticated communications center, and a reinforced cell stretched the length of the back of the hangar. After three sides of the hangar had been completed, Soviet and Cuban construction workers placed steel beams across the top to support a section of playing field in front of the bleachers.

Virtually all construction had taken place at night, with the bright playing lights diffusing the work lights under the well-used ballpark. The excavation process had consumed five months because of the difficulty in disbursing the soil around the air base. Satellite reconnaissance had not detected any changes at San Julian over the course of construction.

Shadow 37 had been towed back onto the runway, then down a specially prepared road to the hangar. The half-mile path to the secret hangar, after the rocks, foliage, fences, and posts had been replaced, disappeared prior to dawn. Steel mats had been used to transport the Stealth to its hiding place, eliminating any telltale ruts in the soft, rain-soaked ground.

The secret bomber now sat in the brightly lighted underground shelter. The sloping ramp into the hangar had been covered and now supported a section of bleachers. Two Cuban workers, wielding high-pressure water hoses, were washing mud off the B-2's modified Boeing 757 landing gear. The right gear door had been damaged slightly during the slide through the muddy field.

Chuck Matthews placed his spoon on the food tray and looked at his watch. "Six-twenty-five. No sleep. Reasonable breakfast. Must be about time for a friendly session with the interrogator."

"I've been thinking about that, Chuck," Evans responded, rubbing the stubble on his cheeks. "No harm, boys, as long as you cooperate."

Matthews snorted. "As long as you sing like magpies, we won't kill you . . . yet." The fatigued bomber pilot ran a hand through his close-cropped hair. "Do you figure the Pentagon believes we're at the bottom of Hudson Day?"

Evans thought about it. "Even if they don't believe that we crashed, where in the hell would they start looking for us?"

Matthews placed his tray on the floor, then met his copilot's eyes. "Paul, do you think the Soviet government is really behind this?"

Evans paused, analyzing the question. "I can't see it . . . not with the Communist empire falling apart."

"But there might still be some hard-liners, some factions holding on. Obviously there are, and our fate is in their hands."

Evans exhaled in frustration. "Who knows what the hell is going on."

"Christ," Matthews said, shaking his head slowly. "I really blew this one."

"Chuck," Evans responded in a comforting tone, "easy on yourself. You did the only thing you could do, short of killing all of us. You're not a suicidal moron."

Matthews looked at his friend. "Well, Paul, we're on our own. We better think about a way—"

Evans placed his right index finger to his lips, then cupped his hand, fingers down, and walked it across the table like a spider, mouthing, Let's be quiet, this place is bugged.

Matthews nodded in agreement as he plucked a pen from the left shoulder pocket of his still-sodden flight suit. He hesitated a moment, then shook his head no and replaced the pen. The Russians would anticipate that move. The pilots had to sign and mouth the words to each other.

Evans nodded yes, then looked for any possible opening for a hidden camera. Matthews tapped his copilot on the shoulder, then used hand signals and exaggerated mouth movements to set their first priority. Reconnoiter in preparation to escape.

MARINE TWO

The gleaming Sikorsky VH-60 Black Hawk lifted off the helicopter pad, turned away from the White House, then accelerated toward the presidential retreat.

Kirk Truesdell picked up the blue leather-bound folder next to his seat, then settled back for the seventy-mile, half-hour trip. Kerchner and Parkinson, along with a military aide and three Secret Service agents, sat quietly while the vice president read the information concerning Shadow 37's crew. The defense secretary and General Parkinson had their own copies.

Truesdell read slowly, writing notes on the scratch pad

attached to the inside of the folder. After ten minutes, the vice president closed the folder, then stared out the cabin window.

Turning back to Kerchner and Parkinson, Truesdell reopened the folder. "Lieutenant Colonel Matthews has a very distinguished background."

"Yes, sir," Parkinson replied, looking closely at Matthews's record. He shifted his gaze to the page with Evans's background. "Major Evans is impressive, too."

"Yes, he is," Truesdell responded, turning a page. The vice president studied the flight record section before speaking again. "They certainly have amassed a great deal of flying experience," he remarked, then looked at his comments. "Both are qualified aircraft commanders, and Colonel Matthews is a B-2 instructor pilot."

The vice president glanced at his folder again, turning a page. "I see that Major Evans had a reprimand for buzzing Falcon Stadium in a B-1."

Parkinson shifted uncomfortably in his seat. "Yes, sir, but it was an authorized flyover before the air force-navy football game. He just made the pass a little low."

Truesdell smiled. "Professional enthusiasm?"

"Yes, sir," Parkinson grinned slightly. "The crews train hard to fly on the deck, and Major Evans wanted to show the taxpayers what kind of capability they were getting for their dollars."

"Apparently the academy brass didn't buy that," Truesdell replied, turning to the background sheet. "Colonel Matthews graduated fourth overall in his class at the academy, then finished first in flight training. Earned a master's in aeronautical engineering at MIT."

"Yes, sir," Parkinson responded. "Evans has a graduate degree, too. Physics."

Kerchner looked up, adjusting his reading glasses. "Both married, have children, and live on base."

"Yes," the vice president replied. "Outstanding flying

records and solid credentials. They appear to be excellent pilots and officers.''

"They are, sir,'' Parkinson responded. "General Donovan told me, in confidence, that both families are happy and well adjusted.''

"We don't have much information about the civilian yet,'' Kerchner added, "but we expect the contractor to provide what they have in the next couple of hours.''

Truesdell acknowledged Kerchner's comment, then looked out the window again, not focusing on anything in particular. He remained quiet, watching the colorful fall foliage pass under the helicopter. His mind shifted back to the present when he saw the presidential retreat come into view. Camp David, nestled in Maryland's Catoctin Mountain Park, was covered with bright gold and red leaves.

As the marine helicopter slowed, then descended toward the landing pad, Truesdell could see the compound clearly. He studied the dining lodge and ten cabins, then gazed at the two swimming pools, horse stables, tennis courts, one-hole golf course, and the stream noted for its trout fishing. The vice president rechecked his seat belt as Marine Two came to a stop in midair, then gently, almost imperceptibly, descended to the ground.

When the main rotor blades began winding down, a marine sergeant in dress blues opened the sliding door, then locked it into position. Truesdell, followed by Kerchner and Parkinson, stepped out of the helicopter and walked past the saluting sergeant. The president of the United States, Alton Glenn "AG" Jarrett, walked forward to greet his three guests.

President Jarrett was a personable, compassionate, family-oriented man who divided his free weekends between Camp David and his home on the New England coast. "We have had word from General Donovan,'' Jarrett said, as they made their way to the presidential retreat. "The airborne search is under way—has been for more than an hour—and they haven't spotted anything thus far.''

"I don't expect they will find anything," the vice president responded, "if my hunch is correct."

Kerchner and Parkinson looked at each other in surprise, then glanced at Truesdell. The president was already forming his words. "What do you mean, Kirk?" Jarrett asked, frowning.

"Let's wait until we have some privacy," Truesdell responded, "if you don't mind, sir."

"I agree, Kirk," the president replied, arching his eyebrows in an unspoken question. "I've had a strange feeling about this since our conversation early this morning."

The group walked the last few yards to the main lodge in quiet contemplation. Each had questions to resolve in the strange mystery of the missing Stealth bomber.

After the four men had settled into the president's office, Jarrett opened the conversation. "Kirk, tell us what's on your mind."

Truesdell reached for the writing pad on the small conference table. "I'm not as well versed about airplanes as General Parkinson," the vice president said, "but I've been a licensed pilot for more than twenty-two years, and this disappearance defies everything I've ever heard of—short of being swallowed by a UFO."

Kerchner and Parkinson glanced at each other, clearly puzzled.

Truesdell paused a moment, contemplating the bizarre situation. "An airplane the size of the B-2 doesn't disappear without any trace. Especially on a designated and precise route segment."

The president turned to Parkinson, waited a moment, then asked a question. "General, what is your professional judgment—what do you think happened to the B-2?"

Parkinson calmly folded his hands together on the conference table. "I'll be very candid, Mister President. I don't know what happened."

Jarrett pressed harder. "You must have a personal feeling, or some intuition, general."

"Yes, sir," Parkinson responded guardedly, "I do. First, and most logical, is that the aircraft strayed off course and crashed in some remote area. It could be anywhere—it's invisible to radar, especially low to the water, or ground."

Kerchner raised his hand slightly, indicating he had a question.

"Bernie," the president acknowledged quietly.

"I'm sorry, general," Kerchner said in a pleasant voice, "but I can't subscribe to that theory. The crew was highly qualified, as we discussed, and they had the most precise navigation system available." He saw Truesdell nod his head in agreement. "Besides," Kerchner continued, "General Donovan says that the emergency code flashed on the Canadian radar screen directly over the route the Stealth was flying, at the exact time the aircraft should have been there."

Kerchner looked at Parkinson, then Jarrett. "Too coincidental."

"You're right, Bernie," Truesdell replied. "I believe that the Stealth was commandeered—hijacked."

"What?" Kerchner said, stunned. "You believe the B-2 was stolen?"

Truesdell waited to respond, seeing the surprised look on everyone's face. "Yes, I do. Our Stealth bomber is one of the most highly classified weapons systems we have. We know the Soviets have been trying, without much success, to develop a Stealth aircraft for the past six years. There are undoubtedly some in the military who aren't willing to accept the loss of power. It would be a real coup to snatch a Stealth aircraft."

Parkinson tensed. "Are you suggesting that our pilots would defect?"

"I'm not accusing anyone, at this point, general," Truesdell said, then turned to Jarrett. "I have a couple of suggestions, with the president's permission."

"Of course, Kirk," Jarrett replied, taken aback by Truesdell's speculation.

"First, we need to run a thorough background check on

all three men aboard the B-2. At the same time, we need to query every air traffic control center and sector in the Stealth's range," Truesdell said calmly, fixing his gaze on General Parkinson. "The aircraft didn't vanish into thin air."

"I concur," Jarrett replied, turning to his secretary of defense. "Bernie, call Fred Adcock at FBI. Make it top priority. We have to have answers in a matter of hours, not days. I want them to concentrate their efforts on the civilian technician."

"Yes, sir," Kerchner responded, shaken by the thought of a B-2 being captured by renegade Russians.

The president turned to Truesdell. "Kirk, have Mel Collins get the FAA moving. We need to know if any FAA facility had anything unusual occur last night. Have him go directly into the system—no passing it down the ranks."

"Yes, sir," the vice president responded, sliding back his chair. "General, check with SAC and see what they've found."

"Yes, sir," Parkinson replied, shaking his head slowly in disbelief. "They should be into their third sweep."

CHAPTER FIVE

SAN JULIAN

Matthews and Evans could hear muted sounds coming from the hangar, but no particular sound was distinguishable. Both men had remained quiet since lunch, resting uncomfortably on the well-worn army cots. Their food trays remained on the small wooden table. The leftovers, hardened in the past four hours, were beginning to emit an offensive odor.

Without warning, the heavy cell door opened with a bang, startling the two pilots. "On your feet now!" the Cuban soldier ordered. "Follow me."

Matthews and Evans looked at each other, shrugged, then walked through the door into the brightly lighted hangar. Two more guards, carrying AK-47 assault rifles, fell in behind the Americans.

Both pilots stole quick looks at the frenzied activity around the Stealth bomber. A power cart had been plugged into the B-2, bringing the aircraft's systems to life. Teams of technicians swarmed over the warplane, taking notes and photographing the interior and exterior. A dozen panels had been removed from the fuselage and wings, exposing the intricacies of the bomber.

Matthews noted that the guards behind them remained at least ten yards away. Well trained, he thought as they reached the entrance to the KGB director's office.

Gennadi Levchenko, sitting behind an olive-drab metal desk, motioned for the pilots to enter. "Have a seat," Levchenko said pleasantly, adjusting his wire-rimmed glasses. His English, after years in the United States, was excellent.

Matthews and Evans sat down on the long bench across from the Soviet agent. The three guards remained standing, blocking the only exit from the room.

"You will have a cigarette?" Levchenko asked, placing a pack of Pall Malls on the front edge of his desk.

"No, thank you," Matthews replied, placing his hands on his knees and arching his stiff back muscles. Evans, remaining quiet, shook his head in a negative response.

"Well," Levchenko continued, then paused while he glanced at Evans, then back to Matthews. "We can make this easy, or we can make this difficult for you. Very difficult. The choice is yours."

Matthews inhaled deeply, measuring his response, then exhaled. "You know our position. We are being held captive—prisoners. You, whomever you represent, have committed a gross violation of international law."

Levchenko smiled slightly, clasped his hands together, then leaned across the desk. "So, major, you elect to make my job more difficult?"

"My rank is lieutenant colonel, and you get nothing but name, rank, and serial number."

"That will soon change, believe me," Levchenko said without emotion. "You will see."

"Cut the crap," Evans said, openly bristling.

Levchenko's watery, pale blue eyes hardened. "You are right, major. We will cut the crap, as you say."

The room remained quiet while Levchenko stood up, walked menacingly around the side of his desk, then sat on the metal top. The KGB director was only two feet away from the Americans. Both pilots could smell his tobacco-tainted breath.

"You will cooperate with me," Levchenko said in a pleasant, even voice, "or I will place you in a very undesirable environment until you change your mind."

"A gulag?" Matthews responded, staring into Levchenko's cold, cloudy eyes.

"Correct, colonel," the Russian replied, unsmiling. "A reconditioning course until you are ready to cooperate. You *will* cooperate, I assure you. It is only a matter of time."

"You're wrong," Matthews said vehemently. "We are prisoners of the Soviet Union, or Cuba, and—understand clearly—we will not cooperate with you."

Levchenko smiled broadly, then lashed out, backhanding Matthews into the side of his copilot.

"You goddamn coward!" Evans shot back, helping Matthews regain his balance.

"Take them to Mantua!" Levchenko shouted to the surprised guards, then yanked both pilots up by the front of their flight suits. "You bastards are going to beg me to let you die before I am finished with you."

CAMP DAVID

The late afternoon sun peeked through the trees as twilight settled over the vast presidential retreat. Two marine corps Sikorsky helicopters, a VH-3D and a VH-60, waited to fly the president and vice president back to Washington.

Alton Jarrett and Kirk Truesdell had agreed the first week of the new administration not to fly together on the same helicopter or aircraft. The risk of losing both the president and vice president in an accident was too great.

Secretary of defense Kerchner talked on a secure telephone as he perused a classified message. He looked up when the vice president walked into the communications room.

"The president is waiting, Bernie," Truesdell said, loosening his tie.

"Yes, sir," Kerchner replied, folding the slip of paper, "be there in a second."

Truesdell gave Kerchner a thumbs-up gesture, then returned to the conference table. "Bernie's on his way," the vice president reported, then sat down in his seat.

"Thank you," Jarrett responded, turning to Parkinson. "General, what is the current status of our search effort?"

"Not a trace, Mister President," Parkinson answered, pausing while Kerchner entered the room and seated himself. Parkinson sipped a glass of water. "They haven't found a single piece of evidence to indicate that the B-2 crashed into the bay."

"General," Kerchner interrupted. "Excuse me, but I have some disturbing news, I'm afraid. That was Fred Adcock on the phone. The background check on the civilian crew member disclosed a link to the KGB."

"What!" Jarrett exclaimed, anger registering on his face. "How could the FBI determine that so quickly?"

Truesdell and Parkinson stared at the secretary in disbelief.

"Fred said—and I quote—," Kerchner looked down at his hastily written notes. "The civilian technician, identified as one Lawrence Maynard Simmons, has categorically been linked to Irina Rykhov, a known KGB agent."

"Jesus Christ," Truesdell said softly, shaking his head in frustration. "How did that information get by the security people?"

"Apparently," Kerchner continued, "from the information Fred has now, Simmons holds a top secret clearance and has worked on the B-2 project for the past three years. He graduated from Cal Poly with honors and is an electronic engineering specialist. The liaison with the KGB agent was nurtured approximately four to five months ago, so the security people had no reason to suspect anything abnormal." Kerchner penned lines through two notations.

"Go on," Jarrett prompted, sitting back in his seat.

"The West Coast bureau," Kerchner continued, placing his pen down, "sent agents to Simmons's workplace, home of record, and usual haunts—the places he is known to frequent." Kerchner looked over the top of his reading glasses at the president. "He had moved from his home into an apartment three months ago. His wife had filed for divorce and left him debt ridden and overextended on all his credit cards. She left town in his only car, taking their daughter with her."

The vice president shook his head. "How did he become associated with the Soviet agent?"

"Well," Kerchner responded, turning to the vice president, "Fred admitted that the bureau backed into the answer. Neighbors and acquaintances of Mrs. Simmons told our agents that she ran away with a boyfriend—a handsome, dark-haired man with a foreign accent."

"I think I have the picture," Jarrett said, glancing at Truesdell.

"One of the FBI agents," Kerchner continued, "remembered a similar situation that happened about a year ago in San Diego."

"Oh, yes," Truesdell said. "The navy submariner—Wilson—the one whose wife jilted him, and he disappeared with his lover and the Trident D-5 information."

"The same team," Kerchner replied. "The FBI agent suspected it was the same KGB couple, and showed pictures to Simmons's neighbors and friends.

"Although Pankyev—Aleksey Pankyev—had altered his appearance since the San Diego operation, it was clearly evident that he was the same person. According to Fred, Pankyev and Rykhov have worked as a team for at least two and a half—possibly three—years."

"So," Jarrett said, "the couple finds a weak individual in a highly classified position, Pankyev romances the wife and destroys the relationship, then the woman—who I assume is very attractive—makes her move on the hapless, distraught husband."

"That is correct," Kerchner responded. "Both Soviet agents are very attractive and charming, and completely ruthless."

"Well," Truesdell replied, clearly disturbed, "we know how the hijacking was set up. Now we need to find out where the aircraft has been taken."

"Yes," the president said, "and who authorized the operation. Pankyev and the woman have to be reporting to someone tied to the KGB."

Truesdell looked at Kerchner, then turned to the president. "I'm sure the answers will fall into place when we locate the bomber."

Jarrett nodded, then reached for his attaché case. "We need to return to the White House and—" the president paused when he saw the intercom light flash, "get organized," he concluded, depressing the switch.

"Yes, Dorothy."

"Melvin Collins, FAA, for Vice President Truesdell."

"He will take the call in here," the president replied, motioning for Truesdell to answer the phone on the credenza behind him.

The vice president swung around and raised the phone receiver. "Hello, Mel. What have you found out?"

Jarrett, lowering his voice, spoke to the defense secretary. "Bernie, I want that airplane back—whatever it takes, whatever we have to do."

"I understand, sir," Kerchner responded, placing his pen in his shirt pocket. "My guess is that they most likely flew due north—over the pole."

"That's probably correct, sir," Parkinson added. "But they would have had to land for fuel. The best place, in my opinion, would have been on the ice cap."

Jarrett nodded in agreement, then opened his attaché case and placed his notes inside.

"We're going to have to . . ." Kerchner trailed off when the vice president placed the phone receiver down and swiveled to face the group.

"Well, gentlemen," Truesdell began, then folded his arms. "I believe I can tell you where our Stealth bomber is located—at the moment."

No one said a word.

"Somewhere in Cuba."

"Cuba?" Parkinson and Kerchner responded simultaneously.

"Yes," the vice president answered, noting that Jarrett had closed his eyes and lowered his head. "Mel Collins," Truesdell continued uneasily, "said that a senior air traffic controller in the Cleveland Center reported a strange occurrence last night. A corporate jet pilot radioed a report of a near midair collision seventy nautical miles south of Detroit, and—this is important—the controller's radar didn't show any other aircraft near the civilian jet."

"Would that be so unusual?" the president asked, raising his head. "I haven't piloted a plane a for a long time, but it seems as if there have been a lot of close calls lately."

"Yes, it is unusual—very unusual," the vice president answered. "As you know, sir, any aircraft flying at the altitude of a civilian jet—they were cruising at fifty-one thousand feet—has to file an instrument flight plan, and be in radar and radio contact."

"Could the crew have been mistaken?" Jarrett asked. "Did they actually see the object?"

Truesdell met the president's eyes. "The FAA contacted the captain of the corporate jet this afternoon, and he was adamant about what happened. He couldn't distinguish what kind of aircraft it was, but he swore that something flew directly under them south of Detroit. It was too dark for him to see the type of airplane, but he reported seeing a dim glow—like cockpit lights—flash under his jet."

"That still leaves a lot of questions unanswered," Parkinson replied.

"Just a moment, general," Truesdell said, turning toward the air force officer. "The civilian jet was traveling east to west, and the object passed under them from right to left—north to south.''

"I understand that, sir,'' Parkinson responded, "but that certainly isn't conclusive evidence that it was the B-2.''

"Perhaps not, general,'' Truesdell said, "but let me ask you a question.''

"Yes, sir.''

The vice president leaned toward the officer. "How fast does the B-2 cruise?''

"The Stealth, as you know,'' Parkinson said, caution creeping into his voice, "is a subsonic aircraft. It cruises in the same range—higher at times—as the majority of commercial airliners. Of course, it does have a substantial dash speed, if needed.''

"I understand, general,'' Truesdell replied. "What is the normal cruise speed, in nautical miles per hour?''

Parkinson thought for a second. "Normal cruise for the B-2 is approximately four hundred fifty to four hundred sixty knots.''

The president raised his hand slightly, indicating a question. "I'm not following you, Kirk. What does speed have to do with establishing the whereabouts of the B-2?''

"My point,'' Truesdell responded, looking directly at Jarrett, "is that the near midair collision happened a little over a thousand statute miles—approximately nine hundred nautical miles—directly south of the last known position of the B-2. Actually, the location of the emergency signal. If you draw a line from that point to the middle of Cuba, the near midair is almost directly on it.''

Jarrett glanced at Parkinson, then back to the vice president. Truesdell absently completed an arithmetic equation while he defended his theory. "General Parkinson states that the Stealth cruises at four hundred fifty—let's say four hundred sixty knots at altitude. So, we can assume that it would take two hours to reach the point of the near collision.''

"Okay,'' Jarrett said, "we can assume that the B-2 would

traverse the nine hundred nautical miles in approximately two hours. What's the bottom line?''

"A little more than two hours," Parkinson corrected, "counting the time to climb. The B-2, like any aircraft, climbs at a slower speed than its cruise speed."

"All right," Jarrett responded, "a little more than two hours. Do we know the time of the close call—the near midair?''

"Yes," Truesdell replied, then paused to look at his quickly written notes. "Cleveland Center has the occurrence on tape, with time hacks. That's normal procedure, and a copy of the tape is being sent to us.''

"What time was it?" Kerchner asked.

"Nine-fifty-seven, local time," Truesdell replied, then looked over to Parkinson. "Two hours, six minutes after the emergency code flashed on Canadian radar.''

THE ROAD TO MANTUA

The last few minutes of daylight were fading away rapidly as the rusted, dented Chevrolet van bounced down the partially paved highway. The torrential rains of the previous evening had washed thick mud and debris across the narrow, winding road.

Lieutenant Colonel Charles Matthews and Maj. Paul Evans sat on a bench in the back of the DAAFAR vehicle. Both men remained quiet, sitting angled away from each other. Their hands had been tied together behind their backs, then tied to each other.

The van lurched to the right to avoid a pothole, then rounded a tree-lined corner into an open expanse of roadway surrounded by grass and stubble. Across an open field, on the far side of a narrow stream, was a small civilian airport.

"Paul," Matthews said under his breath, "look out to your left.''

Evans glanced quickly at the four men in the forward portion of the van. One Cuban guard, sitting behind the steering wheel, was accompanied in the front seat by the chief of KGB security at San Julian. Another Cuban guard and a KGB security officer sat on opposing benches behind the front seats.

Evans studied the guards for a moment, then darted a look at the small private airstrip. He studied the layout of the short runway, then turned to Matthews, smiling.

Both pilots had seen the two ancient, dilapidated DC-3s rotting behind the single hangar. They had also seen an old, radial-engined trainer sporting a huge paddle-bladed propeller. Neither was sure of the country of manufacture, but the aircraft appeared to be of Soviet design.

"The gooney birds," Matthews said, barely moving his lips, "aren't airworthy, but the small plane looks like it's flyable."

Matthews stopped talking when the closest KGB agent looked back at the two pilots. The short, wiry Cuban also glanced at the Americans, then resumed his animated, noisy discussion with the driver. The senior KGB agent carried a 9mm Beretta. The two men in back held their AK-47s across their laps, seemingly unconcerned with the two disheveled Americans.

"Chuck," Evans whispered, straining against the rough ropes binding his wrists. "I think I'm almost out of this lash-up. Can you move your hands farther behind me?"

Matthews darted a quick glance at the guards, then moved his bound hands as far as he could stretch them.

"Just a couple more seconds," Evans said, struggling with the final binding that was cutting into his bruised wrists. "You ready to go for them?"

"Damned right," Matthews replied without moving his bruised lips. "Can you get me loose?"

"Yeah, I think so—just a second."

"Okay," Matthews said, sizing up their four adversaries. "You take scarface, and I'll get the one on the right."

Evans nodded. "Can you pull your left hand loose?"

"Yes," Matthews responded, feeling the cord go slack around his left wrist. "Jesus, Paul, you're amazing."

"You still have the end around your other wrist," Evans whispered, "but you're free."

Matthews, watching the guards, turned slightly to see Evans in his periphery. "When I say 'now,' let's go for their weapons and shove the bastards forward."

"It's our only shot, Chuck."

"You're right, and a damned good one," Matthews replied, feeling the adrenaline surge through his body. "Ready—one, two, three, *now!*"

Both officers catapulted across the van, smashing into the two guards with brutal force. Matthews yanked the AK-47 away from the smaller man, kicking him off his bench into the back of the front passenger seat. Evans had punched the KGB agent straight in the nose and ripped his rifle loose.

"Don't move!" Evans yelled, pointing the barrel into the Russian's face.

The Cuban driver panicked, then slammed on the brakes, sending Evans crashing over the Soviet officer into the back of the driver. Matthews fell on top of the other Cuban as the van slid to a stop.

"Don't move, goddamnit!" Matthews shouted, pointing the assault rifle at the soldier. "You okay, Paul?"

"Yeah," Evans replied, shoving his rifle barrel into the mouth of the KGB guard. "I'm fine."

"Get in the back," Matthews ordered, motioning for the four guards to move to the rear. "Move it, now!"

The Cuban, along with the two Russians, scampered to the back of the battered Chevrolet while Evans yanked the driver between the front seats.

"You heard the man!" Evans barked, gouging the driver in the ribs. "Move it, asshole!"

"Stretch out, face down!" Matthews ordered, shoving the startled men down on their stomachs. "Side by side."

"You, too," Evans said, kicking the driver in the back of his knees. "On the floor."

Evans held his AK-47 on the soldiers while Matthews removed the long, dangling cord from his right wrist. He tied the quartet together quickly, then unzipped the front of his flight suit and tore off his turtleneck. He ripped the soiled pullover into four strips and gagged each man.

"Paul," Matthews said, picking up his assault rifle, "turn this wreck around and let's take that narrow road about three-quarters of a mile back—the one just before the airfield road."

"The one going east into the trees?" Evans asked as he climbed into the driver's seat.

"Yes. We've got to get rid of these bastards, then try the airfield."

Evans pulled over to the side of the road, cranked the wheel hard to the left, then gunned the engine. "Are you going to kill them?" The van spun around, slamming the prisoners against the right side, then straightened out and accelerated.

"No," Matthews answered, leaning against the back of the front passenger seat for balance. "I thought about running over their legs to immobilize them, but that—"

"Oh, shit!" Evans said as another DAAFAR vehicle rounded a curve a quarter mile in front of them. "Grab a couple of their caps."

Matthews scooped the two Cuban military hats off the floor, handing one to Evans. "Paul, if we get stopped for any reason," Matthews said, checking the safety on his Kalashnikov, "we've got to take our chances—we've got to shoot it out."

"I know," Evans replied as he shoved the khaki uniform cap on his head. "I'm with you."

The pilots watched the approaching vehicle. One headlight cast a beam straight toward the van, partially blinding the two Americans; the other headlight pointed slightly downward at the road.

"Uh, oh," Evans said, squinting into the bright beam of the single headlamp. "It's one of the Russian jeeps!"

"Keep going straight," Matthews ordered. "Don't turn off the road."

The Soviet GAZ field car passed the van, continued a hundred meters, then rapidly slowed.

"Son of a bitch," Matthews swore under his breath. "Keep going." At that moment, the brake lights of the DAAFAR field car illuminated.

CHAPTER SIX

CIA HEADQUARTERS

The offices on the top floor of the Central Intelligence Agency (CIA), based at Langley, Virginia, were quiet. The deputy director of the CIA, David Ridgefield, sat staring out the window at the star-filled sky. The reed-thin, partially bald, fifty-three-year-old former attorney turned his gaze toward the twinkling lights of Washington. He waited patiently for his boss, Gen. Norman Lasharr, director of the intelligence agency, to conclude his phone call.

Lasharr, a ruddy-faced, no-nonsense leader, wrote two lines on his scratch pad, tore the page loose, and handed it to his second in command. Ridgefield reached over, grasped the piece of paper, then sat back. He could not believe his eyes.

Lasharr ended his conversation, placed the receiver on its cradle, and turned to his assistant. "I can't believe it either."

Ridgefield shook his head. "A renegade faction in Russia has one of our Stealth bombers?"

"I'm afraid so," the former marine corps commandant

replied with a look of disgust. "Sorry to call you in at this time of the evening, but we have a major hill to take."

"No problem, general. I'm just astounded that anyone in the Soviet Union would even think of capturing a B-2, in light of their reforms."

Lasharr pushed himself back from his desk. "That makes two of us, but there are still hard-liners—many of them wearing stars—who are blatantly resisting the military restructuring."

"How did whoever . . . ," Ridgefield paused, "how did this happen, sir?"

"It's a long story," Lasharr answered as he removed his military-framed reading glasses. Everyone at the intelligence agency called Lasharr either general or sir in his presence. When the director was out of earshot, his associates referred to him as Rambo. "I'll tell you about it later, Dave. Right now, we—the CIA—have a formidable task to accomplish."

"Find the B-2," Ridgefield stated.

Lasharr smiled slightly, then reverted to his normal, dour self. "That was Secretary Kerchner on the phone. The White House wants to use covert means to find out if the B-2 is in Cuba."

"Cuba?" Ridgefield responded, puzzled. "Are they—is the secretary positive it's in Cuba?"

"No, he isn't," the scrappy director answered. "However, all the evidence points to Cuba, and we have our marching orders."

"General," Ridgefield began, formulating a suggestion. "Should we use RAINDANCE?"

"Absolutely," Lasharr replied. "Secretary Kerchner made one thing very clear. The president wants that aircraft back in our hands as expeditiously as possible. The pressure is on the CIA, but we have carte blanche to find the B-2."

"We're not actually being charged with the responsibility to retrieve the aircraft," Ridgefield paused, "are we?"

"No," Lasharr answered, leaning back in his chair. "The White House doesn't want to make any accusations, or confront the Soviets or Cubans, until we know for certain where the Stealth is located. Our job is to find it, and find it fast."

Ridgefield looked concerned. "How far down in the agency are we going to reach, general?"

"You're looking at us, along with the director of covert operations," Lasharr answered, then gathered his messages into a pile. "Secretary Kerchner said to put a lid on it for the time being. Dave, I want you to initiate contact with RAINDANCE as soon as possible."

"Yes, sir."

"We're going to have to use the Vienna loop," Lasharr instructed. "The East German operative has been under surveillance since the wall crumbled, and we can't take the risk of exposing her. We'll have to retrieve her soon, but now isn't the time."

Ridgefield nodded in agreement.

"Also," the director continued, "locate our man with nine lives."

"Will do, general," Ridgefield replied, checking his government-issue watch. "So, you're going to place Wickham back in the saddle?"

Lasharr stopped and looked Ridgefield in the eye. "No one is better qualified, in my opinion, for this kind of operation."

MANTUA AIRFIELD

"Turn into the airfield!" Matthews ordered. "They know something's wrong."

"Chuck," Evans responded, swerving onto the muddy road leading to the small civilian airstrip. "Let's stop here and nail them when they come around the corner."

Matthews glanced down the road at the barely distinguishable hangar, then made a snap decision. "Okay, but we've both got to open up on them."

"Hang on," Evans shouted as he viciously jammed on the brakes, sending the careening van into a four-wheel sideways drift. As the Chevrolet ground to a halt, both pilots jumped out and crouched down in the muddy roadway.

"Go for the windshield!" Matthews ordered, raising the barrel of his rifle. "We have to make this count."

Fourteen seconds elapsed before the Soviet field car lurched through the corner, slid toward the edge of the road, then straightened.

"*Now!*" Matthews barked, squeezing the trigger on his Kalashnikov.

The GAZ swerved to the right in a spray of glass, spun around to the left, then slid to a stop. The driver, badly wounded, fell out of the vehicle and crawled a dozen feet before collapsing.

"Let's check it," Matthews said in a cautious voice. "Back me up, Paul."

"I'm right beside you," Evans responded as he stood erect in the mud. "We better see if—SHIT!"

Both men fired simultaneously when the other Cuban in the GAZ lunged for the mounted machine gun.

"Goddamn," Matthews shouted, watching the soldier slide down into the field car. "Let's move it!"

The pilots threw their weapons into the Chevrolet. Evans jumped into the driver's seat while Matthews pulled the four guards out of the van. He left the bruised men lying in the spongy mud and crawled into the passenger seat. Evans stomped on the accelerator as Matthews swung his door shut. The oversized tires threw up a shower of mud, then found traction.

"Head for that—whatever it is," Matthews ordered, bracing himself when the Chevrolet bounced across the bridge over the narrow stream. The van slewed sideways, then plowed onto the slippery road. Evans kept his foot firmly planted on the accelerator, whipping the steering wheel left and right to straighten the careening van.

"See any activity?" Evans asked as they neared the rusting hangar.

"No," Matthews answered, pointing at the dark-colored single-engine aircraft. "Take it straight across the ramp. Turn off the lights."

Evans pushed in the light switch and turned sharply to the right. "Hold on."

The van hit the edge of the slightly raised tarmac, bounced a foot into the air, landed with a jolt, and shuddered to a stop. Evans and Matthews, carrying the guards' AK-47s, leaped out of the Chevrolet and raced toward the Soviet Yakovlev Yak-18. The Soviet State Industries—manufactured trainer, circa 1957, squatted on its tricycle landing gear. A large white star, bordered in red with a blue stripe on each side, adorned the tail of the tandem seat aircraft.

"What is it?" Evans asked as they slowed to a walk beside the dull black, low-wing airplane.

"Beats me," Matthews responded, looking into the radial engine. "Let's hope we can get it started."

"Right," Evans replied, checking the landing gear and wheels. "It must be flyable—there's grease drippings on the struts and oil residue under the cowling."

"Okay, Paul, let's give it a try."

Matthews ducked under the left wing and raised his right foot up to the step leading to the back of the wing. He pulled himself up, tossed his rifle into the back seat, and turned toward Evans. "I'll fly."

"You'll get no argument from me," Evans replied as he followed Matthews onto the wing. "Let's get the hell out of here."

Both pilots slid back their respective canopies, jumped in, and fastened their webbed seat belts.

"What a bucket of bolts," Matthews remarked as he surveyed the antiquated, well-worn cockpit. "There must be some kind of master switch in here."

"Come on, Chuck," Evans urged, sliding shut his grazed canopy. "I don't like sitting here."

"I'm trying," Matthews replied, feeling hastily around the cockpit. "I need a goddamn flashlight."

Suddenly the silence was shattered when machine-gun fire ripped into the Chevrolet van.

"Oh, shit!" Evans shouted, ducking down into the dark cockpit. "That's coming from the field car. The sonuvabitch is still alive!"

Matthews frantically flipped two more switches, then another. Nothing happened.

"Oh, mother of Jesus," Matthews said, gritting his teeth as another burst of gunfire tore into the van.

"Come on!" Evans shouted, peeking over the edge of the canopy rail. "The bastard is coming up the road!"

"I'm trying!" Matthews yelled, toggling another switch. The cockpit came to life as gyros spun up, pumps surged, and a low hum settled over the interior.

"Go!" Evans shouted. "Let's go!"

Matthews found the well-worn starter engagement, shoved forward the fuel mixture lever, pumped the throttle, then toggled the starter.

"Come on, baby," Matthews said under his breath. "Do it for us."

The big, nine-cylinder, air-cooled, 260-horsepower Ivchenko AI-14R radial cranked over slowly. The fat, two-bladed propeller turned over four times before the engine coughed, then fired momentarily, and quit.

"Shit!" Evans swore, yanking his canopy backward to the open position. He raised his AK-47 and fired his last seven rounds at the approaching field car, then tossed the rifle over the side.

Matthews had the propeller turning again, and was pumping the throttle slightly, when the machine gun rounds ripped into the left wing.

"Oh, God," Matthews groaned a split second before the laboring engine coughed twice, belched a cloud of white smoke from the exhaust stack, then settled into an uneven idle.

"*Go!*" Evans shouted, firing the remaining rounds of the other Kalashnikov at the GAZ.

The Yak-18 surged forward as Matthews shoved the throttle halfway open, then stomped on the right rudder pedal. He had to make the takeoff from the middle of the short runway.

Evans tossed out the second rifle and slammed his canopy closed as the lumbering aircraft slid sideways onto the dark runway. Matthews shoved the throttle all the way forward. The cold engine hesitated, backfired twice, then surged to full power. The paddle-bladed prop slashed the air as the nine cylinders created a deep-throated roar.

The pilot watched the airspeed indicator register slowly, then move steadily faster. "Come on . . . come on . . . ," Matthews urged, watching the airspeed needle move upward. "We don't have much runway left. Go . . . , go . . ."

The Yak-18 was beginning to feel light—ready to fly—when several machine gun rounds tore into the right wing and fuselage. Two more shells sliced through the right main gear, exploding the tire. Shredded rubber slammed into the underside of the wing as the aircraft yawed violently to the right.

"Sonuvabitch!" Matthews shouted as he kicked left rudder, pulled back on the stick, and banked the struggling trainer to the left. The aircraft staggered, then straightened as he fought the controls.

"Hang in there!" Evans encouraged, willing the Yak-18 to fly. "Get the nose down!"

Matthews had already started easing the stick forward. The aircraft settled into ground effect, then accelerated to normal climb airspeed.

"You did it!" Evans screamed over the roaring engine. "Goddamn, you did it!"

Matthews did not reply as he smoothly banked the straining aircraft, then rolled out on a northeasterly heading. Key West,

Florida, home of a naval air station, Matthews reasoned, would be the closest sanctuary.

The Cuban soldier, bleeding profusely from hip and shoulder wounds, cursed the fleeing aircraft. He fired a three-second burst in frustration, then collapsed across the blood-soaked passenger seat. The small man, in shock and pain, grabbed the radio microphone and screamed into it. "*Necesito ayuda, pronto!*" I need help, quick.

The radio crackled. "*Repita, por favor.*"

The soldier shouted "escape" three times, then calmed enough to tell how the Americans had gotten away and what direction they had taken.

Matthews eased back the throttle and lowered the Yak's nose as they skirted along the coastline a hundred feet off the water. The bright moonlight provided good visibility for low flying. The fatigued pilot glanced up at the sparkling stars, thankful that the storm had moved rapidly to the west. He reached up, closed his canopy, and looked around the cockpit.

Evans cupped his hands around his mouth and shouted forward. "We have to stay on the deck!"

Matthews turned his head and shoulders as far as he could to the left. He could see Evans's taut face clearly. "We will." He turned back around and studied the worn cockpit. No radios or navigation gear, he noted, then checked the engine instruments. Uh, oh, he said to himself, then turned back to his copilot. "We don't have any oil pressure."

THE WHITE HOUSE

"Norm Lasharr understands the urgency," Kerchner reported to the president, "and the sensitivity of the situation. The agency expects to make contact with RAINDANCE in a matter of hours."

The Oval Office, at this time of the evening, was as quiet as a tomb. An eerie silence had settled over the White House, replacing the usual hustle and bustle of the staff.

"We have to have confirmation," Jarrett said, "and location, or our hands are tied. I intend to find the B-2 and retrieve it, or destroy it. Those are the only two options I will consider."

The vice president turned to Jarrett. "I have a suggestion that would give us some leverage in Moscow. Even if the Kremlin is not behind the hijacking, they must be aware of the operation."

Jarrett looked at Kerchner, then back to Truesdell. "I'm listening."

"We could seize one of the new Soviet Akula submarines. The Russians regard them as supersecret—their 'Walker-class' boats. The subs are the quietest in the world, with their state-of-the-art propellers and polymer friction systems. They've been tracked underwater at fifty knots." Truesdell glanced at Kerchner. "If an Akula disappeared, I'm positive that Moscow would help us locate our missing B-2."

Jarrett and Kerchner thought for a moment. "Kirk," the president responded, "I have two questions. Do you really believe that we have the capability to snare one of their submarines, and, in the event we are successful, what happens if they don't have the bomber?"

"We have the technical ability—the hardware—to seize an Akula, no question about it." Truesdell paused, evaluating the president's concerns. "Who else would hijack an American B-2? I feel that we need to play hardball with the Kremlin, beginning right now."

"Let me think it over for a while," Jarrett replied, looking at Kerchner. "Bernie?"

"Well, sir," the defense secretary responded, catching Truesdell's eye, "I feel confident that our Moscow informant will be able to ascertain the information we need."

The vice president rose from his chair and walked over to the window. "I suggest we form a contingency plan for every possible scenario we can envision, including the submarine option.''

After a moment, Jarrett responded. "Kirk, I agree with you, and our first priority is to deal with the media. The pressroom has been packed since early this morning, and the rumors are spreading like a plague.''

"True," Kerchner said. "We need some damage control—a press conference—to set the record straight. I recommend that I do that now, before we take any further steps.''

Jarrett, deep in thought, nodded his head in agreement.

"I agree," Truesdell said, walking back to his seat. "It's very simple. The secretary of defense tells the media the truth. A B-2 is missing, and an investigation is under way. More details when they are available. Period.''

"I concur," Jarrett responded, then faced Kerchner again. "Bernie, what about the agent—I've forgotten his name— who Lasharr wants to drop in Cuba?''

"Wickham," Kerchner answered. "Steve Wickham.''

"Oh, yes," Jarrett nodded. "He did a magnificent job rescuing our Kremlin mole when that Russian madman was about to destroy the world.''

Stephen Wickham, former marine corps captain, and decorated combat veteran of the Grenada invasion, was a minor legend in the Central Intelligence Agency. The rugged, dark-haired, six-foot-one-inch agent was considered a real-life hero. Wickham had been reassigned to Clandestine Operations after he had recuperated from injuries sustained during the Moscow rescue.

"General Lasharr," Kerchner continued, "believes that Wickham should reconnoiter the island—actually the location of the bomber, if we can ferret out the information—before we confront the Soviets.''

"I agree," Jarrett said. "We need to move fast, and aggressively. Bernie, I want the latest satellite information, along with aerial reconnaissance of Cuba, at daybreak.''

"Yes, sir," Kerchner responded. "I'll set it in motion, then go to the pressroom."

THE YAKOVLEV-18

"See if there are any life jackets back there!" Matthews shouted over the roar of the big radial. "I'm going to circle close to shore, in case the engine quits."

Evans searched frantically under his seat, along each side, and under the instrument panel. "Nothing back here!" Evans reported. "Anything up front?"

"No!" Matthews said, tapping the oil pressure gauge. It continued to indicate zero pressure. "We may have taken a round in the oil line."

"Chuck, the gauge could be faulty. Let's take our chances and get the hell away from here!"

"Okay," Matthews replied, checking the engine RPMs, then the two fuel gauges. The right wing tank indicated full; the left side showed three-quarters of a tank. "One more circle," he yelled over his shoulder, "and we'll head for Key West. We've got plenty of fuel."

Matthews banked the Yak-18 to the left again, visually checked his height above the water, then rapped the oil pressure gauge with his left fist.

The aircraft, bathed in soft Caribbean moonlight, circled once again over Cayo de Buenavista. Matthews knew that they could glide to the beach if the engine seized. "Here we go!" Matthews said, rolling out again on the northeasterly heading.

The air force pilot flew the Yak-18 along the Cuban coast, skirting the coastline at an altitude of 100 feet. They quickly passed Dimas, Nombre de Dios, and Cayo Ines de Soto, then turned a few degrees to the left, leaving the coastline.

Matthews checked the engine parameters for the thousandth time, looked down at the water, then turned to Evans. "So far, so good."

"Yeah," Evans shouted, "the gauge has to be faulty."

"You doing okay back there?"

"I'd be doing a lot better," Evans yelled, "if we were landing in Key West right now."

Matthews looked at the vibrating airspeed indicator. The large pointer, mounted through an oil-soaked, yellowed card, bounced from 190 to 260 kilometers per hour. "Paul," Matthews said, turning around again to Evans. "I can't tell what we're doing speed-wise."

Evans leaned forward, then shouted. "Feels like one-fifty to one-sixty."

"Yeah," Matthews replied. "From the sound of this engine, you'd think we were makin' three hundred knots."

"I'm counting the minutes," Evans said, looking back at the shrinking island. "How long do you figure before we hit the Keys?"

"I don't know," Matthews answered, cross-checking their altitude. He eased back on the stick to level the Yak-18. "I can't really visualize the distance. I'd say an hour and a half."

"Who cares!" Evans shouted. "We're on our way!"

"Damned right we are!" Matthews responded, watching the erratic wet compass. There was a hole in the instrument panel where the gyrocompass should have been. "This wet compass is all over the place."

"There isn't anything back here," Evans said, searching the instrument panel. "Line up on that constellation at your two o'clock—the one with the bright star in the lower left corner."

"Yeah, just above the horizon," Matthews replied, staring at Capella in the constellation Auriga. "Help me keep it in the same position."

Evans leaned forward in his seat. "I'll handle the nav and you can watch the alti—"

Both pilots were caught off guard when the Yak-18's rumbling Ivchenko radial engine surged, coughed, backfired repeatedly, then surged again.

THE P-3 BLUE SENTINEL

The United States Customs Service Lockheed P-3B Orion, November 91 Lima Charlie, cruised in a seventy-mile racetrack pattern twenty-five nautical miles west of Andros Island.

Two of the reconnaissance aircraft's four turboprop engines had been shut down to increase the loitering time. The gleaming white Orion, with two engines caged, easily maintained an altitude of 20,000 feet. The airborne early warning and control aircraft had been upgraded recently with new APS-138 radar, along with an AYK-14 computer.

Blue Sentinel number one, based at the Corpus Christi Naval Air Station, was flying the second of two eight-hour surveillance missions. The crew, four and a half hours into the shift, were vigilant in their quest to detect drug smugglers amid the Caribbean air traffic. Because Hurricane Bennett had forced the Customs Service to cancel the previous evening's mission, the P-3 crew knew that the smugglers had also been grounded, so they expected the volume of airborne traffic to be greater than usual.

Pete Vecchio, former navy lieutenant and E-2C Hawkeye combat information control officer, sat in front of his radar screen, tweaking the display board continuously in an attempt to filter out false returns from actual air traffic.

Vecchio looked at his friend, Willie Overholser, out of the corner of his eye. The former Coast Guard lieutenant was the P-3's air control officer. Overholser was diligently filling out a stack of official forms required after an intercept. The Orion crew had been instrumental in vectoring a Coast Guard HU-25 jet to a successful bust one hour earlier.

"Willie," Vecchio began, then paused. "I've got something strange here."

Overholser, surprised, glanced at Vecchio with a questioning look. "What?"

"Look at this," Vecchio said, adjusting the brightness of his screen. "Something's fishy here."

Overholser stared at the screen, then punched a computer button to place an overlay of Cuba on the images. The symbology showed coastal boundaries along with cities and all Cuban airports.

"Goddamn, Pete," Overholser commented, placing his headset on. "Those are MiGs coming offshore, see 'em?"

"Yes," Vecchio responded, adjusting the radar image. "Look here . . . just north of the Mariel Naval Air Station. That, Willie, is a flight of two MiGs, no question. Nothing else would accelerate that fast and be in formation."

Overholser was completely absorbed by the fast-moving images on the radarscope. "Pete, see if you can pick up any radio transmissions—scan UHF, VHF, and FM."

"Right," Vecchio replied, resetting the switches on his communications console. "Uh, oh . . . , Willie, take a look-see at this." Vecchio pointed at the APS-138's screen, then listened for radio calls from the MiGs.

"Jesus," Overholser muttered, enthralled by the Cuban Air Defense Force scramble. "There's two more MiGs—they came out of San Julian. They're already moving supersonic—has to be MiG-25s."

"Willie, this must be their target. See . . . right here," Vecchio said, pointing at the slow-moving symbol on his radar screen. "He has to be right down on the water. The returns are intermittent, but both MiG flights are headed for that spot."

"Anything on the radio?" Overholser asked, jotting down the time.

"No," Vecchio answered, then listened an additional fifteen seconds. "Just clutter."

"Where did you first see the low bird?"

Vecchio responded without taking his eyes from the radar console. "Just off the coast, northwest of Bahia Honda. I had a few returns before, but nothing steady. Probably false returns over the offshore coral.''

"We haven't seen this—a four-plane scramble—for a long time,'' Overholser remarked as he concentrated on the aerial intercept. "Look . . . right here. That looks like a helicopter— just off Mariel—going for the slow target.''

"Well, one thing's for certain,'' Vecchio responded. "They're damned serious.''

"Yeah, I'd say so.''

Vecchio watched the two closest Soviet fighters slow, then spread farther apart. "Hell, I thought it was a training hop, or a patrol flight.''

"Pete, not much flics around Cuba at night, believe me. I haven't seen anything like this before—two simultaneous MiG scrambles at night.''

"Well,'' Vecchio said, glancing quickly at Overholser, "whoever it is, he's in deep shit.''

CHAPTER SEVEN

THE YAK-18

"Sonuvabitch!" Matthews swore as he shoved the fuel mixture to full rich and jockeyed the throttle. "Keep running . . . come on . . . do it for us."

"What happened?" Evans shouted. His face was drained of color, and he had a deathgrip on the instrument panel glare shield. "Get the nose up!"

Matthews eased the nose up, climbed thirty feet, then leveled off again. "I don't know, maybe it took a slug of water through the fuel line. Hell of a rain last night—water may have leaked into a tank."

Evans took a deep breath. "Just keep it going, Chuck, and I'll sign over my retirement pay to you."

Matthews monitored closely the vibrating engine instruments—RPMs remained steady, temperature stayed in the green, but still no oil pressure. "Don't touch anything," he said to himself. "Not until we're over Key West."

Matthews raised his gaze, looked around the moonlit sky, then focused on the cluster of stars he had been using for navigation. Capella remained in the same position, winking through his canopy.

Suddenly his mind issued a sharp alert. Something had moved in the sky. Something very fast. He snapped his head back to the right, searching for the source of light.

"Oh, my God . . . ," the pilot said to himself. He yanked open his canopy, straining to hear over the roar of the howling radial engine.

"Paul!" he shouted, simultaneously rechecking his exterior lights. They were turned off. The Yak-18 was blacked out. "They're on us! We've got fighters overhead!"

"Shit!" Evans exclaimed, scanning the star-filled sky. He quickly spotted the MiGs. "They're slowing—coming over the top from the right."

"We're going down!" Matthews said as he shoved the nose over and concentrated on flying. "Right on the deck!"

MIG-25 FOXBAT 28

Lieutenant Colonel Igor S. Zanyathov, in rumpled street clothes and smelling of rum, listened closely to the Cuban radar controller's instructions. The radar specialist had lost the Yak-18 thirty-three miles off the coast, but the track indicated that the escapees were heading for Florida. The controller had calculated where the stolen aircraft should be by the speed and direction of flight.

The former squadron commander in the Soviet Frontovaya Aviatsiya (Tactical Air Force) cursed Levchenko's arrogance and stupidity, then cursed his own bad luck. The boisterous going-away party for Captain Robanov had progressed far into the second hour when the frantic KGB director had called.

Zanyathov checked the spacing between himself and his wingman, Maj. Anatoly V. Sokolviy, then rolled gently into a shallow bank to the left.

"They should be right below you," Zanyathov said to

himself, repeating the controller's words. "No they shouldn't, you idiot," continued the partially inebriated fighter pilot. "The Americans should be under heavy guard in the B-2 hangar, spilling their guts about every operational aspect of the secret bomber."

Zanyathov searched the surface of the ocean, trying to catch any movement. He glanced at his altimeter, then continued his turn until the moon was directly on the tip of his left wing. The Yak-18 would be hard to spot, but it was down there somewhere.

"*Kak pozhivayete*, Major Sokolviy?" Zanyathov radioed to his wingman.

"I am fine, colonel, except for my head."

Zanyathov felt the same effects from the potent rum. "I share your suffering."

Sokolviy looked up through his canopy. "The other interceptors are orbiting overhead. I see their anticollision lights."

"You have young eyes, major. Use them well tonight."

"Yes, colonel."

"Follow me down," Zanyathov ordered, easing back his two throttles. "We will not contact the other flight unless absolutely necessary."

"*Da.*"

The MiG-25's powerful Tumansky turbojets wound down as Zanyathov lowered the nose and rolled into a steeper turn. The Russian pilot knew that he had to be successful in thwarting the Americans' bold escape. The KGB director would pay dearly if the news of this fiasco got out. Zanyathov knew that Levchenko would see him dead if he did not succeed in returning the daring Stealth crew.

Zanyathov could still hear Levchenko swearing over the MiG's radio as the two interceptors had lifted off the runway in afterburner. The message had been clear. If the American pilots were not brought back alive—so their operational and technical knowledge could be gained—Zanyathov and Sokolviy had no reason to return.

"I see the aircraft!" Major Sokolviy radioed his flight leader. "Off your right wing, colonel. Just forward of the wing tip."

Zanyathov searched the area, scanning back and forth, then saw the Yak-18 low over the water. The dark aircraft was bathed in luminous moonlight. "Yes, I have them," Zanyathov acknowledged, steepening his descent. "The Americans are brave—they are almost in the water."

Zanyathov set his armament panel switches, then selected his two 23mm guns. The intercept would be very delicate. He had to turn back the Yakovlev without destroying it. Killing the Americans would seal his own fate.

"How damned ironic," Zanyathov said to himself, spitting out the words. "The Americans are more important to my country than I am." He keyed his radio. "Major Sokolviy, I am descending for a firing pass. Remain in high cover."

"Da, colonel. Be careful."

The lead pilot descended to fifty meters above the water, slowing the MiG-25 to thirty kilometers above the clean configuration stall speed. He rechecked his gun switches, turned slightly to line up on the Yak-18's left side, then added a small amount of power.

"Major, I will make a firing pass to the left, then pull up in front of them. Keep a close watch, in case I lose the Yakovlev in the turn."

"I will not lose them, colonel."

Zanyathov, rapidly approaching the fleeing Americans, pressed lightly on the firing button.

THE YAK-18

"Here he comes!" Matthews shouted over the screaming radial engine. "Goddamnit! We're not turning back!"

Red tracer rounds spewed out of the Foxbat, flashed by

the side of the trainer, arched out in front, then disappeared in the distance.

"Stay low," Evans yelled, watching the MiG-25 approach, "and start jinking!"

Matthews watched his altitude closely, then turned his head to the left. The MiG would be abreast of the unarmed Yak-18 in four seconds. "Hang on!" he warned. "Here goes!"

The desperate pilot pushed the control stick to the left, turning in knife-edged flight directly at the MiG-25.

"Oh, God . . . ," Evans moaned, flinching as the Foxbat's nose snapped up and the two afterburners went to full military power. The roar of the thundering turbojets was earsplitting as the Yak-18 passed twenty feet below the MiG. The small trainer almost rolled inverted before Matthews could snap the wings level.

"They're going to blow our asses off!" Evans shouted, sliding open his canopy. "The MiG driver has to be one mad sonuvabitch."

Matthews was working the controls in an effort to constantly change their path of flight. He guided the Yak-18 through a series of skidded turns, slips, and porpoise maneuvers while maintaining the general heading to Key West. He looked over his left shoulder again, then sideslipped the Yak close to the water. "Keep an eye on him!"

The Foxbat pilot wrapped the fighter around in a tight turn, continuing to slow, then eased the nose toward the fleeing trainer. The MiG pilot was in a perfect guns position.

"Hang on!" Matthews cautioned as he rolled the low-flying Yak-18 into a seventy-degree right turn and chopped the power to idle. The deceleration was instantaneous.

Straining under the g loading, Matthews looked over his right shoulder as the MiG-25 snapped into a tight right turn, stalled, then slammed into the water a split second after the afterburners were lighted. The Foxbat exploded in a blinding flash as cold water rammed through the air intakes into the red-hot turbojets.

"You suckered him in!" Evans shouted, pounding the cockpit glare shield. "You did it!"

Matthews added power and leveled the wings, then looked up and scanned the dark sky. "Where's the other MiG? I've lost him!"

"Ahh . . . okay, I've got him," Evans responded, tightening his seat belt. "Four o'clock and coming down fast."

Anatoly Sokolviy, adrenaline pumping through his veins, was in a frenzy. The pilot knew that Director Levchenko, the omnipotent mastermind of the B-2 operation, would have to answer for the loss of Lieutenant Colonel Zanyathov. Sokolviy's mission had changed. He was driven to stop the wily Americans—any way possible—and avenge the death of his flight leader.

The MiG-25, Sokolviy knew only too well, had not been designed to fight slow-moving light aircraft flying on the deck. Many fine pilots had lost their lives the same way as Zanyathov. He had let his aircraft get behind the power curve, then attempted an abrupt maneuver low and slow.

Sokolviy adjusted his armament panel, selecting his single AA-7 Apex missile. If he missed, he had two more AA–8 Aphids to fire at the fleeing aircraft. He checked the missile arming control, then heard the rescue helicopter.

"*Sudak Chetirnatsat* [perch fourteen] is on station," the excited Soviet helicopter pilot blurted. "Did the runner go in the tank?"

"*Nyet*," Sokolviy growled over the frequency. "Stay off the radio."

The Yak-18 was only three kilometers ahead of Sokolviy when the fighter pilot lowered the MiG's nose. "Kiss your asses goodbye, you clever bastards," Sokolviy said under his breath when the ready-to-fire light glowed. "Come on . . . track . . ."

Sokolviy raised the MiG's nose a couple of degrees, then

rolled into a gentle right turn to line up with the tail of the Yak-18. "Got it!" Sokolviy said triumphantly as he squeezed off the air-to-air missile.

"Break right! Break right," Evans screamed. "Missile!"

Matthews tightened his stomach muscles, then groaned under the snap g load he forced on the trainer. The Yak-18, in knife-edged flight, changed course ninety degrees in three seconds. "Coming back!" Matthews said in a strained voice. "We gotta stay down—"

The pilot's statement was cut off by a flash and a deafening explosion forty yards in front of the aircraft. The AA-7 Apex had missed the trainer and impacted the water, detonating with a thunderous roar.

"Oh, shit!" Matthews swore as he leveled the wings and yanked back the stick.

The Yak-18 flew through the geyser of water and debris, staggered, shuddered, then dropped off on the right wing.

"Hang on!" Matthews shouted, chopping the throttle. "We're goin' in!"

Both pilots grabbed their glare shields and braced themselves for the impact. The Yak-18's right wingtip sliced into the water, sending the trainer into a cartwheeling, end-over-end crash landing. The crumpled fuselage, missing the right wing and three feet of the left wing, came to rest inverted.

Matthews yanked repeatedly at his seat belt, thrashing from side to side. Finally, when his lungs felt as though they had been set on fire, the pilot freed himself and struggled out of the sinking aircraft. Orienting himself with the rising bubbles from the sinking wreckage, he kicked off from the side of the cockpit and clawed his way upward.

Gasping and sucking air, he broke the surface and looked around frantically for Paul Evans. The slightly injured pilot could see bits of floating debris surrounding him, but nothing that resembled his friend.

"Paul!" Matthews shouted, treading water and turning

constantly. He could taste the foul, greasy aviation fuel. ''Paul!''

Matthews, who had been on the swimming team at the Air Force Academy, gulped more air and dove below the surface. He fought his way downward in the pitch-black water, felt the stub of a propeller blade, then crawled along the side of the mangled fuselage. He passed the front cockpit, cutting his right hand on the fractured canopy, and reached into the rear seat. His left hand touched Evans's arm, then moved up to his face. Matthews yanked back his hand, recoiling in horror.

Paul Evans had not suffered long, if at all. His face had slammed into the instrument panel, breaking his neck. Matthews was sickened by the unnatural twist and angle of his friend's head.

Feeling the water pressure build as the Yak-18's fuselage sank below twenty feet, Matthews tugged at Evans's seat belt. The locking device opened easily and Matthews pulled on Evans's torso.

He yanked repeatedly on his copilot, then realized the problem. Evans was trapped in the twisted cockpit, crushed between the seat pan and the glare shield.

Matthews, in agony and frustration, and feeling the onslaught of oxygen starvation, let go of his close friend and shot for the surface. His oxygen-starved mind was slipping into unconsciousness, a kaleidoscope of colored lights dancing in front of his eyes, when his face popped out of the water.

The pilot treaded water instinctively while his lungs heaved in an effort to suck in life-sustaining air. He felt his head clear rapidly and his strength return. His mind shifted from concentrating on survival, to rage.

Four seconds later, Matthews heard the combined sounds. They had been there all along—the MiG-25 overhead and the approaching Soviet helicopter—but he had blocked them out in his mental trauma.

"You SONS OF BITCHES," Matthews bellowed, watching the approaching searchlight from the rescue helicopter.

THE P-3

Pete Vecchio stared at the APS-138 radar screen as he recorded the time and exact location. "Ah . . . Willie, I can't believe this."

"Believe it, Pete," Overholser replied quietly, energizing the LINK-11 secure data communications system. "The MiG flight leader went in the drink, and his wingman, as I see it, splashed the slow mover."

Vecchio turned to the air control officer (ACO). "We better get on the horn."

"Yeah," Overholser responded, keying the communications button. "Stay with 'em." The ACO adjusted his lip microphone, rechecked the radio frequency, then spoke to their operations center. "Corpus Operations, Tar Baby One Five."

"Corpus Ops, One Five," the Texas-based coordinator replied, "go ahead."

"One Five has a priority," Overholser radioed in an even voice. "We just witnessed two aircraft crash in the water seventy nautical miles west of Havana. One of the aircraft, we believe, was a Cuban MiG."

Vecchio and Overholser listened to the surprised operations officer as they watched the three MiGs return to their respective air bases.

SAN JULIAN

Gennadi Levchenko anxiously waited at the control tower for the rescue helicopter to return. The tower chief, *Starshiy Praporshchik* (Senior Warrant Officer) Yevgeny Pogostyan, had just sent word that the helicopter was nine minutes out.

Levchenko had already spoken with Maj. Anatoly Sokolviy, who had been extremely hostile and defiant. The confrontation had ended abruptly when the MiG fighter pilot, encouraged by his fellow aviators, walked away from the contentious KGB director.

Pogostyan ran down the steep stairs of the control tower, then hurried across the tarmac toward Levchenko. "Comrade director, the helicopter pilot reports only one American survivor."

"We only need one," Levchenko snorted. "What condition is he in?"

"He is reported," Pogostyan said cautiously, "to have suffered only cuts and bruises."

"Excellent!" Levchenko spat, turning to the ranking KGB officer now in charge of security. "Talavokine," he shouted at the short, beefy agent. "Come here!"

The security officer turned to the Cuban army lieutenant, said a few quick words, then walked over to Levchenko. "Da, comrade director," the security expert said, standing uneasily.

Levchenko glared at Talavokine. "You will be personally responsible for the confinement of the American. I don't care if you have to guard him yourself—twenty-four hours a day. Do you understand me, Talavokine?"

"Yes, clearly, comrade director."

"Good."

The surprised KGB officer avoided Levchenko's eyes by staring over his right shoulder.

"If there is one screwup," Levchenko said, shaking his right index finger in the officer's face, "I will see that you spend the rest of your miserable career as a clerk on Taymyr Peninsula in Siberia."

The agent swallowed, then nodded his understanding.

"If you allow him to escape again," Levchenko warned, "plan your own escape. You will both be dead men."

"Da, comrade director," the officer stammered. "I will not allow anything to happen."

"Meet the helicopter," Levchenko ordered, seeing the approaching Mil Mi-17's landing light illuminate, "and escort the prisoner to the hangar."

The KGB agent backed away without responding, then turned and walked toward the squad of Cuban soldiers.

Levchenko, shielding his eyes from the rotor wash, watched the Mi-17 descend to a hover in front of the tower. The big Isotov turbines caused the ground to vibrate as the pilot lowered the helicopter gently onto its wheels. Levchenko turned and walked to his field car, then ordered the driver to take him to his office.

NEUNKIRCHEN, AUSTRIA

Fritz Kranz was startled awake when the phone rang. The sixty-eight-year-old, white-haired, heavyset, retired thoracic surgeon struggled with the bed cover, then freed his feet. "One moment, please," Kranz mumbled, fumbling for his robe. He patted his wife. "Sorry, my Katy."

"Who could it be at this hour?" she asked.

"I don't know, dear."

The phone rang again and again, loud and obtrusive in the quiet cottage. Kranz searched for his slippers, then gave up and crossed the bedroom cautiously, opened the door fully, and stepped into the hallway. He turned on the single light and picked up the ringing phone.

"Kranz."

"Herr Doktor," the cheery male voice said, "I am Johann at the cable office."

"Yes."

"I apologize for the untimely intrusion, but we have a cable for you, marked most urgent."

Kranz's mind raced. He had received only four urgent cables during the nine years he had worked with the Central Intelligence Agency. "Oh, yes," Kranz replied, rubbing the sleep from his puffy eyes. "We have been expecting an urgent message. I must be in the city early this morning, so I will stop by your office."

"Very well, Herr Doktor," the pleasant voice said. "Again, my apologies."

"You are very kind," Kranz responded, straining to see the grandfather clock in the living room. The antique time-piece indicated 4:54 A.M. "Good morning."

Kranz replaced the phone receiver, then started for the small bathroom. He replayed the procedures in his mind. Was RAINDANCE still secure?

"Who was it, Fritz?"

"One of my patients, dear They don't seem to understand that I am retired."

Kranz dressed hurriedly, grabbed his medical bag, kissed his dozing wife good-bye, and drove the sixty kilometers into the heart of Vienna.

Entering the city, Kranz slowed near the Hofburg. He glanced at the Lippizaner stallions across the avenue. The beautiful horses turned the cold morning air to steam with their breath.

As he passed the historic imperial palace, Kranz mentally reviewed the CIA code and procedures used to contact RAINDANCE. This type of connection was referred to in the agency as a three-arms'-length transaction. Trust and obscurity held the loop together.

Nearing the cable office, Kranz allowed his mind to drift back a few years. He could clearly see his dear friend and mentor, Doctor William G. Keating, former Dean of Medicine at Harvard University. What wonderful years we had, Kranz thought to himself, remembering how Keating had arranged for Kranz to enter the prestigious medical school.

Fritz Hoffmann Kranz had been one of three highly gifted foreign medical students whom Keating had sponsored in 1948. Keating had respected the young Austrian for his study habits and diligence in pursuing the highest standards of the medical profession. The two men had developed a close relationship—some said like father and son—and Fritz became part of the Keating family.

During the Christmas holidays of 1949, Kranz had married Keating's daughter, Kathryn Lynne, two years his junior. During the spring of 1955, the Kranzes, with their three-year-old daughter, Anna, moved to Austria. Fritz and Kathryn had made it a ritual to return to Cambridge, Massachusetts, every other year for the holiday season.

Kranz had never known about Keating's involvement with the CIA until the day Keating had recruited him. That had been three weeks before Keating died. Fritz and Kathryn had rushed home, accompanied by Anna and her children, to be with the terminally ill doctor. Bill Keating had called his son-in-law into his bedroom, offered him three fingers of Chivas, then laid out his desire for Kranz to accept the responsibility that Keating had been fulfilling for the CIA.

Fritz Kranz had been incredulous initially. The retired Dean of Medicine had explained to Kranz the proposed relationship with the CIA, who the contact would be, the fact that Kranz, with his background, would never be suspected of espionage, and that he would be serving a very worthy cause.

Kranz had resisted politely but firmly until Keating had reminded him of the question he had asked his sponsor upon entering Harvard. Fritz Kranz had remembered the words clearly. "How can I ever repay you, Doctor Keating?" Keating followed the reminder with the disclosure that he could not, under any condition, trust anyone else except his son-in-law. Fritz Kranz had embraced the dying man, then vowed solemnly to continue the service that Keating had been providing for the CIA.

Kranz snapped back to the present as he parked at the cable office. The streets were slowly beginning to fill with people and traffic. The retired surgeon stepped out of his well-worn BMW, shut the door, and walked into the small, unadorned office.

"Good morning," the jovial clerk said.

"Good morning," Kranz replied. "I am Doctor Kranz. You called in regard to a cable."

"Oh, yes," the young man responded. "Have it right here."

Kranz quickly signed for the cable in an unreadable scrawl, then took the envelope and placed it inside his jacket pocket. "Thank you."

"You're quite welcome, Herr Doktor," the clerk replied as Kranz opened the squeaky door and stepped outside.

Well, Fritz, Kranz thought, let us pray no one has been compromised. He returned to his automobile, started the engine, patted his jacket pocket nervously, then drove to the Hotel Sacher at Number 4 Philharmonikerstrasse.

The CIA intermediary, carrying a small overnight bag from his trunk, checked into the elegant hostelry, then hurried to his room on the second floor. He placed the Do Not Disturb sign on the doorknob, locked the door, and reached into his jacket for the cable.

Kranz sat down at the wooden desk, opened the envelope, and spread out the paper. He looked only at the first word in each sentence.

BEA IS DECEASED STOP TWO CEREMONIES PLANNED
STOP
AIRCRAFT ACCIDENT STOP MISSING YOU STOP
CHARLES

Kranz checked his watch, lifted the phone receiver, and rang the switchboard.

"Hotel operator," the soft female voice responded.

"Yes," Kranz said, looking at the cable. "Please connect me with the international operator."

"One moment."

Kranz waited, running RAINDANCE's phone number through his mind. He had had to memorize a new seven-digit number after Mathias Rust, the West German private pilot, landed his Cessna 172 on Red Square. The upper echelon of the Troops of Air Defense had been shuffled, resulting in a new assignment and relocation for RAINDANCE.

"May I help you?" the international operator asked.

"Ah, yes," Kranz responded, looking at his hotel phone number. "I wish to place a call to Moscow. The number is two-four-one-four-four-three-zero." Kranz glanced again at his watch, hoping that his Kremlin contact had not left his quarters.

The phone rang three times, then a fourth, before it was answered. "Lieutenant General Voronoteev."

"I have a person-to-person call for Pyotr Syrokomskiy," Kranz said, then waited for RAINDANCE to respond to the code name.

"You have the wrong number," Yuliy Lavrent'yevich Voronoteev, deputy commander of Rear Services, Troops of Air Defense, replied in heavily accented English.

Kranz hesitated two seconds, allowing Voronoteev time to prepare to write seven numbers. "This is not six-five-four-one-five . . . ah, eight-two?" Kranz asked, giving Voronoteev his five-digit phone number in reverse, then adding his room number in reverse.

"Nyet," Voronoteev answered bluntly, abruptly banging down the phone.

Kranz hung up and looked again at the cable. He knew that Voronoteev would call him back as soon as the Soviet officer could reach a public phone. Kranz got up and walked to his window, feeling uncomfortable with his espionage role. He gazed at the Vienna State Opera House a few moments, then scanned the cable again.

CHAPTER EIGHT

MOSCOW

Lieutenant General Yuliy L. Voronoteev folded the slip of paper containing the numbers, placed it in his shirt pocket, and slipped on his uniform jacket. He brushed back his short-cropped salt and pepper hair, picked up his cap and carefully placed it on his head, then walked out of his seventh-story Kalinin Avenue apartment. After carefully locking the door, he strolled the length of the freshly painted hallway.

The slender, sixty-one-year-old former fighter pilot rode the elevator down to the parking deck, then stepped outside into the brisk morning air. Voronoteev inhaled deeply, glanced across the hazy skyline of Moscow, and walked toward his chauffeur-driven sedan.

Voronoteev's driver, standing beside the Voyska PVO (Troops of Air Defense) Moskvich 412, saluted smartly as he opened the door. "*Zdrastvuytye*, comrade general."

"Good morning, Sergeant Ogorkhov," Voronoteev replied, returning the greeting and salute as he entered the gleaming automobile. "We will make a brief stop at the government department store before going to the Kremlin."

"Da, comrade general," the young driver replied, closing the door carefully.

Yuliy Voronoteev sat quietly, wrestling with his deeply implanted, mixed emotions of loyalty and hostility toward the Rodina—the Motherland. Each time he committed treason, regardless of the magnitude of the offense, Voronoteev justified his act by dredging up his contempt for Soviet ineptness and brutality. After committing treason, the Air Defense officer habitually spent two or three days locked in his Kalinin apartment, drinking Stolichnaya around the clock. After a protracted period of inebriation, he had always managed to purge his disdain for the unnecessary injustices he had endured.

Voronoteev stared out of the Moskvich 412's side window at the overcast sky, lost in the memories of his wife, while Sergeant Ogorkhov negotiated the turn from Kalinin Prospekt onto Manezhnaya Street. The general glanced at *troitskiye vorota*—Trinity Gate—that led to the Palace of Congresses inside the Kremlin compound.

Returning to his thoughts, he remembered the day that his beloved wife had died under the scalpel of an incompetent butcher. Although that had been thirty-four years ago, the events were as clear in his mind as if the tragedy had happened yesterday.

Larissa Innova Voronoteev, eight months pregnant, had suffered severe complications while her *starshiy leytenant* husband had been undergoing flight training three hundred kilometers away. Three days past her twenty-fourth birthday, she had died from a massive hemorrhage when the surgeon bungled the cesarean section. The female infant, deprived of oxygen for more than eight minutes, had died the following afternoon.

Voronoteev recalled vividly the utter helplessness he had felt when his squadron commander had met him at the steps to his MiG-21F. The young fighter pilot's shock and deep sense of loss had turned to rage when the lieutenant colonel explained that Larissa had died two and a half days earlier.

"The stupid bastards," Voronoteev said quietly, unaware that he had spoken. His mind was consumed by the contempt he felt for the doctor and the administrators who had taken almost sixty hours to relay the message of his wife's tragic death.

"Excuse me, comrade general?"

Voronoteev looked up at the face reflected in the rearview mirror. "What, sergeant?"

"I thought the general had asked a question," the driver said, slowing for traffic.

"No," Voronoteev replied in a pleasant voice, "just thinking out loud again."

"Yes, sir."

Voronoteev gazed at the Kremlin Corner Arsenal Tower as his driver accelerated in the flow of traffic. The anguish and hatred swelled in his stomach again, as it always had, when he thought about Larissa's miserably incompetent doctor.

Voronoteev had doggedly pursued a clear explanation of how and why his wife had died. Weeks after his beautiful Larissa had been laid to rest, the young lieutenant had discovered the awful truth. The relatively inexperienced physician had had a record of substandard performance, coupled with a history of frequent transfers and a known drinking problem. The sad part, Voronoteev thought angrily, was the fact that the marginally qualified doctor was still practicing.

Sergeant Ogorkhov eased the Moskvich 412 to a smooth stop in front of the large government department store, better known to Muscovites as GUM. The driver stepped out and hurried around to open his general's door.

"I'll only be a few minutes," Voronoteev said, stepping into the cold air.

The driver acknowledged Voronoteev, then quickly returned to the driver's seat to stay warm.

Lieutenant General Yuliy Voronoteev, ramrod straight, shoulders squared, entered the mammoth department store and walked to a bank of public telephones. He unbuttoned his jacket, reached into his shirt pocket, and glanced around the cavernous building before extracting the piece of paper.

He placed the call, then waited for his contact to answer. Voronoteev could feel his pulse quickening as he continued to scan the interior of the building. No one appeared to be taking any interest in the handsome officer.

HOTEL SACHER

Fritz Kranz sat quietly at the small birch desk, tapping his fingers absently on the smooth top. He looked at the telephone, took a deep breath, then stood and started toward the shuttered window.

Kranz flinched when the phone rang. He hurried back to the desk and lifted the receiver. "Peter Wipplinger," Kranz answered, using the fictitious code name.

"Hello, Peter," Lieutenant General Voronoteev said cheerfully. "Alexei Arbatov, returning your call. It has been a long time."

"Yes, my friend," Kranz responded evenly. "Good to hear your voice again."

"Thank you, professor," Voronoteev replied, carefully scrutinizing the dirigible hangar-shaped building. "What news have you heard?"

"My colleagues at the university," Kranz answered uncomfortably, "have reported that a B-2 Stealth bomber is missing. The speculation is that it did not crash."

"That is very interesting," Voronoteev replied, placing the small strip of paper back in his shirt pocket. He knew what Kranz was alluding to. Some Soviet faction apparently had their hands on the top secret bomber.

"Peter, I have a call on another line," Voronoteev said, seemingly surprised by the news. "I'll contact you when I am not so busy."

"That will be fine, Alexei. I look forward to hearing from

you,'' Kranz replied, then acknowledged Voronoteev's salutation and replaced the receiver in the cradle.

The Austrian physician felt somewhat relieved, knowing that his contact would not call again until the next day. The follow-up calls were always between three and five o'clock in the afternoon, allowing Kranz to return home while he retained the room. He always left toilet articles strewn in the bathroom, and he rumpled the bed, as if it had been slept on.

Kranz walked into the well-appointed bathroom, then stared at his puffy face in the oval mirror. ''Fritz, you're too old and you get too nervous for this kind of nonsense.''

PORT DOUGLAS, QUEENSLAND, AUSTRALIA

The captain of the power catamaran *Quicksilver II* waited patiently, along with his thirteen scuba diving enthusiasts, for one of their companions to complete his telephone conversation. The noisy group, anxious to reach the outer regions of the Great Barrier Reef, had been delayed already by a faulty fuel line.

After receiving a new fuel hose, *Quicksilver II* had cast off scant seconds before the Sheraton Mirage's courtesy van had slid to a grinding halt at the dock. The ensemble had watched curiously as the tanned American had leaped from the catamaran to the pier and run the short distance to the shouting messenger. Most of the passengers had noticed the two large scars on their American diving companion, one on the right shoulder, the other across his lower back.

''I'll go see what the problem is,'' Rebecca Marchand offered, stepping onto the wooden dock.

''Thanks, mate,'' the leathery-skinned captain responded, admiring the beautiful, blond-haired young woman. He could clearly see the skimpy blue and white bikini under her thin cover-up.

The Pan American Airlines flight attendant was only twenty

feet from the small passenger shelter when her fiancé, Stephen Wickham, raced out the door. "Becky, we have to cancel— I'll explain later."

"What's wrong, Steve?"

"I'm not exactly sure," he answered, darting a look at the catamaran. "Let's grab our gear."

Steve turned to the hotel driver. "Hang on, we'll be just a couple of seconds."

"Take your time, Mister Wickham," the easygoing Australian said, leaning against the front fender.

Steve and Becky trotted down to the waiting catamaran, apologized to the skipper and their fellow passengers, retrieved the rented diving gear, then hurried back to the Sheraton's passenger shuttle.

"Honey, I have to go back," Steve said, lowering his voice when the driver opened his door to get in. "Some kind of crisis at the agency."

"You've got to be kidding," Becky responded as the shuttle van accelerated toward the hotel.

"Becky, I know this isn't fair to you, but something very important—really big—has happened. I honestly don't know the particulars, but it's a category one panic."

"Steve, can't they assign someone else? You're on vacation—a well-deserved vacation I might add—and we've only been here three days."

Steve placed his hand on Becky's thigh and patted her in an affectionate manner. "Hey, kiddo, I know you're upset, but it isn't as simple as it sounds."

Becky raised Steve's hand and held it between hers. "I'm not upset with you, Steve. It just seems that every time we arrange anything together . . ."

"I know," Steve responded, "and I can only apologize."

Becky turned slightly to look directly into Steve's sparkling green eyes. "What could be so important that you have to cancel your vacation and race back to Langley?"

Steve remained quiet a moment, selecting his words carefully.

"Stephen," Becky said, tilting her head slightly, "you're holding something back, aren't you?"

"Could we give this a rest," Steve said in a hushed whisper, "until we get to our room?"

Becky paused, giving her fiancé a stern but understanding look. "Yes, Clark Kent. Just one thing."

"I know," Steve replied, trying to suppress a grin.

"Well, why not?" Becky asked in a pleasant manner. "After risking your life in the Marine Corps and damn near getting killed last year in Russia . . . Steve, taking an administrative position isn't the end of the world. You're an excellent manager and leader."

Becky stopped, knowing that this was not the time to discuss her ongoing concern about Steve's profession. "I love you," she said, still clutching his hand, "and I want to spend a long, happy life with you."

Steve Wickham grinned again, revealing his even, white teeth. "Sitting together in our rocking chairs, staring out across the lake?"

"That's right," Becky chuckled, nudging her husband-to-be with her shoulder.

The van stopped at the entrance to the hotel. Steve tipped the driver and followed Becky to their room. Closing the coral pink door of their suite, Steve turned to his fiancé. "Honey, do you want to stay over for a couple of days?"

Becky looked at Steve with a quizzical expression. "No. I want to be with you. We'll go back together and I can spend some time in Washington."

Steve put up his hand, indicating that he needed to explain the situation. "Becky, it isn't quite that easy. I won't be going back on the airline, and . . . I won't be going to Langley."

Becky sat down on the floral print couch and crossed her slender legs. "Okay, Steve, out with it."

Steve walked to the small refrigerator and grabbed a can of Foster's lager. "Care for anything?"

"Yes," Becky replied, pulling a pillow toward her. "An explanation."

Steve popped the top and sat down in a chair across from Becky. "Honey, you don't hold a clearance, but I'm going to tell you as much as I can." Becky nodded, curling her shapely legs under her thin cover-up.

Steve swallowed a quick mouthful of the cold brew. "The Navy is sending a fighter—an F-14 Tomcat—to pick me up and boom me to Key West, Florida. That's all I know right now, honestly."

"Steve," Becky hesitated, "fighter planes don't have the ability to fly nonstop from Australia to Florida."

"Honey," Steve responded, sipping his Foster's, "the Navy is going to aerial refuel the Tomcat all the way across."

"I don't like this, Steve," Becky said, a frown on her attractive face. "The agency doesn't fly CIA agents halfway around the world in a fighter plane if it isn't some kind of crisis."

The former marine corps infantry captain placed his aluminum can on the end table, hesitated a brief second, then leaned forward. "Becky, I haven't explained to you what I'm doing at the present time . . . in the agency."

Becky stood, walked to the refrigerator, and took out a bottle of chilled champagne. "I was saving this for tonight, but I believe now would be an appropriate time to open it. Please go on."

Steve cleared his throat quietly. "I was reassigned to Clandestine Ops after I came back from recuperative leave."

"Clandestine Ops," Becky repeated, popping the cork out of the cold bottle. "That sounds like a nice, safe, long-term career position."

Steve could see the concern on Becky's face. Of all the women he had known in his life, Rebecca Marchand was the first who had made him have second thoughts about marriage and his CIA career. He put his arms around his future wife, then placed her head on his shoulder. "Honey, I promise we'll talk about alternatives when I get home, okay?"

"I'll bet you tell that to all the girls," Becky replied, smiling slightly. "How long until they pick you up?"

Steve looked at his watch. "About two hours. A Tomcat is en route from Cubi Point—it was already airborne when I got the message."

"Well," Becky said as she untied her cover-up and let it drop to the floor, "let's enjoy the time we have."

CHAPTER NINE

LANGLEY, VIRGINIA

Norman Lasharr dropped his linen napkin on his dinner tray, pushed aside the plate holding the remains of his swordfish steak, then ran a rough hand over his white crew cut. "It would damn sure figure," Lasharr said to Hampton B. Milligan, director of CIA Clandestine Operations.

"Yes, sir," Milligan responded, avoiding the gaze of David Ridgefield. "At least we found him."

Ridgefield placed his tray aside and wiped his mouth. "Hamp, in the future—especially where Mister Wickham is concerned—have your people leave an address and phone number where they can be reached in an emergency."

"I've taken care of it, sir," the West Point graduate replied, chagrined. The bags under Milligan's eyes made him look older than his forty-seven years.

Lasharr swallowed the last of his tea. "When will they have Wickham in Key West?"

Milligan, a former Green Beret, looked the CIA director straight in the eyes. "They should be airborne fairly soon, general—CINCPAC estimates the aircraft will arrive at Key

West between seven and eight tomorrow morning.''

"Good," Lasharr replied as he extracted a sheaf of papers from his battered leather briefcase. "Hamp, I want you on the way to Key West as soon as we conclude this brief.''

"Yes, sir," Milligan answered tersely. "I've got a C-20 waiting at Andrews.''

Lasharr did not acknowledge.

"The vice president," Lasharr said, leafing through his papers, "and Secretary Kerchner are in battery. They made one thing very clear this afternoon. Results—now, whatever we have to do to accomplish the objective.''

"Any clues, general?" Ridgefield asked.

Lasharr, unusually exasperated, studied his neatly printed remarks. "We have too many troops stirring this gumbo, but here's the current status.''

The director put on his glasses and repositioned himself in his high-backed chair. "Satellite and reconnaissance photos were negative. The TR-1 made three passes, including a fairly low pass. The recon driver did a great job and the sky was crystal clear, but there wasn't anything that appeared unusual.''

Ridgefield wrote himself a reminder, then looked up at his boss. "General, how do you plan to employ Wickham?''

"That depends," Lasharr replied, underlining one of his remarks, "on whether we receive any information from RAINDANCE before we introduce Wickham to Cuba.''

"Excuse me, general," Ridgefield said with a surprised look, "but I thought we were going with the reconnoiter operation as expeditiously as possible.''

Lasharr rolled his eyes to look at his deputy. "That's correct, Dave, but the vice president has really focused on the western end of the island.''

"Any particular reason," Ridgefield asked, "or just intuition?''

Lasharr removed his military-style glasses and rubbed the bridge of his nose gently. "Seems as if a Customs aircraft— one of our antidrug airborne early warning planes—witnessed something very unusual last night off the northwestern coast of Cuba.''

Milligan's curiosity was aroused. ''Oh?''

''They relayed the incident,'' Lasharr continued, placing his glasses back on, ''through the FAA, and the White House had the story shortly thereafter.''

''What did the Customs people see?'' Ridgefield asked, intrigued by the possibility that the Stealth had been involved.

Lasharr looked at Milligan, then back to Ridgefield. ''They witnessed four MiGs chase a low, slow-flying aircraft out to sea, where a melee occurred. One MiG apparently went into the drink, along with the small aircraft. The Customs crew watched a helicopter hover over the general area where the slow airplane went down, then return to shore.''

''That's rather strange,'' Milligan responded. ''Where did the chopper land?''

''Don't know,'' Lasharr answered. ''The Customs folks lost it in ground clutter. However, they stated that it didn't appear to be returning to the base where the flight originated.''

Ridgefield stood and walked to the lighted wall map displaying the locations of CIA station chiefs. ''Does the vice president think the incident is related to the B-2 disappearance?''

''Yes,'' Lasharr answered, looking at the island of Cuba on the map. ''So docs Secretary Kerchner.''

''What do you think, general?'' Ridgefield asked as he walked back to his chair.

''It does seem mighty unusual,'' Lasharr answered, then thought a moment. ''The Cubans wouldn't send four MiGs after a drug smuggler. Only two reasonable answers come to mind. Either an important person was trying to get away, or our B-2 pilots were attempting to escape—if we follow the theory that the bomber is in Cuba.''

Ridgefield sat down. "Well, we're going to have to depend on Wickham to supply the answer."

"General," Milligan said, "back to RAINDANCE, if you don't mind, sir."

"Sure, Hamp," Lasharr responded pleasantly.

Milligan shifted slightly. "Dave gave me a composite brief on RAINDANCE when I accepted this assignment, but frankly, sir, I'm not clear about the operation. We actually have a source in the Soviet bureaucracy?"

"Two sources," Lasharr answered, nodding slightly to Ridgefield. "Dave, fill Hamp in on RAINDANCE."

"Yes, sir," Ridgefield replied, then faced the surprised Clandestine Operations director. "Hamp, there are a few things that have been buried very deep in the past couple of years. Only a few people in the White House, along with General Lasharr and myself, know about them."

"But," Milligan paused, "I'm the director of Clandestine Operations."

"You've been in this game long enough," Lasharr interjected, "to know some things aren't brought to the surface unless it's absolutely necessary."

Milligan remained silent, agreeing with a nod of his head. He knew the director's penchant for security.

"As the general said," Ridgefield continued, "we have two intelligence sources within the Kremlin military and civilian bureaucracies. One is a rather low-echelon member of the administrative staff to the first deputy chairman of the Council of Ministers."

The deputy director waited a moment, allowing Milligan time to absorb the information. "The other source is a lieutenant general, code name RAINDANCE, on the staff of Troops of Air Defense. He's a recent graduate of the Voroshilov General Staff Academy."

Lasharr rose from his chair, stacked his papers neatly, then turned to his deputy and the director of Clandestine Operations. "Let's take a real detailed look at the Cuba enlargement, then see if we can answer some what-ifs."

CAIRNS, QUEENSLAND

Steve Wickham, feeling uncomfortable in the tight-fitting torso harness, looked out of the right side of the F-14D's rear canopy. He could see Becky standing in the shade next to the Qantas jumbo jet. She was shielding her eyes with one hand and waving with the other.

"Ready back there?" asked Lt. Comdr. Reed Sandoline, swinging the big Grumman Tomcat around to line up with the runway.

"Yeah," Wickham responded absently as he waved back to the beautiful young woman dressed in baggy tropical tans. "I'm ready."

Sandoline held the brakes and advanced the power to 60 percent. He ran through one final check, confident that the Fox 14 was ready to fly.

"Navy Leadfoot One Zero Seven, Cairns tower, cleared for take-off. After lift-off, cleared on course, unrestricted climb."

"Roger," the experienced fighter pilot radioed, "we'll do all that."

Wickham was still craning his neck for a last glimpse of Becky when Sandoline shoved the twin throttles all the way forward. "Navy Leadfoot rolling."

The powerful General Electric F110 turbofans, collectively producing more than 58,000 pounds of thrust, slammed Wickham back into his seat as the F-14D accelerated rapidly. The Mach 2 plus— 1,600 miles per hour—twin-engine air superiority fighter thundered down the runway. The four AIM-9 Sidewinders had been hastily removed, along with the 675 rounds of 20mm cannon shells, leaving the aircraft "clean" except for the external fuel cells.

Sandoline raised the nose slightly, felt the Tomcat break ground, snapped up the landing gear handle, then trimmed the nose down slightly to remain in ground effect. The F-14D hugged the terrain and vibrated the airport structures as it blasted down the runway.

The pilot watched the airspeed increase—190 . . . 210 knots, flaps and slats up . . . 250 . . . 280, variable geometry wings swept back . . . 300, steaming, tweak the nose down.

"Hang on," Sandoline warned two seconds before he eased back on the control stick. The g force crushed Wickham into his ejection seat. His head sagged form the weight of the crash helmet.

The Tomcat's nose kept rising, higher and higher, until the fighter was in the pure vertical. Suddenly the sky rotated counter-clockwise as the pilot rolled the F-14 around its longitudinal axis.

"Nice flyin', Navy," the Australian tower controller radioed. "Contact departure. G'day."

"Roger, going departure," Sandoline responded, watching the altimeter wind through 4,000 feet. He rolled out on heading upside down, hesitated a moment to let the nose fall through the horizon, then continued the roll to an upright attitude.

Wickham heard the fighter jock converse with the air traffic controller as he watched the warm, translucent waters of the Great Barrier Reef slip under the Tomcat's wing. His mind wandered.

"You still with me?" Sandoline asked.

Wickham, who had been thinking about Becky, snapped back to the moment. "Ah . . . yeah," Wickham answered over the intercom. "Do you guys always take off like that?"

The pilot chuckled over the hot mike. "No, only when the Navy and the FAA aren't looking."

"I can just imagine," Wickham replied, enjoying the cool oxygen.

The F-14 trembled slightly as it accelerated through the speed of sound. Sandoline retrimmed the fighter continuously. "I flew with the flight demonstration team—the Blue Angels—for two years, and it's not easy readjusting to the fleet."

Wickham, smiling, watched the airspeed indicator pass 1.2 Mach. "Probably why you got this duty."

"You're right," Sandoline laughed. "What's the scoop? I understand you're with the CIA."

Wickham keyed his ICS. "You know as much as I do at this point."

Sandoline lowered the nose slightly. "I only know that you're going to Key West as fast as we can get you there."

Wickham did not respond, prompting another question from the Tomcat pilot. "Are you at liberty to tell me what the hell you do for the spooks?"

Wickham had become accustomed to answering the question whenever an acquaintance found out he was with the CIA. "Not actually. I do investigative work in specialized areas."

"Well, you must be damned good," Sandoline laughed. "All the staff weenies at Cubi, along with my CO, were jumping through their asses to get me launched."

Wickham checked his watch. "How many times do we have to refuel, commander?"

"Sorry," the pilot replied. "We were in such a hurry, I didn't give you a full brief."

"No problem," Wickham responded.

"It's Steve, isn't it?"

"That's right," the agent answered, adjusting his torso harness.

"Okay, here's the gouge," Sandoline said, then answered a radio call. "We're going high—close to sixty thousand feet—and fast. We'll be leaving a sonic boom the entire trip, except when we slow down to gas."

"What kind of range does this thing have?" Wickham interjected.

"Normally, Steve, approximately three thousand miles with the external tanks. At the speed we'll be averaging— more than a thousand miles an hour—we'll tank twice before we hit the boat."

Wickham looked around the back of the pilot's ejection seat. Sandoline had his helmet visor up and Wickham could see his eyes in one of the rearview mirrors. "Boat? What boat?"

"The aircraft carrier," Sandoline chuckled. "You'll love it, believe me."

Wickham met Sandoline's clear, hazel eyes in the pilot's mirror. "I'm sure."

"We'll rendezvous with a navy tanker out of Guam, then hit a Marine KC-130 six hundred miles south of Hawaii."

"Then the boat?" Wickham asked, taking in the cockpit instruments.

"Yeah, then the boat," Sandoline answered, grinning under his oxygen mask. "We'll deviate slightly north of course and hit the *Ranger* about seven hundred miles off the southern Baja coast."

"If my math is correct," Wickham paused, "that means we'll be landing at night."

"Hey, relax," Sandoline said, sensing Wickham's apprehension. "I've got more than four hundred traps without a scratch. Well, I did slip off the side of a wet cockpit once—twisted my ankle."

Wickham was not convinced. "Didn't I see where insurance actuaries rate being a carrier pilot as the most dangerous profession in the world?"

"Yeah," the aviator replied. "That and being a Tijuana cabdriver."

Sandoline talked with the controller again, signed off, then lowered the Tomcat's nose and leveled at 57,000 feet. The flight would be a quiet ride high above the weather and other air traffic.

The pilot keyed his intercom. "They'll hot-refuel on the *Ranger* and stuff in a fresh pilot. You'll gas again over the Gulf of Mexico, then dash into Key West. Piece of cake."

Wickham waited a few seconds before he responded. "How many night landings have you made?"

"Relax, Steve," Sandoline replied soothingly. "At night you can't see all the things that tend to scare you in the daytime."

Wickham glanced in the mirror again. "Thanks."

SAN JULIAN

Lieutenant Colonel Chuck Matthews had lost track of time. His watch had been smashed during the crash landing and he had discarded it in the Soviet helicopter.

The bruised and battered air force pilot, full of anguish over the loss of his copilot and best friend, looked around the hangar cell. Forcing himself to relax, he walked over to the rumpled bunk and sat down, thinking about his wife and the twins. He was deep in thought, envisioning the pain that Roxanne and the girls, Meredith and Michelle, were experiencing, when the cell door opened abruptly to admit the Stealth project director, accompanied by the KGB security officer and three Cuban soldiers.

Matthews met Gennadi Levchenko's eyes with a cold, unblinking stare. The B-2 pilot's swollen face expressed an intense, unbridled hatred.

"On your feet," the director bellowed.

Matthews remained sitting.

"You will obey me," Levchenko snapped, "or you will pay the consequences."

Matthews stood slowly, not taking his eyes off Levchenko's face. His hair was matted and he had dried blood on his left temple and ear and under his cheek.

Levchenko raised his unfiltered American cigarette to his lips, inhaled deeply, and turned toward Talavokine. "Hand me the list."

The KGB officer stepped forward and gave Levchenko three pieces of paper stapled together. "Now, Lieutenant Colonel Matthews," Levchenko said, exhaling the smoke, "you will answer these questions. If we discover that you have lied about any of them . . . well, let us say that it will not be in your best interest."

"We've been through this before," Matthews replied, controlling his anger, "or have you forgotten?"

Levchenko smiled crookedly, turned halfway around to see

Talavokine, then karate-chopped Matthews viciously across the throat.

The fatigued pilot, caught with his guard down, partially deflected the savage blow, tripped, then fell backward onto the bunk. Two Cuban guards rushed forward and placed the barrels of their AK-47s on Matthews's neck.

"I told you before," Levchenko growled, "that we can make it easy, or we can make it difficult. I mean to get the information I need that you possess."

Levchenko inhaled again, then exhaled while he talked in Matthews's face. "I have decided to move our schedule ahead, so it's your choice. Easy, or difficult? Which will it be, Colonel Matthews?"

Matthews glanced at each guard and Talavokine, then back to Levchenko. "Since we're talking about torture, why don't I just go ahead and give your goons a reason to kill me?"

"They won't kill you, colonel, until I have the information I need. You can attack me right now and they will simply beat you into submission."

Matthews swallowed twice, feeling the end of each barrel in the sides of his throat. "Pride. You must fill the mirror with it."

Levchenko grabbed Matthews's flight suit and yanked the pilot into his face. "It's real simple, swine. We don't have to torture you. We use a much more sophisticated system."

"Drugs," Matthews said, moving his head back slightly.

"That's correct, tough guy," Levchenko growled as he crushed out the Pall Mall on the floor. "We use Versed and Brevital. You will tell us every detail you know about the Stealth, along with the operational data and your command's warfare philosophy." Levchenko grinned again and lighted another cigarette. "You won't remember a thing, so don't be stupid and stubborn."

CHAPTER TEN

MOSCOW

Lieutenant General Yuliy Voronoteev sat in his office at Troops of Air Defense and stared out of the rain-streaked window. His gaze covered the Moskva River and Maurice Thorez Embankment, but his mind was not registering the image.

Voronoteev knew the Soviet military system as well as anyone. If the American Stealth bomber was in Soviet hands, then one of the persons who would know—who would have been included in the logistics—was the commander in chief of Troops of Air Defense, General of the Army Ilych Dankoffevich Borol'kov.

Voronoteev unlocked his desk and retrieved a bottle of vodka from the lower right drawer. He unscrewed the top from the container and took two quick swallows, then recapped the bottle and placed it back in the drawer.

The two-star general, knowing that Borol'kov was on an inspection tour at Kubinka Air Force Base, eighty kilometers west of Moscow, picked up his phone and requested the commanding officer. Voronoteev thought about the animosity that had developed between the two officers.

"General Borol'kov's office," the senior warrant officer answered in a high, nasal voice.

"General Voronoteev for General Borol'kov," Voronoteev said as he placed the latest monthly air defense report in an Eyes Only folder.

The administrative officer responded in his most pleasant manner. "I am sorry, comrade general, but the commander is visiting Kubinka today. May I be of assistance to the general?"

Voronoteev knew the unctuous and politically savvy warrant officer well. "I'm sure you can, Lugayev. I have a readiness report for General Borol'kov, and I need access to the last combat efficiency report."

"Absolutely, comrade general," Lugayev answered smartly. "I will have it delivered to your office immediately."

"No," Voronoteev responded, closing the snap on the classified folder. "It is past time for my morning walk. I will be over in a few minutes."

"As you wish, comrade general."

Voronoteev placed the receiver down and thought back to his first encounter with Borol'kov—the encounter that had cost Voronoteev his first major command and tainted his entire service career.

The date had been September 6, 1976. The place had been Sakharovka Air Force Base, near the village of Chuguyevka, 200 kilometers northeast of Vladivostok. Voronoteev had commanded the 3d Squadron of the 513th Fighter Regiment of the Soviet Air Defense Command. The incident had been the defection to Japan by squadron pilot Lt. Viktor Belenko. He had flown a MiG-25 to asylum in the West, landing out of fuel at Hakodate Airport in northern Japan.

The loss of the highly classified front line interceptor had been difficult enough, but the defection of a Soviet officer and an elite combat pilot had been devastating to the Kremlin leadership.

Heads rolled, including Voronoteev's, Belenko's commanding officer. After the board of inquiry, presided over by then Col. Ilych Borol'kov, Voronoteev had been reassigned to the staff of the deputy commander in chief for Military Schools, Strategic Rocket Forces. The nonflying billet had been humiliating, but the removal from command and subsequent censure had destroyed Voronoteev's career in the military.

Voronoteev cleared his mind, shoved back his chair, stood and placed the Eyes Only folder under his arm. He opened the door to his outer office and spoke to the *starshina* in charge of the clerical staff. "I will return in a few minutes," Voronoteev said as he walked through the cluttered office.

"Yes, comrade general," the chief master sergeant replied, rising to attention.

Voronoteev walked the length of the command and staff offices, passing the first deputy commander and chief's austere quarters, then climbed the wide stairs leading to Borol'kov's spacious suite. The impressive office, replete with bedroom, large bath, walk-in vault, and entertaining salon, was a subject of much discussion among the lower ranking officers.

Voronoteev opened the door to the small outer office and approached Starshiy Praporshchik Lugayev. The smiling senior warrant officer popped to attention and held out a large folder for Voronoteev. "The last combat efficiency report, comrade general."

Voronoteev accepted the bound folder wordlessly, leafed through it, then frowned. "This does not reflect our implementation of Armaments and Aviation Engineering. This report is ambiguous." Voronoteev could see that Lugayev, who blanched, had been taken by complete surprise. "Did you compile this report, Lugayev?"

The short, dapper warrant officer, still at attention, hesitated a moment. "Yes, comrade general."

"At ease," Voronoteev said in a pleasant tone. "Has General Borol'kov read this report?"

"I'm sure the commander has, comrade general," Lugayev answered, clearly uneasy. "I believe that he has endorsed the last page."

Voronoteev thumbed through to the final page. "So he has. It is unusual for the general to miss such a glaring oversight."

Lugayev remained quiet, studying his immaculately manicured fingernails.

"Well, Lugayev, we can let this be our secret. I'll correct your figures as I adjust my readiness report. Open the vault and I'll get the two previous efficiency reports."

"Comrade general," Lugayev said haltingly, "I am expressly forbidden to allow anyone access to the vault, sir."

"Open the vault, Warrant Officer Lugayev," Voronoteev ordered sternly. "I take full responsibility for the security of the contents."

"Yes, comrade general," Lugayev replied as he rounded his desk and entered the spacious office. Voronoteev followed Lugayev into the commander's suite and waited until the vault swung open.

"Comrade general, this is highly irregular, and I must ask you to certify that I was ord—"

"Lugayev," Voronoteev interrupted, "this is official business and I don't have time to waste. We will seal the vault as soon as I compile the figures."

Lugayev nodded his head, stealing a glance toward the outer office entrance, then backed through the open door and closed it behind him.

Voronoteev quickly yanked open the bottom slide-out drawer and began flipping back each SECRET file folder, scanning the content heading. Opening the ninth file, titled ATB, he discovered the B-2 advanced technology bomber scheme.

He was overwhelmed by the complexity of the secret endeavor. The KGB had apparently engineered the operation on its own, and had pulled it off. The supersecret Stealth bomber was in Cuba, secure in the hands of the KGB.

"San Julian," Voronoteev said to himself as he closed the file. He straightened up, opened a larger upper file drawer, then closed it loudly and walked to the door. He opened it and shook his head. "You were right after all. The Armaments and Aviation Engineering data will be included in the annual efficiency report."

"Yes, sir," Lugayev responded as he hurried through the door to close the vault.

Voronoteev tucked his file under his arm and walked out of the small office. He took a few steps, checked his watch, then started down the stairs. He would stop by his office, remember a forgotten meeting in the afternoon, go to the Hotel Metropol for a leisurely lunch, then make his way to the international post office.

Lugayev had paused at the vault and watched Voronoteev leave. Each working day the warrant officer was responsible for checking the security of the secret files in Borol'kov's vault. He kneeled down, opened the bottom drawer, and slid out the secret files. Lugayev checked each folder rapidly. When he looked at the file labeled ATB, he knew that Voronoteev had opened it. Lugayev had no idea what ATB represented—he only placed the folders in the vault for his commander—but he had checked only hours before and the hair-thin, almost invisible thread had been across the seal. The thread now rested on the bottom of the drawer, severed.

Lugayev shut the vault, then rushed out and closed the door between his small office and the hallway. He had been ordered by General Borol'kov to contact the chief of investigations at the KGB—the Committee for State Security—if the vault was compromised or if anything suspicious happened in the general's absence.

Senior Warrant Officer Lugayev had wondered, on more than one occasion, why the general did not want the Glavnoye Razvedyvatelnoye Upravleniye (GRU) to investigate any questionable act. It seemed only logical to Lugayev that military matters should be investigated by Soviet Military Intelligence.

The conscientious administrative officer was not aware that most of Borol'kov's secret files involved KGB clandestine operations outside the Soviet Union. The GRU operations were confined, for the most part, within the boundaries of the Rodina.

Lugayev had been to the KGB headquarters on Dzerzhinsky Square only once, and he did not look forward to a repeat visit. Orders were orders, however, and the general had been explicit. Lugayev could not contact the KGB via phone. He had to present himself in person, along with the proper credentials. He dialed the master sergeant of administration and had a clerk sent to the commanding general's office to answer the phone. Lugayev gave the airman first class clear instructions, grabbed his cap, and raced down the stairs.

LEADFOOT 107

"Are we starting down?" Wickham asked the Tomcat pilot when he felt the F-14D nose down slightly.

Lieutenant Commander Reed Sandoline, quiet for the past fifty minutes, chuckled softly. "Yeah, Steve, you're about to get initiated into the Tailhook Association."

"I can't wait," Wickham laughed, mentally envisioning a fireball tumbling down the flight deck of the carrier. "Can't they just send up another tanker from the carrier?"

"Steve, you're going to have to readjust your thinking," the fighter jock replied. "You're trying to make this mission too simple."

"What do you mean?" Wickham asked as he tightened his shoulder straps.

"We have to land to switch pilots," Sandoline answered, then kidded his VIP passenger. "The Navy doesn't like paying overtime."

"You have some kind of limit to how long you can fly?"

Wickham asked, massaging his tingling calves.

"That's it," Sandoline replied as he slowly reduced power and lowered the F-14's nose further. "We've had new guidelines issued in regard to daily flying and duty times. I'm already illegal."

Wickham returned to his thoughts as he listened to Sandoline communicate with the carrier. Logic told Wickham that Key West could only mean some covert assignment in Central America or the Caribbean. What puzzled him most was the urgency of the operation.

Sandoline lowered the Tomcat's nose even further, eased the twin throttles to idle, and popped the wide speed brakes partially open. The F-14 shuddered slightly and plummeted toward the USS *Ranger*, steaming parallel to the coast of Baja California Norte 600 miles southwest of San Diego.

Wickham's mind returned to the present when he heard his name mentioned on the aircraft radio.

"Leadfoot One Zero Seven," the carrier air traffic controller radioed, "we have a top secret message waiting for Mister Wickham."

"Copy, One Oh Seven," Sandoline replied, then clicked the intercom. "You hear that?"

"Yes," Wickham answered as he snugged his shoulder straps even tighter. "How long until we're down?"

" 'Bout four and a half minutes."

"You gotta be kidding," Wickham responded. "I can't even see anything down there."

"Leadfoot One Zero Seven, come port to zero-four-zero and descend to one-one thousand."

Sandoline checked his altitude, then toggled his throttle-mounted radio switch. "Roger, zero-four-zero, down to one-one thousand, Leadfoot One Oh Seven."

"Leadfoot," a different controller radioed. "We have a change in plans."

"Go," Sandoline replied as he rolled out on heading and prepared to level at 11,000 feet.

The air traffic specialist spoke slowly. "We've got a turkey on the cat ready to launch. Mister Wickham will be escorted to the island, then to the Tomcat.''

"One Oh Seven, copy," Sandoline replied as he closed the speed brakes and added a small amount of power.

"Come port three-five-zero," the original controller ordered. "Descend to three thousand and call the ball."

"One Oh Seven," Sandoline responded as he reduced power and lowered the nose again, "outta one-one thou for three, three-fifty on the heading."

Wickham quietly surveyed the dimly lighted cockpit, then watched the twinkling stars change position as Sandoline turned to the new heading.

"Steve," the pilot offered, "watch over my left shoulder and tell me when you see the orange ball of light."

"I can't see a thing," Wickham responded, straining to locate the carrier. "It's pitch-black out there."

Sandoline swept the wings forward, lowered the flaps, extended the landing gear, set his power, and dropped the tailhook. "When you enter the island," he instructed, "use the head, drink as much water as you're comfortable with—it'll help stave off altitude dehydration—and run in place to get the blood circulating."

"Will do," Wickham responded at the same time he saw the "meatball"—the primary optical landing aid. "I can see the ball, but I don't have the carrier."

"You won't see the boat until we're on deck," Sandoline replied, then keyed his radio. "One Oh Seven Tomcat. Ball. Four point nine."

"Roger, ball," the landing signal officer acknowledged in a studied, nonchalant manner.

"A bit more advice, Steve," Sandoline offered as he extended the speed brakes to stabilize the approach. "Don't ever call a ship a boat around the blue water sailors. The black shoe Navy would have you keelhauled on the spot."

"Yeah," Wickham replied, "they told me that when I joined the Marines."

"Oh, shit," Sandoline said in mock disgust, "how am I going to live this down?"

"You'll make it," Wickham laughed, knowing what the navy fighter pilot was going to say.

"I've been chauffeuring a jarhead around," Sandoline laughed, then concentrated on flying the meatball.

The pilot's labored breathing became erratic gasps as the Tomcat descended through 600 feet, three-quarters of a mile behind the *Ranger*.

"See the horizontal green lights?" Sandoline asked, working the stick and rudder pedals.

"Yes," Wickham answered as he braced himself, "the ball is even with them"

"We gotta . . . keep the ball . . . centered there," Sandoline said, fighting the oxygen mask. "Nailed . . . till we hit . . . the deck."

Wickham stared at the approaching lights but still could not see the carrier. He listened as the *Ranger*'s landing signal officer (LSO) talked to Sandoline.

"Power . . . power," the LSO coached as the F-14 sank slightly below the optimum glide path, then leveled off until Sandoline intercepted the proper descent profile again. "Lookin' good, turkey."

"Hang on!" Sandoline warned three seconds before impact.

Wickham grabbed the sides of the canopy in a death grip and held his breath. The Tomcat, traveling at 145 miles per hour, flashed over the rounddown and slammed into the steel flight deck without flaring. The tailhook screeched down the deck, showering sparks, then snagged the number three wire and snatched the fighter to an abrupt halt.

Wickham, still holding his breath, shot forward violently as his head snapped downward. The shoulder straps dug deep into his shoulder blades. "Holy shit!" he exclaimed as the F-14 rolled backward to allow the arresting cable to fall out of the tailhook. "You people are crazy."

"Yeah," Sandoline responded with a laugh, "being certified crazy is the first qualification."

Wickham quickly unfastened his restraints, unsnapped his oxygen mask, then rubbed his neck. "I think my back is broken."

Sandoline raised the tailhook and flaps, retracted the speed brakes, and added power to follow the two lighted wands beckoning him forward and starboard. He was barely able to see the petty officer holding the soft, glowing lights.

"You got a little CAG to escort you," Sandoline said as he taxied close to the carrier's superstructure.

Wickham held his oxygen mask to his mouth. "What's a little CAG?"

"The deputy carrier air group commander," Sandoline answered as he opened the canopy and shut down the engines. "Good luck, Steve, in whatever it is you do."

"Thanks," Wickham responded as he prepared to remove his helmet. "Hell of a ride."

SAN JULIAN

Lieutenant Colonel Chuck Matthews sat back in the hard, rough chair and watched the Soviet medical technician prepare the syringes. He could see into the hangar through the KGB director's window.

Workers continued to remove components from the Stealth bomber. Larry Simmons stood in the middle of a group of Soviet officials, answering questions and pointing out various components on the B-2.

Matthews, bound to the heavy chair with wide leather wrist straps, flexed his fingers and glanced at the two Cuban guards. They remained impassive, showing no emotion.

Matthews watched as technicians, dressed in light blue smocks, placed thick mats over portions of the wing. They were being extremely careful not to step outside the walkways outlined in white paint. The mats provided protection for the bomber's composite wing.

The American pilot remained quiet when Gennadi Levchenko walked across the hangar, entered his cluttered office, then stepped into the small interrogation cubicle. The chain-smoking director ordered the two guards out, then turned to Matthews.

"Shall we proceed, colonel?" Levchenko asked as he motioned for the gaunt, droopy-eyed technician to inject Matthews with Versed.

"You cowardly bastard," Matthews retorted in a low, hostile voice.

"Do it," Levchenko ordered.

Matthews looked out the window while the skinny Russian pulled up the sleeve of his flight suit and placed a rubber tourniquet around his right bicep. The specialist picked up a freshly opened syringe and leaned over the pilot.

"Goddamnit," Matthews snapped, then winced again when the technician shoved the needle in further.

Levchenko looked at the B-2 aircraft commander, sat down in a chair, lighted a Pall Mall, then turned on a Panasonic cassette tape recorder. "Tell me about the materials that make up the leading edge of your bomber."

Matthews looked Levchenko in the eyes, darting a glance at the needle in his arm. The syringe was almost empty. "My name is Lieutenant Colonel Charles Edward Matthews, United States Air Force. I have been drugged and coerced to compromise my country."

Matthews continued to talk, appearing to be alert and cognizant. His mind, however, failed to record the conversation. The drug-induced amnesia prevented the nerve cells and their fibers from processing and storing the brain's activities.

Levchenko interrogated Matthews for more than two hours, stopping only to allow the medical technician to inject more Versed. Matthews outlined the operating parameters of the B-2, including the dash speed, absolute altitude, range without aerial refueling, armament capability, and maximum load. He also explained the intricacies of the Hughes APQ-118 multimode radar, detailing the penetration, target search, navigation, detection, and tracking capabilities.

Levchenko pressed harder, wanting to know if the aircraft had an Achilles' heel. Matthews cited the Red Team counterstealth study, which indicated that the technology would not be vulnerable for the foreseeable future.

During the second hour, Levchenko had Matthews explain the tactical advantages of the supersecret bomber. "Tell me, Colonel Matthews," Levchenko said, noting the time, "precisely how the B-2 will be deployed in the event of a nuclear war."

Matthews spoke slowly and clearly, pausing at times. "Our primary mission . . . is to seek and destroy mobile Soviet SS-20, SS-24, and SS-25 missiles. We will approach from high altitude, after being refueled en route, and . . . use reconnaissance satellites to pinpoint our targets. We are prepared to do this . . . ," Matthews said, hesitating again, "anywhere in the world . . . ."

"What is the next step?" Levchenko asked, realizing that Matthews was beginning to shake off the effects of the drugs. "Tell me your priorities after you find the mobile weapons."

"We strike the known . . . relocatable targets," the pilot responded in a halting manner, "then continue to other designated areas and attack . . . hardened underground command centers and . . . control installations for space-based reconnaissance satellites." Matthews, attempting to regain consciousness, twisted his face and stuttered slightly.

Levchenko ordered the technician to inject a small amount of Versed, then checked off another line on his list of questions and rechecked the cassette recorder. The second ninety-minute tape was nearing the end of the first side.

The KGB agent leaned closer to Matthews. "What is your

priority after you attack the command centers and satellite control centers?''

''We would search,'' Matthews answered, pausing when his head dropped, ''on our own for missiles . . . and military targets of opportunity.''

Levchenko looked at his watch. ''What are the primary means of detecting Soviet missiles?''

Matthews's face contorted slightly, then relaxed again. ''We use passive . . . infrared, and laser sensors.''

The interrogation expert knew that Matthews needed time to recover from the extended questioning period. ''What weapons would you use against the missiles?'' Levchenko asked, then wrote a quick note.

''Nuclear bombs . . . ,'' Matthews replied with a discernible slur, ''and nuclear . . . armed SRAM Two missiles.''

Levchenko waved the thin medical technician over to Matthews. ''Stay with him until he has recovered. I will send in the guards.''

''Da, comrade director,'' the technician replied, then checked the wide straps holding the American pilot to the chair. ''Will you be conducting another session before—''

''I will let you know,'' Levchenko interrupted, ''when the next session will be.''

''As you say, comrade director.''

Levchenko turned off the recorder, retrieved the two tapes, ground out his cigarette, and walked into his office. He placed the tapes carefully in their original containers, then into watertight bags. After sealing the bags, he placed them in metal containers and locked the square boxes in his desk. The KGB director picked up his phone receiver and punched in three numbers to connect him with the KGB senior security officer.

''Talavokine,'' the agent answered quickly.

''Send in the guards,'' Levchenko ordered, ''and have that other slime—Simmons—sent in.''

"Da, comrade director," Talavokine answered. "The pilot is to return to his cell?"

"Yes," Levchenko responded. "He is to be exercised and fed only—no shower."

"Da, comrade director," the agent replied, spying Larry Simmons. "The guards are on the way and I will escort the traitorous American to your office."

CHAPTER ELEVEN

MOSCOW

Senior Warrant Officer Vitaliy Lugayev had grown impatient
with the snarled traffic. His driver had been trying to negotiate
the approach to Dzerzhinsky Square, but an accident 200
meters in front of them had brought the vehicles to a halt.

Lugayev, exasperated, could see the imposing Komitet
Gosudarstvennoi Bezopasnosti building. The Kremlin spy
headquarters was less than a kilometer away. "I will walk
the rest of the way," Lugayev said as he opened the door
and stepped out. "Park in the Kremlin spaces, and do not
go to lunch."

Lugayev slammed the Moskvich 412's door, muffling the
driver's acknowledgment. The warrant officer hurried toward
the KGB building, darting between the gridlocked cars and
buses. He cursed the ministry of transportation for their in-
efficient traffic system and complex driving regulations.

"What has happened?" a shriveled old man asked as Lugayev passed the window of a faded Zhiguli.

"*Proizoshla avariya*," the warrant officer shouted.
"There's been an accident."

Lugayev stopped and moved between two cars when a motorcycle traffic policeman waved him out of the way. The armed militiaman, dressed in a gray uniform and carrying a white baton, weaved through the narrow passage with ease.

Lugayev raced across the square in front of the spy headquarters, slowed to a walk to recover his wind, and entered the massive structure.

Vitaliy Lugayev nervously removed his hat and approached the information desk. "I am Senior Warrant Officer Lugayev," the dapper administrator announced, proudly flipping open his credentials for inspection. "I am General Borol'kov's aide—Troops of Air Defense—and I must see the chief of investigations immediately."

The white-haired, bleary-eyed man did not respond. He continued to scrutinize Lugayev's papers.

"At once," Lugayev said impatiently.

The information clerk closed Lugayev's credentials and handed the folder back to the warrant officer. "The chief of investigations," the elderly clerk droned slowly, "is out of the city."

"Then I must see his assistant," Lugayev almost shouted, "or someone in charge."

The withered clerk looked up sluggishly, staring into Lugayev's eyes. "You will have to have an appointment to see the assistant chief of—"

"You blubbering old fool!" Lugayev said, trying to control his voice. "This matter is of the greatest concern—I represent General of the Army Borol'kov. I must see an official—immediately!"

"What is the problem?" a senior officer walking by interrupted.

Lugayev quickly explained the situation to the startled bureaucrat.

"Nikolai," the well-groomed KGB officer said to the aging clerk. "Inform investigations that I am on my way to see Akhlomov."

The solemn clerk raised his telephone handset. "Yes, sir, comrade inspector."

The KGB officer, followed by Lugayev, hurried to the elevator. After a brief ride, both men walked at a brisk pace to the office of the deputy chief of investigations.

Natanoly F. Akhlomov, second in command of the department, remained seated while Lugayev introduced himself. "Have a seat, Starshiy Praporshchik Lugayev," the unsmiling deputy said, then turned his attention to the head of the KGB training academy. "Join us, Pyotr."

Both men sat down while Akhlomov energized a recorder built into the front of his desk. Then Lugayev explained, in detail, what had transpired in General Borol'kov's private office.

Akhlomov, without taking his eyes off the warrant officer, wrote quick memos to himself. "Tell me, Comrade Lugayev," Akhlomov said, darting a glance at his KGB associate, "where is General Voronoteev at the present time?"

Lugayev, trying to conceal his anxiety, looked at his shiny black-market watch. "The general is preparing, I'm sure, to go to lunch."

"Thank you," Akhlomov said as he stood from behind his cluttered desk. "We will be in touch if we need further information."

Lugayev rose awkwardly from his chair, grasping his hat with both hands. "Thank you, comrades," he ventured, then walked out the door held open by the other KGB officer.

Akhlomov waited until the door was closed, then turned off the recorder and smiled at his friend. "Well, Pyotr Igoryevich," Akhlomov said quietly, turning serious, "the general finally surfaces for what he is—a treasonous scum."

"I . . . as we have suspected for a long time," the chief of training offered, then lowered his head slightly. "This is a sad day, comrade."

"I agree," Akhlomov replied in a disappointed tone. "We have to move fast—the traitorous bastard knows about the ATB project."

The academy training director looked confused. "The what project, comrade?"

Akhlomov moved quickly around his desk and clasped his friend's shoulders before speaking. The deputy chief of investigations knew that he had made a mistake by blurting out "ATB." "Pyotr Igoryevich," Akhlomov said, convincing in his pretension, "I will explain the project to you when I have authorization."

"I understand, comrade," the training director replied uncomfortably.

Akhlomov walked his associate to the door, then continued down the corridor to the files section. He bypassed the superintendent and personally gathered the dossier of Lt. Gen. Yuliy Lavrent'yevich Voronoteev.

Akhlomov returned to his desk, phoned Voronoteev's office, under the guise of a fellow general, and gleaned the knowledge he needed to locate the traitor. Voronoteev was at lunch and would be out of the office for the afternoon. Voronoteev's aide also provided the names of the places the general normally frequented for lunch.

Akhlomov placed a second call to his subordinate, detailing the description of Voronoteev and his chauffeur-driven automobile. Akhlomov's orders were clear. Locate Voronoteev, using any means available, and report back immediately. Time was extremely critical, Akhlomov explained, then he hung up and rushed downstairs to the transportation section.

USS *RANGER*

Steve Wickham adjusted his oxygen mask and wedged the sealed manila envelope between his ejection seat and the right side of the F-14D's cockpit.

Up front, Comdr. Dalton McDonald eased the howling Tomcat over the catapult shuttle and stopped. The green-shirted catapult crews scurried under the fighter as the blast deflector was raised.

Wickham watched in fascination as a flight deck crewman held up a lighted display board to the pilot. McDonald acknowledged the deckhand with a thumbs-up, indicating that the number on the board corresponded to the F-14's weight.

"Brace your helmet against the headrest," McDonald instructed, simultaneously advancing both throttles to military power.

Wickham, without replying, leaned back his head and braced himself for the night catapult shot. When the nose of the Tomcat dropped, his mind ceased thinking about the top secret message he had read.

"You ready?" McDonald asked as he scanned his engine instruments quickly.

"All set," Wickham responded, breathing heavily.

McDonald moved the control stick and rudder pedals to their full extensions, then returned them to the neutral position. The procedure ensured that the primary flight controls were functioning correctly.

Wickham darted a quick look toward the catapult officer at the center of the flight deck. The yellow-shirted figure was twirling a lighted wand, which signaled the pilot to apply full power. McDonald flipped on his external light master switch, signaling that he was ready to be launched.

The cat officer dropped to one knee as he swung the lighted wand over his head to touch the deck. The big Tomcat, straining under the powerful turbofans, squatted on the main gear and thundered down the starboard bow catapult.

Wickham, unable to breathe during the catapult stroke, felt as though an elephant was sitting on his chest. He groaned, then grayed out as the g forces rendered him helpless. A microsecond later the F-14 roared over the deck edge as Commander McDonald popped up the landing gear handle and trimmed the nose.

Wickham, regaining his vision, felt as though the fighter had decelerated. He sucked in a deep breath of cool oxygen, then realized that the Tomcat was accelerating, but not at the rate it had during the catapult shot.

"Everything okay?" McDonald asked as he cleaned up the aircraft.

"God . . . damn," Wickham answered, releasing the vice grip he had on the side of the canopy. "That makes a roller coaster feel like a merry-go-round."

"Yeah," McDonald replied, then acknowledged a call from *Ranger*.

Wickham reached down and retrieved the large manila envelope, then fumbled for the flashlight he had stuffed into his torso harness. He opened the package as he thought about the cryptic message he had read on board the carrier. The agency had directed him to study the contents of the sealed packet in preparation for a reconnaissance mission in Cuba.

Wickham held the flashlight and read the instructions, then studied the enlarged maps and aerial photographs. His orders stated that he must become familiar with the western tip of Cuba. He studied the detailed picture of Mariel Naval Air Station, then perused photographs of the San Julian military airfield.

What in the hell is going on, Wickham thought to himself. He studied the maps and photographs a few minutes longer, then turned off the flashlight and leaned back to contemplate the situation.

"You might as well get some shut-eye," the pilot said, noticing that the rear cockpit had become dark again. "I've got to keep us subsonic over Mexico—no supersonic footprint over land—so we'll be awhile."

"Okay," Wickham responded. "I understand we have to tank again before Key West."

"Yeah, that's right," McDonald responded, tweaking the nose down. "We'll grab a drink over Brownsville, Texas, and dash into Key West."

"Sounds good," Wickham replied, closing the manila envelope.

"Did the slot man bore you with his A-K stories?" McDonald asked as he leveled the Tomcat at 49,000 feet.

Wickham looked up. "I'm not sure I understand your question."

"Did Commander Sandoline—he flew the slot position with the Blues—bore you with his almost-killed stories?"

"Not really," Wickham laughed, "but the sonuvabitch flies like a maniac."

"Yeah," McDonald replied. "Slots is one of a kind."

Wickham stifled a yawn, then keyed his intercom again. "I'm going to catch a few winks."

"Good idea," the pilot responded. "The in-flight movie is dull anyway."

HOTEL METROPOL

Lieutenant General Yuliy Voronoteev sat quietly in the serene surroundings of the hotel's opulent restaurant. He had elected to bypass his usual luncheon spot, the Kremlin Palace of Congresses, to avoid the crowded conditions. He needed a relaxed, subdued environment to calm his nerves. The facade of being loyal to both the Soviet Union and the KGB had been eating away at his conscience.

The general had begun doubting the moral rectitude of his acts and motives. He was torn between his view of himself and the moribund system in which he was entangled. His immediate desires as well as his future aspirations had become more distorted with each passing year.

Voronoteev, dining alone, looked around the large room and noticed two staff officers having lunch with three civilians. Voronoteev shifted his chair in an effort to avoid being noticed. He needed time for quiet contemplation.

A well-dressed waiter approached his table and hesitated before speaking. "Comrade general, would you care for more vodka?"

"Yes, thank you," Voronoteev answered, then took a small bite of the jellied sturgeon. He chewed slowly, swallowed, then sipped a spoonful of borscht. Voronoteev had lost his appetite and decided against ordering the *lyulya-kebab*. The appetizer and soup would be more than sufficient.

Voronoteev raised his glass and tossed down the last of the chilled vodka. Looking at his watch, he mentally debated making his call to Vienna earlier than scheduled.

"Your vodka, comrade general," the jacketed waiter said as he placed the small glass on the table.

"*Spasibo*," Voronoteev replied, thanking the pleasant young man.

The waiter raised his writing pad. "Would you care to order, comrade general?"

"Nyet," Voronoteev replied, folding his napkin next to his plate. "I'll take another vodka and my bill."

The waiter nodded and hurried to fulfill the request. A Soviet general, the young man had been taught, was not to be kept waiting.

Voronoteev quickly finished the last Stolichnaya, paid his bill, and walked to the cloakroom to retrieve his hat and greatcoat.

Natanoly Akhlomov, deputy chief of investigations, KGB, watched Voronoteev from an alcove off the main dining room. Akhlomov placed his small transmitter to his mouth and alerted the special agents observing Voronoteev's car and driver.

SAN JULIAN

"You have performed in a very distinguished manner," Gennadi Levchenko said in an insincerely smooth voice. "The Soviet Union is proud of your accomplishment."

"Thank you, ah . . . ," Larry Simmons stammered.

"Comrade director," Levchenko prompted the American tech-rep. "You are one of us now, Comrade Simmons."

The technician beamed, feeling more confident with his new countrymen. "Thank you," Simmons paused, "comrade director. I am . . . I feel very privileged to be associated with the Soviet Union. Irina has told me a great deal about your country.''

''We feel the same sentiments,'' Levchenko professed in an unctuous manner. ''Now comrade,'' he smiled, then deftly punched the record button on the tape cassette, ''tell me about the weaknesses of the Stealth bomber.''

''Well . . . ,'' Simmons said uneasily, ''may I ask you a question first?''

''Of course,'' Levchenko replied with another reassuring smile. ''What would you like to know?''

Simmons coughed nervously. ''When will Irina . . . be joining me?''

''Soon, very soon,'' Levchenko answered, then leaned back in his desk chair. ''You are not to worry, my friend. Everything will be fine.''

''I'm just concerned about her,'' Simmons said with an anxious look. ''She said she would meet me here.''

''I understand,'' Levchenko replied patiently as he leaned forward, ''and you will be reunited with Irina soon. Now, we have, let us say, priorities we must meet.''

''Yes . . . comrade director.''

The Stealth project officer leaned forward, fixing his eyes on the apprehensive American. ''I would like for you to outline any problem areas, or weaknesses, in the B-2.''

''Well,'' Simmons began slowly, ''the airframe-mounted accessory drive cases have been a problem.''

''What kind of problem?''

Simmons, feeling more assured, opened up. ''Many of the units have cracked and caused oil leakages, which delayed the flight test phase.''

Levchenko, smiling pleasantly, lighted a cigarette. ''Is it a significant problem?''

''I'm not very knowledgeable in that area,'' Simmons replied uncomfortably. ''I know that the engineers have re-worked the cases, but it is still a concern.''

The KGB officer made a quick notation before he continued

his questioning. "Okay, tell me about any problems or weaknesses in your field of expertise."

"Ah . . . as you know," Simmons responded, taking in the partially dismantled bomber, "the aircraft has very complex electronic and avionic systems."

Levchenko exhaled impatiently. "The electronic systems have been a problem?"

"Yes . . . and still are," Simmons answered hurriedly. "The extreme environment that the B-2 operates in has caused continual reliability problems."

Levchenko's face hardened. "You have to be more specific, Comrade Simmons. Define the nature of the electronic problems you have encountered thus far."

Simmons hesitated, then spoke rapidly. "The weapons systems have been adversely affected by a number of things, including shock, vibration, impact, salt fog, and heat."

Levchenko turned off the recorder and eased back his chair. "Comrade Simmons, your knowledge is invaluable to your new country. I have some business to take care of, so I want you to sit here and list every B-2 strength and weakness you can think of . . . every one."

LEADFOOT 107

Steve Wickham dozed uneasily, dreaming sporadic scenes of Becky and Cuba. Interspersed were flashbacks to his harrowing escape from Russia. The mission to extract the Kremlin mole had almost cost Wickham his life, along with that of the Moscow operative.

"You awake back there?" Commander McDonald asked.

Wickham's eyelids fluttered, then squeezed shut when the early morning sun struck them.

"Reveille," McDonald said over the intercom. "Next stop is Key West."

Wickham groaned as he fumbled for the tinted visor on his helmet. "Key West?" he asked as he attempted to move his cold, stiffened limbs. "Aren't we going to take on fuel first?"

"You must've been out of it," McDonald laughed, "or my flying skills have improved. We tanked about an hour and fifteen minutes ago."

Wickham looked at his watch to confirm the time lapse. "You need to talk to management about these seats."

"Yeah," McDonald replied, "they have to have a solid bottom so your spine won't break if you have to pull the 'loud handle.' Can't allow any compression before the seat slams into your ass."

"How far out are we?" Wickham asked, yawning.

"A hundred and ten nautical miles," McDonald answered between conversations with the air traffic controllers. "We'll be overhead the air station in . . . nine minutes and fifty seconds."

Wickham was amazed. "Nine minutes?"

"And forty-five seconds," McDonald replied. "We're in projectile mode now, but I'll be throwing out the anchor when we approach the beach."

Wickham rubbed his eyes, checked to see that the top secret packet was still in place, then looked down at the Gulf of Mexico. He watched two oil tankers disappear rapidly under the right side of the F-14's fuselage.

"We're starting down," McDonald said as he smoothly lowered the Tomcat's nose. "This will be a steep descent, followed by a rapid decel in close."

"After landing on the carrier," Wickham responded, looking at the water, "I think I can handle about anything."

"You should ride through an ACM gaggle," McDonald replied, lowering the nose further.

Wickham looked in the rearview mirror again, catching the pilot's eyes. "A what?"

"Air combat maneuvering," McDonald explained. "A dogfighting hop."

"I'll pass," Wickham said, then returned to his sight-seeing while the pilot conversed with the controllers.

"Rog, Miami," McDonald radioed, "Key West approach on two-sixty-three-point six, switchin'." McDonald programmed the frequency into his primary UHF radio. "Key Approach, Navy Leadfoot One Oh Seven with you outta one-seven thousand."

"Navy One Zero Seven, Key West Approach." The veteran controller spoke in short, clipped bursts. "Continue descent to three thousand, runway seven currently in use, wind one-two-zero at twelve, gusting to twenty. Altimeter two-niner-niner-eight."

The pilot repeated the instructions. "One Oh Seven down to three K, two-niner-niner-eight." McDonald could see the naval air station rapidly filling his windshield. The F-14, rocketing toward the island at 960 miles per hour (1.25 Mach) descended through 11,000 feet.

Wickham watched, fascinated, while Marquesas Keys and Boca Grande Key flashed under the right wing.

"Navy One Zero Seven," the clipped voice said, "contact Key West tower, three-four-zero point two."

McDonald keyed his radio. "One Oh Seven, switchin' three-forty point two. So long." The pilot reset the UHF frequency, then called the control tower. "Key West tower, Leadfoot One Oh Seven with you outta eight thousand."

"Roger, One Zero Seven," the laconic tower chief replied calmly. "Cleared for a left break, runway seven, wind one-two-zero at fourteen, gusting to twenty-two. No reported traffic."

"Copy, Key tower," McDonald acknowledged, then pressed the intercom switch. "Better brace yourself. I'm gonna slam on the binders."

"I'm ready," Wickham replied as he watched the shoreline rush toward them.

McDonald yanked the twin throttles to idle and popped the speed brakes open. Both men were thrown forward, hanging by their shoulder restraints. Wickham tightened his neck and leg muscles, then gulped a lungful of cool oxygen. He felt as though they had run into a brick wall.

"Hold tight," McDonald warned as the F-14 roared across the beach.

Wickham grasped the canopy rails tightly as the end of the runway flashed under the fighter. His nerves tensed in preparation for the overhead break.

McDonald had the Tomcat slowed to 490 knots by midfield. He tightened his stomach muscles and slapped the stick hard to the left. The F-14 snapped into knife-edged flight, splitting the air in a deafening howl.

Wickham's helmet ricocheted off the right side of the canopy, then slumped onto his chest as McDonald pulled 4½g's through the turn. The g forces rendered each man unable to move their heads.

The pilot waited until the aircraft had completed a 180-degree course reversal before he eased off the g loading. The sensation was that of weightlessness. "Still breathing?" McDonald asked as he leveled the wings and waited for them to sweep forward.

"Well," Wickham paused, taking stock. "If you discount the concussion, I'm fine."

"Navy One Zero Seven," the tower controller said, "check wheels down, cleared to land."

"Cleared to land," McDonald repeated.

The former TOPGUN instructor lowered the flaps, dropped the landing gear, and rolled onto the final approach. Wickham could see the big number 7 painted on the end of the 10,000-foot runway.

"Navy One Zero Seven," the controller radioed. "After rollout, follow the cart at the end of the ramp. They'll park you by the Gulfstream jet—the air force VIP bird sitting by itself."

"Copy," McDonald replied as the hurtling Tomcat thundered onto the concrete, briefly leaving two white puffs of tire smoke.

"Well," McDonald said over the intercom, "I wish you every success in whatever it is you are about to do."

"Thanks," Wickham replied as the F-14 came to a rapid halt. "Just getting here has been a hell of an experience."

CHAPTER TWELVE

MOSCOW

Lieutenant General Yuliy Voronoteev gazed out of the Moskvich 412's window with a vacant stare. *Have I gone too far?* he asked himself. *Would the preening Lugayev say anything to General Borol'kov?*

"To the post office, comrade general?" the sergeant asked as he pulled away from the Hotel Metropol.

"I have some time to spare," Voronoteev replied. "Let's take a slow drive through Sokolniki Park before we stop at the post office."

"As you wish, comrade general."

Voronoteev thought about the privacy of the telephone booths in the international post office. He had known about the secure phone lines for the past three years. The government department store and the post office were two of the three dozen unmonitored trunk lines in Moscow.

The general had resisted the CIA's supposedly more sophisticated means of transmitting classified information. Their method of transfer required a five-step process—three more than he believed necessary. Voronoteev had explained his position to the CIA and they had agreed reluctantly to follow his procedure.

"Did you have lunch?" Voronoteev asked his recently promoted chauffeur.

"No, comrade general," the clean-cut sergeant answered, glancing at the approaching traffic. "The cafeteria was closed for the employees' lunch break."

"We will stop in the park, sergeant," Voronoteev said, shaking his head in exasperation, "and find some proper food for you."

"Thank you, comrade general," the young man responded gratefully, "but I am fine for the time being."

"Nonsense," Voronoteev said, watching the Mayakovsky Museum glide past. "We will stop."

"Da, comrade general."

"Where is he going?" Akhlomov's driver asked as they passed the Kazan railway station.

"How would I know?" Akhlomov said icily. "Concentrate on your job."

The unadorned KGB car followed Voronoteev's Moskvich 412 at a distance of 150 meters. A second vehicle, 50 meters behind the deputy chief of investigations, stayed in contact using a Western-made walkie-talkie. Akhlomov knew that he had to catch Voronoteev in the actual act of passing state secrets. The general was shrewd and had powerful friends in the Kremlin. If the KGB bungled the collar, Akhlomov knew he would be spending a protracted period of time in his own Lefortovo prison.

"Comrade deputy," the gravel-voiced driver said with a hint of sullenness. "They are turning into the park."

"I can see that," Akhlomov replied with a look of disdain. "Slow down."

Both KGB automobiles turned left off Cherkizovskaya Boulevard and followed Voronoteev's car toward the Sokol-niki Exhibition. Akhlomov placed the walkie-talkie to his lips. "He is stopping at the corner food vendor. Park by the knoll and mingle with the people."

"Da, comrade deputy," the agent responded, slowing to a smooth stop under a grove of birch trees.

Akhlomov and his driver remained in their car while his fellow officers got out and blended into the crowd around the portable luncheonette. The four KGB men watched while Voronoteev's driver grabbed a snack, wolfed it down, then hurried back to the car. The general remained in the Moskvich, staring at the paintings propped against the rustling trees. The park was filled with people attending the weekly art fair.

Akhlomov, anticipating some form of information drop, watched Voronoteev closely. He was surprised when the general's car pulled away from the curb and rejoined traffic. "Let's go," Akhlomov ordered, then swore. "The treasonous bastard is up to something. He isn't just joyriding for the sake of it." Akhlomov glanced at the two agents who were scrambling into their car. "Stay close."

Voronoteev remained silent during the short drive to the international post office. He could not shake an apprehension concerning the B-2 bomber. With so many problems confronting the Soviet Union, why had the KGB undertaken such a politically dangerous operation?

Voronoteev focused his eyes as the post office came into view. He forced his mind back to the present and steeled himself for his task. He flexed his fingers nervously as the Moskvich slowed to a stop.

"I'll be a few minutes," Voronoteev said, opening his own door and stepping out.

"Da, comrade general."

Voronoteev walked up the steps, returned a crisp salute from a captain (second rank) of Naval Forces, and entered the deteriorating building. The faded walls and darkened ceiling reflected the state of decline prevalent throughout the sprawling city.

The general of Troops of Air Defense looked around casually before proceeding to a row of antiquated telephone booths. Voronoteev opened his tunic cautiously, pulled out the telephone number for his Vienna connection, then stepped into the dusty opening.

The phone booths did not have doors, making it difficult for the caller to hear over the incessant drone. As everywhere else in Moscow, the international post office had long lines of Muscovites shuffling along slowly.

Voronoteev picked up the receiver, stole a quick glance around the large room, dropped two kopecks into the phone, and waited for the operator.

The general did not see the KGB officer dart across the room and yank the woman out of the booth next to his. Natanoly Akhlomov flashed his credentials in the frightened woman's face and thrust her aside. The KGB still had power to instill fear. The woman gripped her shopping bag and hurried off.

"Operator," the flat-pitched female voice answered.

"*Soyedinite menya s etim nomerom?*" Voronoteev asked. "Can you get me this number?" Voronoteev gave the operator the phone number for the Hotel Sacher in Vienna, then waited, glancing nervously around the large room.

"I am sorry," the operator said after a few seconds. "The wait for international calls is approximately two hours. You can book a reservation, if you like."

"This is official state business," Voronoteev blustered in his most authoritative manner. "I am First Deputy Litvinov, commander in chief of the main inspector staff, Kremlin code one-eight. Put the call through immediately, or give me your supervisor."

"Yes, comrade first deputy," the operator replied with a trembling voice. "I will disconnect a line. One moment, please."

Akhlomov, who had clearly heard the general's bold lie, motioned for his three associates to move closer. The damned fool was going to pass top secret state information over a common telephone line. Enormous stupidity, Akhlomov thought as he leaned closer to the partition separating him from Voronoteev.

"Room twenty-eight," Voronoteev said in passable English as he folded the slip of paper and placed it in his shirt pocket. The phone connection was unusually good. Voronoteev had almost finished buttoning his tunic when Fritz Kranz answered the long distance call.

"Peter Wipplinger," the nervous doctor said as evenly as he could.

"Hello, Peter," Voronoteev responded, cautiously surveying the people in the dimly lighted post office. "The destination is Cuba, at an—"

"You bastard!" Akhlomov yelled as he rushed around the partition and slammed Voronoteev into the side of the dusty booth. "You miserable bastard!"

The other three agents roughly subdued the struggling general as Akhlomov grabbed the dangling phone receiver. The line was dead.

Akhlomov spun around and shoved Voronoteev into the dingy wall. "Who were you talking to?"

Voronoteev paused a moment, trying to regain his shattered composure. "I am Lieutenant General Voronoteev."

"Shut up, you traitorous bastard," Akhlomov shouted, consumed in rage. "Out with it! Who were you talking to?"

Voronoteev, blood dripping from his mouth, remained firmly pinned to the wall. Out of the corner of his eye, the stunned general could see the throng of people rushing out the main entrance of the post office. Muscovites could smell trouble a block away, and they avoided it like the plague.

"You have made a grave mistake," Voronoteev said as evenly as possible, "and your superiors will—"

"You sucking dog!" Akhlomov hissed in Voronoteev's face, then bashed him into the wall again. "Tell me about the ATB. Tell me what you stole from the files this morning."

Voronoteev's eyes gave him away when he tried to recover

from the sudden shock. "I have no idea what you are talking about."

"The hell you don't!" Akhlomov said, positioning the point of his Antipov tactical knife against Voronoteev's throat. "Who were you talking to?"

"I demand—"

"Shut up," Akhlomov said as he pushed the blade against Voronoteev's neck a quarter inch, twisted it, and yanked it away. "You are under arrest, General Voronoteev, for committing treason."

Voronoteev started to speak, then realized that any effort to defend his actions would be in vain. His fate had been sealed when he had forced the issue by checking the contents of General Borol'kov's safe.

The bloodied general held his head high, nodding to his shocked driver, as he was escorted to the KGB automobile.

VIENNA

Fritz Kranz sat staring at the beige telephone on the small desk. His right hand, trembling uncontrollably, still rested on the receiver.

"Oh, god . . . ," Kranz said to himself, then slowly removed his hand from the phone. "It's over."

Kranz sat quietly for a moment, contemplating his predicament, then bolted from his chair and walked to the window. He stared vacantly at the roof of the opera house while he tried to calm his nerves. I've been caught in the middle, he told himself. RAINDANCE had been apprehended. He had heard the commotion and the accusations. Would the KGB—no—how soon would the KGB trace him to Vienna?

He knew that his life was in jeopardy. He had to think clearly, and remember the procedures he had been taught by the CIA instructors at Langley. He paced back and forth between the door and the window, trying to sort out the enormity of what had happened in the past three minutes.

It had not been his fault, he told himself. He had been happily ensconced in his pleasant world, enjoying retirement, before this calamity. He knew now that he was swimming in a sea full of voracious sharks.

Now, Kranz kept telling himself, I must think rationally and clearly. The CIA gave me a telephone number to call in the event of such a disaster. "Use it," he heard himself say as he fumbled in his coat pocket for the matchbook. The cover displayed an advertisement for a seafood restaurant in New Haven, Connecticut.

Kranz walked over to the desk, sat down, and gingerly picked up the receiver. His hands were shaking and his temples throbbed. The emergency code words ran through his mind over and over again. The frightened surgeon dialed the operator and thought about his wife. Christ, Katy had no idea of his involvement in this miserable business.

"Hotel operator," the innocent voice answered.

"I must . . . I need the international operator," Kranz replied, trying to sound calm and businesslike.

"One moment, I will connect you."

"Thank you," Kranz responded, taking deep, even breaths.

Kranz gave the overseas operator the phone number and waited for the call to go through. Finally, after what seemed like an eternity, the number began ringing. One ring. Two rings, then a pause before Kranz heard the recording.

"Thank you for calling. Please leave your name and telephone number at the sound of the tone."

"Good Christ," he blurted out, then heard the beep. "The ship is aground, the ship is aground," Kranz said impulsively, then continued in a hesitant voice, not sure if he should say anything else. "The tie has been—" Kranz stopped in mid-sentence when he heard an urgent voice speak to him.

"This is seafarer control," the vibrant male voice exploded. "Your number?"

"Ah. . . . ," Kranz hesitated, unsure of his response. He

had been told expressly to use code letters. "F . . . K . . . D . . . O . . . M," he said in a shaky voice.

No one said a word for fifteen seconds. Kranz was beginning to have doubts, when the man replied.

"Go ahead, Doctor Kranz," the CIA agent said. "We had to bring you up on the computer."

Kranz inhaled sharply, then gushed forth with the story. "Our connection with RAINDANCE has been severed. He was apprehended in midsentence, after telling me the location of the missing B-2 bomber."

"Say again," the surprised voice said.

The agent was not familiar with RAINDANCE. He only monitored a battery of secret global telephone connections. Most of them never rang, and RAINDANCE was one of four that required top secret handling, Eyes Only, by the director or the deputy director of the Central Intelligence Agency.

"The Stealth bomber—the B-2 bomber that disappeared," Kranz said hurriedly. "It's in Cuba, and the exact location is unknown."

"Got it," the astonished agent replied as he jotted down the message. "Are you okay?"

"No, I'm not," Kranz answered nervously. "I'm sure the KGB is tracing the call from our contact. I need to get out of Austria, quickly."

"You're in a hotel under an assumed name, aren't you?" the Connecticut-based agent asked. He was looking at Kranz's method of operation on the computer screen.

"Yes," Kranz responded uneasily, "but one of the hotel's assistant managers would be able to identify me. His father was a former patient of mine."

"That's not good," the agent replied gravely as he wrote a message for his assistant.

"I didn't know he worked here," Kranz continued, defending himself, "until after I had contacted RAINDANCE. I thought it would complicate matters too much for me to go to another location after the contact. Besides, I had no idea this would happen.''

''We understand,'' the pleasant voice said with genuine feeling. ''You're in a high threat situation. Go directly to the American Embassy.''

Kranz's mind was reeling. His peaceful, tranquil life was coming unwound. ''Damn.''

''What?'' the American asked.

''Nothing,'' Kranz said, then added. ''Can you get us— my family—any protection?''

''My assistant is contacting our field office in Vienna right now. Our immediate concern is your safety,'' the agent paused, ''and that of your family. Go directly to the embassy—it's located at Sixteen Boltzmanngasse—and our people will be there as quickly as possible.''

''Thank you,'' Kranz replied, standing to look out of the window. ''I must hurry.''

''Be careful,'' Krantz heard the agent caution as he placed the receiver down and picked up his jacket. He scurried to gather his toilet articles, then stopped in midstride. To hell with it, he told himself, I've got to get to the embassy. He raced out of his room and down the hallway, then took the stairs two at a time. He walked briskly through the lobby and out into the parking area.

Kranz hurried to his BMW, got in, started the engine, and shifted into reverse. As he turned his head to back out of the parking space, he paused. I have to get Katy, he told himself. I must explain, God help me, what a mess I've gotten myself into. She must go with me to the embassy. She will not be safe at the cottage.

Kranz recalled vividly the CIA briefing about the ruthless means that the KGB utilized to extract information from subjects. His wife, Kranz remembered in agony, would be the primary target of the KGB if he was in the sanctuary of the American Embassy. Kranz backed out, reversed gears, and headed for his home in Neunkirchen.

That decision would prove fatal for Fritz and Katy Kranz. Their charred bodies were found in the remains of their retirement cottage late that evening. A mysterious fire had consumed the entire structure.

CHAPTER THIRTEEN

KEY WEST NAVAL AIR STATION

Steve Wickham sat in the passenger cabin of the C-20 VIP aircraft, listening to Hampton Milligan, director of CIA Clandestine Operations. The former Green Beret officer was pointing out various topographical features on a large relief map of Cuba.

The glistening transport's auxiliary power unit, providing a steady flow of air-conditioning, was barely audible in the quiet cabin. Wickham sat back, eating his breakfast slowly. The air station enlisted mess had been kind enough to send the meal over to the flight line in the duty pickup truck.

"Okay," Wickham said, swallowing the last bite. He placed the dented tray on a fold-out table. "What gives, Hamp? You usually start an ops brief from the beginning."

"Steve," Milligan began slowly, "this comes from the White House—right from the top. The president has ordered us to recon two specific areas in Cuba, and the general has commissioned you to do it . . . alone."

Wickham leaned back and closed his eyes. After a moment he looked out of the window, then turned to Milligan. "Two questions. Why me, when we have a number of clandestine agents who are Hispanic? And, what am I looking for?''

Milligan frowned. ''Steve, when the general gives an order, we pick up our packs and move out. You speak fluent Spanish, along with Russian, and you are the man.''

''Fine,'' Wickham replied, ''but what gives?''

''Your mission,'' Milligan said, enunciating each word carefully, ''is to locate a missing B-2 Stealth bomber.''

''What!'' Wickham exclaimed, sitting upright. ''The Cubans have a Stealth?''

''We have every indication that the aircraft is in Cuba,'' Milligan said as he opened a brown sealed packet.

''How in the name of God did a B-2 end up in Cuba?''

''Read this thoroughly,'' Milligan responded, ''then we'll go over the details.''

Wickham sat back again and studied the agency operations brief. His eyes grew wide at each new paragraph. Milligan sat patiently looking out of the window at the dull gray F-14 parked next to them.

Wickham rested the papers on his thigh and shook his head slowly. ''This is incredible . . . absolutely incredible. I'm expected to snoop a military airfield?''

''You're going in tonight, Steve.'' Milligan had an unusually serious look on his ruddy face. ''The president has made this his number one priority. The ramifications, in regard to relations with the Russians and the Cubans, are incalculable.''

''But, Hamp,'' Wickham said, scratching the coarse stubble on his chin, ''I can't just go waltzing around Cuba—hell, I'll stick out like a sore thumb.''

Milligan, pausing to readjust his glasses, did not respond.

''Hamp, I'm a green-eyed Caucasian.''

The director of Clandestine Operations gave Wickham a blank stare. ''A Caucasian who speaks Spanish and is very innovative under pressure.''

The former marine officer was resigned to the inevitable,

but the selection of an Anglo-Saxon to infiltrate Cuba and reconnoiter a military airfield did not track.

Milligan remained silent. The director continued to look Wickham in the face with an impassive gaze. Wickham knew the look—Milligan always did this when an issue was no longer open for discussion.

"Hamp, this is really stepping over the threshold." Wickham paused, looking at the expressionless face. "Shit . . . how are you proposing to insert me?"

"You will stage out of Cancun tonight." Milligan opened another envelope and handed it to the man considered to be the best clandestine operative in the CIA. "We have a Marine OV-10 en route to Cancun at this time. A young captain, who is regarded as one hell of a pilot, will fly you across the Yucatan Channel and drop you a mile off Bahia de Guadiana."

Wickham shook his head slowly as he looked at the drop location. "We're going to use an active duty pilot?"

"He's a volunteer," Milligan continued, "and he won't have any identification on him. He understands that if anything happens to him, we don't know him. The aircraft will be unmarked. You'll go in," Milligan stopped to point out the exact spot on the large Cuban map, "right here."

"What kind of surf conditions do they have?" Wickham asked, studying the map closely.

"Mild. That's the leeward side of the island." Milligan pointed to San Julian military airfield. "This air base, as you saw in the brief, is the most likely hiding place for the B-2—if it's in Cuba."

"If it isn't there," Wickham said, tapping the map, "or I can't locate it, then what?"

"Wait," Milligan said patiently, holding up both hands. "I'll get to that."

Wickham, showing his disgust, shook his head again. "Hamp, this is goddamned insane."

"Steve," Milligan responded, finally showing some emotion, "you went through Quantico. We don't make the rules, we follow orders."

"Shit!" Wickham exclaimed. "Did the general come up with this plan?"

"Most of it . . . ," Milligan trailed off, then added, "with some input from the National Security Agency."

"Unbelievable," Wickham responded. "Go on."

"San Julian is approximately eight miles inland." Milligan pointed to the map. "We figure you can make the base by sunrise, dig in for the day, then recon the field the following night."

"Wait a second," Wickham said. "Back to the drop. We're going to need some diversionary tactics."

"We're going to cram the channel with a plethora of aircraft." Milligan reached over and picked up the top secret message. "Sixteen, as a matter of fact. It will appear to be heavy drug traffic, and you'll be lost in the shuffle."

"Jesus," Wickham said softly.

"The captain—your pilot—is considered by his CO as the best." Milligan placed the message down. "He's going to be skimming the water all the way in. No way can they pick you up on radar."

Milligan paused when his SecTel 1500 secure phone rang. The director inserted his key that had the identity of the person using it, and pushed the secure button. The key code went to a National Security Agency computer for validation, then selected an encoding algorithm for this particular conversation. The process took fourteen seconds before the call was completed. Milligan heard Norm Lasharr's voice on the line.

"Yes, general," Milligan reported, "he's with me as we speak."

Wickham watched Milligan as he talked to the director of Central Intelligence. A vision of Becky in her bikini crossed his mind, but then his thoughts returned to the recon mission. *I hope the general has another wonderful scheme to extract me,* he told himself.

"Oh, I'm sorry to hear that," Milligan said sadly, "but

we now have the answer . . . at least part of it." Milligan listened a moment longer and bid the director a good day. He severed the secure connection and turned to Wickham. "The Stealth is in Cuba, but the location is unknown."

"How did we confirm it was in Cuba?" Wickham asked, becoming more intrigued with the recon mission.

"I'm not sure of the exact connection," Milligan responded, "but we have . . . had an informant in Moscow fairly high up. The general didn't give me the particulars, but suffice it to say we lost our contact. The KGB had been watching him for quite a while."

Wickham remained silent, mindful of the implications.

"We've got a lot to do," Milligan continued, "so let's get under way. We're going to fly you to Cancun in a chartered cargo jet, then prepare you for the drop. By the way, don't shave . . . we're going to transform you into a gnarled farm worker."

THE WHITE HOUSE

The president walked briskly into the Oval Office, motioning for everyone to remain seated. "Please don't get up," Jarrett said as he crossed the room and sat down at his desk.

Kirk Truesdell and Bernie Kerchner noticed that the president's face was pale. They had become accustomed to this physical sign of trouble.

"Norm Lasharr just received confirmation," Jarrett said, grim faced. "Our B-2 is indeed in Cuba."

Truesdell and Kerchner exchanged stunned looks, then glanced at Brian Gaines, the president's national security adviser. Gaines was speechless for one of the rare moments in his life.

"God . . . damn," Truesdell said emotionally. "We're sitting on a powder keg."

Gaines studied the president before speaking. "Where in Cuba is it located, sir?"

Jarrett sighed, then looked directly at the tall, red-haired security expert. "The exact location is unknown."

"Unknown?" Kerchner asked. "If Lasharr knows—"

"Wait," the president interrupted, seeing Truesdell and Gaines forming words on their lips. "Wait a second, Bernie. We lost our priority contact—the air force general—before he could relay the entire message." Observing the shocked looks, the president poured a glass of water and waited for the gravity of the news to sink in before continuing.

"The CIA's intermediary cutout called an agency crisis line from Vienna. Seems that the general was in midsentence when the conversation was terminated. Our Vienna connection believes that the KGB has the general in custody. And we have no knowledge as to how he confirmed this information."

"Damn," Truesdell said, "we knew that the KGB had been suspicious. Voronoteev had relayed that concern when he gave us the MiG-29 data."

"Well," Jarrett replied, "it's water under the bridge. Norm Lasharr believed we needed to use the general and I agreed. Now, we have an explosive situation on our hands, and I want your suggestions."

"Mister President," Gaines said, shifting uneasily in his chair, "I'm not sure we should continue with the CIA probe into San Julian."

"Why not?" Jarrett inquired before he swallowed a sip of water.

"We already have confirmation that the aircraft is on Cuban soil," Gaines replied uncomfortably. "I believe we are asking for trouble if something goes wrong."

"If our agent is caught?" Kerchner questioned.

"Precisely," the lawyer-turned-security specialist replied in a firm tone. "The Soviets can use that to set up a hell of a smoke screen. My recommendation is that we confront the Kremlin, and Castro, diplomatically, and provide a face-saving solution for the return of our bomber, and the crew."

"I don't agree," Truesdell responded before the president

could speak. "If we don't have positive proof of the exact location of the Stealth, the Kremlin will deny the accusations and buy a lot of time to scrutinize the bomber. Sure, they realize that we know the B-2 is in Cuba, but what the hell are we going to do about it? We can't prove a damned thing."

"Bernie?" the president asked.

"Sir, I have to agree with Kirk. We have to verify the location of the B-2, then confront the Kremlin and Castro. We've got to work both ends of this problem and force Castro to break the logjam."

The defense secretary sat up in his chair and cleared his throat before continuing. "We've spent years developing the Stealth technology, not to mention billions of dollars. We can't afford to lose our technological edge to the Soviets. Castro is providing a shelter for the hijacked airplane, and we must inform him of our intent to recover or destroy the B-2."

Truesdell glanced at Gaines, then turned to Jarrett. "Bernie is right, sir," the vice president said. "We must do our homework, then demand the safe return of the Stealth and her crew—immediately—or Soviet President Ignatyev and Castro will face the consequences."

Jarrett sat quietly for a moment, analyzing the suggestions. "What sort of consequences did you have in mind, Kirk?"

"First, sir," Truesdell began tentatively, "we need to address the Castro issue. We have to know what his position is in relation to the hijacked bomber now hidden somewhere on his island. Castro's relations with the Kremlin turned sour long before Ignatyev surfaced, and they have continued to decline since."

"That's true," Gaines broke in, "but we need to consider an approach to a diplomatic solution."

"Mister Gaines," Truesdell replied sharply, visibly irritated. "Wait a minute. I am proposing that we place two carrier groups close to Cuba, have a battleship stand by to move in as soon as the B-2 is located, then explain our position to Castro and to the Kremlin."

"Kirk," the president said, "I'm not sure we want to take a stance like that, unless we have no alternative."

"Mister President," Truesdell replied, choosing his words carefully, "all I am suggesting is that we put some heat on Castro. He was forced into this—he had to have been. If we find the B-2 in his backyard, and explain our intentions, he damned sure isn't going to sit idle and take a pounding for the Soviet Union, if the Soviets are behind this."

"Sir," Kerchner began slowly, seeing the concern on the president's face. "Again, I have to agree with Kirk. If Castro believes that we're going to flatten his island if the bomber and her crew aren't released, he may quickly convince Ignatyev to change course, or produce the bomber."

The president pushed back his chair, swung around to his right, and stood. "Bernie, that could place us in a very difficult position. We aren't talking about Panama or Noriega. If we're wrong, and Castro can still get Soviet protection, there might be a disastrous about-face in the disarmament talks."

"Mister President," Truesdell interjected, "the Soviets would be responsible. They committed an act of international lawlessness. The Kremlin almost pulled off the hijacking, but they got caught, and we couldn't be in a better position to confront them and their henchman. Castro is going to be sitting on an extremely hot burner."

"If we have the proof," Kerchner said. "We have to have documented evidence—pictures of the B-2 in Cuba—to place in front of the world."

The room remained quiet as Alton Jarrett turned his back to the group and stared out of the window behind his desk. He considered the various solutions for recovering the Stealth bomber, and wondered what it would mean for Soviet-American relations if the Kremlin had initiated the theft. Was President Ignatyev, bent on restoring the glory of the Motherland, returning to the pre-perestroika ideology?

Jarrett turned toward his secretary of defense. "Bernie,

what steps have to be taken before we know where the B-2 is located?''

"First, sir," Kerchner darted a look at Truesdell, who showed no emotion, "we need to be cautious . . business as usual. We can't afford to alarm the Cubans, or the Russians, before our CIA agent is inserted to find the Stealth."

The president nodded his agreement.

"Actually," Kerchner said, placing his pen down, "I recommend we have the carrier groups on normal maneuvers, standing off the East Coast primed to strike. We don't want to do anything until we have the necessary documentation."

Kerchner watched the president's face. Jarrett seemed more relaxed, and the color had returned to his cheeks.

"Also," the secretary continued, "I strongly recommend that we prepare to remove all dependents, civilians, and non-essential personnel from Guantanamo Bay. At the same time, as unobtrusively as possible, we need to reinforce the marine contingent on the base. We'll do that in a routine manner, using C-130s out of Cherry Point."

Jarrett walked to his chair, sat down, and folded his hands together. "Anything else?"

Kerchner looked at the vice president for a moment, then back to Jarrett. "I would like to have the CO of the Naval Strike Warfare Center brief you on the current carrier air wing tactics."

The president agreed with a nod. "Fine, Bernie. Set it up when you have an opportunity."

"I've taken the liberty, sir," Kerchner responded with humility in his voice. "He's on his way now."

The vice president, who remained agitated by the guileless solution that Brian Gaines had put forth, stood and approached the president. "Sir, look at the history of our foreign policy. Every time we've pursued soft formulas, we've lost ground." Truesdell glanced at the chagrined security adviser. "Every time."

"Mister Vice President," Gaines countered, clearly irritated, "I take great umbrage at the insinuation that we are being soft."

"Brian, goddamnit," Truesdell said curtly, "we've just spent billions developing our Stealth technology, and the Soviets are soaking it up. We don't have a second to waste. The Soviets aren't going to respond unless we use a big stick, as we've always had to do."

Gaines, whose face now matched the color of his hair, appeared totally perplexed. He had known of the vice president's disdain for tiptoeing around tough problems. Now he felt the sting of professional embarrassment, and he decided to remain silent.

"Time is of the essence," Kerchner said in an attempt to calm feelings. "But we must have patience for the moment. We have to locate the B-2."

"Step one," Jarrett said calmly. "Then we'll look at our options. Agreed?"

"Yes, sir," Truesdell and Kerchner replied simultaneously.

Brian Gaines, avoiding the vice president's eyes, nodded affirmatively.

Jarrett leaned back and turned his chair slightly sideways again. "Sam Gardner is scheduled to return this afternoon, so we'll plan to meet with him on his arrival. I want an opinion from our secretary of state before we go any further. In the meantime, Bernie, go ahead and implement your suggestions."

"Yes, sir," Kerchner replied.

"I'm going jogging," Jarrett said with determination. "Have some lunch and take a break. We'll get together with Norm Lasharr and Sam at three o'clock."

CANCUN INTERNATIONAL AIRPORT

Steve Wickham sat on the DC-9's cockpit jump seat and watched the airport pass off to his left. The two young pilots, busy preparing the aging aircraft for landing, were in constant motion.

Wickham's mind drifted back to his conversation with the director of Clandestine Operations. More to the point, to the final topic of the covert operation brief—the method to be used to extract Wickham from Cuba.

The cargo jet turned from downwind of the airport to left base as Milligan's voice sounded in Wickham's mind. "We're going to use the skyhook to pick you up offshore the third night, if all goes according to plan."

Wickham, who was basically familiar with the challenging procedure, had listened carefully as Milligan explained the details. Approximately thirty minutes before Wickham was to reach the beach, which was estimated to be 0400 to 0430, the agent would send the signal for extraction. If the time was later than 0500, the pullout would have to be postponed until the following night.

The jet banked gently, turning on final approach for runway 12, as Wickham replayed the skyhook procedure. After sending the extraction signal, which would be transmitted via satellite to the OV-10 pilot orbiting off the Yucatan Peninsula, Wickham would slip back into his wet suit. Next he would don a special parachute harness connected to a 200-foot-long 'bungy' cord. The tough, elastic cord was attached to a 140-foot-long thin nylon line with a modified weather balloon on the end.

After Wickham made his way out to sea, he would wait until he heard the OV-10, then pop the seal on the small cylinder of compressed helium attached to the balloon. The balloon would inflate to approximately 8 feet in diameter, carrying the strong elastic cord up 200 feet. At the end of the elastic cord, beneath a softball-sized rubber attachment, was a large cyalume chemical lightstick. Wickham would have to bend the end of the stick, prior to inflating the balloon, to activate the light.

The OV-10 pilot would be able to see the bright lightstick from a distance of five to eight miles. So would the Cubans.

The risky extraction would have to be swift and flawless.

When the pilot spotted the eerie-looking light, he would head straight for it. He would place the glowing object in the center of a sight ring high on the front of his canopy, warn the winch operator in the back, then begin slowing to 100 knots.

The pilot would drop to 75 feet of altitude in order to be below the light and the rubber stop at the end of the tough elastic cord. The rubber flange would have to slide down from overhead the OV-10 to snag properly in the catch.

The wide, heavy-duty steel fork mounted through the nose of the aircraft would engage the elastic cord approximately 50 feet below the light. The hard rubber ball would snap into the V clutch as the nylon cord and balloon popped free.

Wickham, who would be facing the sound of the aircraft, would start accelerating through the water at a fairly rapid pace, then be snatched out quickly after the line stretched and recoiled. The pilot would add power and raise the Bronco's nose to assist the winch operator in snaring the elastic cord. The taut line, pressed to the belly of the OV-10, would be reeled into the small compartment below and behind the cockpit.

All well and good, Wickham thought as the DC-9 flared for landing, as long as the line did not touch either of the two spinning propellers. The pilot would have to fly perfectly straight until Wickham was safely inside the aircraft.

The jet slowed rapidly, turned off the runway, and taxied smoothly past the terminal building. As the pilots completed their after landing checklist, Wickham surveyed the various hangars. He looked down the shimmering ramp at the wide array of civilian aircraft. There was not a single airplane that looked even remotely like a Marine Corps OV-10 Bronco.

Wickham unbuckled his seat restraints after the cargo jet rolled to a smooth stop in front of a small, pale green hangar. The two sliding doors were open three feet, revealing the camouflaged nose of the OV-10 counterinsurgency (COIN) operations aircraft.

Wickham thanked the cargo crew for the smooth ride, waited for the copilot to open the door, then picked up his canvas bag and walked down the air-stair ladder. The scorching afternoon heat was a shock after the cool, dry atmosphere in the DC-9 cockpit.

Wickham could see a small group of people standing in the hangar. They were all staring at him. He hesitated, then started toward the open doors when a man in a sage green flight suit stepped out into the sun. He was of medium height, with dark brown hair and twinkling brown eyes. His standard issue flight suit was bereft of any insignia, patches, or name tag. There was no visual clue that the man was assigned to the VMO-1 squadron at the Marine Corps Air Station, New River, North Carolina.

"Welcome to our tropical paradise," the cheerful, smiling pilot said as he extended his hand. "I'm Greg Spidel, captain incognito, USMC."

Wickham shook Spidel's hand solidly as he introduced himself. "Steve Wickham. I understand you're the resident ace in OV-10s."

Spidel laughed. "Let's say that's one of a number of things I've been called."

"Know what you mean," Wickham smiled, immediately liking the friendly pilot.

"Hey," Spidel said, displaying his infectious grin, "all my friends call me Spider."

"Spider it is," Wickham replied, noting two agency personnel step through the door.

"You hungry?" Spidel asked as the CIA agents stepped forward to greet Wickham.

"I could go for some chow," Wickham responded as he shook hands with his colleagues. "What's on the menu?"

"South-of-the-border cuisine," Spidel laughed, pointing to a box of greasy enchiladas. "Your friends just introduced me to them . . . and they're great. Besides, we've got a tub of ice-cold Coca-Cola to wash them down."

"Actually, Spider," Wickham said as the group started toward the hangar, "I could use a beer."

"Got some of that, too!" Spidel replied, stepping through the hangar doors. "We'll keep it cold until you're back."

CHAPTER FOURTEEN

THE WHITE HOUSE

President Alton Jarrett watched closely as Bernard Kerchner briefed the secretary of state on the latest developments in and around Cuba. Samuel Gardner, a short, barrel-chested man whose snapping eyes seemed to penetrate their target, listened intently.

Kerchner always felt as though Gardner was silently critiquing his every word. The secretary of state was well known for his dry, humorless personality. "The intelligence reports we have," Kerchner stated, "along with current satellite information, confirm increased activity throughout Cuba and the surrounding waters."

"Excuse me, Bernie," Gardner responded, "but Castro did announce that he had scheduled a large military exercise during this period."

"True," the defense secretary replied, "but the magnitude of these maneuvers is quite different from previous exercises. Sure it may be coincidental that one of our B-2s disappeared at the same time, but it may not be. We simply don't know, so I have to plan for the worst case scenario." Kerchner clicked the slide projector and looked at his briefing agenda. "The Kremlin, we have to assume, knows we're aware of the regional locale of the B-2."

The room remained quiet. The president, the Joint Chiefs of Staff, the national security adviser, the CIA director, and the vice president concentrated on the National Reconnaissance Office photos.

"Here's a Soviet task force," Kerchner pointed to a spot forty miles south of Largo Cay, "and here's a second group of ships."

The first aggregate of Russian warships, bunched tightly, was steaming west 145 miles south of Havana. The second flotilla was 120 miles west of the first group, 80 miles south of the San Julian airfield.

"Normally," Kerchner continued, punching the button on the slide projector, "the Soviet Union sends only one task force a year to Cuban waters. Now we have two Russian task forces, with more ships than usual assigned to each one."

The president leaned forward and addressed his coterie of advisers. "That might not be so odd, knowing the new Soviet leader's penchant for showcasing Russia's military resurgence." Jarrett leaned back and folded his arms. "Please continue, Bernie."

Kerchner flashed another slide on the screen. "This next series of photos causes me a great deal of concern. The Soviet aircraft carrier *Novorossiysk*, normally a Pacific Fleet ship, is operating off the northern coast of Nicaragua with a complement of twenty-seven Yakovlev-38s. As you can see, the carrier has five escort ships."

Kerchner pointed at a ship on the enhanced satellite picture. "This is a Kara-class guided missile cruiser, and this," Kerchner tapped the screen, "is a Kashin-class guided missile destroyer. We believe they are operating with at least two or more hunter-killer submarines."

Kerchner paused for effect. "The carrier task force could be in Cuban waters in a matter of hours. It could become an explosive situation. If an armed conflict erupts, it could spread to American shores very quickly.''

Glancing at Jarrett, Kerchner continued. ''By now, Castro and the Kremlin should know we are damned serious.''

''Bernie,'' the secretary of state spoke finally. ''What's actually happening in Cuba—on the island?''

Kerchner picked up a paper marked top secret. ''The Soviet signal intelligence collection facility at Lourdes has turned into a beehive of activity. They've been soaking up every scrap of military communications, including domestic telephone calls. The increase was noticed within an hour of our notification that the Stealth bomber was in Cuba.''

''Also,'' Kerchner continued, ''the vast majority of Cuban warships have put to sea, or are about to get under way. Bear H and J aircraft—a total of nineteen—have been dispensed all over the island. The Soviets normally have a total of seven or eight Bears in Cuba.''

Kerchner clicked the projector again, showing detailed satellite photos of the entire Communist island. ''Here we have MiG-23s, -25s, and -27s scattered from one end of Cuba to the other. You can see two- and three-plane groups at a number of remote civilian airfields. We also know that the Cubans, since late '89, have acquired at least forty-seven MiG-29s, if not more. There are eight of them dispersed around Havana, but the majority are kept concealed in various forms of camouflage.''

Kerchner flashed his last slide on the screen. ''This is a high-resolution photograph from the latest satellite shots. These concentrations of equipment, including T-62 and T-55 tanks, are moving toward the San Julian air base.''

Kerchner clicked off the projector light and turned on the overhead lights in the basement room. ''We have also seen a number of helicopter gunships and MiGs repositioned close to the Cienfuegos nuclear power station. Ignatyev and Castro know that we aren't going to sit here and wring our hands if we locate our B-2.''

Alton Jarrett leaned forward and clasped his hands together

on the table. "If Ignatyev is bluffing, I'm going to call his bluff."

The president looked at his vice president, then faced Gardner again. "If the B-2 is not at San Julian, we're going to have to step back and reevaluate our position. If it is located at San Julian, and I am convinced it is, we have to respond swiftly and boldly."

"I understand, sir," Gardner replied evenly, "but I recommend that we attempt a diplomatic solution when we have conclusive evidence that the B-2 is in Cuba."

Truesdell softened slightly. "I concur with your diplomatic initiative, but we know that the Soviets are going to disavow everything."

Gardner picked up his pipe and clamped it in his mouth. "If we have clinical evidence—photos—"

Jarrett's intercom buzzed. "Yes?"

"Mister President," the male voice announced, "the reconnaissance aircraft is about to take off from Cancun."

"Very well," Jarrett replied, then looked at his secretary of state. "Sam, go ahead and contact Minister Aksenhov and set up a meeting this evening. Just the three of us—here in the White House."

"Yes, Mister President."

Jarrett turned to Kerchner. "Bernie, let's have the Strike Warfare Center briefing."

"I'll get the captain," Kerchner responded as he finished stacking his slides.

CANCUN

Marine Capt. Greg Spidel taxied the sinister-looking, olive-drab North American Rockwell OV-10D Bronco to the end of runway 12. The fuselage sat between two stubby wings with long engine nacelles. The two nacelles ran the length of the armed reconnaissance aircraft, forming twin tails that connected the tall, wide horizontal stabilizer.

The aerial observer seat behind the pilot was vacant, and the two underwing hardpoints held AIM-9 Sidewinder missiles. Every indication of country of origin, along with the serial number, had been sanded clean or otherwise removed.

Steve Wickham sat alone in the cramped compartment behind and below the cockpit. He was isolated in the dark interior except for his communications link with Spidel. The rear quick-disconnect cargo door had been removed, allowing Wickham an unobstructed view out the back of the aircraft.

Wickham, uncomfortable in his wet suit, sat on a sliding seat mounted flat on the floor. He was restrained by a seat strap and a shoulder harness. Greg Spidel would inform him when to unbuckle and prepare for the paradrop.

"All set, Mister Wickham?" Spidel asked as he cycled his flight controls.

"Hey, Spider, drop the Mister," Wickham replied, adjusting his Clark headset. "I'm ready when you are."

"We'll be rolling in a couple of seconds," Spidel said over the intercom.

"Cancun tower, Tailback One is ready to roll," Spidel radioed as he pressed on the brakes and walked the throttles forward, checking his engines and propellers.

"Taxi into position and hold," the controller instructed with a pronounced accent.

"Posit and hold," Spidel radioed, taxiing to the center of the active runway.

"Tailback One, wind one-three-zero at seven, cleared for takeoff," the tower operator replied, then added a cheerful send-off. "Tell 'em hello in Pensacola."

"Will do," Spidel replied into his lip microphone as he rechecked his engine instruments. His visual flight rules (VFR) flight plan showed his destination to be Pensacola Naval Air Station. After Wickham parachuted out of the Bronco, Spidel would return to Cancun from the north with a purported engine problem.

"Tailback One rolling," Spidel radioed as he shoved the twin throttles forward. Both Garrett T-76 turboprop engines, producing a collective 2,080-shaft horsepower, howled in unison as the camouflaged Bronco accelerated rapidly down the 11,483-foot runway.

Spidel, feeling the composite propellers clawing the air, watched the airspeed indicator race past his takeoff speed as he eased back smoothly on the stick.

Wickham watched the runway drop away, then felt the landing gear bang into the wheel wells. He could see the last purple and gold rays of the shimmering tropical sun sinking below the horizon.

Spidel leveled the OV-10D at 300 feet above the dark Yucatan Channel and rechecked his global navigation display. The readout corresponded precisely with the manual navigation plot he had completed before his passenger had arrived.

He turned north and remained on course to Pensacola, Florida, until he was out of sight. At that point, he dropped to 100 feet over the smooth water and turned east toward Cuba. The Bronco would not be visible to radar at their transition altitude.

Spidel cast a quick glance at his vertical tape engine instruments, then concentrated on keeping the OV-10D at the prescribed altitude. He could tell he would have good moonlight for low-level flying.

Wickham sat with his arms folded on top of his equipment pack and thought about his mission. He had checked and rechecked his gear a half-dozen times. He adjusted his camouflage parachute and felt again for the static line snap. Hooked properly and free to slide.

The waterproof equipment bag connected to Wickham's chest straps contained his extraction harness and balloon. It also contained worn-looking dark khaki trousers and a soiled green peasant shirt. A tattered straw hat and scuffed work boots completed the outfit. Wickham also carried a 9-mm Excam with a clip containing fifteen rounds, along with a Burbour tactical knife.

Cushioned inside the clothing were two very important items—a small transmitter to signal for his extraction, and a compact Sony television camera. The lightweight camera, a fraction of the size of the Sony Betacam, had a built-in power pack capable of generating a continuous picture for eight to ten minutes. Provided he could locate the Stealth bomber, Wickham would be able to send real-time photos of the B-2, via satellite. The picture would go to a Transat-16 satellite receiver before being flashed to a monitor in the National Reconnaissance Office.

The last piece of equipment Wickham had attached to his harness was a small hydrogen-powered tow vehicle. The underwater tow conveyance had been designed for covert operations by Ingenieurkontor Lubeck. Small fuel cells produced electricity by combining hydrogen and oxygen in a quiet electrochemical reaction. The energy turned a shielded propeller, which supplied the swimmer or scuba diver with an effortless ride. Wickham knew that the tow vehicle would take him to the beach from one mile offshore. Returning to his extraction point would expend the limited fuel and require him to swim most of the way.

Wickham keyed his intercom. "Spider, let me know when we're five minutes from the drop."

"Will do," Spidel replied from the darkened cockpit.

The pilot could see a half-dozen aircraft navigation and recognition lights traveling north and south over the channel. The diversionary aircraft flew at staggered altitudes ranging from 4,500 to 16,500 feet. He knew that there were at least another ten aircraft crisscrossing over the Bronco's flight path with their lights extinguished.

Cuban radar hopefully would not be able to pick out the low-flying OV-10 in the mass of airborne traffic. The string of small prop and turboprop aircraft provided a screen to fully occupy the Cuban radar operators. The CIA pilots would make their trips every night while Wickham was in Cuba.

Spidel carefully reset his specially mounted Collins AL-101 radio altimeter at seventy-five feet and lowered the OV-10's nose. The precision instrument provided the pilot with altitude accuracy within plus or minus two feet, or 2 percent accuracy, below 500 feet.

"I'm stepping down to seventy-five feet," Spidel informed his passenger. "I'll take it down on the deck in a couple of minutes."

"You're the expert," Wickham responded as he slipped on his swim fins. "Just don't doze off."

GUANTANAMO BAY, CUBA

The United States Naval Base, referred to as Gitmo, was almost deserted except for the contingent of marines and the essential personnel of CompRon Ten.

The naval air composite squadron VC-10, who claimed to work in a Communist country every day, was on full alert. The unique squadron, charged with the dual mission of serving the fleet and providing base defense, had its eight TA-4J Skyhawks loaded with ordnance. Three of the single-engine jets, affectionately known as scooters, had been configured for close air support. The remaining five aircraft were loaded with weapons for air defense, including two AIM-9 Sidewinder missiles and twin 20mm cannons concealed in the wing roots. Each cannon held 200 rounds of ammunition.

The VC-10 Challengers maintained a high state of readiness in air-to-ground ordnance delivery by flying almost daily weapons training missions. The unit, acting as an adversary squadron, also provided air combat training for fleet fighter pilots. Each VC-10 pilot had to refine his tactics skills continually, with an emphasis on countering the types of MiGs deployed in Cuba.

The naval aviators of VC-10 were typical of their breed— excellent pilots and proud of the fact. Three of the current pilots were Navy Fighter Weapons School graduates who added to the lean and mean reputation the squadron enjoyed.

Lieutenant Commander Jim "Flaps" Flannagan, VC-10's operations officer, sat alone in his TA-4J at the end of the

naval air station's 8,000-foot runway. His wingman, Lt.
Frank "Doc" Wellby, taxied into position for the night section takeoff. Both of the attack aircraft had been configured
for air defense. A standby Skyhawk, manned and with the
engine running, sat on the taxiway adjacent to the runway.

Flannagan checked his master armament switch to ensure
that it was in the off position, then glanced back at Wellby's
Skyhawk. He could not see Wellby in the cockpit, but he
knew that his partner was going through his final checks.
Frank Wellby was one of the best in the fighter business.

Wellby's red anticollision lights flashed back and forth in
an eerie, pulsating glow. Flannagan, flying the lead position,
had his anticollision lights off so he wouldn't blind his wingman.

"Gunsmoke Four is ready," Wellby radioed Flannagan.
The tower had already cleared the flight of two for takeoff
before the pilots taxied onto the runway.

"Rog," Flannagan replied, advancing the throttle of the
Pratt & Whitney J-52 turbojet. "Power coming up to ninety-
six percent." The lead pilot did not use full power for takeoff
so his wingman would have extra thrust to stay in position.
"Gunsmoke Three rolling," Flannagan announced as he released the brakes and concentrated on tracking straight down
the left side of the dark runway.

Wellby, jockeying his throttle slightly, maintained perfect
position to the right of his flight leader. The two Skyhawks
blasted down the concrete strip, sending a thundering roar
reverberating across Guantanamo Bay. Wellby watched the
lead Skyhawk and responded identically to every move Flannagan initiated. The actions and responses of the two pilots
were only an eighth of a second from being mirror images.

The lead TA-4J lifted smoothly from the runway. Two
seconds later the landing gear was retracting and the aircraft
settled slightly as the flaps were raised. Flannagan felt a
wobble as one of the leading edge slats on each wing seated
before the other was in place.

"Gunsmoke Three," the tower controller radioed, "contact Gunsmoke One on three-two-seven point six.''

"Smoke Three, switching three-twenty-seven-six," Flannagan responded as he banked gently to the left and watched his airspeed approach 250 knots.

"Gunsmoke One, Smoke Three and Four up."

"Roger," the orbiting flight leader replied. "I have a tally. We're at your nine o'clock, four miles, descending through eight thousand."

Flannagan, scanning back and forth above his left wing, saw the flashing red lights. "I have you in sight."

Flannagan and Wellby would replace their two squadron mates as the duty air base combat air patrol (CAP). Since Cuban MiG activity had increased sharply during the massive personnel evacuation airlift—two MiG-23s had flown directly over the base during the late afternoon—a continuous combat air patrol was necessary.

The Skyhawk flights were operating under the guise of normal training missions. They would refuel from a Navy KA-6D tanker fifty-five minutes into the mission, then remain on station for another hour. The two TA-4Js now landing would be their reliefs. Fresh pilots were being rotated on each mission, allowing the previous two pilots an opportunity to grab a quick meal and a few hours of sleep.

"Okay, Doc," Flannagan said into his mask, "let's go upstairs. Cross under and go loose deuce."

"Roger," Wellby replied, raising the nose to match his leader as he transitioned to the tactical formation.

"The Hawkeye is RTB," Gunsmoke One radioed, then spoke to his wingman. "Smoke Two, boards . . . now." Both descending pilots popped their speed brakes to hasten their letdown.

"What's with the E-2?" Flannagan asked, concerned about not having the Hawkeye airborne early warning aircraft to call targets for them. The Grumman E-2C all-weather surveillance aircraft provided the eyes for fleet defense. Fighter and attack crews relied on the twin-engine turboprop to warn them early about bogies in the area.

"Their starboard engine went south on 'em," Gunsmoke One answered. "Gitmo approach is up this freq, so they'll work you as Strike."

"Copy," Flannagan replied, rolling out on a heading of ninety degrees three miles south of the runway.

"Strike," Flannagan radioed, glancing at his wingman. "Smoke Three and Four with you."

"Roger, Smoke," the controller acknowledged calmly. "We have confirmed MiG activity over Antonio Maceo. The Strike officer is on his way over from the Hawkeye. Your orbit is the Gitmo two-nine-zero radial, angels fifteen at twelve DME. Squawk one-four-two-seven."

"Wilco," Flannagan responded as he banked the Skyhawk smoothly to the left and set the new transponder code. "Check switches safe."

"Four . . . safe," Wellby radioed, interrupting his thoughts about a cancelled leave. He had been scheduled to be the best man at his brother's wedding in two days.

Neither pilot had any idea what had caused the sudden alert. The ready room speculation had ranged from a terrorist attack to a possible invasion of the naval base. A senior navy captain from CINCLANT headquarters had arrived during the afternoon. He had immediately assumed the responsibility of on-site commander for the base and acted as Strike control.

Flannagan and Wellby leveled their Skyhawks at 15,000 feet and settled into a racetrack pattern twelve nautical miles west of the air base.

"Smoke Three and Four," the controller radioed, "Strike has arrived, and we show new MiG activity eighteen miles southeast of Holguin."

"Roger," Flannagan responded, checking his fuel supply. "I have a visual on three MiGs over Tony Mack."

"We show four targets," the controller said. "The two high contacts are flying a triangle pattern, and the low targets are meandering around north of the city."

Flannagan banked slightly to focus on the fast mover closest to the ground. "We've got a good moon, but I only see one down low. His buddy must have his lights off."

"Roger that."

The two Skyhawk fighter and attack pilots continued their orbit as Flannagan concentrated on the MiGs and counted the minutes till refueling.

"Ah . . . Smoke," the controller said cautiously, "we've got multiple bogies—looks like three targets—closing from three-one-zero."

Flannagan's head snapped to his four o'clock position. "How far out?"

"Sixty-five miles," the radar operator said. "They're the MiGs from Holguin."

"Roger," Flannagan replied, thinking about the afternoon rules of engagement (ROE) briefing. The pilots could not fire unless fired upon. "We're going to the tanker."

"Roger, Smoke," the tense controller replied, offering assistance. "The Texaco is at your ten o'clock, angels one-seven."

Flannagan shoved his throttle forward and looked out of his canopy to the left. He could see clearly the Grumman KA-6D's oscillating anticollision lights. "Smoke has a tally on the tanker."

The bright moonlight would be a godsend for the Skyhawk pilots. Night refueling required a great deal of concentration and coordination. Any light would help the pilots' depth perception.

"Gunsmoke Three and Four," the tanker pilot radioed, "we're heading zero-seven-zero, two hundred fifty indicated, coming port."

Flannagan checked his airspeed. He would have to bleed off the extra forty-five knots as he closed quickly inside the tanker. "Smoke flight," Flannagan radioed, "will take four grand each."

The KA-6D pilot clicked his mike twice and extended the refueling drogue. The shuttlecock basket, attached to the fueling hose, slid out from under the twin jet and extended fifty feet.

"Call stabilized," the tanker pilot ordered as he disengaged the autopilot. He would hand fly the aircraft during the refueling procedure.

"Wilco," Flannagan replied, then spoke to his close friend and wingman. "Doc, cross under and plug first."

"Roger," Wellby said, adding a small amount of power and lowering the TA-4J's nose. He passed under his leader, emerging on Flannagan's right wing.

One minute later both aircraft eased into position on the Intruder's left wing. Flannagan checked his wingman's position, then keyed his radio. "Stabilized."

"Cleared to plug," the tanker pilot radioed as he rechecked the fuel-transfer panel. It was set to pump two tons of fuel into each TA-4J.

Wellby moved forward and flew his fixed probe smoothly into the drogue on the first try. The delicate maneuver required a tremendous degree of finesse with the stick and throttle. The fuel transfer went quickly, and Wellby slid out of the basket, moved seventy feet from the KA-6D's right wing, and watched his flight leader.

Flannagan tanked without a hitch. He watched the refueling light wink off, then disengaged from the basket and slid astern. "Thanks for the drink," Flannagan radioed as Wellby eased back into position on his right wing. "Strike, Smoke flight is returning to our CAP posit."

"Roger," the controller answered. "The inbound contacts are three north of Dos Caminos, closing rapidly."

Flannagan eased his throttle to 98 percent. "Coming up on the power."

"Four," Wellby responded, staring at Flannagan's dull gray Skyhawk.

"Smoke, Strike," the controller said with a hint of anxiety. "The two high targets over Antonio Maceo appear to be joining the inbound flight of three."

Flannagan scanned the sky to the northwest as he descended back to 15,000 feet. After a few seconds he picked out the MiGs' blinking anticollision lights. "Tally on the flight of two," Flannagan reported, then spotted the other three bogies. "I have the Holguin inbounds, too."

The two MiG groups rendezvoused in a staggered trail formation and made a wide, sweeping pass two miles west of the Navy TA-4Js. Flannagan and Wellby watched the MiGs pass 3,000 feet higher as they settled back into their pattern.

"Four, let's step up two thou—" Flannagan stopped abruptly, not believing his eyes. Had the Cuban MiGs flown into a cloud? Hell no, he realized quickly—the thin wisps of clouds were well above them.

"Strike, Smoke flight," Flannagan radioed uneasily. "The comrades just turned off all their exterior lights. I've lost them."

"Copy, Smoke. Stand by—"

"Negative," Flannagan said brusquely. "Launch the spare, and get the other two shooters back up."

"Gunsmoke Three," a different voice said, "this is Captain Murchison. Return to base and orbit. Smoke Five is rolling and will join up overhead."

"Wilco," Flannagan replied as he banked smoothly toward the naval base.

Seven seconds passed before the original voice sounded in Flannagan's helmet. "Smoke flight, we have two targets breaking away from the MiG flight. They are approaching you at . . . they're accelerating at your seven o'clock, twelve miles."

"Shit," Flannagan said inadvertently over the radio. "Doc, come hard port and go combat spread."

CHAPTER FIFTEEN

THE OV-10

"We're five minutes out," Greg Spidel said over the intercom. He was concentrating intently on remaining thirty feet above the calm sea.

"Okay," Wickham replied, steeling himself for the night parachute jump. He looked up at his static line, checking the hook again. "I'll unstrap at the one-minute mark."

"I won't forget," the pilot replied.

The camouflaged Bronco raced across the sea at full power, black against the dark water. Spidel could see the twinkling lights of Peninsula de Guanahacabibes approaching rapidly on the right. He searched for any sign of boats or low-flying aircraft, then checked his position. Two minutes to go. He glanced ahead at the surface of the water and watched for a sign of land.

"Oh, shit," Spidel exclaimed to himself as he noticed the white mast light of a small boat off to his right. "Too late now." He continued on course, watching the time and searching for the beach. The bright Caribbean moonlight was both a curse and a blessing.

"One minute, Steve," Spidel warned at the same instant he spotted the curved beach where Wickham would go ashore. Spidel retarded the throttles to slow the Bronco to paradrop speed.

"All set," Wickham replied as he unstrapped his restraining harness. He was free to slide out the rear when the pilot pulled up the OV-10's nose. Wickham made a last check to ensure that his static line was secure, then froze into the brace position. He could feel the aircraft decelerating.

"Thirty seconds, Steve," Spidel said calmly, watching his airspeed. "Good luck."

"Thanks," Wickham replied, clamping his mouth shut and removing the Clark headset. His heart raced and he could feel the adrenaline surge.

Spidel stared at the shore, judging it to be a mile and a quarter from the drop point. He paused a second, checked his speed at 210 knots, then eased back on the stick. "Here we go," the pilot said to himself as he pulled the speeding OV-10 into the vertical.

Wickham flew out the back at 200 feet, cleared the overhead horizontal stabilizer, then stopped in midair when the parachute popped open. The chute deployment, at more than 200 miles per hour, sounded like a shotgun blast. Afraid of becoming entangled in the parachute shroud lines, he closely watched the surface of the water. He did not want to drown under the heavy, wet canopy.

Wickham waited until he judged the sea to be about thirty feet below him, then unsnapped his parachute risers and plunged into the cool water. The violent impact almost tore off his right swim fin.

"Sonuvabitch," Wickham sputtered as he resurfaced. His first thought was to get clear of the falling canopy. After swimming twenty yards, he rolled on his back and rested as he watched the parachute sink beneath the sea. His thick wet suit provided as much flotation as a small life vest. He listened for a moment, hearing only the OV-10 departing to the northwest.

He secured his swim fin, then unstrapped the water tow vehicle and rolled onto his stomach. He looked around, pointed the water tow, then focused on the beach and pulled the trigger on the right handle.

OVER GUANTANAMO BAY

The two TA-4J Skyhawks raced head-on toward the unseen adversaries. Lieutenant Frank Wellby, flying Gunsmoke Four, was three-quarters of a mile off his flight leader's starboard wing. He was stepped up 2,000 feet from Flannagan's aircraft.

"Smoke flight," the anxious controller radioed, "your bogies—at twelve o'clock, three miles. Warning Yellow, Weapons Hold."

"Smoke looking," Flannagan replied, scanning straight ahead. "Tallyho!"

"Two miles," Strike warned. "Right down the middle." Both TA-4Js were easy to see with their navigation lights and bright red anticollision beacons blinking.

"Four has 'em," Wellby radioed. The two Cuban MiG-23s (NATO code name Flogger) slashed between the two American jets and snapped into a tight climbing turn to the left.

"Vertical reverse," Flannagan called, then pitched up and turned toward his wingman. "I'll get some angle on."

"I've got ya'," Wellby replied as he passed head-on to his leader. "Five, say posit."

"I have you at one o'clock," the third Skyhawk pilot radioed. "Keep it comin' around—I'll join on your inside."

"Smokes," the radar controller said with an edge of tension in his voice, "the other three bogies are turning. They're accelerating toward you."

"Roger," Flannagan replied, straining under the g load he

forced on the Skyhawk. "They're turning into me . . . master arm on . . . going to be close—oh!"

Flannagan snapped the stick into his stomach, but it was too late to avoid colliding with the MiG wingman. The right wing of each jet impacted in a blinding flash, sending both aircraft plummeting out of control.

"Lead is hit!" Wellby radioed in stunned disbelief. "I'm engaging, arm 'em up—cover me!"

Strike tried to transmit at the same instant as Smoke Five, blocking each other's calls. Flannagan ejected from his wildly spinning jet and floated down in the middle of the aerial combat. He watched both crippled fighters tumble to the ground five miles northwest of the runway.

"Smoke, Strike," the controller shouted, "cleared to engage—engage!"

"Lights, lights, Doc!" Lt. Guy Elliot radioed to the new lead pilot as he flipped off his own exterior lights. He saw Wellby's Skyhawk disappear momentarily, then reacquired the aircraft. "Break right, hard right . . . he's turning inside . . . reverse . . . hard port—bring your nose up, now!"

The Strike controller broke in. "The three bogies closing from due west, six miles, angels one-six!"

"Okay, Doc," Elliot shouted, "I'm goin' with a winder. Break hard starboard, now!"

"Fox Two!" Elliot radioed, squeezing the firing button a split second after Wellby snapped his Skyhawk into a gut-wrenching right turn. The Sidewinder heat-seeking missile, appearing to track low, curved into the vertical and slammed into the MiG-23's tailpipe. The Flogger continued to fly, spewing a thin vapor trail, as the pilot fought to control the fighter. He headed straight for Holguin.

"Doc!" Elliot yelled. "I'm at your nine o'clock, low— we've got three on the nose. Let's burn 'em."

"Tally, tally," Wellby shouted, "they're breakin' right . . . in trail . . . let's go high." Both Skyhawks, separated 1,200 feet horizontally, pulled up in tandem, then rolled almost inverted to track the MiGs.

"I'm going for the lead!" Wellby radioed. "Get one on
. . . put it on tail end Charlie."

"Wilco," Elliot said, lining up 600 yards behind the last
Flogger. He was beginning to feel a sensory overload.

"Fox Two!" Wellby radioed, squeezing off his first Sidewinder. The missile, pointed at the hot exhaust of the lead
MiG-23, made two erratic corrections, missed its target, and
collided with the second MiG fighter. The Flogger disintegrated in a rapid series of pulsing explosions.

Elliot fired his remaining Sidewinder and watched it track
unerringly toward its prey. "Fox Two!"

Wellby, realizing that the Cuban MiGs were attempting to
disengage, called his wingman. "Break it off, break off!
Strike, we're RTB—"

His statement was interrupted by the explosion and orange
fireball created by the destruction of the trailing MiG. The
pilot ejected from the burning jet, forcing Elliot to barrel roll
over the parachute.

"Jesus," Wellby shouted over the radio. "Strike, recommend you get Smoke One and Two back up to cover the
tanker."

"Yeah," the shocked KA-6D pilot interjected, "we'd go
for that."

"We're working them now," the controller responded.
"Smoke flight, report to Captain Murchison in the ready room
after you land. Switch to the tower."

"Wilco," Wellby replied, feeling the stress of the combat
engagement. "Did Flannagan get out?"

A long pause followed before the stunned controller answered. "We don't know. The SAR helo is launching—it's
airborne now."

THE BEACH

Steve Wickham released the trigger on his water tow, slowing
to a halt forty yards from the gently sloping beach. He had

worked his way cautiously through a narrow gap in the coral reef. Now he let his legs sink, feeling for the sandy bottom of the small inlet.

His swim fins touched bottom in what Wickham figured to be about four feet of water. The agent purged the saltwater from his nostrils and mouth, then listened for any sign of activity. He studied the beach carefully in both directions and spotted the point where he wanted to slip out of the water. Pulling the trigger again, he aimed for a wide stretch of sand leading to a large guava thicket.

When he felt his knees drag bottom, Wickham stopped, slipped off his fins, and walked ashore. He hurried across the beach, carrying his fins and tow vehicle, then slowed at the edge of the sand dunes adjacent to the guava thicket. He flinched as he walked through an area of salt grass and prickly pears. Swatting away a couple of sand fleas, he trotted the last few yards to the thicket.

The agent caught a whiff of eucalyptus as he settled into the thick foliage. The scent reminded him of Grenada. After catching his breath, he stripped off the wet suit, opened his sealed equipment bag, and changed into the dry peasant clothing. After tying his boots, he concealed his gear carefully, strapped his tactical knife to the calf of his right leg, then placed the 9mm Excam into the holster at the small of his back.

Wickham looked at his watch, unstrapped it, and placed it in his shirt pocket. He checked his small compass and dropped it in the pocket, too. He felt confident that he could traverse the distance to San Julian by 3 A.M.

He placed the small, lightweight satellite transmitter in a pocket of his baggy khaki trousers and donned his tattered straw hat. He slid the compact television camera into the specially sewn pocket in his pants, checked his camouflaged tow vehicle and wet suit, then set off for the Cuban air base.

THE SITUATION ROOM

The president, vice president, secretary of defense, security adviser, CIA director, and Joint Chiefs of Staff listened to the seasoned, articulate commanding officer of the Naval Strike Warfare Center, referred to as Strike University.

The rugged-looking captain, who had been initially taken aback by the disclosure of the B-2's whereabouts, explained the intricacies of the various missions the carrier groups could support. He outlined the latest improvements implemented to standardize air wing training, then explained their basic strategy.

"In this type of situation," the confident pilot said, "we would use two carrier battle groups. One group, augmented by shore-based forces, would be assigned the task of defending our southern coastline. The second group would support the type of operation selected to neutralize or recover the B-2. We can fly air strikes, or supply close air support if you elect to shell the airfield . . . or invade the island."

The captain hesitated, waiting for an indication of the preferred course of action.

"Captain," the president said in a friendly tone, "Secretary Kerchner and the Joint Chiefs have expressed their opinions in this matter. You're the current expert. What do you recommend?"

The captain paused a moment, seeking to formulate a politically astute answer.

"I apologize for putting you on the spot," Jarrett said when he saw the officer tense. "We recognize your splendid record, including combat duty, and I would appreciate your thoughts on the situation."

"Mister President," the captain replied, measuring his words carefully, "our naval and marine forces can provide three basic capabilities in this particular situation. One, we can use a battleship to shell San Julian . . . take the least number of casualties. However, we cannot predict the outcome if we don't have precise targeting coordinates. Even if we did know the exact location of the B-2, it might be fortified beyond our conventional capability.'' The pilot glanced at the chief of naval operations, who nodded in agreement.

"Second, we can fly heavy strike missions against the base. Again, we can't be sure of the results, and we run the risk of losing a lot of aircraft, and the crews. And there's an additional factor to consider with this type of operation—some of the pilots would undoubtedly become prisoners.''

The captain concealed his uneasiness. "The third option, in my opinion, is the most desirable and provides the best chance for success.''

"Please continue," the president said, seeing the officer hesitate again.

"The best approach," the captain continued, "is to have two marine expeditionary units assault San Julian. Navy and marine aircraft will provide close air support and air cover while the grunts secure the base.''

The marine commandant leaned back and squinted at the naval officer. "Captain, while I agree with your basic approach, I must point out that battalion landing teams are too light to conduct sustained combat operations.''

"Yes, general," the pilot responded, "I realize that. I'm suggesting that we go in fast, secure the base, destroy the Stealth, free the crew, and withdraw.''

"What is our chance for success?" Jarrett asked in an interested tone.

"Mister President," the captain replied, "as the general knows, we've been working with two of his crack battalion landing teams. They're primed for this type of mission. We can have them on station in a matter of hours, and with increased helo and Harrier support, I believe we can successfully accomplish the objective.''

"Thank you, captain," the president said, then stood. Everyone followed his lead as the commander in chief walked over to the surprised officer and extended his hand. "We appreciate your brief, and your recommendation. I feel more comfortable—and knowledgeable about—our current capabilities.''

''Thank you, Mister President,'' the captain replied, shaking Jarrett's hand solidly.

The president walked the officer to the entrance, wished him a safe flight home, then returned to his chair. ''Well, gentlemen,'' Jarrett said, ''Secretary Gardner and I have a meeting with Minister Aksenhov. We will discuss our options in—''

The president stopped when the vice chairman of the Joint Chiefs stepped into the room. His face was flushed and he was carrying a message hard copy. ''Mister President,'' the four-star general said, ''three navy jets based at Guantanamo Bay have engaged in a dogfight with five Cuban MiGs.''

''Jesus . . . Christ,'' Jarrett replied, trying to stifle his irritation and surprise. ''When?''

''Only minutes ago, sir. We just received the flash message.''

The president broke the shocked silence that had settled over the room. ''What's the present situation, general?'' Jarrett asked, casting a glance at his secretary of defense.

''The on-site commander's report states that our pilots were forced to defend themselves. The navy flight leader was apparently shot down.''

''Are the other two pilots okay?''

''As far as I know, sir.''

Jarrett turned to his secretary of defense. ''Bernie, I want a thorough brief as soon as you can glean the details.''

''Yes, sir,'' Kerchner replied, nodding soberly. ''I suggest we have the on-site commander, along with the pilots involved, flown here immediately to get a clear picture of exactly what happened before we react.''

''I agree,'' Jarrett responded, then added, ''and expedite getting them here.'' The president was angry—and not in the best frame of mind to confront the Soviet foreign minister.

THE AGENT

Steve Wickham slowed his pace, then stopped at the edge of a tobacco field. He had heard a vehicle approaching and now saw the glaring headlights. He squatted down and checked his watch. Twenty-five minutes after eleven and he was already more than halfway to San Julian. Just three more miles to the MiG base.

Wickham watched the dilapidated automobile go past his hiding place and disappear down the winding dirt road. He waited another minute, silently cursing his wet feet. He had been forced to wade across a wide, stagnant marsh a half hour earlier.

A donkey suddenly brayed, startling Wickham. His senses tensed as he scanned his concealment. The bright moonlight made blending into the surroundings extremely difficult.

He could see a thatched roof lean-to sixty yards away. Directly behind it, next to the encroaching jungle, stood a small ramshackle house. The rickety-looking structure had rusted sheets of tin nailed to the exterior.

The donkey brayed again, causing the agent to freeze in his hiding place. He could see the animal moving around next to the lean-to. Wickham stood, hot and sweaty, and started walking slowly toward the road. He had taken only nine steps when a naked light bulb flashed on in the shanty.

"Shit," Wickham said as he crouched down and ran for the sanctuary of the jungle on the far side of the road. Without warning, his right ankle snagged a trip wire designed to foil thieves.

"Goddamnit," Wickham swore when he heard the tin cans topple off the front porch of the shack. He broke into a sprint for the jungle as the donkey brayed loudly and a dog barked excitedly.

He had barely crossed the narrow road when a man stepped out of the front entrance to the house. The figure tucked in his shirttail and looked around. A moment later, he spoke to someone inside and a small boy appeared. The youngster carried a rifle and a flashlight.

Wickham bent down into the thick foliage and watched the man disappear around the back of his house. The Cuban reappeared with the barking dog on a leash, then took the rifle and flashlight from the boy.

Wickham's mind raced, seeking an avenue of escape. He reached behind his back, lifted the baggy shirt bottom, and eased his Excam out of the holster.

The youngster remained close to the house while the man and his dog started around the property. Wickham followed the search, then froze when the Cuban reached the point where the agent had entered the field. The man and his yelping dog hesitated a few seconds, then started across the tobacco field on the same course Wickham had taken. The agent knew that the Cuban could see his boot prints in the moist soil.

"Oh, Christ," Wickham whispered as he watched the Cuban and his dog approach his hiding place. The man carefully splayed the flashlight beam twenty feet in front of him. It would be only a matter of seconds before Wickham would be discovered.

WILLARD INTERCONTINENTAL HOTEL, Washington, D.C.

The quaint hotel, located one and a half blocks from the White House, had become a meeting place for heads of state and foreign diplomats.

A group of the late night crowd, many attired in their native dress, gathered around the television set in the cocktail lounge. A Special Report sign had just been flashed on the screen by ABC news. The lively, noisy chatter hushed when the commentator appeared.

"Good evening," the anchor said, unsmiling. "Sources inside the government, who are familiar with the growing tension in Cuba, have told ABC news that Cuban fighter planes attacked three Navy A-4 Skyhawk jets over their base at Guantanamo Bay. The exact time of the aerial attack is unknown. Pentagon officials have confirmed that a confrontation between U.S. and Cuban jet fighters did take place. The number of aircraft involved, according to officials, is not available for release at this time. The cause of the attack is still unknown.

"A White House staff member, who insisted on anonymity, stated that a downed Cuban fighter, which crashed near Guantanamo Bay Naval Base, contained the remains of a Russian pilot."

The anchor continued in a somber manner, glancing to someone off camera. "Elsewhere in Washington, the United Nations Security Council has been summoned for an emergency session regarding the attack."

The cocktail lounge began to buzz with speculation as to what might have caused the aerial attack. The crowd continued drinking while the commentator paused to receive new material.

"I have just been handed a release from the Cuban news agency Prensa Latina," the well-groomed man said, scanning the page quickly before he continued. "A Cuban Air Force MiG-23 fighter jet crashed into a suburb of Holguin this evening, killing seventeen people on the ground. Witnesses in the neighborhood where the jet came down reported that the airplane was trailing fire before it plowed through five houses. Residents of the Loma de la Cruz section of Holguin said that the pilot ejected moments before the crash."

The anchor stared at the copy a moment, then looked back into the eye of the camera. "Cuban government officials have accused the U.S. of precipitating the attack."

Murmurs filled the room as the commentator switched to a White House correspondent for a series of questions.

CHAPTER SIXTEEN

THE OVAL OFFICE

President Jarrett, looking haggard and irritable, sat behind his desk. Samuel Gardner was seated at one end of two oversized sofas that faced each other in the middle of the room. Bernard Kerchner, reading a readiness report, sat at the other end.

"The son of a bitch is consistent," Jarrett spat. "Late as usual."

Gardner, frowning, nodded in agreement. "It's a game, sir. He has to convince you that his time is more important than yours."

Sergey Aksenhov was a typical career diplomat, having served his entire adult life in the Russian Foreign Department. This was his seventh tour in Washington, his first as foreign minister. He prided himself on being unflappable and emotionless. His cold, stony eyes never revealed what his devious mind was thinking.

"I apologize, gentlemen," the tall, heavyset foreign minister said in an orchestrated display of rushing to remove his overcoat. "This evening has been difficult for me."

The three Americans remained silent. The Russian seemed surprised at their lack of cordiality. The usual handshakes and polite banter had been replaced by an icy silence.

"Minister Aksenhov," Jarrett began as the diplomat sat down facing Gardner and Kerchner, "I have received some very distressing news in regard to American-Soviet relations."

Aksenhov feigned surprise. "If you are referring to this evening's unfortunate events, Mister President, I must inform you that we have no other choice than to file an official complaint with the—"

"Minister Aksenhov," the president interrupted tersely. "I suggest you cut the formality and listen for a change."

Aksenhov, genuinely surprised, showed only a flicker of emotion. Years of training and practice had almost eliminated any external signs of stress. Undaunted by the hostility in the president's tone, Aksenhov spoke slowly and evenly. "As you wish, Mister President."

"We have been advised," Jarrett began, staring into Aksenhov's eyes, "that Russia—actually a faction of the KGB—is responsible for commandeering . . . hijacking one of our B-2 bombers."

Aksenhov remained poker-faced, but the statement had had a profound impact on the diplomat.

"Furthermore," Jarrett continued harshly, "the bomber is in Cuba—a Soviet satellite—and I intend to recover the aircraft if it is not released immediately."

"Mister President, gentlemen," Aksenhov said sincerely, "your accusation is preposterous—outrageous."

Gardner sat straight up. "Goddamnit, Sergey, we're past the point of pretending that the Soviet Union isn't involved. I insist that you notify your superiors in Moscow—now. I have championed the cause for a diplomatic resolution to this unprecedented violation, but the president is adamant. We are going to recover the aircraft, or destroy it."

Aksenhov remained silent, but his mind was spinning. He

knew nothing of the hijacking. He had recognized the MiG attacks as a planned diversion to focus attention on Guantanamo Bay, but he assumed it had been ordered by Castro for reasons he did not yet understand. If the American bomber had indeed been hijacked to Cuba, that might be reason enough—an attempt to scare them off, divert them. The Americans had mentioned the KGB. Did the Kremlin know? He would have to contact them immediately.

The president was speaking to him. "Minister Aksenhov, it is up to you. We want to know what the Soviet position is in this affair, and we want our bomber back."

Aksenhov placed a chunky hand on his topcoat and heaved himself up. "Mister President, gentlemen, I can only convey your message."

"I will expect an answer," the president said, "by nine o'clock tomorrow morning, Washington time."

WICKHAM

The CIA agent watched the advancing man and his dog. Wickham crawled forward to the edge of the dirt road and grabbed a fist-sized rock. After pushing himself back into the thick vines and leaves, he stood and heaved the rock in desperation.

Wickham waited, his heart pounding, as the rock sailed toward the small house. The quiet, humid night was shattered when the projectile slammed into the tin siding with a resounding crack.

The Cuban spun around and yelled and the dog went wild, barking savagely. "*Cuidado!* Watch out!" the man shouted, running toward the house.

Wickham leaped out of the foliage and sprinted down the road toward San Julian. He distanced himself rapidly from the confusion he had created at the small tobacco farm. He slowed to a trot, then walked as the braying and barking dissipated behind him. His lungs heaved as he surveyed the sugarcane fields to his left. They would provide excellent camouflage if needed.

Wickham hurried along the barren road, passing a number of dilapidated, cheerless small shacks. He stopped occasionally, blending into the fields when a vehicle approached. An individual walking down an isolated stretch of road this late at night would draw attention. Not being recognized as a local resident would make matters worse.

One of his off-road excursions found Wickham lying next to a pen full of hogs. The agent's eyes had watered from the repugnant stench emanating from the hog trough. Another stop, only a mile and a quarter from San Julian, had placed Wickham in a precarious position close to a weathered house. A raucous late night party was in its final, drunken stages when the agent had seen an approaching vehicle and been forced to slide under a rusted '60 Pontiac.

Three men, standing under a dim yellow light on the front porch, were arguing loudly. A quartet of people inside the clapboard residence yelled at the three inebriated men on the porch. The Cubans ignored the foursome inside, swilling beer and arguing at the top of their lungs.

Wickham waited until the approaching pickup truck careened past before he crawled back out to the edge of the road. Another drunk driver, Wickham thought to himself as he jogged across another tobacco field and rejoined the dirt road a quarter of a mile from the ongoing party.

Wickham slowed to a cautious walk when he glimpsed the lights of the military airfield. He checked the time again and decided to reconnoiter the base in the darkness available to him. If he got lucky, he thought, he might spot the Stealth bomber, televise the evidence, and get out of the immediate area before daybreak.

He hurried toward the base, constantly checking the road behind him, then stopped at the edge of the tree line fifty yards from the perimeter fence. He looked up and down the barbed-wire barrier, which he judged to be about four feet high. The agent was surprised by the lack of guard towers, and he did not see any sign of perimeter sentries. The Soviets had done a good job of making the base appear not to have increased security.

The end of the runway was less than 300 yards from the fence. Wickham could see MiG fighters lined up on the ramp in front of the control tower. They were bathed in bright light from fixtures on top of the tower and adjacent hangars.

He studied the ramp and the two hangars. He was shocked to see the enclosures open and lighted. Inside each hangar a crew of maintenance personnel was busy working on the MiGs. The agent also saw what he had been looking for initially. Four sentries patrolled the two hangars and another two guards walked the line of MiGs.

Wickham also examined the tall building containing two fire trucks. Three fuel trucks sat next to the base of the control tower. Two MiGs and their support carts were positioned at the far end of the runway. Wickham could not tell whether the pilots were in the two aircraft, but he could faintly see activity around the fighters.

Christ, Wickham thought, looking at the wooden barracks and other buildings, there's no place to conceal a Stealth bomber. His thoughts turned to retracing his route and aborting the reconnaissance mission when he noticed the baseball park. It sat on a rise off to the south of the main section of the base. Something seemed strange about the park, but Wickham did not grasp the oddity at first.

Then it struck him. Why, at this hour of the early morning, would the bright field lights be on? He could not distinguish any movement on the field or in the spectator bleachers. A second later, Wickham remembered a part of Milligan's briefing. The director had told him that San Julian appeared to be a carbon copy of every other base, including a ball diamond lighted all night. Satellite photographs had revealed games in progress at 3:30 A.M.

The agent decided to investigate. He approached the perimeter fence slowly and examined the barbed wire closely, noting a small strand of wire wrapped around the top line. He reasoned that it had to be electrified.

He folded his straw hat and shoved it into his back pocket, backed fifteen feet from the fence, inhaled deeply, then raced toward the barrier and high-jumped over the top strand. He landed on his back and rolled to a sitting position, then stood and brushed himself off.

Wickham jogged along the edge of the fence until it made a right turn. At that point he paused, listening and looking for any signs of activity, before heading toward the open field leading to the ballpark.

Halfway across the grassy expanse, Wickham saw movement by the bleachers. He stopped and knelt down, partially hidden by the palm trees that dotted the area. He counted three guards in and around the tiered seats. Two were sitting on the fourth row, smoking cigarettes and talking. The third was walking around the perimeter of the stands. All three were Cubans carrying AK-47s.

Why, Wickham asked himself, would armed guards be patrolling a fully lighted ballpark in the wee hours of the morning? He scurried across the field, darting between palm trees, until he was sixty feet from the west end of the bleachers. The two guards sitting and talking were on the opposite side, engrossed in their conversation. The patrolling sentry had stopped to relieve himself, standing stationary near third base.

Wickham dropped to a prone position, then crawled under the bleachers and rested a moment. As his breathing slowed, he heard a peculiar sound—one that he could not associate with a ballpark. The noise reminded him of an attic fan or a commercial heat ventilator.

He crawled toward the sound. It appeared to come from the end of the stands, close to the dugout. Wickham inched forward, then stopped abruptly as he saw the telltale signs of a photocell security system. He grabbed a pinch of loose dirt, ground it between his thumb and forefinger, then tossed the fine dust between the sensors. The powdery particles were illuminated in the beam of light.

He stood, moving to the edge of the right photocell, paused a moment, then gingerly stepped over the beam of light. He straddled the invisible light a moment before bringing his other foot over.

"Jesus," Wickham said under his breath. He could see a metal grate under the bleachers at the very edge of the steel supports. Hot, humid air was being forced up through the iron bars.

It took a second for the enormity of the message to register on the agent. The Stealth was under the baseball field.

The next thought Wickham had was the lesson he remembered from Clandestine Operations training. He could still picture the burly instructor pounding home the same point: Covert operations never go according to schedule or plan. You must learn to improvise if you plan to survive.

Wickham eased forward to the iron bars, checked the positions of the sentries, then lifted the heavy grate cautiously. The metal cover, which he judged to weight thirty pounds, was about three feet long by two and a half feet wide. The air that rushed from the opening blasted Wickham in the face, causing his eyes to burn.

He swung his legs carefully over the edge of the opening, holding up the grate at a forty-five-degree angle. He judged the underground compartment to be close to three feet deep. He dropped into the shaft and lowered the cover.

He leaned down, then froze like a statue. "I'll be damned," Wickham swore under his breath. There in front of him, not thirty feet away, was the missing B-2 Stealth bomber.

A large fan, enclosed in protective metal screening, sucked air out of the underground hangar. Wickham could see three other ventilation fans at the back of the enclosure and two on the opposite wall. Since he could see easily through the spinning blades of the fan that separated him from the bomber, he knew that the camera would send a reasonable picture.

Wickham extracted the compact Sony television camera as he surveyed the interior of the hangar. Four guards surrounded the bomber while two other sentries walked around the perimeter of the enclosure. Six technicians, dressed in powder blue smocks, worked in teams of two at different places on the Stealth aircraft.

The agent was surprised that components and panels from the bomber were strewn all over the hangar. Tubular scaffolding encompassed the cockpit, and padding had been placed across the wings. The aircraft, though partially dismantled, still looked sinister.

He checked the small camera and took the thin antenna out of its padded container. The twelve-foot-long antenna was folded like a carpenter's rule. Wickham extended the antenna up through the grate, then maneuvered it between the bleacher seats.

He dropped to his knees, steadied himself, aimed the camera, then pressed the button. He knew that the bright ceiling lights would enhance the picture quality. He also knew that his life would be in greater jeopardy the moment the Soviets found out about the pictures.

NATIONAL RECONNAISSANCE OFFICE

The duty watch officer was sitting in front of the row of blank television screens, penning a letter to his daughter in boarding school, when the transmission announcer beeped three times, indicating that an imminent television signal would appear on the screens.

"What the hell is going on?" he asked himself, placing his pen down. He was not expecting any visual transmissions until the following evening, at the earliest. A moment later a slightly blurred image of the Stealth bomber appeared on all three television monitors.

"Good God!" he said to his assistant. "He's in there. Look at this!"

His friend hurried to the bank of monitors and let out a whistle. "Hit the tape."

"Got it," the officer replied. "Call the comm chief."

"I'm dialing now," the wide-eyed assistant responded, mesmerized by the picture on the screens. The resolution was only fair, but the B-2 was clearly visible.

"Jesus," the officer said, "we've got to get a tape to the White House, on the double."

SAN JULIAN

The bored Cuban guard standing near third base buttoned his fly, hitched up his assault rifle, and turned to resume his monotonous patrol duty. He waked walked toward the pitching mound, noticing his two companions sitting in the stands behind home plate. They outranked him, so he was obligated to walk around the ball field and report in every half hour.

The potbellied guard ambled across the slightly raised mound and continued toward first base. He was about to step on the bag when his eye caught something move. He stopped and scanned the bleachers. Sure enough, there was a small, thin strip of metal protruding through the stadium seats.

The Cuban soldier approached the end of the bleachers cautiously. Had the Soviet technicians added something new to their array of gadgets? He walked between the dugout and the end of the stands, stepped under the stadium, and flipped on his flashlight.

Directly in front of him, not two meters away, was a sliver of metal sticking out of the ventilation duct. Odd, he thought as he stepped closer to peer through the iron grate.

Steve Wickham, concentrating intently on slowly moving

the camera from the front of the B-2 to the back, sensed danger, then caught the flicker of light. He placed the camera down and turned around in the cramped space. He could feel his heartbeat surge when he saw the soldier step over the grate, lean down, and point the flashlight into the duct.

NATIONAL RECONNAISSANCE OFFICE

"Uh, oh," the watch officer said, feeling uneasy. "We've got a problem. I've lost the feed."

His assistant, holding the phone to his ear, rolled his chair over to the monitors. "What happened?"

"I don't know," the officer answered, staring at the blank screens. "He was giving us a long sweep when the picture angled down and went blank."

"Maybe he thought that would be enough to—" The assistant stopped when his call was answered in the communications center. "Sir, Wozniak at recon ops. We've received a visual on the B-2."

"We have tape," the excited watch officer prompted.

His assistant acknowledged with a nod of his head, then spoke again. "Yes, sir. We have it on tape."

SAN JULIAN

Wickham braced himself, felt a fleeting moment of near panic, then exploded upward, slamming the heavy iron grate into the Cuban's face.

The adrenaline-fueled effort smashed the soldier's nose, broke three of his teeth, and rendered him semiconscious. The guard stumbled backward, holding his face and moaning in agony, then fell between the photocell security system. A high-pitched siren immediately blasted the quiet night with a pulsating shriek. The guard, in shock and pain, never saw his attacker.

Wickham leaped out of the duct, yanked up the television

camera, grabbed the squirming guard's rifle, and raced toward the palm tree-studded field. He glanced back and saw the other two sentries running across the ball field. They were headed toward the spot where their companion had disappeared.

The agent stopped suddenly when bright searchlights winked on around the perimeter of the air base. He dropped to the ground and searched frantically for a way out. Seconds passed before he realized he was trapped. The entire base was coming to life.

In desperation, Wickham jumped to his feet and ran toward the nearest cluster of administration buildings. He stopped halfway to the nearest structure, dropping to the ground as he saw a dozen Cuban soldiers pile out of the adjacent barracks. Then he belly-crawled as fast as he could toward the first building in the row.

CHAPTER SEVENTEEN

THE WHITE HOUSE

Alton Jarrett walked into the Oval Office wearing a navy blue robe over his gray pajamas. The groggy president accepted a cup of steaming coffee from Brian Gaines, then sat down on one of the two facing sofas. The national security adviser, looking rumpled and tired, returned to his seat next to Bernard Kerchner.

The secretary of defense rubbed his bloodshot eyes before speaking to the president. "Is Sam joining us?"

Jarrett nodded, tasting his coffee. "Sam is on his way over. Should be here any minute."

"Good," Kerchner replied, sipping his hot tea.

The president settled into the sofa. "First I want to address Aksenhov personally. When will we have a copy of the B-2 tape?"

Kerchner glanced at the small clock sitting on the president's desk. He had forgotten his wristwatch during the mad dash to the White House. "I expected it here a few minutes ago, sir."

The three men heard an exchange of voices outside the

main entrance to the Oval Office. ''Thank you,'' the secretary of state said to the military courier as he grasped the tape container. Samuel Gardner closed the door and turned to the president. ''Sir, Aksenhov is on his way.''

''He better be,'' the president replied as Gaines accepted the tape from Gardner.

The national security adviser walked to the VCR, inserted the tape, and punched the play button. Gaines backed away a few steps and remained standing as Gardner took a seat next to the president.

The small screen remained blank a few seconds, then the Stealth bomber appeared in a well-lighted hangar. The black and white picture focused on the aircraft, then moved to the right and swept the entire enclosure. Soldiers and technicians surrounded the secret bomber. A few seconds later the picture returned to the stolen B-2, moving slowly from one section to another.

The nose of the Stealth came into view. Then there was a pause before the picture moved down the length of the bomber. A split second before the aircraft's trailing edge would have come into view, the picture stopped a moment, then tilted down and went blank.

''I'll be damned,'' the president said, placing his cup and saucer on the coffee table. ''Brian, run that back.''

''Yes, sir.''

Jarrett turned to his secretary of defense. ''Bernie, I'm going with the captain's recommendation, from the Strike Center. I believe we should assault San Julian with marine expeditionary units.'' The president leaned back. ''We've got to have concentrated close air support and solid air cover. The Marines have to hit quickly, secure the airfield, destroy the bomber, and rescue the pilots—if they can locate them.''

Jarrett paused, mentally reviewing the operation. ''This is a different situation from what we had in Panama. I think we have to soften up San Julian before the Marines go in. Let's use a combination of carrier attack aircraft and air force bombers." The president removed his glasses. "Do you have any qualms about that?"

"No, sir, none whatsoever," Kerchner answered truthfully. "I fully endorse that course of action, as does the chairman of the Joint Chiefs. We have already discussed the option."

The president thought for a second. "How soon will our carrier battle groups be on station?"

"Approximately fifteen to twenty hours, sir," Kerchner answered. "*America* and her group departed Norfolk this— yesterday afternoon, and *Kitty Hawk* is preparing to get under way from Pensacola. We have an emergency recall out for her crew.

"The marine expeditionary units are en route to the *Wasp* and the *Essex*. I anticipate both assault carriers will be in the Gulf by early this evening. The commandant insisted we incorporate a third amphibious assault ship, *Nassau*, with an additional battalion landing team. It left Puerto Rico a little more than two hours ago. The general is also adding additional Harrier jets and helicopters to each carrier."

"Very well," the president replied, facing his secretary of state. "Sam, you know Aksenhov better than any of us. Any suggestions?"

Gardner paused, chewing on his pipe. "Mister President, we're well past the gamesmanship stage. We simply have to throw it on the table and take a stand."

The president nodded in agreement. "Almost the exact words Kirk used."

"Is the vice president coming over?" Kerchner asked as the Soviet foreign minister was announced.

"No," Jarrett answered. "I spoke with him before I came down—told him to get a good night's rest. We'll need a fresh, clear mind later this morning."

Gaines pulled a large stuffed chair to the opening between the two sofas. Aksenhov, visibly irritated and looking disheveled, walked to the chair and sat down heavily. "May

I ask what this is about? We agreed on nine o'clock this morning, did we not, Mister President?''

"I have something special to show you," the president replied, stone faced.

The Soviet foreign minister, feeling the cold looks, steeled himself cautiously to contest any accusations. His face, concealing his trepidation, was deadpan.

"Brian," the president said calmly, "please run the tape again."

"Yes, sir," Gaines replied as he punched the VCR play button.

Aksenhov attempted to remain impassive as the commandeered Stealth bomber appeared on the screen. His expression gave way to a sudden uneasiness when he realized that the Americans had a spy in San Julian. He was caught completely off guard and unprepared. He had not been informed about any operation involving the American bomber. Was the KGB involved, or had Castro acted alone?

Aksenhov knew that he had to transmit the shocking news to the Kremlin as quickly as possible. He watched the rest of the short tape without concentrating on the picture, searching frantically for a carefully phrased lie to refute the visual evidence.

The room remained quiet when the VCR clicked off. Aksenhov turned slowly to the president. "What is the point of this film, Mister President? I have seen pictures of your Stealth bomber many times."

Jarrett looked Aksenhov in the eyes, shaking his head in amazement. "My point, Minister Aksenhov, is that our missing B-2 bomber is sitting in a hangar at San Julian Air Base in Cuba—a satellite of the Soviet Union."

Aksenhov, confused and knowing the futility of continuing the charade, let out a convincing sigh. "Mister President, I have no knowledge of any operation involving your B-2 aircraft."

"Well," Jarrett responded coldly, "I strongly suggest that you contact your superiors in Moscow and find out who is responsible for the hijacking. We know that the individual who commandeered the B-2 had ties to the KGB.''

Jarrett could see the question on Aksenhov's face. All Russian diplomats were suspicious by nature, untrusting of everyone, including their own countrymen. ''I believe you understand,'' Jarrett continued. ''We are on a collision course, Minister Aksenhov, and I urge you to intervene before we face off militarily.''

Aksenhov, feeling a growing alarm, stood and inhaled. ''I will contact Moscow immediately, Mister President.''

''I will expect to hear from the Kremlin, Minister Aksenhov, as soon as you do.''

SAN JULIAN

Steve Wickham peeked out cautiously from an opening in the foundation of the administration building. The air base was crawling with Cuban soldiers, all looking for the intruder.

The dank, mildewed hiding place was a maze of spiderwebs and rotting wood supports. Wickham thought about his options, knowing that it would be daylight soon. He replayed the lessons from the CIA covert operations classes, especially the chameleon course. If you are surrounded, and have access to the resources, blend into the environment.

''Great,'' Wickham said to himself, easing away from the opening. ''What I need is a Russian uniform.'' He reasoned that the search would intensify once the sun topped the horizon. He had to think of a way to escape from sure death.

Surveying the activity, he forced his mind to be calm. He watched a GAZ field car approach the building and stop next to a group of Cuban soldiers. A Soviet officer stepped out of the vehicle and walked to the cluster of men. Wickham listened intently, trying to catch what the Russian was saying. Suddenly, the soldiers formed two groups and approached the barracks and administration building.

Wickham swore to himself and scooted back three feet.

He wedged the camera and the assault rifle between the cracked foundation and a support beam, then braced his toes on the concrete ledge. Placing his fingers through a rotted hole in the wooden beam, he yanked himself up between the supports.

He held his breath, listening to the men, as two of the soldiers looked under the building with flashlights. Seconds became an eternity as Wickham's arms began to quiver from the strain of holding his body horizontal.

THE WHITE HOUSE

Alton Jarrett, unable to sleep, had showered, shaved, and donned a fresh suit. He was nibbling his breakfast and reading an update brief when the vice president entered the Oval Office.

"Any word, Mister President?" Kirklin Truesdell asked, carrying two file folders.

"Nothing yet," Jarrett answered, motioning Truesdell to a chair. "Sam is talking with the Soviet ambassador, but I don't anticipate much progress from that avenue. . . . Take a look at this," the president continued, handing Truesdell a sheaf of confidential briefing notes.

The vice president sat down, read each section thoroughly, then looked at Jarrett. "They executed Voronoteev?"

"Afraid so," the president said, grim faced. "Norm Lasharr confirmed it fifteen minutes ago. He said that the execution was open to certain individuals—media representatives and dissidents—in order to send a message."

Jarrett slid aside his tray. "The United Nations Security Council has come out against our position, as usual."

"The UN is an open embarrassment," Truesdell replied in a disgusted voice. "They have voted against us eighty-three percent of the time in the past year. It really peeves me."

The president tossed his napkin on the breakfast tray.

"Kirk," he said as he leaned forward in his chair, "I have ordered a third carrier group to rendezvous in the Caribbean. The *Abraham Lincoln* and her escorts will stand off the western shore of Andros Island. They're southwest of Bermuda, moving at flank speed. We also have three attack submarines en route to the area, and the Air Force, Navy, and Marines are concentrating fighter aircraft along our southern bases.

"Also," Jarrett continued, glancing at his page of personal notes, "I have ordered the *Wisconsin* and her support ships to get under way as quickly as possible. Two destroyers have already left Ingleside and cleared Corpus Christi Bay. They'll loiter until the battleship is in open water."

Jarrett turned his paper over. "The *Lexington* is in the gulf conducting carrier qualifications, so Bernie decided to attach it to the *Wisconsin*, along with two reserve frigates and a combat support ship. He wants the flight deck available for emergencies."

The president massaged his chin. "Bernie and the Joint Chiefs are concerned because we won't have any element of surprise. The Cubans have more than seventy thousand troops on the island, plus several hundred leftover Soviet advisers."

Truesdell nodded. "I recommend strongly that we strengthen our southern flanks, too."

"Bernie is coordinating the effort as we speak." The president handed Truesdell another piece of paper. "He also debriefed the onsite commander and his three pilots from the Guantanamo skirmish."

"Oh?" Truesdell paused, keenly interested. "What happened?"

Jarrett shrugged. "The MiGs slashed right though the navy formation—on the outskirts of our base—and entered an attack posture."

"Did they fire at out pilots?"

"No," Jarrett replied, removing his glasses. "The first two aircraft that went down—an A-4 and a MiG–23—collided in a head-on pass. Our pilot ejected and the other pilot, a Soviet, as you know, never got out. The two aviators who shot down the other MiGs thought their leader had been fired upon. They engaged, with the on-site's permission, immediately after the collision.''

The president stopped a few seconds to allow Truesdell to skim the brief. "The point is that the MiGs forced the issue . . . pushed us against the wall.''

Truesdell shook his head in acknowledgement. "An open effort to divert attention.''

"That's how I see it,'' Jarrett replied, glancing at his watch. "Have to run—the press conference is scheduled in nine minutes.''

"What do you plan to say?'' the vice president asked with a concerned look on his face.

"The truth—as much as I can reveal,'' the president answered as he stood. "I'm not going to start deceiving people at this stage.''

SAN JULIAN

Steve Wickham, breathing deeply, sagged to the ground and crawled next to the small opening in the foundation. He ventured a quick look outside, then retreated to a corner of the building. The soldiers had moved on to another structure and the Soviet officer was driving away.

Wickham considered his options as his pulse returned to normal. Five minutes later, after analyzing his limited choices, the agent resigned himself to the only viable possibility. He would have to wait until nightfall to attempt an escape.

USS *KITTY HAWK* (CV-63)

The 80,000-ton warship, carrying less than half of her air group, was increasing speed eight miles southeast of Pensacola beach. On board *Kitty Hawk*, the sailors and officers of Carrier Air Wing 3 prepared for the arrival of the rest of

CVW-3's warplanes. The crew emergency recall had produced a 92 percent manning level when the giant ship put to sea.

The refurbished carrier sported new flush deck catapult launch equipment, MK-7 blast deflectors, arresting gear, and state-of-the-art AN/SPS-49(V) radar. The veteran ship had also been equipped with an advanced combat direction system (ACDS), formerly referred to as the combat information center (CIC), to improve the tactical decision process.

Kitty Hawk would join her escort ships thirty-four miles south of Fort Walton Beach, Florida. The support ships, consisting of four missile destroyers, two cruisers, and two frigates, were home-ported at Mobile, Alabama, and Pascagoula, Mississippi.

The carrier air wing commander embarked on *Kitty Hawk* had received his operations orders directing the wing to initially provide attack and fighter combat air patrols (CAP). When the carrier and escort ships arrived on station 150 miles northwest of San Julian, their mission would intensify. The air wing would be tasked with normal CAP duties, along with surface combat patrol (SUCAP) and war-at-sea contingencies.

Sixty miles north of *Kitty Hawk*, Comdr. Doug "Frogman" Karns, commanding officer of fighter squadron VF-102, led the first six F-14D Tomcats toward the carrier. His executive officer, ten miles in trail, led four more VF-102 Diamondback fighters.

Karns, a TOPGUN graduate, had been in command of the Diamondbacks less than two months. His reputation had preceded him and he was well respected by every member of his squadron.

The CO had been tagged with his peculiar nickname when he was a lieutenant (junior grade) nugget pilot—a new aviator, to the uninitiated. Karns had erred on a difficult terrain reconnaissance mission off the carrier *Coral Sea*, missed the rendezvous point with the "boat," ran out of fuel, and ditched five miles astern of the carrier. His fellow squadron pilots immediately began calling Karns "Frogman."

The VF-102, along with a second F-14D squadron—VF-41 Black Aces—would provide combat air patrol. Two F/A-18 Hornet squadrons would fly aboard later to provide additional fighter strength.

The Warhawks from VA-97 and the Marauders from VA-82 would fly SUCAP in their A-6E Intruder medium bombers. The surface patrol would be augmented by the Zappers of VAQ-130 in their EA-6B Prowler electronic warfare Intruders.

The Cyclops of VAW-123, flying the E-2C Hawkeye Hummer airborne early warning turboprop, would provide the eyes for the fleet. The Sea Wolves of VS-27 would support the antisubmarine warfare effort in their twin-jet S-3B Vikings.

Karns started a slow descent, keyed his radio mike, and waited for the scramble to sync. "Wolfpack, Diamond One Oh Three inbound with a flight of six."

"Roger, Diamond flight," the controller said, watching his radar-scope in the bowels of *Kitty Hawk*. "Squawk four-one-three-three."

"Forty-one-thirty-three," Karns acknowledged, reprogramming his transponder.

The controller watched the new code appear on his scope, then keyed his mike. "I have you at five-two DME, descending through three-three thousand." The Tomcats, passing through 33,000 feet, were fifty-two nautical miles from the carrier.

"That's affirm," Karns replied. "Diamond One Oh Four had a hydraulic pump go south on him. Request priority deck—he'll be a straight-in."

"Copy, Diamond One Zero Three." A short pause followed. "Diamond One Zero Four," the controller radioed, "is number one for the deck."

"Roger," Karns responded, steepening the descent. The sky under the high overcast was beginning to show signs of dawn. The fighter pilots would not have to make a night landing.

"Diamond One Oh Four," the F-14 jock replied, "number one on arrival."

"Diamond One Zero Three," the controller radioed with professional aplomb, "Wolfpack directs two Diamond aircraft to hit the tanker and BARCAP at seventy DME. The Hummer reports MiG activity at one-six-five degrees for two-four-zero, angels three-one-zero."

CHAPTER EIGHTEEN

THE WHITE HOUSE PRESSROOM

President Alton Jarrett, fresh and trim looking, stepped to the podium in the crowded, noisy room. A hush fell over the tightly packed press corps. This was the earliest that anyone could remember attending an unscheduled press briefing.

The president, setting the tone for his message, raised both hands, palms facing the crowd, to stop any questions until he had an opportunity to complete his opening statement.

"Good morning," the president said in a staid, perfunctory manner. "Before I take your questions, I want to bring you up to date on a couple of items." There was complete silence.

"First, the unfortunate encounter our navy pilots had last night, we believe, is tied to the disappearance of our Stealth bomber." He paused as a loud murmur swept through the crowd, with four people attempting to ask questions at the same time.

"Now, wait," the president said, holding his hands aloft again, "wait a second. Remember, we all agreed as to how we would handle these meetings. Let me finish. I can confirm that our missing B-2 bomber is in Cuba." No one said a word, listening intently and writing.

"Furthermore," Jarrett continued, "we have unequivocal proof of the exact location of the B-2, and," the president raised his hands again, seeing words form on the sea of faces, "we are taking diplomatic steps to have the aircraft and crew returned immediately.

"I intend to be candid with you," Jarrett said, "and explain the circumstances surrounding this bizarre and unprecedented situation. Our preliminary findings, based on CIA and FBI investigations, indicate that the B-2 was commandeered by a civilian technician recruited by the KGB." The audience erupted in turmoil.

"Let me finish," Jarrett said, somewhat irritated. "I'll take your questions in a minute. There have been reports and rumors that our pilots defected, and that they are seeking political asylum in Cuba. This is not correct, and we deny any accusation to that effect. Our fine pilots categorically did not defect. I do not know the condition of the crew, but we hold the Soviet Union, and Premier Castro, responsible for their safety and well-being.

"I have just had a conversation with Minister Aksenhov," the president said, adjusting his glasses. "He hinted at the existence of factions, probably of the KGB operating outside the jurisdiction of the Kremlin, but this does not absolve them of all responsibility. We expect to hear from President Ignatyev soon, and no, we have not ruled out a military intervention.

"I will take your questions now," Jarrett said, pointing to a woman in the first row, "in an orderly fashion." The noise intensity increased in the room.

"Mister President," the tall reporter said, ignoring the clicking cameras, "exactly what measures do you intend to take if the B-2 isn't returned? Are you saying that the U.S. is prepared to invade Cuba?"

"I am not going to discuss what our intentions are at this point, nor am I going to reveal our intelligence sources,"

Jarrett answered, as he pointed to an NBC network representative.

"Can you confirm that the Cuban MiGs were flown by Soviet pilots?"

"I can only say," Jarrett looked at Kerchner, "that the MiG fighter that crashed close to our base at Guantanamo was flown by a Soviet Air Force captain."

A reporter shouted over the group. "Has Castro been involved in the negotiations? Where does he stand?"

Jarrett gave the television reporter a stern look. "Premier Castro has been notified of our position and intent. He obviously is a partner in this violation of international law, and I hold him accountable—as I do the Soviets—for the well-being of our crew.

"Margaret," the president said, gesturing at a newspaper reporter.

"Mister President," an attractive woman stood, "reports have it that you are positioning aircraft carriers in the Gulf of Mexico. What action are you prepared to take if the Stealth bomber is not returned, and what time frame are you talking about?"

"I am not in a position to discuss any military matters," Jarrett answered, "nor can I tell you our time frame. Suffice it to say, we will make decisions based on the reply we receive from Moscow. It's that simple. We have placed President Ignatyev on notice, and I will respond accordingly when we receive his answer.

"One more question," Jarrett said, motioning toward an old friend, "and then I have to leave. Secretary Kerchner and Secretary Gardner will answer further questions."

"Sir," the respected journalist said, "are you prepared to confront the Cubans . . . militarily?"

Jarrett set his jaw, paused and inhaled, then addressed the entire group. "I am prepared to do what is necessary to preserve our fundamental rights, and protect international law."

USS *AMERICA* (CV-66)

The Norfolk, Virginia-based carrier, powered by four Westinghouse steam turbines, cruised thirty miles southwest of Plantation Key, Florida. Her combined energy of 280,000 shaft horsepower propelled the mammoth ship through the pristine waters at twenty-nine knots. *America* could achieve thirty-three knots at flank speed.

The carrier and her battle group would rendezvous with an attack submarine, the Los Angeles-class USS *Baton Rouge* (SSN 689), sixty-five miles southwest of Key West, Florida.

The carrier air wing assigned to *America* had flown aboard five hours after the ship left home port. *America*, originally scheduled to depart the following day for a routine deployment, had her entire crew aboard.

Two F/A-18 Hornet squadrons, including the Silver Eagles of VMFA-115, were sharing CAP duties with two F-14D Tomcat squadrons. The marine fighter/attack pilots of VMFA-115 thoroughly enjoyed having the opportunity to hone their skills aboard the huge carrier.

Forty-five miles south of the ship, Marine Maj. Vince Cangemi, along with his wingman, Capt. Chuck Bellvue, orbited at 22,000 feet. The two fighter pilots had been assigned to Barrier Combat Air Patrol with two navy pilots flying F-14Ds. The Tomcat pilots were twenty miles west and two thousand feet higher than the Marine F/A-18 Hornets. The McDonnell-Douglas F/A-18s, powered by twin General Electric F404 afterburning turbofans, were capable of reaching speeds in excess of 1.8 Mach.

The combination fighter/attack aircraft sported the powerful liquid-cooled Hughes APG-65 radar, along with a nose-mounted 20mm M-61 cannon containing 570 rounds. The Hornets also had two advanced AIM-9 Sidewinder missiles slung under the wings and an AIM-9 mounted on each wing tip.

Cangemi was checking his three multifunction displays,

which replaced most of the conventional cockpit instruments, when he heard the E-2C Hawkeye call.

"Animal flight, Phoenix," the airborne warning and control officer said. "We hold multiple bogies at your three o'clock, forty-five miles, climbing out of eight thousand."

"Roger the bogies," Cangemi radioed, squinting into the early morning sun. "Bullet flight, Animal."

The F-14D pilots, orbiting in a lazy circle, were on the same radio frequency. "Go, Animal," the navy flight leader replied.

Cangemi keyed his mike. "Care to come on down here?"

"We're comin' starboard," the deep voice responded. "Be there in a minute."

"Ah . . . negative, Bullets," Phoenix ordered. "You have three bogies thirty right for forty-seven. CAP aircraft Warning Yellow, Weapons Hold."

"Animals copy," Cangemi radioed at the same instant his Hughes radar locked onto the four aircraft approaching his flight. "I have four on the scope," Cangemi said. "Animals, go combat spread."

"Roger," Bellvue replied as he moved out to the right and up 1,000 feet.

"Bullet Two Oh Two has a lock," the navy flight leader reported. "Copy Yellow, Weapons Hold."

Both CAP flights attempted to maneuver to place themselves in advantageous positions. Each move was countered by the approaching Cuban MiGs. The Hawkeye controller, watching the four flights close on each other, ordered the Ready Two CAP pilots to launch from *America*. After the acknowledgment, Phoenix called the BARCAP fighter crews.

"They have good GCI [ground control intercept]. Countering every move you make. Bullets, come starboard sixty—we need more separation."

"Comin' right sixty," the VF-2 squadron executive officer replied, then called his wingman. "Barry, step up another three grand and cover me."

"Movin' up, boss."

Cangemi watched on the heads up display (HUD) the four radar targets rapidly approaching. The MiGs were straight off the Hornet's nose, closing at 700 knots. "Animals go burner, now," Cangemi ordered, shoving his twin throttles into afterburner.

"Two," Bellvue replied as he checked his radar. "I've got 'em locked."

Seven seconds later, Cangemi and his wingman saw the MiG-25 Foxbats silhouetted against a puffy cumulonimbus cloud. "Tally," Cangemi radioed. "They're Foxbats—State Iron Works twenty-fives."

"Bullet has a tally," the navy pilot radioed. "We've got three Foxbats, one o'clock low, comin' up."

Cangemi started to raise his F/A-18's nose when two of the MiGs launched missiles. "Hard port!" Cangemi shouted as he slammed the stick to the left. "They fired—MiGs launched missiles!" he gasped in the 8½-g turn. He felt his tight g suit inflate, squeezing his legs and stomach in a vise grip.

"Weapons Hot!" the Hawkeye controller ordered. "CAP flights engage! Repeat, CAP flights engage!"

Bellvue reacted immediately, breaking hard left to get on the tail of the lead Foxbat. He snapped down his tinted helmet visor, selected heat, and waited a second for the lock-on tone. Cangemi saw a missile flash past his canopy, then snapped hard over to track the last MiG.

The Foxbats split into two sections, providing excellent coverage for each flight. It was obvious that the Cuban MiG-25s were being flown by well-trained fighter pilots.

Cangemi got into a turning fight with the leader of the second section, then noticed a MiG slipping behind him for the kill. The marine aviator unloaded his Hornet, throwing the number two bandit off a split second, then snatched the stick back. The F/A-18 slashed between the Foxbats as Cangemi searched frantically for his wingman.

"Chuck," Cangemi groaned, feeling the effects of grayout

as he saw Bellvue twisting through the sky, "break hard starboard, now!"

Cangemi watched as his wingman wrapped the Hornet into a gut-wrenching, vapor-producing right turn. A second later, Cangemi heard a rasping sound in his headset, indicating that the selected AIM-9 Sidewinder missile was tracking the infrared signature of the lead MiG.

"Fox Two!" Cangemi said as he pulled the trigger.

The heat-seeking missile rocketed straight at the Foxbat, colliding with the right tailpipe of the twin-engine fighter. The impact blew off the entire aft section of the aircraft in a black pulsing explosion.

The MiG's nose yawed to the right, then tucked under, sending the fighter tumbling out of control through the sky. Cangemi glimpsed the canopy separate from the crippled aircraft, but he never saw the pilot eject. Cangemi whipped the stick to the right to avoid debris, then pulled into the vertical. He rolled the Hornet slowly, scanning the hazy sky.

"Chuck," Cangemi radioed, hanging in his straps as he pulled the F/A 18 through the horizon, "check your six— you've got a gomer settin' up."

"Goin' for knots," Bellvue replied as he forced the Hornet into an 8-g "Bat Turn," followed by a zero-g unload. The fighter accelerated downward, then snapped straight up when Bellvue sighted two of the Foxbats attempting to turn inside his leader.

"Vince!" Bellvue shouted. "Break left now! Fox Two!"

Bellvue waited a second, then fired two of his Sidewinder missiles in a head-on pass at the two MiGs. The advanced air-to-air weapons, three seconds apart, slammed into the first Foxbat. The doomed fighter emerged from the orange fireball trailing debris, smoke, and blazing jet fuel.

The second MiG popped up instantly to miss the colossal explosion and raining debris. The pilot caught the upper edge of the black cloud, disintegrating his right engine with foreign object damage. The MiG, turning tight, unloaded and raced for Cuban airspace.

"Reverse, Chuck!" Cangemi ordered, working the remaining MiG into a vertical scissors. "Set him up—I'm going to disengage. Call it!"

"Stay on him a couple of seconds," Bellvue responded, rechecking heat while he rolled into a firing position. He searched the sky quickly for other bandits, then heard his AIM-9 missiles track the MiG-25. "Turn him loose!"

Cangemi snatched the stick back violently, then rolled the agile Hornet 180 degrees and unloaded the g forces. Going supersonic, Cangemi snapped into the vertical again and watched both of Bellvue's missiles miss the Foxbat. He stared, transfixed, as both heat-seeking missiles tracked straight at the blazing sun low on the horizon.

"Shit!" Bellvue said, selecting his 20mm M-61 cannon. "I'm guns!"

"Wrap him up," Cangemi shouted, watching Bellvue close inside the tight-turning MiG.

Suddenly the Foxbat snapped out of the punishing turn, allowing the Hornet pilot to fall into trail—a perfect firing solution.

Cangemi's mind sounded a warning a split second before the Soviet missile erupted from under the MiG's tail. "Break, break!" Cangemi radioed as he watched the Hornet explode into a million flaming pieces. His eyes witnessed the carnage, but it took his brain a second to record the blazing image.

"Chuck!" Cangemi shouted, flashing by the black puff, "get out! Eject! Eject!"

Three seconds passed as Cangemi looked frantically for the Foxbat. He spotted the MiG turning tight and diving toward the water. "Sonuvabitch!" Cangemi swore to himself, realizing that his wingman was part of the smoking wreckage falling toward the ocean.

The MiG had disengaged and was running for home. Cangemi eased the Hornet's nose slightly in front of the Foxbat, selected another missile, waited for it to lock on, then squeezed the trigger gently.

"Fox Two!" Cangemi radioed as he watched the missile

undulate toward the bastard who had killed his friend. "Go
. . . go . . . be there . . ."

The heat-seeking weapon missed the MiG's twin exhausts,
hitting the left wing root. The wing separated from the fuselage, sending the Foxbat spinning out of control. Cangemi
watched the MiG pilot eject as he heard a Mayday call from
one of the F-14 pilots. Stunned and absorbed in the drama,
Cangemi made an age-old mistake. He allowed his F/A-18
to fly through the debris of his kill.

SAN JULIAN

Seven armed guards surrounded the partially dismantled
Stealth bomber. All activity had ceased in the hangar while
everyone involved in the secret operation was interrogated
by the KGB director.

The technicians, scientists, and KGB personnel were se-
questered in two adjoining rooms. Gennadi Levchenko, sitting in his small office, was questioning each man
individually.

Natanoly Obukhov, the assistant KGB director, approached Levchenko's door.

"Have you found the infiltrator?" Levchenko barked.

"Comrade director," Obukhov bowed slightly in a highly
respectful manner, "our men are scouring the base and surrounding area. We have three helicopters and two spotter
planes in the air, and we are—"

"Don't give me long-winded reports," Levchenko spat.
"Give me results."

"Yes, comrade director," Obukhov replied, averting his
eyes to the colorless concrete walls in the spartan office. He
always felt apprehension when his eyes crossed the Mon-
golian features of Levchenko's face.

"What did the guard see?" Levchenko asked, dismissing
a technician with a wave of his arm.

"He never saw the assailant," Obukhov answered, then

added quickly, "he doesn't remember anything after he bent over."

Levchenko fixed his eyes on his assistant. "I want every inch of this base searched again."

ANIMAL ONE

Major Vince Cangemi, turning toward his carrier, USS *America*, looked back at his right wing. He could clearly see two deep slices in the leading edge, along with numerous dents and scars close to the fuselage.

The marine pilot quickly scanned his annunciator panel and engine instruments. "Oh, shit," Cangemi muttered when he noticed the right engine was cooking at the maximum temperature limit. The damaged F/A-18 had ingested the MiG's debris through the starboard engine.

Cangemi waited while the outbound combat air patrol pilots talked with the E-2C Hawkeye, then keyed his radio switch. "Phoenix, Animal One is inbound with engine damage."

"Copy, Animal One," the controller responded in a professional, low-key manner. "You have a ready deck. Come port fifteen degrees."

"Port fifteen," Cangemi radioed, watching the right engine gauges cautiously.

The Hornet continued flying, rock steady, for another minute and a half. Cangemi was just starting to relax when the F/A-18 yawed violently to the right.

"Ah . . . Phoenix," Cangemi radioed as he checked the hydraulic pressure. "Animal One has a problem."

"Roger, Animal," the controller said in a detached tone. "Say nature of your problem."

Cangemi watched the main hydraulic pressure fluctuate, then drop rapidly toward zero. "I'm losin' my hydraulics."

"Are you declaring an emergency?" the controller asked with an edge in his voice.

"That's affirm, Phoenix," Cangemi answered as he

watched the primary hydraulic pressure reach zero. "Animal One is declaring an emer—"

Without warning, the Hornet's nose pitched up seventy degrees. Cangemi shoved in full left rudder, forcing the aircraft into knife-edged flight. The nose fell through the horizon as Cangemi pushed in full right rudder, bringing the fighter wings-level.

The nose pitched skyward again, forcing the pilot to repeat the unusual procedure to control the Hornet. During the third rudder roll maneuver, Cangemi selected emergency hydraulic power and recovered control of his wounded fighter. He also noticed that he had lost more than 2,000 feet of altitude during the wild gyrations.

"Understand emergency," Phoenix radioed. "Can you make the ship?"

Cangemi studied his instruments and checked his DME. Forty-two nautical miles to go. "I think so. Looks okay . . . at the moment."

"Do you want the barricade?" the concerned controller asked as he rechecked the flight deck status.

Cangemi raised the nose slightly and mentally reviewed his NATOPS emergency procedures. "Ah . . . negative. Not at this time."

"Roger."

Cangemi glanced at his fuel gauges, knowing he needed to plug into a tanker. He also knew he could not risk close formation flying with a questionable control problem.

The pilot rechecked his DME, fuel burn, and rate of descent. He would arrive over the carrier with 700 to 800 pounds of fuel—only a few minutes in the thirsty fighter. He could not afford a bolter. He had to trap aboard *America* on his first pass.

Cangemi watched the right engine parameters as the seconds ticked away. He listened while Bullet Two Oh Two, the sole returning navy Tomcat, checked in for a push time. He eased back on the left throttle, held his breath, then pulled the right throttle slowly back to match the reduced power.

"Animal," Phoenix radioed, "your deck is eleven o'clock, twenty miles."

"I have a visual," Cangemi responded, squinting through the early morning haze. He could see the long white wake of the fast-moving carrier. "I'm setting up for an overhead two-seventy."

"Roger," the controller replied. "CAG paddles will wave you." The senior landing signal officer (LSO) would guide the marine aviator through the emergency landing. "Switch button five," the controller instructed.

Cangemi clicked his mike twice to acknowledge the radio transmission, switched to the Carrier Air Traffic Control Center (CATCC), then switched again to the LSO standing on the side of the flight deck. The LSO platform was adjacent to the arresting gear at the stern of the carrier.

"Animal One with a sick right engine, and ah . . . hydraulic problems."

"Okay, Animal," the senior LSO said in a reassuring tone, "hang onto it. Left two-seventy into the grove."

"Animal One," Cangemi replied a second before the right engine fire warning light flashed on and off momentarily.

"Oh . . . no," Cangemi said to himself as he approached the carrier at 3,000 feet and 360 knots. "Just two more minutes . . . give me two more minutes."

The fighter pilot watched the ship pass under him as he started slowing and banking to the left. "I'm going to trap on this pass," Cangemi said to himself, "if I have to taxi to the one wire." He lowered the flaps as the leading edge slats deployed automatically.

The F/A-18 continued to decelerate as Cangemi lowered the landing gear and tailhook. He increased power on both engines to compensate for the drag, glanced at his angle-of-attack indicator, then looked out at the wake of the carrier.

Concentrating on his approach, he did not see the right engine fire warning light flicker twice, then glow steadily.

"Animal One," the LSO radioed urgently, "you have smoke—negative, you're on fire! You're burnin' Vince!"

Cangemi snatched the right throttle to cutoff and activated the fire extinguishing system. The fire light remained illuminated as he tightened his turn toward the carrier.

"Hornet ball!" Cangemi radioed as he added more power on the left engine. The angle-of-attack indicator continued to rise, forcing the pilot to ease up the port throttle further.

"Roger, ball," the LSO replied, trying to quell his apprehension. "You're lookin' good."

Cangemi, concentrating intently on the bright orange meatball, angle of attack, and lineup, did not detect the drop in emergency hydraulic pressure.

"You're going low...too low!" the LSO shouted. "Power! POWER!"

Animal One, seconds from touchdown, shoved the left throttle forward. The stricken fighter plane climbed through the glide slope as Cangemi tried frantically to force down the Hornet's nose. He recognized that the controls were frozen as the carrier deck rushed up to meet him.

"Oh, God, I'm sinking like a rock!" Cangemi yanked the left throttle to idle and shoved on the control stick, diving for the deck. The burning fighter sank toward the end of the mammoth ship as Cangemi fought desperately to salvage the landing.

"Wave off! Wave off!" the LSO shouted as the F/A-18, flying left wing low, slammed into the rounddown at the aft end of the flight deck.

The fighter shed its landing gear, along with the left wing, then caught the number one arresting wire. The crushing impact, followed by the violent arrestment, separated the fuselage three feet behind the cockpit. The Hornet's nose and cockpit, minus the canopy, continued up the flight deck on its left side, stopping four feet from the angled deck edge.

Cangemi, rendered semiconscious during the 160 mile-per-hour crash, struggled to free himself from the smoking wreckage. He could see waves passing almost directly below him.

Three hot-suit firefighters and a paramedic reached Cangemi at the same time. They assisted the stunned aviator out of the remains of his cockpit, then placed him on a stretcher. The paramedic helped remove Cangemi's helmet, then placed it on the fighter pilot's chest.

Cangemi looked at the helmet in astonishment, then said a silent prayer. The left side of the marine red and gold helmet had been ground paper thin where Cangemi's head had slid on the rough flight deck.

CHAPTER NINETEEN

CABLE NEWS NETWORK

The CNN anchorman adjusted his tie for the third time, smoothed back his hair, and waited for his cue.

"Tensions in the Gulf of Mexico continue to escalate as President Jarrett attempts to resolve the B-2 hijacking. CNN has learned that another air battle has taken place, this time over the Straits of Florida. Initial reports indicate that American carrier planes were attacked only minutes ago by Cuban-based MiG fighters.

"A Pentagon source confirmed that two fighters from the carrier *America* were lost. The fate of the crews is unknown. Cuban losses are unconfirmed at this time.

"Premier Fidel Castro has issued a harsh warning to the White House, prompting legislators to call for immediate sanctions against Cuba. In a statement released minutes ago, Premier Castro stated that any further aggression on behalf of the United States will result in a state of war being declared by his government.

"The official newspaper of the Cuban Communist party, *Granma*, announced that any airplanes, including civilian aircraft, violating Cuban airspace will be shot down.

"In related news, a bipartisan group of congressional leaders is calling for an investigation into the Stealth hijacking." The newscaster paused as fresh information was placed on his desk outside the view of the camera.

"White House sources have confirmed that President Jarrett has increased the military alert status," he continued. "Our White House correspondent, Evelynn Myers, is standing by with an update. Evelynn?"

The pleasant-looking, short-haired woman stepped a few feet to the right to allow a better camera angle. "I just spoke to a White House staff member who confirmed the increased alert status. Fighter aircraft and helicopters from every branch of the services are congregating at Homestead, MacDill, and England Air Force Bases. Unconfirmed reports indicate that B-1 bombers from Dyess and Ellsworth Air Force Bases are en route to Barksdale Air Force Base near Bossier City, Louisiana.

"Reporters have been given a short release stating that the Army 82d Airborne Division at Fort Bragg, along with the 101st Air Assault Division at Fort Campbell, are on full alert. Secretary Kerchner also informed us that a marine corps special landing force, Amphibious Squadron Three, is embarked on the assault carrier *Wasp*. Another marine landing team is boarding a sister ship, the *Essex*."

The television picture switched back to the anchorman. "Evelynn, what is the current status of the Marines at Guantanamo Bay? Is there any provision to extract them from the base?"

"As far as we've been told," the reporter replied, switching her microphone to her other hand, "they will remain in place for the time being. The military does not want to risk flying any aircraft in or out of Guantanamo Bay. I spoke with a Pentagon source who said that the navy fighter planes at the base are remaining on the ground. The aircraft are manned—on immediate alert—to provide air cover if the Marines come under attack.

"One other note. White House sources have indicated that President Jarrett has demanded clarification of Russian involvement from President Ignatyev. Secretary Kerchner, who has scheduled a news conference later today, stated that he would address this subject, John?"

The anchorman waited a moment, adjusted his papers, then looked into the camera. "This item just in. The Kremlin has issued a statement denying any culpability in the Stealth disappearance. According to Soviet Foreign Minister Sergey Aksenhov, they are interrogating officials of the KGB and Cuban General Counterintelligence Directorate. Kremlin officials have issued an additional statement, saying that they will not participate in any military action we take against Cuba.

"In related news, NATO forces have been placed on alert, pending the outcome of the B-2 situation.

"We'll be right back," the anchor said without emotion, "so stay with us for the latest in headline news."

When a weather update flashed on the monitor, the anchorman turned to a staff member. "You think this is the excuse they've wanted . . . to eliminate Castro and communism in Cuba?"

"Hell, who knows what goes on in the puzzle palace."

SAN JULIAN

Gennadi Levchenko angrily dismissed the senior Soviet aeronautical engineer and turned to his assistant. "What is it, Natanoly Vitelevich?"

Obukhov, standing outside the director's door, stepped inside. "Comrade director, the American—Simmons—is becoming a problem for us."

"Get him in here," Levchenko blurted, too preoccupied with the security breach to concentrate on the American. "Are they searching the base again?"

"Da, comrade director," Obukhov answered. "The entire

base is sealed tight.'' As Levchenko shook his head in disgust, Obukhov stepped back through the door and motioned for Simmons to approach the director's office. ''You're making things difficult for yourself, comrade,'' Obukhov warned the frightened defector sternly as he ushered him into Levchenko's office.

''Sit down, Comrade Simmons,'' Levchenko said firmly. ''What is your problem?''

Simmons, sitting rigidly on the bench in front of the impatient KGB director, darted a glance at the small photo he held of Irina Rykhov. She had given him the black-and-white picture the afternoon prior to his commandeering the Stealth bomber.

The pretty face smiled at Simmons, giving him strength. He remembered vividly Irina's clear, provocative hazel eyes. Her face had a pronounced Slavic tilt that set off her full, sensuous mouth.

''Comrade director,'' Simmons began cautiously, ''I am concerned about Irina . . . for her safety.''

Levchenko half listened to the scared defector, his mind busy with the repercussions of the breach in security. If the truth reached the Kremlin . . .

''I am afraid,'' Simmons continued, unsure of himself, ''for Irina. She promised we would be together here, in San Julian. Is something wrong?''

Levchenko heard Simmons's last words. ''Yes, comrade,'' Levchenko answered in his grim, specious manner. ''Irina will be reunited with you in Moscow, for security reasons. We have had a security breach here, as you well know, and we cannot place Irina at risk.''

Simmons, showing fear and confusion, looked at the picture again. ''When will I be able to go to Moscow?''

''In a matter of days,'' Levchenko answered, trying to contain his anger and frustration. ''Right now, Comrade Simmons, we have work to do, and I am counting on you.''

Simmons rose slowly. ''Yes, comrade director.''

CIA HEADQUARTERS

Norman Lasharr and his deputy, David Ridgefield, sat quietly, waiting to hear from Hampton Milligan in Key West. Ridgefield refilled their coffee mugs while Lasharr reviewed the latest message traffic. Both men glanced occasionally at the television monitor in the corner of Lasharr's office.

"Well, general," Ridgefield said, picking up the discarded messages, "Wickham pulled it off."

Lasharr remained silent a few seconds, then placed the messages down. "Yes, he did . . . the crazy son of a bitch. I wish we had another fifty like him."

Ridgefield smiled slightly as he sat down catty-corner from the tenacious director. "I agree, sir."

Lasharr started to speak at the same moment a special report flashed on the television monitor. "Dave, turn it up."

Ridgefield pressed the volume button on the remote control next to his chair. Both men watched a harried, well-known commentator, tie askew, struggle to insert an earpiece.

The anchorman looked into the camera. "Cuban President Fidel Castro, moments ago, issued a declaration of war aimed at the United States. Speaking from his home at Varadero Beach, Castro lashed out vehemently at President Jarrett and vowed to confront any military threat to Cuba."

The newsman paused to adjust his earpiece, then continued quickly. "Castro has dispatched his brother, Army Commander Raul Castro, to personally take command of Cuban army troops advancing toward the San Julian Air Base. San Julian is the purported location of the missing B-2 Stealth bomber. White House sources have refused to comment."

The commentator, seeing new information being rushed to him, followed the director's cue. "CBS will continue our coverage of the Cuban crisis after this word."

Lasharr and Ridgefield looked at each other in astonishment. "Dave, get in touch with Hamp," Lasharr instructed, "and put a priority on getting Wickham out."

"Yes, sir," Ridgefield replied as he reached for his SecTel 1500 secure phone.

"I'll be at the White House," Lasharr said as he closed his thin attaché case. "Dave, I don't want any screwups. Keep a lid on it."

THE WHITE HOUSE
9:18 A.M. Eastern Standard Time

The situation room was crowded when President Jarrett and the secretary of state entered. "Gentlemen," Jarrett began, grim faced, "Secretary Gardner and I have issued a statement to world leaders. As you know, the Kremlin is denying any involvement in the hijacking."

Alton Jarrett adjusted his glasses carefully and read the dispatch.

"The president of the United States of America denounces Cuba's refusal to release our B-2 bomber and crew.

"The government of the United States recognizes the declaration of war issued by Cuban President Fidel Castro.

"The United States of America is, and will continue to be, committed to recovering our commandeered Stealth bomber and her crew."

Jarrett removed his glasses and placed the message faceup on the table. "This episode is a tremendous embarrassment for Castro. The Soviets—Ignatyev—are sidestepping the issue and leaving Castro caught in the middle. There may be a rogue faction operating in the KGB, but Ignatyev apparently isn't going to admit it.

"The dictatorial society that Castro has created is undergoing a major economic and ideological crisis. Moscow has withdrawn support, and Castro is feeling the pressure."

The president looked around the table before speaking again. "It is my opinion that we can expect stiff resistance from Castro. He is a desperate man, caught standing alone or with whatever support he can muster in this hemisphere.''

Jarrett sat back. The Joint Chiefs, the CIA director, and the cabinet members waited to see who would speak first.

''Mister President,'' the secretary of state said solemnly, ''may I have a word with you . . . in private?''

Jarrett paused, then looked at Gardner. ''Sam, if you have a comment—any comment—you can speak candidly to the entire group.''

Gardner, displaying a twinge of irritation, leaned on the table and clasped his hands together. ''Sir, if we—if you insist on pursuing your plan to invade Cuba,'' Gardner said cautiously, then stopped and shifted in his seat, ''the ramifications—the Vietnam syndrome—will be devastating to your political career.''

The president, taking time to compose himself, propped his elbows on the table. He attempted to suppress his usual wry smile. ''Sam, I don't give a damn about my political career. What office am I going to run for?'' In his peripheral vision, Jarrett could see that all eyes were averted. ''My responsibility, Sam, is to the American people—the people who voted me into office. Sure, there will be dissenters, as there always have been, but the vast majority of Americans know the difference between right and wrong.''

The president looked at his secretary of defense, then back to Gardner. ''Some Soviet faction has, with or without their government's knowledge or approval, commandeered our bomber, and we have to get it back.''

Jarrett paused when he saw the reaction on the faces surrounding him. He leaned back in his chair. ''What the United States government is engaged in is a recovery mission, pure and simple. When we have reclaimed our B-2, or destroyed it, the encroachment on Cuba is over.''

The vice president, silent until now, swiveled to face Gardner. ''Sam, we lose more than Stealth technology if we sit idle and exchange diatribe. As world leaders, we lose face and support.''

The secretary of state displayed a rare show of condescension but remained silent. He had disagreed openly with Truesdell on a number of occasions.

Jarrett caught a glance from his defense secretary but addressed his remarks to Gardner. "Sam," the president said more softly, "this issue is much bigger than a single B-2 or its technical secrets. This administration is being challenged openly, and we are not going to take the bashing."

Gardner remained unconvinced but said nothing.

The president looked at his watch and focused on his defense secretary. "Bernie, I want a maximum effort from our forces, with minimum collateral damage."

"The Joint Chiefs," Kerchner replied, glancing at the JCS chairman, "and I feel confident that we can achieve the objective, and keep the situation contained."

"Very well," Jarrett responded, then stood. "I have to meet with the families of the B-2 pilots. Bernie, I want a solid, continuous blanket of air cover over our battle groups until they have returned to our coastal waters."

"Yes, sir," Kerchner replied, standing with the rest of the group. "We're concentrating our resources to provide a constant barrier."

Jarrett walked to the door, then stopped and turned to the assemblage. "Let's not forget that Cuban soldiers shot down two U.S. helicopters, in Grenada, killing three Marines. Now, we have more losses caused by Communist Cubans." Jarrett stiffened slightly. "Losses because Castro is sheltering our commandeered bomber."

USS *WASP* (LHD-1)

The 40,500-ton amphibious assault ship, commissioned in July 1989, steamed south toward the western tip of Cuba. The carrier was the tenth navy ship to bear the name *Wasp*.

Embarked on board the 844-foot ship were 1,966 Marines, supported by eighteen AV-8B Harrier II jets, four LAMPS III helicopters, and four CH-53E Marine Super Stallion helicopters. On the well deck, below the 2.2-acre flight deck, three air-cushioned landing craft (LCAC) waited to transport the marine expeditionary force ashore near San Julian.

The heavy transport CH-53s, powered by three 4,380-shaft horsepower General Electric turboshafts, would supplement the air cushion landing craft. The four helicopters, each carrying fifty-five Marines, would land at strategic points around San Julian air base.

The LAMPS III helicopters, with their long-range air-to-surface radar and advanced data link, would manage the over-the-horizon assault. Two LAMPS IIIs, backed by two assault LAMPS IIIs, would track the amphibious landing craft, maintain communications with the LHD, and transmit the LCACs' progress to the *Wasp*'s large screen displays in the Combat Information Center.

The eighteen Marine AV-8B close support attack fighters, armed with Snakeye bombs, rockets, and one 25mm cannon, would provide air cover for the marine landing force.

Wasp's sister ship, USS *Essex* (LHD-2), followed the lead assault carrier at a distance of seventy nautical miles. *Essex* was in the final stages of receiving her marine special landing force, along with their AV-8B Harriers from Cherry Point Marine Corps Air Station. A continuous stream of helicopters landed, disgorged Marines and supplies, then flew back to shore to pick up more men.

Essex would land her assault force three-quarters of a mile north of *Wasp*'s unit. Both assault groups would go ashore at Bahia de Guadiana, then forge east to San Julian. The USS *Nassau* would provide a third marine amphibious assault force. Eight CH-53s, carrying full loads of Marines, would augment the helicopters from *Wasp* and *Essex*. *Nassau* would also provide UH-1 Huey helicopters and AH-1 Cobra gun ships for the assault.

Navy F-14s and Navy/Marine F/A-18 fighter/attack jets, operating from the decks of *Kitty Hawk, America,* and *Abraham Lincoln,* would fly high air cover for the Harrier jets and helicopters.

Wasp continued on course, reducing speed to allow *Essex* and *Nassau* to close the gap. Her escort ships moved closer as the assault carrier approached Cuban waters. Supported by F-14D Tomcats from *Kitty Hawk,* S-3B Viking antisubmarine aircraft patrolled around the *Wasp* assault group.

Each minute increased the danger and tension aboard the amphibious aircraft carrier. Every crew member knew that they were sailing toward a Communist country that had declared war on the United States.

SAN JULIAN

Gennadi Levchenko, seething and shouting commands, stormed into his office. He had been informed only minutes earlier that he had a double agent in his midst—an agent who had relayed live pictures of the B-2 bomber to Washington.

Levchenko, absorbed in ferreting out the spy, yanked his telephone across the desk and sat down heavily. "Who the hell am I supposed to call?" he bellowed at the skinny clerk/medical technician.

The gaunt, hollow-eyed man flinched. "President Castro—Fidel Castro, comrade dir—"

"Bullshit!" Levchenko raged, eyes bulging. The director had a moment of pure panic, then attempted to recover as his racing heart pounded. He was boxed in between KGB chief Golodnikov and Castro. Levchenko knew that he would face a firing squad if he could not isolate the traitor under his command. Now, with his life on the line, Fidel Castro was meddling in the Stealth operation.

"I don't report to Castro," Levchenko continued, breathing heavily. "Who took the call?"

"I did, comrade director," the frightened man answered. "He said immediately. That's why the lieutenant chased after you . . . comrade director."

"Get out!" Levchenko yelled as he scribbled notes on a scratch pad. "Get out!"

The clerk hurried through the door, knocking papers off a low filing cabinet.

Levchenko's mind raced. Shit, what does Castro want? Does he know about the security leak? Levchenko picked up the receiver, adjusted his wire-rimmed glasses, then looked at the phone number on the message.

He placed the call. If he could only capture the treasonous member of his contingent. Who the hell was the bastard? Levchenko waited, fidgeting, while the phone rang three times. He yanked out a cigarette pack and snapped open his lighter.

"President Castro's residence," the pleasingly mild male voice said. "May I have your name and the purpose of your call?"

Levchenko, glancing over the rim of his glasses into the hangar, fought frustration and disdain. "Gennadi Levchenko, director of KGB operations in Cuba, returning President Castro's communication."

"Yes, comrade director. The president will only be a moment."

Levchenko, drumming his stubby fingers on the desk, did not acknowledge the comment. His thoughts were concentrated on retaining control of the situation at San Julian.

The KGB agent had met Fidel Castro on two occasions. He knew how quickly the Cuban dictator's personality could change from charming and hospitable to belligerent and raging.

"Levchenko," Castro's voice was loud and abrupt. "Have the American bomber ready to fly by the time my brother arrives at San Julian."

Levchenko was stunned by the order. "Comrade president, you cannot make such a demand."

"Have the B-2 ready to fly!" Castro ordered in a highly agitated voice. "Raul is on the way to San Julian."

Levchenko sat staring into the hangar after Castro had terminated the conversation. "Goddamned fanatic," Levchenko growled in disgust. He loathed the Cuban dictator, as did the majority of Russians remaining on the island, but he knew he had to be careful around Castro.

Levchenko's stomach churned as he considered his options. First, the director reasoned, he had to contact KGB headquarters in Moscow. Vladimir Golodnikov, the volatile chief of the KGB, would be incensed when he received word that Castro had assumed command of the Stealth bomber.

Levchenko sat quietly, pondering other options and thinking about Castro. He recalled clearly Castro's annual national holiday speech at Camaguey, Cuba. The Cuban dictator, accused by many of becoming an aged museum piece, had ranted for more than three hours to a throng of thousands. Clinging to Stalinist-style communism and ideology, Castro had delivered a bitter and emotional discourse to the sweltering crowd. The Cuban leader, yelling loudly, had stated that he would never surrender his brand of communism. Speaking on the anniversary of the revolution he had led, Castro talked about the civil conflict and national strife in the Soviet Union.

Levchenko could hear Castro's words clearly in his mind. "Cuba, our great and wonderful country, can expect serious shortages in Soviet economic aid."

Levchenko, like most Soviet officials, paid little attention to Castro's agitated, lectern-pounding speeches, in which he generally spotlighted past triumphs and focused on the 1953 Moncado barracks attack that had launched his revolution.

Now, Levchenko thought, Castro was on the verge of cutting ties with Moscow and directing communism in the West. The Stealth hijacking, now exposed, could destroy him.

Levchenko stood to go to the communications room, then stopped when he remembered what else Castro had said. It all tied together for Levchenko. The Cuban president had lashed out vociferously against the United States, saying, "We can survive and overcome any challenge by the imperialist Americans, be it blockade, invasion, or full-fledged war. If the Yankee troops invade or try to occupy Cuba, we will be on our own, forgotten by our Soviet benefactors, but we will prevail.''

Levchenko walked out of the office and headed toward the communications center. He replayed Castro's speech in his mind. The Cuban dictator, a fervent Stalin purist in Levchenko's estimation, was going to present some difficult problems.

The KGB director, developing a strategy to protect himself, entered the sophisticated message center. He walked to one of two direct lines to KGB headquarters, dismissed the communications officer brusquely, then sat down and lighted a cigarette before he initiated the voice-scrambled call.

CHAPTER TWENTY

THE *GENERAL ABELARDO ALVAREZ*

The Soviet Foxtrot-class submarine, crewed by Cuban sailors and a KGB political officer, moved slowly through the depths of the Gulf of Mexico. The diesel-electric-powered attack submarine, quieter than her nuclear-powered counterparts, slipped through the water using freshly charged batteries.

Three and a half hours had passed since the *General Abelardo Alvarez* had submerged 280 kilometers northwest of Havana. The captain, Ricardo Esteban, had ascended to periscope depth twice during that time to receive messages informing him that President Castro had declared war on the United States.

The grizzled captain, three months from retirement, had been astounded. He had been thoroughly briefed about the war contingency but never dreamed it would happen. He told himself to remain calm, but he could not quell the thought that Castro must be senile, or crazy. The United States, the submarine skipper knew, could crush Cuba like an eggshell.

The KGB officer, a veteran submariner, showed little emotion when the message had been transmitted. Esteban, who privately had no desire to engage the Americans, knew that the Soviet political officer would label him a coward and traitor if he did not attack American targets of opportunity.

The *General Abelardo Alvarez*, freshly painted in dark gray, carried three Soviet-manufactured antiship torpedoes. The devastating weapons, fired from the bow tubes, had the power to sink an aircraft carrier. The reconditioned torpedoes, stowed aboard the *Alvarez* less than a month earlier, had replaced older, less powerful weapons.

Esteban, dripping with perspiration, hovered over the chart table. He was sure that the Soviet officer could sense his trepidation.

"Captain," the sonar operator said in a loud whisper, "I have a contact, bearing three-four-zero. Two propellers, turning at high speed."

Esteban turned white, glancing nervously at the KGB officer. "Right twenty degrees." The *Alvarez*, creeping along at two and a half knots, eased around to place the torpedo tubes on the unknown ship.

"The contact is big," the intent Cuban sonarman reported. "Very big, captain . . . wait—I have more propellers to the . . . a contact in front of the large ship."

The political officer, openly irritated, stepped forward to the sonar station. "Range, what's the goddamn range!"

The sonar operator hunkered down and pressed his earphones tightly to his head. "Twenty kilometers, possibly less, comrade."

"Stand by forward tubes," the Soviet officer ordered, aggressively taking command. "Come to periscope depth."

Esteban, openly embarrassed, shrugged his shoulders and retreated against the bulkhead.

The control room talker, apprehension in his eyes, turned

to the Soviet officer. "Forward tubes ready to fire, comrade."

The KGB officer, ignoring the report, watched the depth gauge. "Bearing and distance," the Russian commanded in a harsh tone. "Give me bearing and distance at one-minute intervals."

"Three-three-seven," the perspiring sonarman reported, keeping his eyes forward. "Eighteen kilometers, comrade."

The tension in the control room mounted as the range of the contact closed. The Cuban sailors, who went to sea only three to four weeks a year, had never even fired a torpedo. The military budget did not allow firing weapons for training purposes.

The *Alvarez*, rigged for silent running, moved only fast enough to maintain depth control. The propeller, driven by the silent batteries, turned very slowly.

"Bearing three-three-five," the Cuban sonar specialist said in a hushed whisper. "Fourteen kilometers."

"Up periscope," the grim-faced Russian ordered.

The sonarman stole a glance at Esteban as the thin attack scope slid into position. The Cuban captain only frowned, then looked blankly at the deck. He despised the arrogant Russian, but he had adjusted to the fact that the Soviet Union supplied the submarines and the expertise.

The Russian grasped the periscope handles and swung the scope around the horizon, stopping on the large contact. "It's a carrier—an American troop carrier!"

Esteban flinched inwardly, catching the frightened sailors looking at him for some indication of command.

The Soviet officer moved the periscope slightly to the left, then reversed to the right, scanning both sides of the big warship. "I hold three frigates," he said quietly, "and one . . . destroyer. Down scope." The relentless officer watched the periscope retract, then turned to Esteban. "You will give the order to fire, comrade captain."

THE *WASP* (LHD-1)

The amphibious assault carrier, steaming at 20 knots, was preparing to land a flight of four Marine AV-8B Harrier II jets. The vertical/short takeoff and landing (VSTOL) attack aircraft, seven miles astern, were approaching the *Wasp* at 400 knots.

Two S-3B Viking antisubmarine warfare (ASW) aircraft, supplemented by three LAMPS III ASW helicopters, orbited around the carrier at varying distances. The four escort ships bracketed the *Wasp* on all points. Two frigates were deployed on each side of the carrier, along with a frigate 2,000 yards in front of the bow. A single destroyer followed the assault ship at a distance of 1,600 yards. High above the carrier, thirty-five miles off the port and starboard bow, two flights of F-14D Tomcats patrolled the sky.

Wasp's combat information center, tracking multiple targets close to Cuban shores, had been working closely with the E-2C Hawkeye from *Kitty Hawk*'s VAW-123 squadron. The Hawkeye was due to be relieved on station in twelve minutes.

Wasp's CIC came to life when one of the LAMPS III ASW helicopters radioed a report. "Crossbow, Cold Water Three has a contact," the pilot said in an excited voice. "We're coming around for another pass, but we had a solid contact."

"Roger, Cold Water Three," the CIC officer replied as he sounded general quarters. "Drop a marker and stand clear."

"Ah . . . roger," the pilot radioed, searching the water around and below the helicopter. "Cold Water Three is marking . . . solid contact . . . confirmed."

Less than five seconds passed before the ASW pilot shouted and pointed below. His copilot saw the periscope a second later. "We have a periscope! We have a scope below us!"

The CIC officer glanced at the two large screens in front

of his console. "Sea Wolf Seven One Two cleared for a drop. Repeat, Sea Wolf Seven One Two cleared for a live drop. Warning Red, Weapons Free."

"Copy, copy," the S-3B Viking pilot radioed. "Tally on the smoke. We're comin' downhill."

"Roger," the CIC officer replied as the *Wasp* and her escort ships assumed battle stations. "Call the drop."

"Seven-twelve," the Viking pilot replied as he lined up slightly upwind from the smoke.

THE *GENERAL ALVAREZ*

Captain Ricardo Esteban squinted through the attack periscope. The American assault carrier would be at the optimum torpedo attack position in less than half a minute.

Esteban, aware of the KGB officer standing behind him, wiped perspiration from his glistening forehead. The interior temperature of the Soviet submarine was approaching eighty-three degrees Fahrenheit.

"Stand by to fire on my command," Esteban ordered, tracking the carrier. He rotated the periscope quickly to check the horizon around the battle group, then stopped in panic when he saw the canister. It was eighty meters off the starboard bow, pumping out billowing clouds of bright yellow smoke.

"Smoke!" Esteban said, swinging the periscope forward. They're on us!" The crew tensed as the Russian exchanged a concerned glance with the Cuban captain.

"Down scope!" Esteban ordered, backing away from the attack periscope as if it were a ghost. "Dive! Dive!"

"Negative!" the Russian countermanded sharply. "Negative! Up scope!"

The Soviet officer grasped the periscope handles firmly, made a slight adjustment, then waited patiently. "Fire One!" the tense, sweating KGB officer ordered, then looked at the firing board lights. The bright green launch light winked on.

A second elapsed before the *General Alvarez* shuddered as the powerful torpedo shot out of the flooded tube. "Fire Two!" the Russian barked. "Down scope, dive! Dive! Right full rudder! All ahead flank!" The Soviet officer shot Esteban a contemptuous glance, cold and accusing. "Rig for depth charges."

SEA WOLF 712

"We have screws! We've got contacts!" the Viking sensor operator shouted over the intercom system. "Two targets confirmed . . . ah, shit—tracking the carrier!"

"We've got torpedoes!" the pilot broadcast as he prepared to drop two depth charges. "Two targets tracking *Wasp*!"

The pilot of the twin-jet submarine killer, figuring that the submerged enemy would turn away from the carrier battle group, lined up his pass.

"Seven Oh Eight," the pilot radioed to the second S-3B Viking, "make a run! Drop two hundred yards southeast of my shot."

"Roger," the aircraft commander replied. "We're rolling in now."

The first sub killer dropped his ordnance, bottomed out, then pulled up steeply for another pass. "One is off, clearing port."

"Two has a tally," the second Viking pilot responded, concentrating on his lineup. He was a split second from his release point when the first two depth charges exploded, sending two huge geysers blasting out of the water.

The pilot and copilot of the lead Viking focused on the *Wasp* as they rolled out of their steep, climbing turn. They could see that the assault carrier had changed course, along with the escort ships, to place the bow straight toward the torpedoes.

"The old man," the copilot said, "is giving them the least amount to hit."

"Yeah," the pilot replied in a tight voice. "We'll know in a few seconds."

"Two's off," the second Viking pilot radioed, then snapped into a climbing left turn. "One's in!"

THE *WASP* (LHD-1)

The 40,500-ton carrier, bow on to the Russian-manufactured torpedoes, was slowing steadily. A senior chief petty officer ran down the length of the flight deck waving his arms, yelling for everyone to hit the deck.

A LAMPS III pilot raced across the bow of the carrier, turned steeply, waited two seconds, then jettisoned his full load of depth charges. The heroic effort had no effect on the two fast-moving torpedoes as they sped toward the assault ship. The flight of four marine Harriers, warned about the torpedo launch, had turned away and were orbiting.

The first torpedo, traveling at twenty-three knots, rammed the carrier and detonated in a blinding white flash. The underwater blast ripped off the bottom third of the *Wasp*'s bow. The second Russian torpedo hit the starboard side forty yards aft of the initial impact. The explosion sent another blast and shock wave over the flight deck.

The effects of the attack were devastating. *Wasp* plowed to a stop with two gaping holes in her bow. The scene on the flight deck was chaotic, as all hands attempted to help each other secure aircraft and equipment. The tall island structure, unaffected by the devastating explosions, was crammed with personnel hurrying to their battle stations.

The huge ship, bow down twelve degrees, was taking on water rapidly. Debris rained down on the heavily damaged carrier as water surged through her forward compartments.

A group of stunned sailors, working on the lowered flight deck elevator, had been blown overboard by the second explosion. One of the LAMPS III helicopters hovered over the men and dropped a life raft. Two of the LAMPS III helicopters, skimming low over the water, were dropping ordnance on the attack submarine.

Wasp's escort ships moved closer to the stricken carrier while both Viking antisubmarine jets continued to track the submarine. The Viking crews, enraged by the unexpected blasts, were determined to sink the enemy sub.

THE *GENERAL ALVAREZ*

''We have to surface!'' Captain Esteban shouted as water sprayed from two overhead pipes.

''Nyet!'' the Soviet officer shot back, nervously watching the water rise around his ankles. ''We can't surface—they're on top of us.''

The sailors, fear showing in their eyes, were desperately trying to contain the leaks caused by the pressure surges from the depth charges. The air, smelling like oil, was stagnant, humid, and warm.

''Torpedo room reports heavy flooding,'' the frightened control room talker reported to Esteban. ''They . . . they want out, captain.''

''Negative!'' the Russian ordered. ''If they open the watertight door, we might flood the whole boat.''

Esteban paused, looking at the depth gauge, then faced the sullen Russian. ''We have to take pressure off the hull before something fails.''

''We will remain at this depth,'' the Soviet officer commanded angrily, ''until we are clear of the area.''

The hull creaked, then groaned loudly, instilling in the Cuban crew uncontrollable fear.

''Captain,'' the sailor manning the diving planes said in a panic-choked voice. ''I can't control . . . the bow is going down.''

Esteban stared at the diving plane indicator. The controls were in the full up position and the depth was increasing.

The stricken submarine was beginning to plunge toward the bottom of the Gulf of Mexico.

"Blow forward tanks!" Esteban ordered, ignoring the Russian. "All ahead two thirds."

"I am in command!" the Soviet officer shouted. "I will decide when we sur—"

CRRRAACK!

His statement was cut off when a weld joint on the side of the inner hull split, spraying cold water into the control room. The high-pressure discharge was like a stream from a fire hose.

"Surface! Emergency surface!" Esteban shouted above the confusion. "Blow all tanks!"

A rumbling noise reverberated through the submarine as the lights flickered twice and went out. "Emergency power!" the Soviet officer shouted. "Give me emergency lights!"

"We're sinking," the diving plane operator cried. "Oh, mother of God, we're—"

"Shut up!" the Russian bellowed. "All ahead full, blow tanks, blow tanks!"

The crew, hysterical in the dark, sinking submarine, cried out in a high-pitched wailing. The hull creaked loudly, then ripped open in a terrifying screech, sending tons of seawater crashing into the control room.

SAN JULIAN

Gennadi Levchenko listened to the scrambler switch off, then placed the phone receiver down and pushed back his chair. His hands shook as he lighted a cigarette and stood.

"Idiots," he said absently, brushing an ash off his sleeve. "Stupid bumbling idiots."

Levchenko walked out of the communications center and headed for his office. He had ordered his deputy to return to the hangar immediately. Levchenko had major problems to solve and needed the assistance of Obukhov.

The KGB director walked into his office, ground out his cigarette, and sat down, seething. Levchenko continuously flexed his fingers and balled his fists. His world, the career he had developed so painstakingly, was rapidly coming unraveled.

Obukhov hurried down the hangar stairs, almost tripping on the bottom step, and rushed into Levchenko's office.

"Sit down," Levchenko ordered, placing his forearms on the desk. "We have big problems, Natanoly Vitelevich. This operation is disintegrating, and now Castro is interfering."

Obukhov leaned back slightly, started to speak, then decided to remain silent. He had known Levchenko long enough to become conditioned to the director's moods.

"Castro called me," Levchenko announced, anger written across his craggy face. His eyes were like cold blue marbles embedded in the puffy white face.

"Castro," Obukhov said wide-eyed, "called here?"

"He ordered me," Levchenko replied bitterly, "to have the Stealth ready to fly when his brother arrives."

Obukhov sat petrified, uncomprehending, trying to sort out what the foreboding call meant. "What is he doing?"

Levchenko ignored the question and smashed out his cigarette. "Castro has declared war on the United States!"

"War?" Obukhov responded, tilting his head slightly. "Castro declared war? Why?..."

"He believes that the Americans are preparing to invade Cuba...," Levchenko answered, then leaned back, "to retrieve their bomber." The KGB director slammed his fist on the desk. "The sonuvabitch is like a polar bear. Castro has no fear of anything or anyone."

Obukhov was speechless.

"I have contacted Moscow," Levchenko said, "and our goddamned director—the hotheaded idiot who didn't want extra security here—who wanted the base to look like every other base so the satellite photos wouldn't show any change—ordered me to protect the bomber."

Levchenko rubbed his neck. "Golodnikov said that the B-

2 must be secured at any cost. The bomber is scheduled to fly a top priority secret mission. Our orders are to keep Castro's people away from the B-2,'' Levchenko continued, pausing to control himself, ''until Golodnikov decides what action to take.''

Obukhov squeezed his knees. ''You actually spoke with Golodnikov?''

''No, goddamnit. I talked with the operations director.''

''What about the bomber?'' Obukhov asked cautiously. ''Are you going to prepare it for flight?''

''Da,'' Levchenko answered, taking off his wire-rimmed glasses to rub the bridge of his bulbous nose. ''It may climinate the military conflict with the United States.''

Obukhov peered into the hangar. The dark charcoal-colored bomber, entrails exposed, looked forlorn. ''When is Raul scheduled to arrive?''

''I don't know. Who knows what those lunatics will do next?'' Levchenko replied harshly, then changed to his unctuous manner. ''Natanoly Vitelevich, I am going to need your help, to salvage what we can of this goddamned mess.''

CHAPTER TWENTY-ONE

THE WHITE HOUSE

President Alton Jarrett, interrupted at the beginning of a meeting with the Advisory Committee for Trade Policy and Negotiations, rushed down the long corridor to the situation room.

He met his secretary of defense a few steps from the entrance. The Joint Chiefs, along with the other members of the security team, were discussing military options available for use against Cuba. Kerchner wanted to talk with the president alone before Jarrett entered the room.

"What happened, Bernie?" the president asked, stopping to quiz his friend.

"AJ," Kerchner replied in a somber, strained voice, "the *Wasp* has been torpedoed, and we have sustained heavy casualties."

The president's face turned ashen as the magnitude of the tragedy registered in his mind. Jarrett, who normally analyzed information carefully before approaching a decision, went from shock to rage in five seconds. "Goddamn, Bernie," the president said with open emotion, "what the hell happened? Is it in danger of sinking?"

"The flash message said that the ship was struck," Kerchner answered with a tremor in his voice, "by a submarine-fired torpedo. It isn't in danger of sinking, but the report indicates that *Wasp* is listing to starboard. We'll have more information in a few minutes, after the crew completes the damage control assessment."

"Jesus Christ," Jarrett responded, grim faced. His color was deadly pale, almost gray. "Why, Bernie? What happened to our ASW cover—our air cover?"

"I don't know, Mister President," Kerchner answered, shaking his head in frustration. "The submarine was apparently detected at the same time the torpedoes were fired."

"Did they get the sub?"

Kerchner looked straight into the president's eyes. "They aren't sure, sir. We'll have to wait for a detailed report."

"Heavy casualties?" the chief of state asked.

Kerchner's face quivered slightly. "That is the report, sir. The surface escorts reported men in the water."

The president remained quiet, as if in a trance. Kerchner waited a few seconds, expecting Jarrett to say something. It was highly unusual for this outgoing man to be openly withdrawn.

The president, jaw set rigid, closed his eyes a moment, then opened them. "I want Castro's military installations reduced to rubble—all of them," Jarrett said, violently agitated. "Every goddamned airfield, port, ship, airplane, radar site—everything destroyed—flattened."

The president paused a moment, seeing the surprised look on Kerchner's face. "I want to keep this military—understand, Bernie? No cities, or civilians—just military targets."

"Yes, sir," Kerchner replied, placing a comforting hand on his friend's shoulder. "The Joint Chiefs are working on the operation now. We will submit it for your approval as soon as the plans are finalized.''

''Bernie,'' the president said, glancing at the entrance to the situation room, ''I want a maximum effort.''

HARTSFIELD INTERNATIONAL AIRPORT,
Atlanta, Georgia

Hundreds of travelers crowded around the cocktail lounge television monitors when the president of the United States appeared on the screen. Continuous news reports, updating the *Wasp* tragedy, had angered and shocked people around the world. Calls for retribution had filled the airwaves as diplomatic efforts were cast aside.

The president, looking drawn and tired, faced the television cameras. ''My fellow citizens, and friends around the world, I share your grief in the *Wasp* tragedy. We mourn the fine young American patriots who gave their lives today . . . in a state of war declared by Cuba. We must band together to make it clear that America will exact a price from those who cause war, and from those who support them.''

Jarrett stared intently into the group of cameras. ''I assure you, as president of the United States of America, that I will take the appropriate steps to stop Castro's aggression.''

Cheers and applause thundered through the huge airport, drowning out the president's final words.

Jarrett stepped away from the podium, joining his defense secretary and other staff members, as the secretary of state stepped in front of the cameras.

''Mister President,'' Kerchner said quietly, ''the Joint Chiefs are prepared to present their recommendations for targeting.''

''Very well,'' Jarrett responded, walking rapidly out of the room.

DIAMOND FLIGHT

The four F-14D Tomcats from VF-102, led by Comdr. Doug "Frogman" Karns, rendezvoused over the *Kitty Hawk* and headed for their barrier combat air patrol station. The pilots and their radar intercept officers, reacting to the news of the *Wasp*, were keyed to a fever pitch.

The expedited catapult launches and the quick ready room brief, covering the change in the rules of engagement (ROE), had heightened tensions. The new ROE stated that a pilot had to visually identify his target as an enemy aircraft, or ship, before he could fire.

Everyone felt the visceral impact of being thrust into a shooting conflict. The strain was magnified by the close proximity to American shores.

"Diamond One Zero Three, Wolfpack," the carrier controller radioed, "contact Phoenix, button seven."

"Copy, button seven," Karns acknowledged, then transmitted, "Diamonds switch, now."

The fighter pilots simultaneously switched to the new frequency and checked in with their leader.

"Two."

"Three."

"Four."

"Phoenix, Diamond One Oh Three," Karns reported to the E-2C Hawkeye airborne early warning and control aircraft. "Four Fox Fourteens."

"Roger, Diamonds," the controller responded. "Stand by for your quadrant."

"Diamond One Oh Three."

The Hawkeye, one of three circling over the Gulf, would handle the fighter aircraft from the carriers *Kitty Hawk* and USS *America*.

"Diamonds," the controller said calmly, "we have bogies in whiskey one-seven-four bravo. Flight of three . . . looks low. Your eleven o'clock for forty-five."

"Diamond One Oh Three," Karns responded, then talked

to his charges. "Frank, take your section out a mile and step up three thousand."

"Diamonds Three and Four movin' out," the second section flight leader replied, banking gently to the right.

"Okay, Two," Karns radioed, "combat spread."

"Two."

"Diamond," the laconic Hawkeye controller paused, "your . . . ah . . . bogies at twelve for thirty-five, maneuvering."

"Roger," Karns responded, scanning the horizon. He raised his tinted visor a few seconds, examining the sea and sky, then lowered it back in place and twisted the tension knob. "Heads up, Diamonds."

"Warning Red," the controller called. "Weapons Hot!"

"Arm 'em up!" Karns ordered his pilots as he leveled at 17,000 feet. "It's show time."

"Two."

"Three."

"Four's hot."

Karns keyed the intercom and queried his radio intercept officer (RIO) about the radar return on the bogies.

"Got 'em locked, skipper."

The F-14s, receiving continuous updates from the Hawkeye flew straight at the MiGs. At eighteen miles Karns rechecked his firing switches and fuel state, then keyed his radio. "Diamonds, let's go burner."

At seven miles the Hawkeye called. "Check starboard, one o'clock low!"

Karns rolled the big Grumman fighter inverted, scanning the hazy sky below his Tomcat. "Tallyho—One has a tally! MiG twenty-fives . . . confirmed."

The Foxbats, guided by their own ground control radar site, were in trail with the third MiG weaving back and forth. They were level at 12,000 feet, going supersonic.

"Diamond One is engaged!" Karns radioed, shoving the Tomcat's nose down.

Karns's wingman rolled inverted and followed the lead F-

14 into the fight. As Karns plunged toward the camouflaged MiGs, the lead Foxbat turned hard into the two Tomcats. The two trailing MiGs continued straight ahead, building speed, then pulled into the vertical.

Karns, recognizing an overshoot, pulled his throttles to idle and deployed his speed brakes. "I've got him . . . come on, lock up!"

"Shoot! Shoot!" Karns's backseater yelled. "The other two are . . . they're takin' us!"

Karns squeezed off an AIM-9 missile, slammed the throttles into afterburner, retracted the speed brakes, unloaded the aircraft, and dove for separation. "Fox Two!"

The VF-102 commanding officer caught a glimpse of the exploding MiG-25 as his Tomcat slashed by the cartwheeling fuselage at 670 knots. The lead MiG, minus sections of the wings, tumbled across the sky, exploded again, then spun straight into the Gulf of Mexico.

"Good hit! Good shot!" the RIO shouted as he checked the other two Foxbats. "They're pulling lead!"

"Skipper," the second section leader radioed, "break hard starboard, bring your nose up!"

Karns popped the Tomcat into knife-edged flight and snatched the stick into his stomach, groaning under the 6½ g's. He saw why the section leader had called. Karns's wingman was in a perfect position to attack the two remaining MiGs.

"Two has . . . we're locked!" the wingman radioed as he fired a missile. "Fox Two!" The missile tracked straight to the second MiG, flew up the left tailpipe, and exploded in a mushrooming fireball.

"I'm in!" Karns radioed, pitching the F-14 to the left and rolling up into a high yo-yo. "Good shot!" He looked down just in time to see the cockpit of the Foxbat fly out of the fireball. No wings, no tail—just the cockpit. The canopy separated and the pilot ejected a second later, falling out of sight when his parachute failed to open.

"Come on, lock it up," Karns said, pulling through the

top of his climb. He looked into the late afternoon sun, losing the MiG in the glare. "Sonuvabitch!"

"Skipper!" the section leader, who was calling the fight, radioed frantically. "The gomer reversed, coming inside your five o'clock."

"Okay," Karns groaned, twisting the F-14 through a displacement roll. "I've lost him!"

"Break hard starboard!" Karns's wingman called. "I can't get a shot into the sun!"

"He's firing!" the section leader yelled to the CO. "Get on him, Two!"

Karns, breaking right and up into the vertical, felt the thudding impact of the MiG's twin 23mm cannons. Red streaks flashed by the canopy as tracer rounds worked across the left wing, blasting access plates off the fighter. Karns whipped the stick over, snapping the Tomcat through three tight rolls, then unloaded the F-14, going for separation.

The MiG, flown with great expertise and wild abandon, pulled in behind Karns, leaving Diamond Two a difficult shot. If the missile missed the Foxbat, highly possible in combat, it might track to the Tomcat.

"Doug! Break, break!" the section leader radioed, flipping his armament switch to guns. "Three is engaged—gonna drag his ass off."

"Bring it on!" Karns groaned, jerking the accelerating Tomcat into a 6½-g, neck-wrenching turn.

The section leader, turning inside the third MiG, placed the pipper slightly ahead of the Foxbat and squeezed the trigger gently. The Vulcan cannon growled, pouring more than 100 shells a second into the Russian fighter. The pilot released the trigger a split second, then squeezed it again, causing the Tomcat to vibrate. He watched, fascinated, as the M-61 multibarrel cannon, spewing molten lead, knocked large pieces off the stricken MiG.

"Fox Two!" Karns's wingman shouted, punching off another Sidewinder. The missile tucked down, made a correction, and plowed into the MiG's right wing a millisecond after the pilot ejected.

The section leader, caught off guard, slammed his stick hard over in an attempt to miss the explosion and debris. Both F-14 crew members felt the thump when they collided with the MiG pilot's body.

"Good shot!" Karns said, elated. He scanned the milky sky quickly then called the Hawkeye. "Phoenix," Karns sucked pure oxygen, "Diamond flight with three splashes. Any more bandits?"

The Hawkeye controller, busy vectoring another flight of Tomcats, completed his radio call and acknowledged Karns. "Negative, Diamond One Zero Three." The controller checked his radarscope, leaving the mike keyed. "Nothing in your sector at this time. RTB for recycle. Rattler and Snake flights are inbound—comin' up your port side, ten o'clock high."

"Roger," Karns responded, looking for his executive officer in Snake One. He caught a glint of sunlight off a canopy as the XO rocked his wings. "I have a tally."

"Skipper," Karns's RIO said over the intercom, "check fuel."

Karns glanced at the fuel gauge, surprised by the amount the thirsty Tomcat had consumed during the combat engagement. He was down to 5,900 pounds of fuel—enough to reach the carrier if he conserved the precious fluid.

"Diamonds, let's go max conserve and join up," Karns ordered, easing back the twin throttles. "Call fuel states."

The other three pilots acknowledged, giving their respective fuel loads, as Karns slowed the Tomcat. As the F-14 decelerated through 0.72 Mach, Karns felt a strange sensation. Something was definitely wrong. The Tomcat wobbled unsteadily.

"Skipper, we've got a control problem." Karns glanced back over his right shoulder, swearing to himself. The wings, swept back to the full aft position, had not reprogrammed forward. Karns tried the wing-sweep button, emergency handle, and circuit breakers. Nothing worked.

"Diamond Two," Karns radioed, reviewing his pocket checklist, "come aboard and check me over. My wings are frozen in the full aft position."

"Roger, movin' up."

Karns waited, cursing his luck, while his wingman rendezvoused on the starboard side. Karns knew he could not land aboard the carrier with full wing sweep; the engagement speed would be close to 200 miles an hour. It was prohibited, even during a time of war.

If the emergency developed during Blue Water operations—in the middle of an ocean—the pilot and RIO would have to fly by the carrier and make a controlled ejection. In this case, Karns prepared to divert to Key West Naval Air Station, the closest field with the arresting equipment he needed.

The Diamondback CO watched his wingman's Tomcat slide up to his wounded fighter. He could see the rivets, the oil streaks, and the pilot's eyes. Karns waited patiently while his wingman slid under the Tomcat, appearing on the other side.

"Okay, skipper," the pilot radioed, knowing they had only one option, "we're going to have to go to Key Worst."

"Yeah," Karns replied calmly. "What does it look like?"

"You've got hydraulic fluid pouring down the port side of the aircraft." The wingman moved in closer. "Skipper, you took some rounds. Looks like the area around the wing sweep actuator is shot up."

SAN JULIAN

Gennadi Levchenko checked on the bomber assembly and walked into the communications center.

"Comrade director," the chief communications officer

said in a hesitant voice, "Castro has attacked an American aircraft carrier."

Levchenko's thick neck muscles bulged, distorting his craggy face. "That goddamned idiot!" Levchenko raged savagely. "When?"

"Earlier today, comrade dir—"

"And you just heard about it?" Levchenko yanked a cigarette pack from his pocket. He had a momentary thought that the communications chief might be the double agent. The officer had been off duty at the time the guard had been attacked. "What the hell is wrong here? Why didn't Moscow contact us?"

The officer recoiled, feeling the sting of Levchenko's wrath. "I don't know, comrade director."

"Get KGB operations on the scrambler, NOW!"

Levchenko slumped into the seat next to the Moscow lines, discouraged and angry. His perilous situation had degenerated even further. "Moscow is going to have to stop Castro," Levchenko said to himself as the communications specialist nervously contacted KGB headquarters.

Steve Wickham, hearing his stomach growl, crawled to the small opening in the crumbling foundation. He peered out cautiously, noting the long shadows of late afternoon, then he slid around to the other side, taking in the hangars and flight line area.

The agent was surprised by the amount of activity on the air base. He counted eleven antiaircraft guns and four tanks, along with hundreds of soldiers digging in around the outer boundaries of the field.

He rolled over and leaned against the cool cement support. He felt exhausted but forced himself to stay alert. His only chance for survival was to attempt a daring escape during the early morning hours.

CHAPTER TWENTY-TWO

THE WHITE HOUSE

The Joint Chiefs of Staff, secretary of defense, and director of the CIA stood when the president entered the room, followed by the vice president, secretary of state, and national security adviser.

"Be seated, gentlemen," Jarrett said somberly, then sat down between Bernard Kerchner and the chairman of the Joint Chiefs of Staff. The president adjusted his glasses before addressing the assemblage. "As you know, the skipper of the *Wasp* has confirmed sixty-one casualties, with four sailors and one marine missing.

"We are embarking on an ominous, challenging struggle with an unpredictable foe—an adversary who will not hesitate to use every weapon available to him, as we have tragically witnessed. You have read the CIA reports and seen the afternoon news. Fidel Castro, for whatever reason, has turned into an Hispanic Ayatollah Khomeini. Secretary Kerchner has just received a report confirming that the submarine was sunk. The flotsam, along with the bodies that surfaced, indicate clearly that the submarine was operated by the Cubans."

Jarrett removed his glasses. "I want to be perfectly clear in regard to my position. I will not tolerate a long, protracted operation. We have to ensure that we use the correct weapons, and enough of them, to accomplish the objective in one or two strikes. The stakes are high and we cannot afford any tactical blunders, or we could find ourselves defending our southern shores."

Jarrett looked around the table, reading the response, before continuing. "We have telegraphed our intentions to Castro, as you well know, so our strike will have to be a maximum effort. I will contact President Ignatyev minutes before the first strike aircraft reach their targets. The Soviets will be on notice not to interfere on behalf of their nationals. If they do become involved, which is a grave possibility, we will not hesitate to destroy them."

The president swallowed a sip of water, glancing around the polished mahogany table. "We will go on global alert five minutes before our first attack aircraft reach Cuban soil." Jarrett replaced his glasses. "Are there any questions, gentlemen?"

The national security adviser cleared his throat. "Mister President, what is your feeling about the B-2? Do you intend to destroy the aircraft, or retrieve it?"

"Brian," the president began slowly, catching the disdainful look on the vice president's face, "we are about to engage Cuba militarily. At this point, we don't have the luxury of recovering the B-2 intact."

The secretary of defense knew, as did the other men in the room, that Brian Gaines had been a disappointment as the national security adviser. Kerchner faced the red-headed attorney. "The airfield—San Julian—where the B-2 is concealed, will be heavily bombed, so that may solve the problem for us."

Jarrett opened his briefing folder, prompting the group to join him. "Bernie," the president said, turning to his defense secretary, "let's look at the entire operation."

"Yes, sir," Kerchner replied, standing to walk to a map of Cuba and the Gulf of Mexico. He picked up an expandable metal pointer. "We intend to use three carriers—*Kitty Hawk*, *America*, and *Abraham Lincoln*, with the *Lexington* as a spare deck—supplemented by eighteen B-1Bs and three attack submarines."

Kerchner pointed to the highly detailed planning chart. "*Kitty Hawk* and her battle group," he made a small circle with the tipped pointer, "will be located here—about one hundred forty miles northwest of San Julian. Her group will be solely responsible for San Julian and any surface vessels in the vicinity. They will also suppress radar and GCI sites, then provide close air support when the Marines hit the beach."

The secretary of state caught Kerchner's attention. "Yes, Sam."

"At what point will the Marines go ashore?"

Kerchner paused a moment, glancing at the marine commandant. "We will make that decision after the first air strike. We may have to go back in and soften up the area, depending on what kind of resistance Castro puts up. At any rate, Sam, the Marines will have plenty of close air support when they take the beach."

Gardner, chewing on his unlighted pipe, acknowledged the explanation silently.

"Satellite photos," Kerchner continued, "indicate that a number of SAM sites have been installed around San Julian, along with a variety of triple A guns. They also have a number of ZSU-X motorized antiaircraft guns, so we can anticipate heavy fire from around San Julian."

Kerchner looked back at the chart. "*America* will be here, eighty miles northeast of Havana. Her mission is to attack radar and GCI sites, then clobber the military airfields around Havana, including Mariel, Playa Baracoa, Ciudad Libertad, San Pedro, San Antonio de Los Banos, Managua, and San Jose de Las Lajas. The carrier will also supply air defense for *Kitty Hawk*, the tanker aircraft, and the Hawkeyes.''

Kerchner moved the pointer over to a circle by the Great Bahama Bank. ''*Lincoln* will be one hundred ten miles southeast of Andros Island . . . right here.'' The defense secretary tapped the map, then looked at the president. ''Her responsibility will be to bomb Santa Clara airfield and provide air cover for the Marine KC-130 cargo planes going into Guantanamo Bay—to extract the Marines marooned there.''

Jarrett nodded his approval and wrote a lengthy note on his folder.

''We have three attack submarines,'' Kerchner continued, facing the president, ''*Albuquerque, Jacksonville*, and *Baton Rouge*, operating with the carrier battle groups . . . one to a ship. Two of the submarines will have designated shore targets—military barracks, supply depots, and naval ports, including any ships in port. They will use conventional Tomahawk cruise missiles.''

Kerchner stopped when he saw the president indicate that he had a question. ''Yes, sir.''

''Bernie, how comfortable are we with one submarine to protect each carrier? I mean, we can't afford another tragedy, and possibly lose a carrier.''

Kerchner inhaled deeply. ''Mister President, we—the Joint Chiefs and I—feel comfortable with one submarine each, since Cuba has lost one third of her submarine force. As you mentioned, two ASW helicopters confirmed surface debris, including bodies, from the submarine that torpedoed *Wasp*.''

''What about the suspected submarines,'' Jarrett asked, looking at the chief of naval operations, then back to Kerchner, ''that are operating with the Soviet aircraft carrier? Where is the carrier—the Russian one?''

Kerchner moved the end of the pointer to a spot thirty miles south of the western tip of Cuba. ''The *Novorossiysk* has moved to a position between the two Soviet task forces. Mister President,'' Kerchner continued confidently, ''we have doubled our ASW coverage, and I feel comfortable with our protection.''

"I want to be absolutely certain, Bernie," Jarrett replied, grim faced. "I want overkill built into everything we do from now on." Jarrett paused for emphasis. "Can we get two more submarines into place before morning?"

Kerchner paused, contemplating the logistics. "We can add one submarine, but not two, by early morning. Sir, we don't have the time, unless we delay the operation."

"No, we can't afford to delay our strike," the president said, pleased with the additional submarine coverage. "Let's get the other attack submarine on station as quickly as possible."

"Yes, sir," the defense secretary responded, facing the chief of naval operations (CNO). "Admiral, will you take care of that and rejoin us?"

"Yes, Mister Secretary."

Kerchner waited until the CNO shut the door before he resumed the briefing. "Our B-1Bs will stage out of Barksdale," Kerchner said, pointing out their route of flight across the Gulf of Mexico, "flying high over the Yucatan Peninsula, then drop down south of Cuba. They'll split into three groups and make supersonic, low-level penetrations—one group going to San Julian and the other two flights hitting military installations in the Havana area."

Kerchner turned to face the president. "We believe it's best if the bombers approach from the south, drop their ordnance, and depart straight ahead—no turning while coming off the targets."

Kirk Truesdell indicated that he had a question. "Mister Vice President?" Kerchner asked, compressing his pointer.

"Bernie, I have a couple of questions in regard to coordination. First, it appears to me as if we're going to have a lot of aircraft converging over the same targets at the same time, not to mention the Cuban fighters."

Truesdell looked at his briefing folder, tapping his pen lightly on the paper. "Another thought I had—a concern actually—what kind of protection will the B-1s have going into the target?"

Kerchner waited to answer when he saw the CNO step back into the room.

"The *Birmingham* will be in the Gulf," the admiral reported, sitting down, "by oh-four-hundred, Mister President."

"Very well, admiral," Jarrett responded. "Please continue, Bernie."

"The B-1 strike force, fourteen aircraft, will follow the initial carrier-based strikes by four minutes. We'll have two B-1 spares airborne and two on alert at Barksdale."

Kerchner drew a breath. "The skies over Cuba, especially the Havana area, will be saturated with aircraft. All the strike aircraft have precise routes of ingress and egress, but we have no way of telling how many enemy aircraft will be airborne."

"I understand that," Truesdell responded, shifting uncomfortably in his seat. "But it sure looks like a gaggle ripe for disaster."

Kerchner caught two of the Joint Chiefs bristle openly, working hard to contain their comments.

"Sir," the defense secretary said, "our crews are highly qualified and extremely well trained. I have every confidence in our military leadership and their planning—and no doubt about the outcome of this mission."

Truesdell showed a tinge of embarrassment. "I apologize, Bernie. I didn't mean to question anyone's competency. It just appears as if the skies over Cuba are going to be very crowded."

"No offense taken, sir," Kerchner responded, glancing at the Joint Chiefs. "And you're right, we will have a large number of aircraft in and off the targets in a compressed period of time. We want to hit Castro hard and be gone in seconds.

"The B-1s," Kerchner continued, "will be escorted to and from the targets by their own fighters. The F-15s and -16s will tank over the Gulf—from two KC-10s—and fly cover all the way in and out, recovering at Homestead Air Force Base."

Truesdell nodded his understanding.

"Any questions, gentlemen?" Kerchner asked, returning to his seat.

The secretary of state turned to the president. "Sir, I would like one clarification, concerning logistics."

"Certainly, Sam," Jarrett responded, closing his briefing folder.

"When are you leaving for 'kneecap'?" Gardner asked, referring to the National Emergency Airborne Command Post (NEACP). Jarrett and the secretary of defense had agreed that it would be best to have the president airborne, ready for any contingency.

The president leaned back, reopened his folder, then looked at Kerchner. "Bernie, let's cover our command, control, and communications plans."

"Yes, sir," Kerchner replied, turning to the "c-cubed" page in his folder. "The president will board the crown helo at five in the morning and be airborne in kneecap at five-thirty. The vice president will leave after this meeting for Raven Rock. He will be in the communications loop at Site R at five-fifteen in the morning."

Kerchner looked at the secretary of state. "Sam, you'll be driven to Mount Weather later this evening. I'll remain here, along with the Joint Chiefs. However, we'll have another kneecap standing by at Andrews, if needed."

The discussion was over. "Well, gentlemen," the president said in a firm tone, "I must excuse myself." Jarrett stood, remaining in place until the men followed a second later.

"Before I leave," the president said as he grasped his briefing folder, "I want to express my appreciation for all your fine work. America has a long and proud history of being the de facto leader of the free world. Now, we have the responsibility to defend our nation and people. We must face a fundamental fact. To remain a free nation, we may have to sacrifice more lives in order to preserve our future, and the future of our children."

Jarrett walked out of the room as the remaining men looked at each other, concern etched on their faces.

DIAMOND 103

Commander Doug Karns slowed the battered Tomcat in preparation for a controllability check. He had sent the second section of F-14s back to *Kitty Hawk*. He checked the horizon, then watched the airspeed indicator—215 . . . 210 . . . 205 . . . The F-14's right wing dropped sharply.

"Oh, shit!" Karns said over the intercom, slamming the throttles into afterburner. The Tomcat accelerated quickly through 230 knots as he leveled the wings again. "On speed is two-oh-five."

Karns's new radar intercept officer, Lt. (jg) Dean "Scurvy" Ricketts, keyed his intercom. "Skipper, you want to dump some gas—lighten us up a tad?"

"I'm in the process," Karns answered, flipping the fuel dump switch. Jet fuel streamed back from the fighter as Karns switched from approach control to Key West tower. "Navy Key West tower, Diamond One Oh Three with you on a wide, modified right base."

"Roger, Diamond One Zero Three," the tower chief replied, apprised of the inbound emergency aircraft. "Cleared straight in, runway seven, wind one-one-zero at twelve. We have the equipment standing by."

"Thanks," Karns radioed, then talked to his wingman. "Two, go ahead and land, in case I crater the runway."

"Copy, skipper," the pilot responded, lowering his flaps and landing gear.

"Key tower," Karns called, rolling into a shallow turn, "Diamond Two is going to land first."

The tower controller looked down at the fire trucks, then keyed his radio. "Diamond Two cleared to land. Roll out to the end of the runway."

The wingman clicked his mike twice as he slowed the Tomcat to his on-speed angle of attack.

Karns completed two wide 360-degree turns, streaming white vapor trails of jet fuel, as he briefed his radar intercept officer. "Scurve, if we don't grab the wire, I'll go burner and we'll come around for another crack at it."

"Ah . . . skipper," Ricketts ventured, "think we should stop dump?"

"Oh, shit," Karns replied, snapping off the fuel dump switch. He had 1,400 pounds left—enough for two passes. "Scurve, you want to go ahead and jump out? I'm having a hell of a day."

"Naw," Ricketts responded, looking down at the ocean, "I didn't bring my bathing suit."

Karns watched the other Tomcat land, roll out, and turn off at the end of the runway. He lined up with the center line, dropped the gear, and lowered the tailhook. The squadron commander flew a shallow, low approach at 210 knots, then brought the throttles to idle and flared the F-14 gently over the runway threshold.

The fighter landed on the numbers, but the hook slammed into the pavement and bounced over the wire. Karns shoved the throttles into afterburner, feeling the Tomcat vibrate. The master caution light flashed on, but Karns could not look down for the cause. His feet danced on the rudder pedals, correcting the F-14's path down the runway.

He rotated the speeding jet and shot a quick glance at the annunciator panel. "Sonuvabitch!" Karns swore over the intercom, seeing that the combined hydraulics had dropped to zero. "Scurve, we're in deep shit."

"What now, coach?" Ricketts asked in an unsteady voice. The ejection option was looking better.

"Diamond One Zero Three," the tower controller radioed urgently, "looks like you blew one of your main mounts. Appears to be rubber on the runway."

"Copy," Karns replied, wrestling with the sluggish

fighter. "We're coming around for a final pass—we'll have to keep it on the ground this time."

Karns keyed his intercom as the tower acknowledged the radio transmission. "Scurve, we're outta gas and hydraulic fluid. If we miss the wire, I'll try to keep us on the runway."

"You've got my vote," Ricketts responded, cinching his straps as tight as they would go.

Karns, watching the sun sink below the horizon, flew an extended downwind and turned final. "If we go off the runway, or it looks like we're gonna take out any obstacles, I'll call for ejection."

"I'm ready," Ricketts replied, taking the ink pens out of the arm pocket of his flight suit. He unstrapped his knee board and stowed it on the side console, then placed his sunglasses in his right breast pocket. The young officer said a silent prayer as the end of the runway flashed under the stricken Tomcat.

Karns pulled the power to idle, touched down hard at 190 knots, sensed the tailhook skip, then fought the rudders to keep the F-14 on the runway.

"Uh, oh!" Karns exclaimed when the left main mount, minus the tire, collapsed. The Tomcat's left wing dug into the pavement, trailing a shower of sparks and metal.

Karns fought to keep the big Grumman on the runway, then realized they were headed for a fire truck that was backing away at full throttle.

"Eject! Eject!" Karns shouted as he pulled the alternate ejection handle between his legs.

Both men rocketed out of the speeding Tomcat, arcing through the air. Their chutes opened a split second before the F-14 slashed by the fire truck, exploded in a blinding flash, then tumbled across the field.

CHAPTER TWENTY-THREE

SAN JULIAN

The air base had been placed under total blackout conditions, as had all of Cuba. President Castro had issued a warning over national radio. Simply stated, any light showing after dark would be shot out by the army.

The perimeter of San Julian was bustling with activity as additional weapons were placed in strategic locations. Four squads of Cuban soldiers rushed from site to site, camou-flaging the armament.

Portable surface-to-air (SAM) missiles ringed the air base, along with radar-controlled 57mm and 85mm antiaircraft guns. By late evening, twenty-three motorized ZSU-X anti-aircraft weapons had joined the original twelve ZSU-Xs that had been sent to San Julian earlier. The assembled firepower represented a major obstacle to the American pilots.

Seven MiG-23s, eight MiG-25 Foxbats, and twelve MiG-29 Fulcrums had been fueled and loaded with ordnance in preparation for the expected American assault. The fighters were lined up on the runway and taxiway, ready to be airborne in five minutes.

The first eight aircraft on the runway, six Fulcrums and two MiG-25s, were manned. The rest of the pilots, including three Russian instructors, waited in the ready tent erected hastily next to their fighters.

Gennadi Levchenko sat on the small bunk in the cramped quarters behind his office. The wait for instructions from Moscow was taking its toll on the KGB director.

Levchenko leaned over his footlocker, grabbed the neck of a rum bottle, and poured a liberal amount of the amber fluid into his coffee mug. He tossed down the room-temperature libation, grimaced, and reached into his pocket for a cigarette. His hand froze when the chief communications officer rapped on the edge of his open door.

"Comrade director," the man said cautiously, "I have an urgent message for you."

"Moscow called?" Levchenko asked impatiently. "What is it?"

The communications officer swallowed. "Raul Castro is en route to our base, comrade dir—"

"Goddamnit!" Levchenko bellowed, leaping up. "Get Moscow on the line! I want answers!"

The flustered officer, exhausted from lack of sleep and the mounting tension, hurried out of the small office and ran toward the communications center.

Levchenko hastily slipped on his boots and marched into the hangar. He surveyed the B-2, noting it was in the final stages of reassembly. The fuselage was still open, exposing the complex array of electronic equipment, but the few remaining access panels were being replaced.

Levchenko, kicking a loose hose out of his way, walked over to the senior airframe technician. The scowl on the director's face reflected his foul mood. "When will the Stealth be ready to fly?"

The aircraft engineer, matching Levchenko's serious look, calculated quickly how much longer it would take to restore the bomber to flying condition. "Two and a half—possibly three hours at the most, comrade director."

Levchenko looked at his watch, thoroughly disgruntled with the change of events. "It damned sure better be," Levchenko growled, then spun around and headed for the communications center.

The Soviet airframe technician, upset by Levchenko's rebuke, turned around and barked orders to his crew. Intimidated and uneasy, the men went back to work at an increased pace.

Levchenko was about to enter the communications room when the harried comm officer rushed out: "Comrade director, Moscow is on the line," he gushed, "and Castro's helicopter just landed at base operations."

"Sonuvabitch!" Levchenko yelped, brushing the officer out of his way. He stormed into the room and glanced at the sergeant manning the main console.

The portly young man, showing his anxiety, looked toward Levchenko. "Castro is on his way over, comrade director."

Levchenko ignored him and yanked up the receiver next to the blinking yellow light. "Levchenko!"

The KGB director was paralyzed momentarily when he heard the voice on the discreet phone. He sat down, fumbled for a cigarette, snapped open his lighter, and listened to the chief of the KGB. Not a subordinate, division chief, or operations director. THE director of Komitet Gosudarstvennoi Bezopasnosti.

Levchenko forgot about the cigarette. "Da, comrade director." He listened intently to Vladimir Golodnikov, motioning for the communications officer to close the door, then scribbled a note to the surprised man.

"Da, I understand, comrade director," Levchenko said as the comm officer read the scrawl and rushed out to find Obukhov.

"Da, comrade director," Levchenko continued, surprised by the order he had been given. "I will keep you informed, comrade director.'' Levchenko listened to the final statement, then said good-bye. ''*Do svidanya*, comrade director.''

KEY WEST NAVAL AIR STATION

Commander Doug Karns taxied his ''borrowed'' F-14D onto the runway and swung into position for takeoff. He had been cleared to hold in position until the A-6F Intruder that had landed cleared the runway.

The commanding officer of the Diamondbacks, along with his radar intercept officer, had received a thorough physical after their narrow escape. They were in excellent condition, except for strained muscles and contusions, and had been pronounced fit for flight duty.

Karns had made arrangements to have his wingman and RIO flown to the *Kitty Hawk*. He checked with the carrier air boss for an overhead time, then crawled into Diamond 107 and taxied to the duty runway.

''You ready, Scurve?''

Ricketts thought of an appropriate answer but decided not to utter the obscene expression to his CO. Instead, he voiced what he really felt. ''A triple martini would help.''

Karns grinned, keying his radio when the Intruder cleared the duty runway. ''Key tower, Diamond One Oh Seven, ready to roll.''

''Diamond One Zero Seven, wind one-zero-zero at eight, cleared for takeoff.''

Karns rechecked his flight controls, navigation and anti-collision lights, and engine instruments. He released the brakes, shoved the throttles into afterburner, then felt the powerful g forces push his helmet back against the headrest. ''Diamond One Oh Seven on the roll.''

The Tomcat accelerated down the 10,000-foot runway, after-burners lighting the night, then rotated smoothly and headed for the *Kitty Hawk*.

SAN JULIAN

Levchenko glanced at the Stealth bomber, then saw Obukhov rushing across the hangar. Both men arrived at Levchenko's office at the same time.

"We have more problems . . . , shit," Levchenko snarled, slamming the door. "Raul Castro is here."

"I was informed," Obukhov responded, sitting down on the hard metal bench.

Levchenko sat down at his desk and wearily removed his glasses. "I just had a conversation with our stubborn director—THE man."

Obukhov sensed trouble. The KGB chief's reputation for recalcitrance was known widely throughout the organization.

"He ordered us to cooperate with Castro," Levchenko sighed heavily. "They are backing off . . . washing their hands of the operation now that we have the goddamned airplane."

Obukhov, clearly uncomfortable, fidgeted for a moment. "I'm not sure I understand, comrade director."

"Damnit!" Levchenko snapped, showing his growing frustration. "The situation is out of control. Golodnikov knows the operation has collapsed. They can't contain or control Castro, and they have turned their backs on the operation . . . and us. I don't know what the hell is going on, but the Kremlin is not to be involved further. Golodnikov inferred that I am a man without a country—persona non grata in Moscow."

Levchenko yanked out a cigarette, lighted it, and inhaled deeply. "We are out of the picture. The Stealth belongs to Castro, as of now."

Both men sat in dumbfounded silence. So many months of intense work, training, and planning had been erased in one split second.

Levchenko started to speak, then noticed a commotion in the hangar. He stood, then walked to the door and opened it. "He's here," Levchenko said in a resigned voice. "I will need your assistance, Natanoly Vietlevich."

"You have it, comrade director."

Levchenko and Obukhov silently observed Raul Castro and his small procession enter the hangar, stop for a moment to take in the secret bomber, then walk slowly toward the work spaces and office.

Levchenko, watching Raul Castro, wondered about Fidel Castro's motivation. The dictator had always harbored a grudge against the Soviet Union for excluding him during the 1961 missile crisis—the October crisis in Cuban history. Stifling his rage and looking pleasant, Levchenko walked toward the commander of the Cuban army and extended his hand.

Raul Castro gave Levchenko an obligatory handshake. He was imposing as he stared at Levchenko, eyes focused, riveting. Beads of sweat glistened on his forehead and sideburns. His olive green utility uniform was damp with perspiration. "You do not have the bomber ready to fly," Castro accused.

"Comrade general," Levchenko replied uncomfortably, "the bomber will be ready to fly in three hours. The men are working as fast as they can."

Raul Castro remained silent a moment before he leaned into Levchenko's face. "I will be back in three hours—have it ready!"

Levchenko flinched, feeling the warm spittle hit his cheek. "Yes, comrade general."

USS *KITTY HAWK* (CV-63)

Sparks flew from the tailhook of Diamond 107 as Comdr. Doug Karns screeched to a halt in the number three arresting cable. The CO let the Tomcat roll back a few feet, dropped the wire, raised the tailhook, and followed the lighted wands held aloft by the flight deck petty officer. The pitch-black deck was alive with ordnance handlers and fueling crews.

Kitty Hawk began slowing as the plane guard helicopter, a Kaman SH-2F Seasprite, entered a hover over the angle deck, then settled to a gentle landing. Two F-14Ds sat on the forward catapults, manned and ready to launch at a moment's notice.

Seventy-five miles ahead of *Kitty Hawk*, off the port quarter, two Diamondback Tomcats flew barrier air combat patrol. They would refuel one more time from two KA-6D Intruders before being relieved by two F-14Ds from the Black Aces of VF-41.

On board *Kitty Hawk*, in flag plot, the carrier air wing commander had received the tactical air operations order. The battle plans had been approved by the Joint Chiefs of Staff before being forwarded to the three carrier groups. The operations order tasked the three air wings with attack and combat air patrol missions, along with a war-at-sea contingency.

SAN JULIAN

Gennadi Levchenko, unshaven and feeling the effects of fatigue, supervised the final assembly of the Stealth bomber. He had Simmons, who had become even more withdrawn, in the cockpit checking the avionics and weapons systems.

Levchenko had watched the time closely, expecting the Cuban general to return at the end of three hours. He observed the tired technicians reconnect the last avionics system and replace the last access panel, then went into the lavatory and washed his face with cold water. He was drying his neck vigorously when Natanoly Obukhov rushed in.

"Comrade director," Obukhov said breathlessly, "Raul Castro called. He wants an engine run-up on the Stealth, and then have it towed to the flight line."

Levchenko looked at his assistant through tired, bloodshot eyes. "What are you waiting for? It's his airplane now . . . we're out of the picture."

"Da, comrade director," Obukhov replied respectfully, turning to leave. "I will take care of everything."

Levchenko finished drying his face and flung the towel into a corner hamper. He was about to lie down when the sergeant from the communications center appeared at the door.

"Comrade director, you have an urgent call from Moscow!"

Steve Wickham, hearing the loud sound of jet engines being started, inched next to the opening in the foundation. The base was completely blacked out except for a group of men working with flashlights.

He studied the soldiers, unsure of what they were trying to accomplish. The men worked rapidly, moving rocks and fence posts. Wickham continued to observe the group until they had passed his position. Three minutes later the jet engines reached a howling crescendo, then throttled down and shut off. Wickham, having forgotten his hunger pangs, waited impatiently for an opportunity to escape from his hiding place.

Finally, after the soldiers had completed their task, Wickham grabbed the assault rifle and ventured out of the small hole. He remained on his stomach and looked cautiously around the immediate area. The bright, luminous moon would spotlight any dark object and make his escape more dangerous.

Wickham listened intently for any sign of soldiers, then crawled to the corner of the building. He edged around the side and froze when he saw the B-2. Realizing what the soldiers had been doing, he watched the bomber as it was towed down the cleared path. Then he crawled back to the opening in the foundation and returned to his place of concealment. If they were going to fly the B-2 out of Cuba, Wickham reasoned, the roar during takeoff would help cover his escape.

Gennadi Levchenko replaced the phone receiver and sat quietly at the communications console. He shook his head and turned to the watch officer. "Get Talavokine up," Levchenko ordered, "and have General Brotskharnov report to me immediately."

"Da, comrade director," the comm chief replied, motioning to the sergeant. "Wake Leytenant Talavokine." The stocky young man hurried out the door as the officer called base operations.

"Have them report to my office," Levchenko said, then stood and walked out the door. Feeling mixed emotions, he entered his office and called his deputy.

"Natanoly Vitelevich," Levchenko said in an even voice, "come to my office."

Starshiy Leytenant Talavokine, groggy and disheveled, walked into the office as Levchenko completed his call.

"Sit down, Talavokine."

"Da, comrade director," the security chief responded, then rubbed his swollen eyes and tucked his shirttail into his trousers.

Levchenko pulled out the bottom drawer of his desk and propped his feet on the compartment as he noticed Obukhov at the door. He motioned him in. "Headquarters," Levchenko said as Obukhov sat down, "has decreed a change in plans in regard to the bomber."

Talavokine and Obukhov glanced at each other with apprehension, but remained silent.

"General Brotskharnov is on his way over," Levchenko continued, "so I'll wait until he gets here to brief you." Levchenko stood, then walked into his cramped quarters and placed a fresh pack of cigarettes in his shirt pocket.

General Petr V. Brotskharnov, irritation written on his face, walked through the door as Levchenko reentered his office.

"Have a seat, general," Levchenko said as he returned to his desk. He lighted a cigarette and propped his feet on the drawer again. "We have received new orders, general."

Brotskharnov looked puzzled. "And? . . ."

"We—more to the point—you, general, are going to be

responsible for flying the bomber out of Cuba.''

The three men looked at Levchenko with equal amazement. Brotskharnov leaned forward. "What am I—"

"We have much to accomplish," Levchenko interrupted, "in a short span of time. I'm going to explain the situation, then we'll discuss particulars.

"First," Levchenko continued, "this change of plans originated at the highest level of KGB and word is being sent to Fidel Castro as we speak. Castro is screaming about getting the bomber off his island immediately. He and Raul are convinced that the Americans are going to invade Cuba to get the Stealth bomber back, so Moscow has decided to fly it to the Soviet Union."

Levchenko looked directly at Talavokine. "Also, our director is outraged over the breach of security here—the pictures that were relayed to the Americans."

Talavokine nodded his head.

"You, Leytenant Talavokine," Levchenko said in his menacing voice, "are going to sequester every single person involved in this project until I give you further orders."

Talavokine swallowed, brushing back his hair. "Da, comrade director."

"You will gather everyone in the middle of the hangar—everyone—including my deputy, until I give you the word."

Obukhov turned pale.

"Now," Levchenko continued, "I will explain our orders. General Brotskharnov, along with the American pilot and the defector—Simmons—are going to fly the bomber to Russia."

Talavokine and Obukhov shot a glance at Brotskharnov. The self-styled commanding officer of what remained of Soviet air forces in Cuba appeared to be dazed.

"General," Levchenko said slowly and clearly, "your orders are to fly straight west over Mexico and the Pacific Ocean to a point twelve hundred miles east of Hawaii. From there," Levchenko said, exhaling, "you will turn northwest and land at Yelizovo on Kamchatka Peninsula."

Levchenko leaned back and looked at Talavokine. "Get Simmons in here, then take four guards and bring the pilot to my office."

"Da, comrade director."

As Talavokine hurried out the door, Levchenko turned to Brotskharnov. "You will take off as soon as the bomber is fueled."

The air force commander, trying to assimilate the drastic change in plans, appeared perplexed. "I do not have any idea how many miles it is to our destination. We will be running a very high risk that—"

"General," Levchenko interrupted tersely, "the logistics have been worked out in Moscow. These orders were communicated to me by the director of the KGB. You will have approximately one hour of fuel left when you reach the Yelizovo airfield."

Brotskharnov started to speak but fell silent when Talavokine and the Cuban guards rushed by the door.

"Moscow," Levchenko continued, "wants you airborne as quickly as possible to take advantage of the dark. You will not be exposed to daylight until you are northeast of the Hawaiian Islands. They are confident that you will not be detected."

Brotskharnov inhaled deeply, then let the air out. "What are they thinking about in Moscow? This is crazy—if we get caught, it will jeopardize all the gains we have made."

"Goddamnit!" Levchenko exploded. "I'm not going to argue with you. The orders originated from the director of the KGB. You either comply, or contact Golodnikov."

Brotskharnov sat mute.

The KGB officer turned to Larry Simmons when he appeared at the door. "Come in and have a seat, Comrade Simmons."

Brotskharnov shook his head. "We're digging ourselves a deeper hole, comrade director."

"We," Levchenko shot back, "do not question our orders."

CHAPTER TWENTY-FOUR

SAN JULIAN

Steve Wickham peeked out from the opening in the foundation of the administration building. The agent had been surprised by the escalating activity around the perimeter of the air base. The Cubans were amassing a tremendous amount of antiaircraft weapons.

Wickham leaned back and closed his eyes. The longer he had to wait, the more fatigued he would become. His best chance for escape was now. Besides, he reasoned, if an air strike was scheduled, San Julian would be pulverized.

The sound of approaching vehicles snapped Wickham back to the present. He watched a GAZ field car, followed by two motorized antiaircraft guns, approach the building from the path the B-2 had traveled. He suddenly realized that he would have to do something very unorthodox if he were to have any chance for survival. He would also have to hurry if he was going to make the rendezvous with the OV-10.

Wickham slid the assault rifle behind him and quietly eased out from under his hiding place. The agent stood, quickly brushed himself off, and walked boldly toward the GAZ.

• • •

Chuck Matthews, accompanied by Talavokine and the Cuban guards, walked unsteadily into Levchenko's office. He had been drifting in and out of sleep before Talavokine marched into the cell. The pilot's hands, bound securely behind him, had become painfully swollen.

"Sit down," the KGB director ordered brusquely. "You are going to fly your bomber again . . . to the Soviet Union."

Matthews, glancing at Simmons and the Soviet general, was stupefied. He noted the look of surprise on Simmons's face. Matthews was speechless, confronted by this unexpected turn of events.

"Take him to the van," Levchenko ordered as he turned his attention to Brotskharnov. "We'll be there in a minute."

Matthews had a premonition of impending disaster as he walked out of the office and started across the hangar. Talavokine walked next to him as they climbed the stairs and went out the entrance. Matthews stepped into the dark brown van, still absolutely silent. His mind searched for a clue to his fate. Listening to the guards converse in their native language, he contemplated his possible options.

Two minutes later, Levchenko, accompanied by Brotskharnov and Simmons, hurried out of the hangar and rushed to the van. Three soldiers boarded the vehicle as the fourth Cuban slid behind the steering wheel.

Steve Wickham stepped in front of the GAZ field car and raised his right arm. The Cuban driver mashed the brake pedal as Wickham hurried to the vehicle.

The GAZ shuddered to a halt at the same instant that Wickham recognized a Soviet officer in the passenger seat. The agent, thinking rapidly, approached the door and spoke to the officer in fluent Russian.

"Kapitan, I am Yuri Kuyev, KGB special operations."

The Soviet officer, taken unaware, looked at Wickham with suspicion.

Wickham continued quickly, seeing the doubt on the officer's face. "We have had another serious breach in base security. Take me to the director of the KGB—we do not have a second to waste."

"Yes, comrade," the captain replied as a brown van raced past the field car.

The Russian knew that the KGB had infiltrated most units at San Julian. The officer reasoned that the scruffy-looking agent was assigned to perimeter security. He would blend easily into the civilian atmosphere on the outskirts of the air base.

Wickham, speaking in Spanish, motioned to the Cuban soldier behind the wheel. "Out—get out."

The soldier stared at Wickham, uncomprehending, until the Soviet officer reinforced the order. "KGB—I will drive." The Cuban acknowledged the command and jumped out of the field car as the officer quickly switched seats.

"Hurry!" Wickham ordered, leaping into the vacated passenger seat. "The American bomber is in jeopardy."

The Soviet officer, now convinced that Wickham was indeed a senior KGB operative, floored the vehicle.

Wickham, who wanted to be near the edge of the base when he made his move, leaned closer to the driver. "Stop at the hangar first, comrade kapitan. The B-2 hangar."

The Russian glanced at Wickham suspiciously. "The director's office is in the B-2 hangar."

Wickham saw the officer's hand flash toward his leather holster.

The van weaved between the control tower and a fuel truck, stopping twenty meters from the Stealth bomber. A second fuel truck was pumping jet fuel into Shadow 37.

Matthews scrutinized the B-2, observing that it was squatting heavily on the main landing gears. The pilot could tell they were filling the fuel tanks to capacity. He also noticed the increased activity around the airfield, along with the vast number of antiaircraft batteries that had been installed. It was clear to Matthews why Levchenko was frantic to get the

B-2 airborne. The U.S. had apparently located the Stealth bomber and planned to level San Julian.

The van came to a stop near the entrance to an underground bomb shelter. Levchenko opened his door as the guards slid open the side door.

"General Brotskharnov," Levchenko said, slamming the door, "check the aircraft carefully."

Brotskharnov hesitated, accepting a flashlight from one of the guards. "I don't even have a flight suit."

"There isn't time," Levchenko shot back. "Moscow wants you in the air immediately."

The general swore to himself, then flicked on the flashlight and walked to the aircraft.

If only, Matthews thought, he could find a way to thwart the plan. He felt frustrated and defeated.

Levchenko, as if reading the pilot's mind, stepped in front of Matthews. His eyes reflected pure animal hostility. "If you try one thing—anything—to hinder us, I will have you shot on the spot."

Matthews remained motionless, staring past the perspiring Russian. He was anxious to get airborne. Then he might have a chance to alter the outcome of the flight.

Levchenko turned to Simmons, startling the technician.

"If he tries anything in the air," Levchenko hissed, handing his revolver to Simmons, "you are ordered to shoot him. General Brotskharnov can fly the plane once it is airborne."

Simmons nodded quietly, accepted the weapon, then walked to the bomber and released the crew entrance hatch.

"Keep the pilot here," Levchenko said to the guards, "until I get back."

Matthews watched Levchenko enter the underground shelter, then looked around cautiously. The fuel truck had stopped pumping and two men were unplugging the hose.

Steve Wickham backhanded the Soviet officer viciously in the larynx, then slammed his head into the steering wheel. The blow stunned the captain momentarily.

The agent shoved the inert officer against the car door and continued driving, steering from the passenger seat. He moved his foot over to the accelerator and stomped on the pedal. Two hundred yards away, he turned toward the palm-studded field at the west end of the runway.

Without warning, the Soviet captain pushed himself off the door and struck Wickham in the face with the back of his elbow. The force of the impact knocked Wickham's foot off the accelerator. The agent, bleeding profusely from his cut lip, struggled with the Russian as the GAZ rolled to a stop.

The violent fight continued as both men fought for leverage. Wickham lost his balance and fell against his door, releasing the handle. He slid out of the field car, kneeing the Russian in the groin. The captain groaned as he landed on the American, knocking the wind out of the agent.

The Russian, taking advantage of his opportunity, repeatedly pounded Wickham's head into the hard ground. Wickham balled his fists tightly, then slammed them into the captain's temples. The bone-crushing blow sent the Russian headfirst into the ground.

Wickham, heaving for air, rolled the Soviet officer off him and scrambled into the idling GAZ. He floored the accelerator as the captain rolled on his side and drew his weapon.

Three rounds ricocheted off the GAZ as it raced through the trees. The agent flicked off the dim lights and pressed firmly on the gas pedal. Puffs of dirt flew up beside the speeding car as Wickham approached the perimeter fence.

Chuck Matthews, startled by the gunfire, felt a nudge in his lower back.

"Get down!" a Cuban guard ordered. "On your stomach."

Matthews dropped to his knees, then rolled on his right shoulder and spread out. He could hear more shots being fired from the far end of the airfield.

Gennadi Levchenko, followed by Raul Castro and two

senior Cuban officers, ran up the stairs and out of the underground command post.

Total confusion reigned as Castro heard a report over his hand-held radio. A field car, traveling at high speed, was being shot at by an unknown person. Castro turned to his officers. "Secure the perimeter and get the gunships airborne!" Gesturing wildly, he turned to Levchenko. "Take off—get the bomber out of here!"

"Untie the pilot!" Levchenko shouted to the guards. "Get him in the plane!"

A split second later, the command radio crackled again. Someone had seized the field car and was about to crash through the fence. "Fire on the GAZ!" Raul Castro barked over the radio. "Stop the car!"

An automatic weapon opened fire, causing Steve Wickham to swerve to miss a falling palm shaft. He straightened the vehicle and braced himself for a collision with the barbed-wire fence.

Mashing the accelerator with all his strength Wickham aimed the field car between two support posts and gripped the steering wheel. He ducked his head as the GAZ plowed through the wire fence, sending the barbed strands snapping over his head. Tasting the salty blood from his lip, Wickham fought to control the careening automobile.

The GAZ slid across the dirt road, bounced through a small ditch, went up on two wheels, then righted and skidded sideways through a sugarcane field.

"Go!" Wickham shouted to himself over the roar of the engine and gunfire. "Go!" On the brink of losing control of the car, the agent drove off the right side of the narrow road. He snapped the wheel to the left and slowed down in the darkness.

Wickham, now straddling the middle of the road, looked back toward the airfield. "Shit!" he said, spotting two Soviet helicopter gunships closing rapidly on him.

He concentrated on his driving, glancing back often. The

fourth time Wickham looked, both helicopters appeared to twinkle. A millisecond later the ground in front of the GAZ erupted in a shower of flying dirt and debris.

Wickham wrenched the wheel hard to the left, straightened it momentarily, then rocketed into the deep jungle foliage. The field car smashed through the thick entanglement and ground to an abrupt halt.

The agent leaped out of his seat and grasped the overhead-mounted machine gun. One of the Mi-24 gunships pulled up for another firing pass as the second helicopter orbited to call the firing runs.

The gunship pilot, tracking the GAZ with his four-barrel 12.7mm gun, hurtled toward the field car. The Mi-24's turret gunner commenced firing, sending a stream of high-velocity shells into the ground twelve meters in front of the vehicle.

Wickham pointed the machine gun at the first helicopter. He squeezed the trigger, holding it tightly, until the red-hot gun jammed. "Come on!" the agent yelled as the lead gunship, trailing fire, nosed over and exploded in the trees seventy meters from the GAZ.

Wickham leaped to the ground and ran through the thick jungle for 150 meters, then stopped and changed direction. He knew he had to hurry to reach the beach where he had come ashore. The OV-10 extraction was his only hope of avoiding a firing squad.

The agent, hearing the second gunship rake the GAZ with cannon fire, sprinted toward the beach as the vehicle's fuel tank exploded. Rushing breathlessly through the dense foliage, Wickham had no idea he was headed straight for an advancing company of Cuban infantrymen.

Matthews rubbed his sore wrists as he stepped quickly to the crew entrance hatch of the Stealth bomber. He stopped abruptly when Larry Simmons appeared, backing down the steps.

"Get back in the plane!" Levchenko barked.

The frightened tech-rep raced up the steps and into the cockpit.

"Move it," Levchenko shouted as Matthews climbed into the dark cockpit to join Simmons.

The pilot of Shadow 37 paused for a second, working rapidly to untangle his shoulder restraints, then eased into the left seat.

Major General Petr Brotskharnov, after his quick walk around the B-2, climbed into the bomber and sat down in the copilot's seat. He busied himself strapping in as Simmons locked the crew entrance hatch, twisted around, then sat down in the third seat.

"You have checklist?" Brotskharnov asked, glancing at his side panel.

"The checklist," Matthews replied as he slipped on his helmet, "will come up on the screen over the center console when we have power."

The general looked at the dark screen, then replied in competent English. "I do not read English so good."

"I'll take care of it," Matthews responded as he adjusted his seat.

Brotskharnov suddenly turned to the pilot. "We do not have maps—charts prepared for flight."

Matthews glanced at the Soviet officer. "We won't need them. Our navigation system will take care of everything."

The American pilot, desperate to foil the mission, looked over his right shoulder. Larry Simmons, holding a flashlight, had Levchenko's revolver drawn.

"Larry," Matthews said quietly, "how about helping me with the prestart."

Simmons, with a tight grip on the pistol, wordlessly went through the motions he had completed dozens of times, re-checking his avionics systems before Matthews, using the ground power unit, brought the B-2's dark cockpit to life.

Steve Wickham, short of breath, dropped to the ground. He rested on his stomach as he looked around cautiously. The agent had heard the voices of soldiers walking down the road.

Wickham, wringing wet and exhausted, was fifteen yards from the edge of a clearing. He crawled forward to get a better view of the activity on the road. The long line of men stretched around a curve on the same dirt road the agent had traversed going to San Julian. He had to cross the narrow route to get to his escape point.

Another sound caught the agent's attention. He could hear the subdued conversation of a group of soldiers making their way along the path the American had just traveled. Wickham swore to himself, knowing that the trail he had savagely forced through the jungle would not be hard to follow, even in the dark. The agent was caught between the column of troops on the road and the search party advancing on his position.

Lieutenant Colonel Chuck Matthews taxied the sinister-looking bomber toward the runway. He studied the eight multipurpose optical displays as he punched in four navigational waypoints. After the information was stored in memory, Matthews placed the master mode switch in the takeoff position.

He watched the display units switch from mission data readouts to performance information. The radios were checked automatically as the flight controls switched to the takeoff mode.

Matthews turned the bomber onto the runway, pointed the nose into the easterly wind toward Ensenada de Cortes, checked the engine instruments a third time, then glanced at Brotskharnov and Simmons. "Ready?" Matthews asked as he held the brakes and walked the throttles forward.

Simmons, fastening his helmet tighter, nodded yes.

Brotskharnov, unsure what his flying responsibilities would entail, looked at the American pilot. "You will tell me what I need to do?"

Matthews simultaneously released the brakes and shoved

the four throttles forward. "Just sit tight and don't touch anything until I tell you."

Simmons, listening to the pilots over the intercom, held his revolver on his thigh.

Shadow 37, heavily laden with fuel, gathered speed slowly as the four General Electric turbofans split the air with a deafening roar. At sixty knots, tracking the runway centerline, the B-2 rumbled when the left main gear ran over a depression.

Matthews, mentally calculating the runway distance needed for takeoff, watched the airspeed increase. It would be close at their heavy weight. The speeding bomber passed 130 knots, then 140 . . . 145 . . . 150 . . . 155 . . . Matthews pulled back on the stick, feeling the aircraft vibrate when it ran over another rough spot on the runway.

"Come on . . . ," Matthews coaxed as the last 500 feet of runway flashed under the hurtling bomber. The main gear skipped across the runway overrun as the heavy B-2 lumbered into the air, then shuddered as the left wing dropped. The wing tip scraped the ground before Matthews could level the staggering aircraft.

"Gear up!" Matthews ordered, pointing to the landing gear handle.

Brotskharnov raised the handle, then felt the wheels thump into the gear wells. He could hear himself breathing heavily over the open intercom.

Matthews, busy with the transition to flight, flew straight ahead. The bomber accelerated in ground effect through 230 knots before the pilot started a gentle climb.

Wickham glanced around quickly, then crawled three meters to an area of dense foliage. His ability to hear the approaching soldiers was nullified temporarily during the B-2's takeoff. There was no mistaking the earthshaking roar of the four jet engines. Now, as the thundering bomber climbed away, Wickham could clearly hear the approaching search party.

The agent worked at camouflaging himself in the foliage,

pulling leaves over his body. His spot was precarious, but it afforded the only chance he had. His position was totally surrounded by Cuban and Russian soldiers.

Wickham lay perfectly still, his heart racing wildly, as the soldiers advanced on the clump of vegetation. Wickham, eyes locked in one position, looked out from a small opening. He could see three Cubans, wielding machetes, moving steadily toward his concealment. Six additional soldiers followed close behind, their assault rifles at the ready.

The seconds turned into minutes for the agent as the search patrol reached his chancy hiding place. Two soldiers, with flashlights, walked within two meters of Wickham's head, paused, looked left and right, then continued toward the road.

Four minutes passed before Wickham ventured a move. He raised his head slightly and peered through the camouflage. The soldiers had moved out of view of his position. He sat up cautiously, then quietly rolled over onto his stomach.

An Mi-24 Hind D gunship flew slowly overhead, masking any noise on the ground. The helicopter's powerful Isotov turboshafts, turning the five-blade main rotor, whipped the tops of the trees with gale force winds while a spotlight probed the jungle canopy.

Wickham decided to retrace his trail and conceal himself until the search patrol moved down the road. Remaining on his stomach, he began backing away.

He felt a searing pain when the back of his head collided with a sharp, solid object. The agent stopped, feeling a flash of panic, then turned his head slowly. He froze in stark terror as he stared at the barrel of an AK-47 assault rifle.

CHAPTER TWENTY-FIVE

THE B-2

Matthews watched the shoreline pass under the B-2's nose, checked his airspeed and rate of climb, then rolled into a gentle left turn. After reversing course, he engaged the autopilot and reprogrammed the first navigational waypoint. The screen lighted with the time and distance to the checkpoint.

Major General Brotskharnov watched Matthews closely but remained silent as the aircraft climbed through 7,000 feet.

"We'll level," Matthews announced over the intercom, "at thirty-six thousand . . . until we've burned off some fuel. We'll stay between cardinal altitudes to avoid traffic."

Brotskharnov nodded, feeling anxiety beginning to creep into his mind. He was no longer in the relative safety and anonymity of San Julian. He was in an American Stealth aircraft—a stolen B-2 bomber—on his way to Russia.

Matthews, thinking about the arduous flight ahead, looked at the instrument panel. The clock read 4:02 A.M. He made a slight adjustment to the autopilot, then settled back in his seat. He tried to think if there was any way to extract himself from his perilous situation.

WICKHAM

The lone Cuban soldier, holding his cap in the helicopter downwash, stepped back and motioned with his rifle for Wickham to stand. The fat, sweat-soaked man had been a straggler who had fallen behind his patrol. Now, the gap-toothed soldier would be a hero to those who ridiculed him constantly about his size.

Wickham raised to one knee, caught the Cuban looking ahead for his unit, then leaped at the soldier like a sprinter out of the starting blocks. The agent hit the obese man square in the chest at the same time the soldier pulled the trigger.

A resounding crack filled the air as the round blasted through the trees, sounding an alarm. The Cuban, gasping for breath, dropped his rifle and fell to the ground with a thud. Wickham scooped up the rifle and slammed the butt into the soldier's head, knocking him unconscious.

Wickham turned and raced through the heavy foliage, using the assault rifle to bash his way through the dense growth. He stopped abruptly at the edge of the clearing. He could see that Cuban troops had him surrounded. There was no way out except across the open field. He cursed the bright Caribbean moonlight.

"Oh, sweet Jesus," Wickham exclaimed in desperation, then dropped the rifle and fell to his knees. He watched the column of troops, then analyzed his choices. If I can reach the bend, he thought, I'll have a chance.

The sound of voices, closer than before, made the decision easier. Wickham leaped to his feet and crashed through the thick growth, then sprinted across the field. Shots rang out, kicking up sprays of dirt, as the American zigzagged in a low crouch.

Wickham reached the far side of the clearing at the same instant a high-velocity round slammed into his right boot. The impact knocked Wickham's leg out from under him, sending the agent sprawling to the ground.

• • •

Over the Yucatan Channel, Marine Capt. Greg Spidel checked the time as he prepared to select his main gas tanks. The auxiliary fuel cell was almost depleted, but the pilot waited three more minutes before he toggled the fuel switch.

Aware that Wickham had transmitted pictures of the B-2, Spidel was prepared to extract the agent at any point prior to 5 A.M. He flew the OV-10 Bronco in a lazy circle with the Garrett turboprops throttled back to conserve fuel.

Spidel, talking occasionally with his winch operator, waited impatiently for the signal from the CIA agent. The extraction call would have to come soon if he was going to complete the mission this morning.

Wickham rolled over and sat up. He pulled up his tingling leg and looked at his right boot. The thick heel had been partially blown off, but the round had not hit his foot.

He jumped to his feet, raced into the jungle, then turned toward the road, determined to get across and head for the beach. Rapidly outflanking the soldiers, he came to the roadside.

"Shit," Wickham said under his breath as he watched a large patrol, rifles at the ready, walking cautiously down the road.

The sound of the search party behind him forced a bold decision. Seeing a Russian staff sergeant at the head of the Cuban column, Wickham ran out in the road. "Mladshiy serzhant," Wickham said in Russian, "I am Kapitan Kuyev, KGB. Get your men back up the road," he ordered, pointing at the open field he had crossed, "and cover that field. We have a foreign agent trapped somewhere in the middle."

"Da, comrade kapitan," the sergeant replied, turning to his patrol. "Move out!"

Wickham hesitated, watching the soldiers hurry back along the road, then turned and sprinted for his life. The weary agent ran until his lungs felt as though they were on fire. He slowed momentarily, checked behind him, and ran into a tobacco field.

The agent yanked out his small watch, noting that he had less than forty-five minutes to make the extraction deadline. Walking rapidly, he replaced the timepiece and pulled out the satellite transmitter. It was time to send Spidel the extraction signal.

Greg Spidel cast a glance at his vertical tape engine instruments. The turboprops were humming quietly, producing only 65 percent of their rated power.

The pilot looked at the time again, checked the dwindling fuel supply, then spoke to his volunteer winch operator. "Gunny, you awake back there?"

"Yes, sir . . . barely."

Spidel was startled when the high-pitched beep-beep, beep-beep, beep-beep sounded in his earphones. "Here we go," Spidel announced, pushing the throttles and stick forward simultaneously. "We're gonna be tight on time and fuel."

The OV-10 Bronco, flying more than 300 miles per hour, descended to 150 feet over the peninsula and raced for the extraction coordinates. Ten minutes later, Spidel reduced power and eased down to 100 feet. He would be on station, off the Gulf of Guanahacabibes, in fifteen minutes.

USS KITTY HAWK

Planning had intensified into the wee hours of the morning before the air strike to Cuba was in hard copy. Senior, highly experienced aircrews had been selected for the combat air patrol/escort, attack, and surface combat air patrol (SUCAP) missions.

The pilots and other aircrew members had begun to gather at 0315 to prepare for the launch thirty minutes before first light. At 0455 the war-at-sea strike would shift into their fifteen-minute alert status, ready to pounce on any invading surface ships.

The A-6F Intruders and F/A-18 Hornets had been armed

with Walleyes, Harpoons, Rockeyes, Skippers, and assorted multipurpose bomb loads. The combat air patrol aircraft, F-14Ds, supplemented by four F/A-18s, carried upgraded AIM-9 Sidewinders and Sparrow AIM-7M air-to-air missiles. Both types of CAP fighters held maximum rounds in their 20mm M-61 cannons.

Aerial refueling would be minimal, due to the short flight distances involved in the air strike. Two KA-6Ds would be airborne, with two standing by on deck.

The Air Force would supply three KC-10 refueling aircraft—one per aircraft carrier—as standoff safety tankers. Each of the three-engine behemoths carried more than 350,000 pounds of total fuel. They could give away 270,000 pounds and still have the reserve fuel to fly to an inland U.S. base.

Two E-2C Hawkeye early warning aircraft, working as a team, would sweep the entire gulf area around Cuba. A third Hawkeye would orbit sixty miles closer to the U.S. coast, acting as a spare warning platform. The E-2Cs would be critical in providing the big picture for aircrews and the battle staff.

The amphibious assault carriers *Essex* and *Nassau*, carrying the two marine expeditionary units, would be held in reserve. After the initial air strike, including the Air Force B-1Bs, the joint task force commander would evaluate the need for a second strike before landing the Marines.

Two of the four Los Angeles–class attack submarines operating in the Gulf had been tasked to launch BGM-109C Tomahawk cruise missiles at Cuban shore installations and inland targets. USS *Jacksonville* (SSN 699) would concentrate her missiles at military sites along the shore west of Havana. USS *Albuquerque* (SSN 706) would direct her ordnance at targets east of the capital city. All four of the nuclear-powered submarines had been cleared to attack unidentified submarines and fire MK-48 torpedoes at Cuban surface combatants.

The *Kitty Hawk*–based flight crews were in the final stages of preparing their aircraft for combat. The effort was being duplicated aboard the supercarriers *America* and *Abraham Lincoln*.

BOSSIER CITY, LOUISIANA

At Barksdale Air Force Base, final preparations were in progress to launch the Rockwell International B-1B strategic bombers. The eighteen aircraft had been loaded with a variety of conventional bombs and air-launched cruise missiles (ALCM).

The first sixteen bombers were taxiing for takeoff. Two of the supersonic B-1Bs, serving as spares, would return to the base if all the strike aircraft were functioning properly at the midway point. The bomber crews would rendezvous with their fighter escorts over the Gulf of Mexico 105 miles south of Lafayette, Louisiana.

At 0445 the first B-1B began its takeoff roll, thundering down the runway in a pouring rainstorm. Operation Metal Scorpion was under way.

THE AGENT

Steve Wickham, breathing heavily, jogged at a steady pace past the weathered houses he had seen en route to San Julian. He noted that the area was in total blackout conditions, which made it easier for him to move rapidly. "God," Wickham said, panting, "let the OV-10 be there."

The agent left the dirt road, splashing noisily across the shallow marsh he had waded through going to the airfield. The warm, stagnant water splattered his face as he ran out of the swamp.

Wickham could hear gunships spreading out to the south and west of San Julian. He also saw the glowing afterburners of two MiG-29s as they climbed out of the airfield.

Checking the time on the run, the agent realized that he

was not going to make the beach by the 0500 deadline. He had only eight minutes to traverse the final half mile to the rescue point. He slowed, yanked out the satellite transmitter, and punched in the extraction code again. He pointed the miniscule antenna over his head and squeezed the send button.

Greg Spidel had just entered his first orbit in the OV-10 when he heard Wickham's signal again. He scanned the sky frantically, looking for the bright cyalume lightstick.

The gunnery sergeant had also heard the second extraction signal. "Skipper, you figure he's ready for the snatch?"

"I don't know, gunny," Spidel answered, keeping his eyes moving. "We don't have a visual." The pilot continued turning the Bronco until the cockpit was beginning to point out to sea. "Check behind us," Spidel ordered, "while I set up for another pass."

"Copy."

Fifteen seconds passed while the OV-10 completed the course change. "Skipper," the sergeant paused, searching the water and coastline, "I can't see jack shit."

Spidel set his Collins AL-101 radio altimeter for seventy-five feet of altitude. "Okay, we'll make two more orbits, then I'm gonna make a pass down the coast."

"We got the gas, cap'n?"

Spidel hesitated, making a quick calculation. "We're standing on the wire now."

ANDREWS AIR FORCE BASE

The crown helo touched down softly on the main ramp. President Jarrett emerged with his aides and walked straight to the specially configured Boeing 747. After a short discussion with two air force generals, the president and his party entered the National Emergency Airborne Command Post.

The "kneecap," utilizing aerial refueling, could remain airborne for days, allowing the president to direct military strikes and coordinate emergency relief efforts.

The big Boeing E-4B, tail number 31676, lumbered to the runway, taxied into position, and roared down the pavement, rising smoothly into the early morning sky. As the huge jet climbed to altitude on its classified route, bouncing lightly in the turbulence, Jarrett checked in with the National Security Council. The jumbo jet leveled at 39,000 feet on a course for Burlington, Vermont.

SAN JULIAN

Raul Castro, cursing and gesturing wildly to his subordinates, stood next to a battle phone in the underground command post. His brother, President Fidel Castro, had just completed an emotionally charged conversation with the army general. The angry dictator had reminded his brother what the northern imperialist had done to Panama and Noriega.

"Get our Bear bombers aloft," Raul Castro ordered, then added, "and launch our air cover! The Americans may use their Stealth aircraft again." His rage increased as further reconnaissance reports cast a bleak picture. Three of the four-engine turboprop bombers, carrying long-range cruise missiles, were airborne eight minutes later.

Raul Castro, after concluding the conversation with his brother, walked over to Maj. Anatoly V. Sokolviy, the wingman of the deceased Lt. Col. Igor Zanyathov. "Major," the army commander said quietly, "the president wants you to man your aircraft and lead our pilots. We have a feeling the air will be full of American planes very soon."

Sokolviy, dressed in his gray-green flight suit, nodded his understanding, saluted, and slipped quietly away from the turmoil. The Cubans would be ecstatic to have one of the Soviet Union's premier fighter pilots leading them into aerial combat.

• • •

Two combat air patrol Tomcats had been launched early from the USS *America* (CV-66). Now, fifteen minutes later, the flight deck was again buzzing with activity. Green-shirted catapult crews checked the surface combat patrol F-14Ds on the two bow catapults.

Behind the raised jet blast deflectors, two additional Tomcats waited in line, followed by four F/A-18s, two A-6F Intruders, and two EA-6B advanced capability (ADVCAP) Prowler electronic countermeasure aircraft. The Prowlers sported a new receiver processor group for passive detection, along with the ALQ-149 communications intercept and jamming system.

The yellow-shirted catapult officer, standing between the howling F-14s, supervised the launch preparations. He listened to the air boss in PRI-FLY and waited for the green light to illuminate on the crowded island structure.

"Launch aircraft! Launch aircraft!" the cat officer heard through his "mickey mouse" headphones. He made a final check of the Tomcats and turned toward the pilot on the starboard catapult.

The F-14 aviator was looking at the officer, anticipating the full-power signal. The cat officer raised his arm, then formed a vee with his index and middle fingers and shook them vigorously back and forth.

The Tomcat's two engines increased to full power, splitting the air with a savage howl. The pilot checked his engine instruments, then saluted the catapult officer smartly and placed his helmet back against the head restraint. The cat officer brought his arm down quickly—the signal to launch the Tomcat.

The big fighter squatted down and rocketed off the end of the catapult track, sinking slightly as it left the deck. The pilot snapped the gear up and turned to the right, climbing to his assigned rendezvous altitude. Thirty-five seconds later the second Tomcat, on the port catapult, roared down the flight deck in a cloud of superheated steam.

Marine Maj. Vince Cangemi, cleared for flight duty by the squadron flight surgeon, sat in the lead F/A-18 waiting to taxi onto the port bow catapult. His Hornet, loaded with twelve Mark-82 five-hundred-pound bombs, two AIM-9 Sidewinder missiles, and 570 rounds of 20mm ammunition, had been configured for a ground attack mission. With a flick of a button on his control stick, Cangemi could switch instantaneously from air-to-ground mode to air-to-air capability.

The marine pilot looked to his right, checking his wingman's aircraft for any obvious problems. He watched his friend taxi the VMFA-115 Silver Eagles Hornet up to the blast deflector, stop while the jet exhaust shield was lowered, then taxi onto the starboard catapult.

Twenty seconds later, Cangemi taxied into place on the left catapult. He felt the catapult take tension, checked his controls, and went to full power, then afterburner. He checked the engine gauges, saluted the cat officer, and placed his new helmet against the headrest.

BOOM!

Cangemi, feeling the effects of grayout, blasted down the flight deck and off the bow. His vision returned as he snapped the landing gear up and accelerated straight ahead. He would rendezvous with the other Marine F/A-18s and join the Navy A-6F Intruders. Their mission was to bomb and strafe military targets, including radar sites and targets of opportunity, in the vicinity of Havana. The Hornets would strike first, then revert to a fighter mission.

CHAPTER TWENTY-SIX

SHADOW 37

The blacked-out bomber, now 390 miles east of Tampico, Mexico, cruised at 36,000 feet in calm air. Shadow 37 remained in total darkness, racing the morning light westward.

Chuck Matthews punched in the latitude and longitude of their next waypoint. The B-2 would pass 28 miles south of Cabo San Lucas before turning northwest to Russia. Matthews checked the navigational display, noting the current fuel burn. In forty-five minutes, the Stealth bomber would be light enough to climb to 40,000 feet.

General Brotskharnov continued to study the sophisticated cockpit as he watched Matthews very closely. Larry Simmons remained quiet, fingering his revolver constantly. He appeared to be dispirited but remained keenly alert.

Unknown to Matthews, Shadow 37 had passed within twelve miles of two F-14s from USS *Kitty Hawk*. The radar screens in the combat air patrol fighters had remained blank as the bomber crossed the gulf in front of the Tomcats.

ABRAHAM LINCOLN (CVN-72)

The Nimitz-class carrier, launched in February 1989, turned to place the wind down the flight deck. The nuclear-powered ship, stretching 1,092 feet, cut through the pristine water at thirty-one knots.

Two miles in front of the carrier, the AEGIS cruiser *Gettysburg* (CG-64) led the task force past the coast of Andros Island.

A pair of F-14s raced down *Lincoln*'s bow catapults, then climbed rapidly to their station seventy miles ahead of the carrier. Six additional Tomcats blasted off the flight deck to join the MiG combat air patrol.

Two A-6F Intruders, heavily laden with bombs and fuel, taxied onto the steaming catapults. The strike flight leader launched safely and turned toward his target. His wingman was not as fortunate. He lost his starboard engine during the catapult stroke. The frantic pilot, desperate to save his aircraft, jettisoned his entire bomb load while the bombardier/navigator attempted to dump fuel. The bombs, still attached to the ordnance racks, fell harmlessly into the water.

Flight deck crew members watched helplessly as the A-6F settled precariously low, blew spray from the port engine, then exploded on contact with the water. The 96,000-ton carrier continued straight ahead, plowing through the Intruder's debris, as the spare A-6F taxied forward.

THE AGENT

Steve Wickham, noticing the first hint of daylight, ran through a dense guava thicket and stumbled onto the beach. He fell forward, landing on his hands and knees, as his lungs heaved.

The agent rested a moment, listening to the water lap against the shoreline. He could smell the strong, sweet scent of eucalyptus.

His breathing was slowing when he heard the OV-10 in the distance. ''Oh, shit,'' Wickham muttered, lurching to his feet. He ran through the salt grass, crossed a pair of sand dunes, and plopped down at the edge of a large guava thicket. The thick foliage concealed the wet suit, skyhook harness, and water tow vehicle he had hidden there earlier.

Abandoning the wet suit, Wickham tore at the harness as the OV-10 made a pass down the beach. The aircraft, barely discernible in the faint light, appeared to be a mile offshore.

"Goddamnit," Wickham swore as he struggled into the converted parachute harness. "Get it together."

Greg Spidel banked the OV-10 into a tight right turn and raced out to sea. He swore to himself, checked the fuel again, and pressed the intercom. "Gunny, I'm gonna make one more pass . . . ."

"Cap'n," the sergeant replied in a resigned voice, "we ain't got the fuel."

Spidel, ignoring the remark, concentrated on his instruments as he flew a wide arc to start the second pass. He was not going to leave the CIA agent stranded.

Wickham snapped the last ring on his harness, grabbed the water tow, scooped up his swim fins, and ran down the beach. He plunged into the water, slipped on the fins, and pressed the trigger on the water tow. After quickly negotiating the narrow gap in the coral reef, he relaxed his legs and let the water tow propel him out of the cove.

Two minutes later, Wickham again heard the OV-10. He released the water tow, snapped the cyalume lightstick, and popped the cylinder of compressed helium. The balloon inflated rapidly, dragging the elastic cord and chemical lightstick to 200 feet.

Wickham kicked off his swim fins, rolled on his back, and searched frantically for the approaching Bronco. "Come on . . . ," Wickham sputtered as he saw the eerie-looking light. "Don't miss."

"I've got him!" Spidel said over the intercom. "I've got a visual on the light!" Spidel checked his altitude at seventy-five feet and slowed to 100 knots. "Stand by!"

"Set, cap'n."

Spidel banked slightly to line up on his target. His mouth was dry as he fixated on the lightstick. "He's close in!" Watching the glowing light approach the center of his canopy sight ring, the pilot eased in a touch of right rudder and waited for the impact.

Four seconds later the nose-mounted steel fork slammed into the elastic cord. Spidel shoved the throttles forward at the same instant the hard rubber ball snapped into the V clutch, severing the lightstick and balloon.

Wickham, gasping for air, accelerated through the water, then popped into the air. He twisted and turned uncontrollably in the OV-10's propeller wash. During a moment of stability, he caught a glimpse of the lightstick floating skyward at the end of the balloon.

Six miles to the east, the pilot of an Mi-24 gunship also saw the strange, glowing light.

SAN JULIAN

Major Anatoly Sokolviy, flying one of the newest MiG-29 Fulcrums on the island, taxied to the runway. The advanced MiG-29s had been stored secretly for seven months in a heavily guarded hangar at Ciudad Libertad Air Base. The other MiG-29s, flown by Cuban pilots who had recently transitioned to the Fulcrum in Russia, taxied in trail behind Sokolviy.

The MiGs were equipped with six AA-11 Archer air-to-air missiles and full loads of 30mm ammunition. The fighter cockpits, at Fidel Castro's insistence, had been reinforced with armor plating. The Cuban president had lost a good friend who had been shot in the stomach during an aerial engagement.

Sokolviy energized his pulse-Doppler radar, glanced at his engine instruments, then shoved his twin throttles forward into afterburner. The two Tumansky R-33D turbofans belched flames thirty feet behind the Fulcrum as it rocketed down the pavement in the growing dawn.

Sokolviy caught a glimpse of the line of MiG-25s and -23s taxiing in the opposite direction. He watched his airspeed increase rapidly, then raised the Fulcrum's nose wheel gently off the rough runway.

His wingman was halfway through his takeoff roll when Sokolviy snatched the landing gear up and banked into a rendezvous turn. He waited for the airspeed to build before deselecting afterburner, then checked in with the ground control intercept radar unit and armed his missiles.

Sokolviy was surprised when the radar operator informed him that numerous contacts were approaching San Julian from the northwest. The Soviet fighter weapons instructor waited for his wingman to join off his right wing. Both MiGs increased power and began a steep climb as Sokolviy talked to the radar controller.

Partway through the radio communication, Sokolviy heard static followed by a humming noise. He swore to himself, knowing that the American EA-6B ADVCAP Prowlers were jamming the airwaves. Sokolviy also knew that the U.S. ELINT aircraft would have a detrimental effect on the radar-controlled 57mm and 85mm antiaircraft guns.

The Soviet fighter pilot leveled the Fulcrum at 14,000 feet and carefully scanned the sky to the northwest. He vowed to avenge the death of his close friend and fellow pilot, Igor Zanyathov.

USS *KITTY HAWK* (CV-63)

The last strike aircraft, a VF-41 Tomcat sporting a black ace on the tail, thundered down the starboard catapult into the glare of the rising sun. The pilot left the F-14D in afterburner, accelerating above the speed of sound, as he pursued his flight leader. Two manned CAP Tomcats were towed to the bow catapults as the barren flight deck was respotted for the recovery cycle.

The catapult crews, keenly aware of the sudden silence on the flight deck, went below to have a cup of coffee and discuss the upcoming strike. Most of the crew in the coffee locker were in their late teens and early twenties. They had never actually seen aircraft launched with the intent of striking an enemy. The attack on the *Wasp*, along with the aerial engagements of the previous day, had cast a new feeling aboard *Kitty Hawk*. The crew of the giant carrier wanted Castro and Cuba blown off the map.

Commander Doug Karns, CO of the VF-102 Diamondbacks, led a flight of four F-14s toward San Julian. He had selected his two best pilots to lead another four-ship and three-plane fighter mission. Their job was to fly MiG cover for the A-6s and F/A-18s that would bomb San Julian. Each Tomcat had eight advanced AIM-9 Sidewinder missiles and 675 rounds of 20mm ammunition in the multi-barrel M-61 cannon.

Karns listened to the E-2C early warning controller vector another flight toward surface ships off the western tip of Cuba. The E-2C had the San Julian strike group turn to a new heading to avoid flying close to the Cuban ships and patrol craft.

Karns could see two of the attack elements 4,000 feet below his Tomcat. The lead A-6F Intruder was being flown by CAG, the *Kitty Hawk*'s air group commander; his deputy led the escort F-14s. The cockpit load and communications intensified as the strike force approached the Cuban shoreline.

THE OV-10

Greg Spidel, climbing at a reduced airspeed of 120 knots, focused on flying perfectly straight until the agent was aboard. Wickham, dangling twenty-five feet behind and below the Bronco, watched the Mi-24 helicopter pass by the ascending lightstick and turn directly toward the OV-10. He knew that the gunship pilot could see the low-flying turboprop in the pale morning light.

Thirty seconds later, Wickham was in the grasp of the winch operator. After he was pulled inside the aircraft, Wickham leaned next to the sergeant. "We've got a gunship closing on us!" Wickham shouted, gesturing wildly out the back of the OV-10.

The startled sergeant looked at the helicopter, then turned to Wickham. "Strap in!"

Wickham scrambled forward and locked himself into a crew seat. The winch operator severed the elastic cord, crawled into his seat, secured his restraints, and keyed his intercom.

"Cap'n!" the sergeant yelled, "our man's aboard and we've got a shooter—a gunship closin' from five o'clock!"

Spidel, feeling his adrenaline surge, shoved the throttles forward. "How far out?"

"I can't see him now," the sergeant reported, checking his parachute straps. "He's comin' up your right side."

Spidel, glancing back to his right, saw the gunship. "Are you both strapped in tight?"

"That's affirm," the sergeant responded, bracing himself.

Wickham, taking his cues from the gunnery sergeant, grabbed the handholds over his head.

"Hang tight!" Spidel ordered as he flipped on his master arm and wheeled the accelerating Bronco into a tight wingover. Coming down the inside of the face-sagging turn, Spidel saw a flash of flame and smoke erupt from the gunship. The pilot, recognizing the launch of an air-to-air missile, fired both of his Sidewinders and shoved the nose down violently.

Passing 250 feet above the water, Spidel whipped the OV-10 into a steep turn and recoiled from the shock of a proximity detonation. He leveled the wings and felt the Bronco yaw to the left as the port engine disintegrated in a fireball. Spidel yanked the left throttle back and initiated an emergency shutdown to contain the fuel and hydraulic systems.

Wickham, looking out the back, caught a glimpse of the Mi-24 as one of the Sidewinders hit it head-on. The gunship shed the main rotor blades and plummeted into the water. The agent grabbed the spare headset and clamped it over his ears. He heard Spidel, in midsentence, talking to the sergeant.

". . . lost the left engine, but we're okay for the moment."

Wickham keyed his intercom. "The gunship went in."

Spidel recognized Wickham's voice. "Yeah, I saw the impact flash. You okay?"

"Fine," Wickham replied, feeling his heart pound. "We gonna make it?"

Spidel hesitated before answering. "We're a little tight on fuel. We may have to ditch off the Yucatan coast."

Wickham glanced at the sergeant, then spoke to the pilot again. "Spider, are you in contact with Cancun?"

"I can be," the pilot answered. "What's up?"

Wickham felt the winch operator staring at him. "The B-2 took off . . . about four this morning."

"You saw it?" Spidel asked in a surprised voice.

"No, but I heard it."

"Okay," the pilot said, switching on his scrambler. "You can talk by pushing the radio button on the cord. Let me check in and . . . uh, oh."

Spidel was quiet for a few seconds, adjusting the two radios. "We've lost our comm. Probably knocked the antennas off when the engine shelled."

"Do you have any other means of communication?" Wickham asked.

"Afraid not," Spidel replied calmly. "We'll have to wait until we land."

ANIMAL ONE

Vince Cangemi listened closely to the excited chatter between the Hawkeye and the F-14 lead pilot from the VF-202 Superheaters. The Tomcat flight, four miles ahead of the strike aircraft, was less than two minutes from tangling with five sections of Cuban MiGs.

Cangemi, not wanting to add to the radio clutter, rocked his wings and started a shallow descent. His flight, locked in perfect formation, followed their leader toward the deck.

Animal flight did not need to converse to accomplish its mission. The marine aviators had briefed the mission and memorized their targets, airspeeds, altitudes, headings, timing, separation, tactics, and egress procedures. The pilots had studied their charts and flown the attack mission a dozen times in their minds.

Cangemi heard Heater One, the VF-202 CO, acknowledge the Weapons Red and Free call from the E-2C. Seconds later the sky ahead and above the F/A-18s filled with white, fast-moving streaks as the Tomcat pilots fired their missiles at the Cuban MiGs.

The radio was saturated with calls to break, shoot, reverse, and pull up. Cangemi saw two, then three explosions as two MiGs and an F-14 became large black puffs in the clear morning sky.

Cangemi shoved the Hornet's nose down further, streaking across the water at sixty feet and 510 knots. He checked his switchology—air/ground in master mode, inertial navigation system set to display the target offset point in the heads up display—then kicked in the afterburners.

The F/A-18 accelerated to 530 knots as the coast rapidly filled Cangemi's windshield. Forty seconds to "feet dry." Cangemi saw the piers approach, then flash under the Hornet in a blur as he snapped into a 6-g knife-edged turn and looked for his target. He resisted the insidious g-LOC (g-induced loss of consciousness).

Eight seconds later, Cangemi saw the San Antonio de Los Banos Air Base appear in his canopy. Concentrating on altitude, he waited until he was abreast of the pop-up point, then snatched the stick back and shot skyward. The tight-fitting g suit squeezed his abdomen and legs, then deflated as he unloaded the Hornet.

Cangemi, simultaneously rolling inverted and turning ninety degrees to the left, let the nose fall through until the pipper was on the main runway.

The radar-guided 57mm and 85mm antiaircraft guns opened up in unison, filling the sky with black shrouds of flak. The ground and pavement rushed toward the marine pilot at a breathtaking speed. Cangemi finessed the Hornet's pipper up, capturing the first third of the runway, held it a second, then pickled the twelve Mark-82 bombs.

The 500-pound explosives came off the racks in timed sequence, blasting twelve huge craters in the runway as Cangemi pulled out of the dive. Clouds of dust and debris boiled into the sky as Animal Two laid his twelve bombs down a row of hangars.

The third Hornet was blasting an assortment of parked aircraft as Cangemi snapped into another "fangs out" turn to the left. The Hornet bounced upward when a shell exploded under the fuselage. Cangemi checked his warning lights. They remained blank as he let out his breath.

He rechecked the gun position for a strafing run on the egress portion of the attack mission. The flight had been briefed to hose down the San Pedro and Ciudad Libertad military airfields on the way out. The sky was filled with black puffs of flak and red tracers slashing past the fighters.

Cangemi lined up with the first field, approaching from the south at 480 knots, then spotted two MiG-23 Floggers on their takeoff roll. They were pointed straight at him, one gaining speed and the second beginning to roll.

Cangemi lowered the Hornet's nose four degrees and pulled the trigger. The M-61 cannon spewed more than 320 rounds into the runway, through the center of the MiG-23 leader and across the right wing of Dash Two.

The first MiG, with a dead Cuban pilot in the cockpit, veered off the runway, crossed the ramp under full power, and plowed into a maintenance hangar. The explosion created an enormous fireball that engulfed four additional aircraft.

The wingman, stunned by the sudden attack, aborted his

takeoff roll and stood on the brakes. His Flogger, damaged heavily by the cannon fire, had jet fuel pouring out of the right wing root.

Cangemi yanked the stick into his stomach as he passed over the explosion, jinking as hard as he could. The antiaircraft fire was devastating and concentrated. "Oh, Jesus!" the marine fighter pilot said to himself as three lines of tracers crisscrossed in front of the Hornet's canopy.

Cangemi lowered the nose for a pass across the third airfield. He knew he was pushing his luck well beyond the boundaries of reason. The Marine banked the agile F/A-18 to the right, placing the nose straight at Ciudad Libertad, then glanced around. The morning sky, clear and blue, was filled with aircraft and rising plumes of black smoke.

CHAPTER TWENTY-SEVEN

DIAMOND ONE

Karns tuned out the wild chatter in his earphones. There was total confusion as each pilot, straining to keep track of all the hurtling aircraft, snapped his head continuously from side to side.

"Skipper," Ricketts said over the intercom, "break right! We've got two gomers comin' down from four o'clock."

Karns tightened his stomach muscles to counter g-LOC, then whipped the Tomcat into a painful 6½-g turn and slammed the throttles into afterburner. He switched from missiles to guns, worried that a Sidewinder might miss so close in and hit another F-14 or Hornet.

Transonic vapor appeared over the wing roots as the Tomcat dug into the savage turn. "I . . . have 'em . . . ," Karns groaned in agony, easing off the crushing g load. "They're reversing . . . coming over . . . the top. Come on, just a few more seconds."

Karns slapped the stick hard to the left and yanked the nose up, placing the pipper just behind the second MiG-25 Foxbat. Two camouflaged MiGs flashed below the Foxbat, firing missiles at two F-14s engaged with three MiG-23s. One of the Tomcats erupted in flame and smoke, breaking hard into the pursuers.

Karns squeezed the trigger and let the M-61 Vulcan roar, vibrating the Tomcat. A blazing reddish white streak walked up the MiG's fuselage, tearing off pieces of metal. The Foxbat headed for the deck, diving steeply while trailing white smoke and jet fuel vapor.

Karns rolled inverted and let the F-14's nose drop, following the wounded Foxbat. He switched back to missiles, heard the tone, waited, and punched off a Sidewinder.

"Fox Two!"

The missile tracked straight to the MiG, exploding on the right side of the fuselage. A brilliant flame trailed down the side of the Foxbat.

Karns recognized the magnesium fire at the same instant the pilot ejected. "We got him!" Karns said to his RIO as he pulled the throttles out of afterburner. "We'll extend and pull back into this furball."

"Yeah," Ricketts responded, scanning the sky above and below the Tomcat.

They could see two distinct groups of aircraft engaged in separate fights. Ricketts spotted three sections of MiGs, high above the melee, traveling supersonic.

"Skipper!" Ricketts warned, snapping his visor up for a better view. "Bogies...oh, Jesus...MiG-29s at eight o'clock. They're comin' right down the tube."

Karns was shocked by the sight of the high-performance Fulcrums. They had superior armament and look-down, shoot-down capability. He wrapped the Tomcat into a crushing bat turn, placing the nose on the MiG-29s.

"MiG-29s high!" Karns warned the other fighter pilots over the radio. "Fulcrums—MiG-29s high to the east!"

"Lock 'em up, skipper!" Ricketts shouted.

Diamond One looked up at the diving MiGs, heard the tone, then fired two Sidewinders. His wingman fired one missile, waited a second, and fired a second missile.

• • •

Anatoly Sokolviy saw the missiles come off the Tomcats. He
punched the chaff button, sending out bright flares to deflect
the onrushing Sidewinders, then broke hard to the left. His
Cuban wingman, unprepared for the sudden attack, hesitated
a second before he yanked his Fulcrum around. It was a costly
mistake for the experienced pilot.

The American missile hit the wingman's tail, blowing off
the entire aft section of the MiG. The aircraft tumbled end
over end, then exploded at the same instant the pilot ejected.
His parachute, engulfed in the horrendous fireball, was partially destroyed when the pilot separated from his ejection
seat. Strapped in the streaming parachute, the flash-burned
fighter pilot fell four miles to his death.

Sokolviy completed his evasive maneuver and banked the
Fulcrum around, tracking the elusive Americans. He fired
two AA-11 Archer missiles at Diamond One, then shot into
the vertical and snap-rolled the Fulcrum 180 degrees. Shoving
his throttles to the stops, he arched his head back to follow
the two missiles. The Russian was surprised to see the two
F-14s facing him canopy to canopy.

SAN JULIAN

Raul Castro, enraged and shouting orders to everyone in sight,
heard the antiaircraft guns start firing. He dashed to the control
tower windows and shook his fist at the A-6Fs and Hornets
approaching the airfield.

The aircraft were on the deck, screaming toward the air
base in left echelon. The flight leader, flying so low he caused
the tops of trees to sway when he roared overhead, was
pointed straight at the hangars.

The Cuban general watched, stunned, as the strike aircraft
leveled a dozen radar-controlled guns. The second wave of
attack aircraft boomed across the field, dropping huge loads
of bombs on the flight line, runway, and hangars. The win-

dows blew in, knocking Castro to the floor. He picked himself up, partially blinded by the dust and debris, and grabbed his command phone.

Vince Cangemi blasted down the length of Ciudad Libertad, spraying 20mm shells into parked aircraft, hangars, and a large fuel storage area. The fuel farm exploded, sending billowing black smoke and orange flames into the early morning sky.

Cangemi fired a last burst at a taxiing Cubana de Aviacion Ilyushin-62M transport. The four-engine jet shuddered to a halt with the right wing and both engines engulfed in blazing jet fuel.

The fighter pilot flashed over the perimeter of the airfield, scooting down in his cockpit as the cannon shells whizzed by the canopy. He shoved the twin General Electric turbofans into afterburner and pushed the nose down. The tracers were still sweeping past the cockpit when the F/A-18 screeched across the coastline at 550 knots.

Cangemi stayed on the deck for another minute, hugging the water and flying as low as he dared. He raised the nose slowly and started to breathe normally. The marine aviator quickly checked his annunciator panel and eased back on the power. He decided he had just enough fuel to return to the carrier without tanking when he sensed something ahead of his Hornet. He looked up and blinked, not believing his eyes. A Bear bomber, slightly to the right, filled his windshield. Cangemi judged the lumbering bomber to be one and a half miles in front of his fighter.

The pilot hit the air/ground button, switching to air-to-air missiles. He waited a second, swinging the pipper gently on the bomber, then locked up the Tupolev Tu-142.

"Ivan," Cangemi said to himself, bringing the power back further, "the dance is over." He squeezed off a Sidewinder and jinked the Hornet around, checking for his wingman and MiGs.

"Fox Two!" Cangemi broadcast over the radio. He snapped his head forward a split second after the AIM-9 struck the Bear's left outboard turboprop. The big engine came apart in slow motion, flinging blades into the fuselage and tearing into the inboard engine. The huge bomber continued to fly, streaming smoke and fluid.

Cangemi was startled when two cruise missiles, mounted one to a wing, dropped off and ignited. The weapons quickly accelerated out in front of the heavily damaged Bear, steadying at a cruise speed of 0.74 Mach.

"Shit!" Cangemi said to himself as he squeezed off his last Sidewinder. "Fox Two!" he warned, watching the missile plow into the stricken bomber's left wing.

"Animal One," the distressed pilot of the number four Hornet radioed his leader, "Dash Three went in . . . comin' off the last target."

"Oh, sweet Jesus," Cangemi replied as the Bear, missing the outer half of the left wing, rolled inverted and plunged for the Gulf.

The marine flight leader saw two figures jump out of the spinning bomber, then pop open their parachutes. Cangemi knew that his armament was almost depleted, but he had to intercept and destroy the two Soviet-made cruise missiles.

Karns had a quick glimpse of the two AA-11 missiles flash under him as he watched the MiG-29, canopy to canopy, pull into his Tomcat.

Anatoly Sokolviy rudder-rolled the Fulcrum into the F-14, firing his 30mm cannon. He could see the tracers arc under the Tomcat's tail.

Karns dropped the F-14's nose, going for knots and separation, then snapped into the pure vertical. Vapor trailed off the wings, signaling the severe positive g load being imposed on the fighter.

The MiG pilot, matching Karns's every move, pulled hard into the F-14 and fired a short burst.

"Holy shit!" Karns yelled, breathing hard. "This sonuvabitch is good!"

"Too good," the RIO grunted as Karns unloaded the straining Tomcat.

"Boss," Karns's wingman radioed, "we're workin' him for a shot."

Karns rolled over the top, separated from the fight, turned hard into the MiG, and engaged again.

"Skipper," Ricketts said, growing more concerned, "you better take him . . . before we're sea level minus six."

"Yeah," Karns groaned, committing his nose up again. "He's bound to get lucky . . . matter of time."

Sokolviy watched the American, waiting for the fatal mistake that would give the wily MiG pilot the advantage in the deadly aerial duel. Sokolviy smiled to himself when he saw the Tomcat commit too soon for the vertical engagement. The Russian pilot shoved hard on the throttles, still in burner, and snapped the MiG's nose up.

Karns, anticipating the maneuver, slammed his throttles to idle and popped the speed brakes for a split second. The MiG shot out in front of the Tomcat, twisting violently to spoil the F-14's gun-tracking envelope.

"Son . . . of . . . a . . . bitch!" Ricketts gasped, trying vainly to raise his head under the fierce g load. He had never experienced such a punishing engagement.

"I'm gonna light the pipes," Karns grunted, fighting g-LOC, "and take him out." He shoved the throttles forward into burner, retracted his speed brakes, and fired 290 rounds at the twisting Fulcrum. He aimed ahead of the MiG, expecting the talented pilot to break into the F-14.

Sokolviy, caught off guard, pulled into the fast-turning Tomcat. The MiG pilot, sustaining a gut-wrenching 8½ g's, flew through the devastating cannon fire, shedding large wing panels and part of the vertical stabilizers.

Karns yanked the F-14 up into a barrel roll and watched the Soviet pilot eject from the uncontrollable fighter. "Ivan jettisoned his airplane," Karns said, checking for other MiGs.

"Two," the CO radioed, "you've got a gomer closin' at your seven o'clock . . . low."

THE E-2C HAWKEYE

"Wolfpack, I hold four contacts," the airborne warning and control officer urgently radioed *Kitty Hawk*. He felt the draining stress of coordinating multiple aerial engagements.

There was no immediate response. "No," the controller paused, "make that five bogies. They came from the Bears . . . have to be cruise missiles."

"Ah . . . copy, Phoenix," the CIC officer replied, pushing the launch signal on his console. "Ready One CAP will be up your freq in a minute."

"Roger that," the Hawkeye controller responded. "Two bogies tracking Wolfpack, one-niner-zero for forty-five, low."

"Wolfpack copies," the strained officer replied, feeling the first catapult shot reverberate through the carrier. "Say targets of the other three."

"Stand by."

Seven seconds elapsed before the harried control officer replied. "They appear to be tracking the tip of Florida."

The CIC officer paused a moment, checking the location of the surface combat patrol flights. "Scramble the fighters from Key West and Homestead," the officer ordered, feeling the second catapult slam into the water brakes.

The lead B-1B strategic bomber, wings fully swept and traveling supersonic, blasted over Cabo Corrientas at 150 feet. The shoreline was rocked by six shock waves as the lethal bombers raced toward San Julian.

One hundred twenty miles east-northeast, two flights of four B-1Bs passed northwest of Cayos del Hambre, then separated to attack targets around Havana. Vulture 25 made a slight course correction as San Julian filled the windshield. A wall of ground fire, antiaircraft fire, and surface-to-air missiles filled the air.

The B-1B flight leader had heard the frantic radio calls from the navy strike force. The pilot could clearly see the damage they had caused as he tweaked the nose to the right to line up on the hangars. "Vultures . . . defense," the pilot radioed, then hesitated a second. "Now!"

The six bombers, thundering toward San Julian, filled the sky with chaff and flare decoys.

Raul Castro, warned of the rapidly approaching bombers by Cuban and Soviet warships, had sought refuge in the bomb shelter at the base of the control tower. The damp, musty-smelling shelter was full of personnel seeking cover from the air raids.

Gennadi Levchenko had dropped to the floor and covered his head when the antiaircraft weapons commenced firing. The Stealth project officer gritted his teeth and cursed in frustration.

The bombers screamed toward San Julian with an ear-shattering, high-pitched screech. Seconds from bomb release, Vulture 25 flew into a surface-to-air missile and exploded, spreading flaming debris for a mile and three quarters.

Two more B-1Bs succumbed to the devastating barrage of antiaircraft weapons, crashing across San Julian in terrifying fireballs. The remaining three aircraft released their bomb loads and flew straight across the center of the field.

Clouds of churning dust, smoke, and debris shot into the air as the deadly clusters of bombs pounded the air base. The hail of antiaircraft fire followed the fleeing planes, damaging two of the strategic bombers. Overhead, the B-1Bs' fighter escorts fired missiles at the MiGs, then chased after the surviving bombers.

ANIMAL ONE

Marine Maj. Vince Cangemi heard the frantic call from the Hawkeye. The two cruise missiles, launched from the Bear bomber he had shot down, were heading for the *Kitty Hawk*.

"Phoenix! Phoenix!" Cangemi radioed, shoving his throttles to the stops. "Animal One has a tally on the cruise missiles—the ones heading for *Kitty Hawk*."

"Phoenix, copy!" the controller said in a taut voice. "Can you get a shot?"

"I'm closing now!" Cangemi answered, unsure of how many rounds he had left in his M-61 cannon. "Two and Four, close up and say ordnance."

"Two has one missile," Cangemi's wingman answered, trying to catch his flight leader. "Vince, you'll have to ease off the power."

"Four is winchester," the marine pilot radioed, indicating that he was out of ammunition and missiles.

"Okay, Two," Cangemi replied, easing back on his throttles as he rapidly approached the closest AS-15 missile. "Come up on my starboard wing and drop the cruiser off to the right." Cangemi jinked his Hornet violently, checking his six o'clock for Cuban MiGs.

"On the way," the wingman radioed, sliding out to the side of his leader. "I have a tally." The sleek F/A-18 drew abreast of Animal One, reduced power to stay aligned, waited for the missile side tone, then squeezed the trigger.

"Fox Two!" the pilot radioed, watching the lethal air-to-air missile belch fire and accelerate toward the deadly prey. The Sidewinder went slightly high, then corrected downward and slammed into the cruise missile.

Cangemi saw the flash, then watched tensely as the missile exploded in an orange fireball. "Phoenix!" Cangemi radioed excitedly, "we dropped one—going for the second."

"Copy, copy!"

Cangemi looked at his wingman. "Good show, Torch. Slide back and cover my six."

"Rog," Animal Two acknowledged. "Go for it!"

Cangemi moved closer to the camouflaged cruise missile, now only twenty-eight nautical miles from *Kitty Hawk*. He could see the two descending CAP F-14s pull hard into a rendezvous turn with his flight.

The marine aviator lined up the pipper, adjusted his aim, and pulled the trigger. The Vulcan vibrated a split second, spewing out the last eighty-nine rounds at the small target. "Shit!" Cangemi swore to himself as he watched the red stream of lead pass under the AS-15.

Time was running out rapidly. The Hornet flight leader, checking the position of the closing Tomcats, made a snap decision. He rammed his throttles into afterburner and accelerated toward the deadly missile.

"What the hell are you doing?" Animal Two asked, breathing heavily.

Cangemi, concentrating intently on his target, did not reply as he pulled into tight formation with the speeding Soviet cruise missile.

"Holy shit, Vince," the wingman called. "You're gonna kill yourself!"

Cangemi remained quiet and concentrated, adrenaline coursing through his veins, as he eased his left wing tip under the tail of the AS-15. He steadied the Hornet for a second, then snatched the stick hard to the right. The F/A-18 snapped over violently, flipping the cruise missile end over end. The AS-15, tumbling and twisting out of control, plummeted toward the ocean.

"CAP Tomcats and Animals," Cangemi ordered loudly, "let's go high!" The five pilots shoved their throttles into burner and reefed their fighters into the vertical.

Twelve seconds passed before the missile impacted the water. The high-explosive detonation erupted in a geyser.

"Jesus Christ!" an unidentified voice shouted over the radio. "He did it!"

The pilots, their fighters running out of energy, began recovering from vertical flight.

"Phoenix," Cangemi radioed, feeling the shock wave buffet his fighter, "Animals are winchester . . . we're heading for the boat."

"Roger that," the Hawkeye controller said, then added, "and thanks."

Cangemi, rolling into level flight, hesitated a moment, then concentrated on his charges. "Animals, close up."

"Two."

"Four."

The Tomcat pilots extended their thanks and banked toward *Kitty Hawk*. Cangemi forced himself not to think about his lost friend. Animal Three, Cangemi's former flight student, had been shot down on the northern perimeter of Ciudad Libertad.

CHAPTER TWENTY-EIGHT

GUANTANAMO BAY

Lieutenant Commander Jim Flannagan, followed by his wingman, Lt. Frank Wellby, circled high over the naval base. Two additional sections of VC-10 TA-4J Skyhawks, including the commanding officer in Gunsmoke One, orbited the sprawling complex.

The navy fighter pilots listened as nine Marine KC-130 Hercules approached the runway. The big, four-engine transports raced low over the water at 360 miles per hour. Their mission was to extract the Marines and naval personnel pinned down on the base.

"This should be worth the price of admission," Flannagan radioed, banking steeply over the center of the 8,000-foot runway.

"Yeah," Wellby answered. "I've watched them do this before."

Gunsmoke flight remained quiet, searching for MiGs. The Skyhawk pilots could hear other flights engaged in aerial combat, but the sky over Gitmo had remained clear of enemy fighters. The Guantanamo control tower and air traffic radar facility had been shut down minutes before, allowing personnel to reach the debarkation point before the rescue aircraft landed.

The six Skyhawks, joining with the Hercules F/A-18 fighter escorts, would accompany the KC-130s out to sea, refuel, then trap aboard the *Abraham Lincoln*.

Flannagan looked seaward, searching for the rugged transports. "I have a tally . . . three o'clock, low."

"I have 'em," Wellby radioed.

The nine aircraft, separated in trail at one-mile intervals, waited until the lead pilot, the CO of VMGR-252, was two miles from the end of the runway.

"Watch this," Wellby said over the fighter frequency.

The pilots of the nine KC-130s simultaneously pulled their power to idle, decelerated to flap speed, dropped the flaps and landing gear, then adjusted power to hold their interval at approach speed. Every transition was performed at the same instant by every pilot.

Flannagan and Wellby banked their Skyhawks tighter and watched the first Hercules cross the runway threshold and touch down on centerline halfway down the landing strip. The transport CO waited until he passed the 3,000-foot remaining marker on runway 28, then yanked the four Allison turboprops into full reverse. The speeding transport slowed quickly as the second Hercules landed a thousand feet behind the touchdown point of the commanding officer.

The first KC-130 reached the end of the runway and executed a right 180-degree turn onto the parallel taxiway.

"Here they are," Flannagan radioed, spotting the four Marine F/A-18s streak overhead in tight formation and enter the defensive circle.

The VMFA-323 Death Rattlers, on detachment to Roosevelt Roads Naval Air Station, Puerto Rico, checked in with the VC-10 Skyhawks. The Hornets would maintain high station during the evacuation.

Below, the last KC-130 was touching down as the first

Hercules, crammed quickly with personnel, added power for takeoff from the taxiway.

The transport squadron CO passed the landing Hercules, accelerated rapidly past the control tower, then hauled the straining KC-130 into the air. The pilot, hugging the deck, raised the landing gear as the aircraft roared over the Hot Cargo area. The aircraft commander of the second Hercules was commencing his takeoff run when the first transport passed over the end of the taxiway.

Both groups of fighter escorts circled lazily overhead, watching the evacuation operation while keeping a vigilant eye open for MiGs.

The orderly scene was shattered by a frantic call from Frank Wellby. "Bogies! Bogies at . . . comin' in high from the northwest!"

"Weapons Hot!" the VC-10 commanding officer ordered.

SAN JULIAN

The stagnant air in the bomb shelter was thick with suffocating dust. Raul Castro, boiling with anger, stormed up the steps and kicked open the dented door. He was unprepared for the magnitude of destruction that lay around him. The hangars and support facilities, burning furiously, had been reduced to rubble.

The control tower had toppled to the ground, crushing the Cuban general's personal helicopter. Two fuel trucks at the base of the tower added to the inferno. Flames licked skyward from the fuel storage area, sending billowing clouds of coal black smoke rising over the ruins of San Julian.

Raul also noticed that the baseball stadium had been destroyed. The walls of the underground hangar had caved in, touching off a fuel tank fire. Castro walked a few steps and stopped as two MiG-29s, followed by three MiG-25s, flew over the field to survey the damaged landing strip.

The contingent of Cuban and Russian military personnel,

including Gennadi Levchenko, emerged from the underground shelter. They stared at the devastation, coughing as they brushed the dust from their faces. Levchenko, seeing the blazing fire, knew that the intense heat had melted the tapes containing the secret Stealth information.

The Cuban general, shaking with rage, lunged toward Levchenko. "The Soviet Union," Castro hissed in the Russian's face, "is responsible for this!"

The MiGs, looking for a divert field, added power and flew northeast.

THE KNEECAP 747

President Jarrett, wearing a blue windbreaker, sat across from two air force generals. He held a phone to his ear, listening intently to his secretary of defense.

"Mister President," Kerchner said over the secure net, "we have lost a number of aircraft, but the strike was successful . . . in our estimation."

Jarrett shifted around to glance at a message, nodding his head in agreement. "Bernie," the president replied, turning back around, "give me a quick synopsis."

Kerchner measured his words carefully. "San Julian was damaged heavily, but we don't know if the B-2 was there or had departed, as the Cubans claim."

"Okay, Bernie," Jarrett said impatiently, "let's get some photoreconnaisance—see if we can detect the B-2 in the rubble."

"Yes, sir."

The president paused. "What were our losses?"

"At the moment," Kerchner replied uncomfortably, loosening his tie, "we show six aircraft at San Julian, along with three F-14s, two additional Hornets, one F-16, and an A-4 at Guantanamo Bay."

"Did the Marines get out okay?" the president asked as he totaled the number of aircraft lost on his code reference book.

"Yes, sir," Kerchner answered quickly, "but one of the trailing C-130s was shot up before our fighters downed the MiGs. The Hercules lost an engine, but they're limping home with a fighter escort."

"What about our aircrews?" Jarrett asked, experiencing the pressure of command. "Did we have anyone . . . any crewmen captured?"

"Not that we are aware of," Kerchner answered, deeply concerned about the lack of timely information. "However, the aircrews have not been debriefed yet, so we'll know more in about an hour and a half."

The president sighed. "Okay, Bernie . . . oh, what happened to the Soviet ship—the *Marshal Ustinov?*"

"We're not sure, sir," Kerchner responded, glancing at his message notes. "We think a Cuban pilot erroneously thought it was one of ours, and strafed it. We'll get the credit, though."

"Well, Bernie," the president paused, "what is your recommendation?"

Both men were interrupted almost simultaneously as the flash message appeared on monitors. "Uh, oh," Kerchner said first. "Sir, we have an emergency condition—cruise missiles approaching Florida! We have to alert the—"

"I see it!" Jarrett said excitedly, turning to the four-star general. "Get everything up! They have to knock down those missiles!"

HOMESTEAD AIR FORCE BASE

Two F-16s from the 308th Tactical Fighter Squadron, afterburners blazing, hurtled down the runway. The Fighting Falcons left a trail of shimmering heat waves as they scrambled to intercept the incoming cruise missiles.

The fighters passed smoke generators, fake aircraft, and false runway surfaces that had been hurriedly deployed by the camouflage, concealment, and deception personnel.

Two more F-16s rolled at the precise second that the first

section lifted off the pavement and snapped up their landing gear. The thundering Pratt & Whitney turbojets, producing more than 23,800 pounds of thrust, slammed the highly experienced pilots into their seat backs. Each F-16 was armed with four AIM-9 missiles and 515 rounds of 20mm ammunition.

One hundred ten miles southwest of Homestead, two Navy Tomcats lifted off from Key West Naval Air Station and banked into a tight, climbing turn. The fighter crews contacted the airborne warning and control aircraft for snap vectors to the intruding cruise missiles.

Both flights, air force and navy, left their fighters in afterburner, pushing their aircraft to 1.5 Mach. The pilots knew they had less than seven minutes to locate and destroy the missiles.

KNEECAP

The president, sitting stiffly at the command console, pressed his headset tightly against his ears. He could hear the airborne controller vectoring the air force and navy fighters toward the three cruise missiles.

"Come on . . . ," Jarrett said to himself, feeling his hands ball tightly. "Knock them down."

The three air-launched cruise missiles (ALCMs) were forty-five miles south of Key Largo, Florida, when the F-14s spotted the intruding weapons. Both pilots circled to approach the streaking missiles from behind. Seconds later the air force fighter pilots had a tally on the Tomcats.

The radio chatter, incomprehensible at times, increased dramatically when the airborne controller and the flight leaders attempted to coordinate the attack. Jarrett felt his neck and shoulders become rigid when the four-star general slammed down his fist and swore out loud.

The F-16s moved to the east of the missiles, allowing the Tomcat crews a clear shot. Time was ticking away as the weapons, traveling more than 480 miles per hour, hurtled toward the southern Florida coastline. Both Tomcat pilots closed on the AS-15s, each firing two AIM-9s, then pulled into the vertical to clear the target area.

"They splashed one!" the F-16 flight leader radioed as he led his three squadron mates into their firing run.

The president listened, his eyes closed, as the F-16 pilots initiated their attack. He could hear them call their missile launches.

"Oh . . . my God!" the navy flight leader shouted through the confusion. "One of the sixteens is down—his Sidewinder detonated coming off the rail!"

The president grimaced, pressing his earphones tighter. He could hear the anguish in the pilot's voice.

"We got another cruiser dow—" a voice radioed, cut off by a separate radio transmission.

"He's in his chute—good chute!"

"Ghostrider's in!" the VF-142 Tomcat leader radioed, seeing the Air Force F-16s pull up. "They got another missile down." The second AS-15, like the first, had exploded in a blazing fireball.

Jarrett looked over at the general, then listened with heightened anxiety. He heard the navy flight leader announce that their missiles were away.

"Fox Two!"

The president held his breath, waiting.

"Miss!" the pilot radioed. "Two—get it!"

"Come on, damnit," Jarrett said under his breath. He was unaware that he was clutching the edge of his console in a death grip. The seconds passed slowly as the radio chatter quieted, then ceased.

"Okay," the F-14 wingman called. "We had a proximity explosion . . . don't know if we have a kill."

"Say again," the Hawkeye controller ordered, unsure of the situation. The ALCM, now seven miles east of Key Largo, was still on his radarscope.

"The missile—our Sidewinder," the Tomcat pilot said,

"exploded close to the target. The cruise missile appeared to oscillate, then flew into these buildups."

"Do you have a visual?" the distraught Hawkeye coordinator asked, knowing that the fighters were too close to the coast to launch more missiles.

"Negative!" the navy flight leader radioed. "It flew into the clouds—appeared to be descending. Keep us in trail, and we'll nail it when it comes out the bottom."

The president listened to the frantic E-2C controller give the F-14 crews, joined by the three remaining F-16 pilots, vectors to the west of the AS-15. The seconds continued to stretch into a minute before the ALCM descended below the billowing cumulonimbus cloud.

"Tally! Tally!" the air force flight leader yelled. "Cajun lead is in!" The pilot raced across Biscayne Bay, closing on the ALCM at 520 knots. He placed the pipper on the descending missile, squeezed the trigger, twitched the control stick gently, and expended his entire 515 rounds at the cruise missile.

"Got it!" the jubilant pilot radioed, watching the ALCM, minus the tail, cartwheel out of the sky. "It's going into the bay!"

"Go vertical!" the Tomcat leader radioed, reefing his F-14 into a chest-crushing 6½-g climb. "It may deto—"

His warning was cut short when the conventional-warhead missile, nine miles south of the Miami Seaquarium, exploded in Biscayne Bay.

THE B-2

Lieutenant Colonel Chuck Matthews, growing more weary by the minute, prepared to alter course toward the Soviet airfield on Kamchatka Peninsula. He had watched the distant lights of Cabo San Lucas pass off the right wing fifteen minutes earlier.

Matthews, noticing that the Russian general was beginning

to show the effects of fatigue, glanced back at Simmons. The technician's eyes were wide open and he sat up straight in his seat, still vigilant and cautious. Matthews, knowing that daylight would catch them in approximately three hours, had to figure a way to stop the flight.

THE KNEECAP 747
7:22 A.M.

A haggard President Jarrett sat alone in his suite, listening to his defense secretary on a secure line. The vice president, at Raven Rock, and the secretary of state, at Mount Weather, were also listening. The Joint Chiefs of Staff were monitoring the conversation.

"Goddamnit, Bernie," the president said, hunched over his desk, "I want containment . . . saturation bombing until Castro is completely neutralized . . . on his knees. He's going to pay a heavy price for the men we've lost."

"Yes, Mister President," Kerchner replied, resting his head on his left hand. "We have twenty-three more B-1s en route to Barksd—"

"I'm aware of that," Jarrett interrupted tersely. "I also want the Navy to deep-six—to sink every Cuban warship and patrol vessel. I don't want anything flying or floating when we're finished."

"Yes, sir," Kerchner responded, glancing across the table at the tense faces of the Joint Chiefs. "Mister President," the defense secretary continued, "the carrier battle groups are preparing for a second Alpha Strike. We anticipate a launch in two hours fifteen minutes. The strike will be a maximum effort, utilizing the reserve aircraft, too."

"Sam," Jarrett said without acknowledging his defense secretary, "what is Ignatyev's position?"

"Mister President," Gardner answered from Mount Weather, "the Kremlin is pursuing an investigation of KGB officials, but they are flatly refuting any involvement. President Ignatyev contends that our pilots defected to Cuba, and that Castro is operating on his own.''

Gardner hesitated a moment, expecting the president to reply. The secretary of state cleared his throat and continued. ''Sir, Ignatyev has completely absolved the Soviet Union from any responsibility in the B-2 affair.''

The secretary of defense was listening to Sam Gardner when his CIA line buzzed. He switched off the speaker phone and picked up the receiver. ''Kerchner.''

''Norm Lasharr,'' the director said, sounding out of breath. ''We've just heard from our operative—from San Julian.''

''Just a second, Norm,'' Kerchner interrupted. ''The president is on the line . . . I'll put you through.'' Kerchner punched the conference call button and waited for a pause. ''Mister President, Norm Lasharr is on the line with an update from our San Julian operative.''

The president spoke quickly. ''Go ahead, Norm.''

''Sir, we have recovered our agent,'' Lasharr said hurriedly. ''They crash-landed off the coast near Cancun . . . out of gas, but they're okay. The agent confirms that the B-2 departed San Julian around four o'clock this morning. He couldn't tell the direction of flight, but he's positive it took off.''

''Okay,'' Jarrett responded. ''Stay on the line.''

''Yes, sir.''

The president addressed the entire group. ''Gentlemen, we've got an entirely different situation now. A hundred and eighty out. Bernie, let's stand down from the second air strike and concentrate on finding the B-2.''

''Yes, sir,'' Kerchner replied. ''We need to be very cautious though, in regard to retaliatory strikes.''

''Of course,'' Jarrett agreed, remembering what General Rafael del Pino, who had defected from Cuba during 1986, had told the CIA. Fidel Castro had planned an air strike against a nuclear power installation in southern Florida if the United States had blockaded Cuba during the Grenada invasion.

''Bernie,'' the president continued, ''we want to maintain our battle groups on station for the time being. Do you have any idea where the B-2 might be at the present time?''

Kerchner had been calculating the possibilities but kept coming back to one point. ''Sir, my bet is that they're flying away from the sun, to stay in the dark as long as possible. We have to assume,'' Kerchner said slowly, ''that they're counting on getting the bomber to a safe haven before we have time to find out it hasn't been destroyed in Cuba.''

Jarrett thought a moment. ''Any other theories?''

''Mister President,'' the vice president said from Raven Rock, ''Secretary Kerchner is probably on the money. My guess is they're traveling west, or northwest—the quickest way to another hiding place with the least exposure to daylight.''

''Bernie,'' Jarrett said calmly, ''the B-2 has been airborne about three and a half hours. That has to put them out somewhere around seventeen to eighteen hundred miles.''

''Yes, sir,'' Kerchner replied, thinking about possible contingencies.

Jarrett, sounding more upbeat, continued. ''Okay, let's move. Bernie, get every aircraft we can muster airborne. We have to have a semicircle of airplanes, from the mid-Atlantic across North America to the western Pacific, beginning at a radius of two thousand miles from San Julian.''

Jarrett, thoroughly engaged, continued. ''I want layers of aircraft all the way to the territorial limits of the Soviet Union. Sam, you notify the Kremlin . . . just in case . . . and make our position crystal clear.''

''Yes, sir,'' Gardner answered, harboring reservations.

Kerchner was already scratching a note for the chairman of the Joint Chiefs.

''Bernie,'' the president said sternly, ''the only way we're going to find the B-2 is to spot it visually in the daylight.''

''You're right, sir,'' Kerchner responded, then added a question. ''What action do you want to take when we locate the B-2?''

Jarrett responded without hesitation. ''If the pilot doesn't respond to the order to land, shoot it down.''

CHAPTER TWENTY-NINE

SHADOW 37

The Stealth bomber cruised serenely at 44,000 feet as Matthews and Brotskharnov monitored the radios for converging air traffic. Matthews, to avoid a possible midair collision, continued to fly between cardinal flight levels. Simmons, exercising his numb limbs in the confined space, remained alert and uncommunicative.

The morning light was rapidly overtaking the B-2 as it passed a point 1,180 miles northeast of Honolulu. Shadow 37 would be visible to aerial observers in forty-five minutes.

Matthews was surprised when he heard a Northwest Airlines pilot call another Northwest flight. "Ah . . . Northwest Sixty-Seven, Northwest Three-Twenty-Nine."

"Sixty-Seven, good morning."

Brotskharnov cocked his head, listening to the exchange.

"Morning," the pilot responded, then hesitated a moment. "We just had a call from operations. Seems the word is being passed to look out for the B-2—the Stealth bomber that disappeared."

Matthews sensed Brotskharnov glance at him. He looked

over at the officer, noticing the Russian gripping his armrest.

"Okay," the astonished copilot radioed. "Any idea of the general location?"

"Negative," the 747 captain answered. "The military has a full-scale search under way. They believe the B-2 is airborne somewhere between the North Atlantic and the western Pacific, and the commercial crews are being asked to be on the alert."

"Ah . . . Six Seven," the copilot said, then paused and keyed his radio again. "Any news on Cuba?"

"All we know," the captain answered in his gravel voice, "is that Jarrett kicked 'em in the dirt this morning."

"Copy, Northwest Six Seven. Have a good flight."

"Three Two Nine."

Matthews, concealing his emotions, began to hope. If he could only enhance the possibility of being intercepted. He needed to induce an engine failure in order to descend to an altitude where most of the traffic flew.

USS *CARL VINSON* (CVN-70)

The supercarrier, 420 miles southeast of King Cove, Alaska, turned into the wind in preparation to launch aircraft. Every available airplane assigned to Carrier Air Wing 15 had been prepared for the extensive search mission. Locating the B-2, as the air wing commander had said, was a White House priority.

The navy carrier-based aerial tankers would be augmented by Air Force KC-135s operating from Elmendorf Air Force Base. The F-14s from the VF–51 Screaming Eagles blasted down the bow catapults, followed by Tomcats from the VF-111 Sundowners.

The remainder of the carrier air wing launched in rapid succession and raced for their respective patrol sectors. *Carl Vinson* had been assigned a surveillance area that extended from 200 miles southeast of the carrier to 600 miles west-southwest.

HICKAM AIR FORCE BASE, Oahu, Hawaii

Four Hawaiian Air National Guard F-15 Eagles, afterburners blazing in the predawn, scrambled into the early morning air and turned northeast. The fighters, from the 199th Tactical Fighter Squadron, thundered over Halawa Heights as they headed for the shoreline of Oahu. Their mission was to split into two sections and patrol the outer boundaries of the Hawaiian air defense area. They would be refueled twice by a KC-10 tanker. The pilots had been briefed to shoot down the B-2, in the event they located the bomber, if the Stealth crew did not comply with orders to turn toward Hawaii.

Ten miles to the east, four F/A-18s from Kaneohe Bay Marine Corps Air Station lifted off the runway. The VMFA-232 Red Devils, backed by a KC-130 tanker, would provide search coverage in a separate patrol zone. Two Boeing E-3C airborne warning and control aircraft were en route to central and northern Pacific stations. The AWACS would provide sector coordination for the fighters.

THE B-2

The first rays of sunlight began to illuminate the cockpit as Matthews prepared to execute his daring plan. He waited until Brotskharnov was occupied scanning the horizon, then eased his left hand down to the circuit breaker panel next to his seat.

Matthews felt along the rows of buttons, pinched the number three engine oil pressure breaker, and popped it out. He moved his hand back to his thigh as the engine instrument and crew alerting system annunciator lights flashed on, lighting the dim cockpit with a reddish amber glow. The synoptic display projected a diagram of the number three engine oil system, indicating a failure.

"Goddamnit," Matthews exclaimed as convincingly as possible, "we've lost oil pressure on number three." He retarded the number three throttle as he programmed the flight director to descend to a lower altitude.

Matthews turned to Brotskharnov, who sat transfixed, staring at the color-coded electronic displays. "General, watch our rate of descent while I go through the shutdown checklist."

Brotskharnov nodded, watching the altitude readout as Matthews followed the engine shutdown list on the bright display screen.

Simmons, leaning forward in his straps, was tense and jumpy. He suspected that Matthews had caused the malfunction deliberately, but he was confused by the sudden failure.

"I think—" Matthews started, then caught Simmons leaning to his left. The pilot snapped his left hand down, shoved the oil pressure breaker in, and yanked his hand back to the controls. "We should . . . , I think we can maintain forty thousand."

Brotskharnov, who did not suspect any chicanery, answered with a strained voice. "Whatever you have to do."

The Stealth bomber descended slowly toward 40,000 feet as sunlight filled the cockpit.

The new jumbo jet on Cathay Pacific Flight 12 flying eastbound at 41,000 feet, left four distinctive white contrails in the morning sky. The captain and first officer, enjoying fresh coffee and breakfast pastries, had pulled down their glare shields to block out the bright sunlight.

Both pilots, relaxed and monitoring their navigation plot, discussed the air strike to Cuba and the political unrest in Singapore. The veteran pilots were unprepared for what they were about to witness.

• • •

Chuck Matthews looked out to the horizon, studying the growing cloud cover in front of the bomber. He could tell that a major winter storm was developing over the northern Pacific.

Matthews selected cross-feed to balance the fuel load, then looked out of the windshield again. He was caught unprepared when he saw contrails approaching the B-2 from eleven o'clock high. The white trails, closing rapidly, appeared to be five to six miles away.

Matthews shot a glance at Brotskharnov, who seemed to be deep in thought. Simmons had his head lowered and was staring at the flight deck.

The B-2 pilot, knowing that the bomber did not generate contrails, had to do something to make the aircraft visible. He manipulated the fuel controls again, deliberately taking extra steps to conceal his next move. He raised his hand an inch, then activated the fuel dump switch. The caution light illuminated, but no one noticed. Hundreds of pounds of fuel streamed out of the bomber in two frothy white trails.

The first officer on Cathay Pacific Flight 12 handed his breakfast tray to the smiling flight attendant, then turned in his seat. He was peering out of the windshield as the B-2 commenced dumping fuel. The two white trails showcased the Stealth bomber directly in front of the 747.

"Look!" the copilot pointed. "That's a . . . it's a B-2!"

The captain focused outside. "Good God . . . you're right. Looks like they're at three-nine-oh."

Both pilots remained silent, staring at the sinister-looking bomber as it passed to the left and disappeared under the wing.

"They're higher than thirty-nine . . . gotta be," the first officer said as he turned to the captain. "Think we should notify someone?"

The pilot thought a second, then nodded his head. "Yeah, I think so. Kinda strange dumping fuel over the middle of the pond . . . and being at the wrong altitude."

• • •

Matthews discreetly deselected fuel dump and tuned the VHF radio to 121.5 and the UHF sets to 243.0, the international distress frequencies. He knew that if anyone attempted to contact Shadow 37, they would most likely try the Guard emergency frequency.

Matthews sat back, staring at the murky clouds and contemplating what action he should take if they were contacted or intercepted.

THE AWACS

"We have a sighting," the airborne controller said over the intercom, then keyed his radio and talked to the Air Guard F-15 flight leader.

"Rainbow leader, we have a confirmation on the B-2. You're three-five-two, angels three-nine-zero to four-zero-zero at two hundred ten miles. Heading approximately three-four-zero."

The radar operator waited a moment, receiving further information through his headset. "You are cleared to intercept. Repeat, you are cleared to intercept."

"Copy," the Air Guard flight leader radioed, shoving his throttles into afterburner. "Rainbows, let's move it out."

A minute passed before the controller contacted the Marine F/A-18s. "Devil flight, take up a heading of three-three-zero. We'll hold you fifty south of Rainbow flight."

"Devil copy."

THE WHITE HOUSE

Marine One, transporting Jarrett back from the Kneecap E-4, was touching down as the secretary of state hurried out of the White House. Kerchner waited until the president stepped off the helicopter and saluted the marine sergeant.

"Mister President," Kerchner said as he fell in step with

Jarrett, "the B-2 has been spotted over the northern Pacific, north of the Hawaiian Islands."

Jarrett, smiling and waving at the throng of media representatives, did not change his expression. "Who spotted it?"

"An airliner . . . a Cathay Pacific flight," Kerchner answered as they approached the entrance to the White House. "We're vectoring air force fighters for an intercept."

"Excellent," Jarrett responded with a final wave to the shouting press corps. "Let's get everyone in the situation room as soon as possible."

"They're standing by, sir," Kerchner replied as he slowed to let the president step through the open door. "And the Soviets—Ignatyev—just offered to assist us in locating the B-2."

Jarrett looked surprised. "Interesting."

As if in confirmation of that fact, at that point the 65,000-metric-ton Soviet aircraft carrier, *Tiblisi*, operating 370 miles south of Amchitka Island, was plowing through heavy seas. The large-deck carrier was on a direct line between the American Stealth bomber and Yelizovo airfield on Kamchatka Peninsula.

Sukhoi Su-27 Flankers and MiG-29 Fulcrums, using the ski-jump bow, were being launched to search for the elusive Stealth bomber. The pilots had been briefed, in the event they spotted the bomber, to keep it in sight until an American aircraft could be vectored for an intercept.

The Soviet fighters would spread out from 220 to 310 miles ahead of the *Tiblisi*, refuel from one of five tankers, then orbit at staggered intervals.

SHADOW 37

The sun was high in the sky when Matthews felt the first bumps of rough air. The looming storm had grown darker in the past forty minutes.

Matthews, who was feeling the effects of dehydration, turned to General Brotskharnov. "We're going to need the weather radar, or we're in for a rough ride."

The Russian pilot looked at the display units, then back at Simmons.

The technician shook his head. "We have to keep the airplane cold—no emissions."

Brotskharnov shrugged and turned to Matthews. "I am not the expert."

Matthews, tired and irritated, cinched his straps tighter as the B-2 bounced through the lower layers of the cloud bank.

THE AWACS

"Rainbow leader," the controller radioed, staring at his radar console, "continue present course and spread your flight another ten miles. We believe you should be overtaking the B-2 soon."

"Ah . . . roger," the Air Guard flight leader responded, checking his wingman's position. "You'll have to space us—we're starting to encounter some weather."

"Copy," the AWACS officer replied. "Come left ten degrees and I'll call your separation."

"Roger, comin' left ten."

The F-15 pilot eased his stick to the left and glanced out at the horizon. He froze when he saw the Stealth bomber whisk through a layer of stringy dark clouds.

"Sonuvabitch," the fighter pilot said in his oxygen mask, then keyed his radio. "Pelican, Rainbow lead has a tally on the B-2!"

"Roger, roger," the excited AWACS officer replied. "Rainbow Two, turn left twenty degrees—lead is seven miles at your nine o'clock."

"Two comin' left twenty. Call me at three miles."

"Wilco," the controller radioed. "Rainbow lead, close on the B-2 and contact on Guard."

''Roger,'' the startled pilot said. ''Confirm the call sign.''

''Ah . . . Shadow Three Seven.''

''Copy.''

THE BOMBER

Matthews twisted his head back and forth, exercising his stiff neck muscles. He was thinking about taking off his helmet when something out of the side window caught his eye.

He snapped his head to the left and stared at the cockpit of an F-15 Eagle. Matthews saw the Hawaiian Air National Guard lettering on the aircraft at the same instant the fighter pilot transmitted over the radio.

''Shadow Three Seven, Shadow Three Seven, Rainbow leader on Guard. Do you copy?''

Simmons bolted upright as Brotskharnov leaned over the console and stared at the American fighter in wide-eyed astonishment.

''We better talk to him,'' Matthews cautioned, turning to Simmons. ''The game is over.''

Simmons looked at Brotskharnov, who was in shock.

''Shadow Three Seven, Shadow Three Seven, Rainbow lead on Guard,'' the F-15 pilot radioed, easing closer to the nose of the B-2. ''We have orders to shoot you down if you do not comply. Do you copy?''

Matthews shot a glance at the Eagle pilot and turned to Brotskharnov. ''They've got us, goddamnit!''

The Russian blanched, snapped off the autopilot, grabbed his set of controls, and shoved the three throttles forward. ''The hell they do!'' the Russian pilot barked, yanking the bomber into a tight, climbing turn to the right.

Matthews reached for his controls at the same instant that Simmons pressed the revolver against the pilot's ribs.

The stunned fighter pilot, unprepared for the B-2's abrupt maneuver, tried to close on the bomber. When the two aircraft entered the dense clouds, the F-15 pilot, concerned about a midair collision, pulled his throttles back and shoved the nose over.

"Pelican, Rainbow lead. I've lost the target—he pulled into the clouds."

"Stand by," the controller radioed in a frustrated voice. "Are you in a position to try another intercept?"

"Negative—I'm not painting anything on the scope. They just disappeared in the soup."

The radio remained quiet for a moment before another voice spoke. "Rainbow leader, say fuel state."

"Three point nine," the pilot replied as his wingman rendezvoused on the right side. "We're gonna have to drop back and tank."

"Get the nose down!" Matthews ordered, watching the airspeed decrease rapidly. "We're going to stall!"

Brotskharnov, having changed course forty degrees and climbed 2,300 feet, shoved the nose down and turned back to the original heading. The Russian pilot's hands were shaking as he leveled the bomber at 42,300 feet.

Shadow 37, bouncing lightly in the dense clouds, accelerated to cruise speed again.

"They're going to shoot us down!" Matthews said, feeling the revolver in his side. "It's only a matter of time!"

Simmons shoved harder on the barrel of the gun. "Shut up, colonel!"

Matthews, ignoring the technician, leaned closer to Brotskharnov. "There's no way out . . . they've got us surrounded."

The wily Russian slowly turned his head. "Engage the autopilot. We will be okay if we can remain in the clouds."

CHAPTER THIRTY

THE AWACS

The airborne command and control officer called Shadow 37 on Guard a dozen times, then radioed the E-2C Hawkeye controlling the navy aircraft from *Carl Vinson*.

The Hawkeye radar controller plotted the coordinates of the B-2 sighting and vectored two sections of F-14s toward a rendezvous with the bomber. "Sundowners, come port fifteen degrees and climb to angels four-five-zero. We've got a B-2 coming down the pike."

"Roger," the operations officer of VF-111 radioed. "Any idea when we'll intercept?"

"Stand by," the controller answered as he conferred with another radar operator. "We're projecting that you'll overfly the B-2 in twenty . . . say twenty-one minutes."

The Tomcat pilot, easing his throttles forward in the climb, looked over his glare shield. "We've got a thick cloud cover out here."

"Copy," the Hawkeye officer replied. "Don't show a thing . . . not a trace of the B-2. We're just extrapolating at this point."

"Roger."

The radios remained quiet for a few seconds before the controller spoke again. "Sundowners, we show MiG activity at your four o'clock, climbing out of two-seven-zero. Looks like three aircraft at twenty-eight miles."

The F-14 flight leader checked his armament panel. "Keep us informed."

"Roger that," the controller said as he adjusted his scope. "They're off the *Tiblisi*—supposed to be helping us—but we haven't received permission to work them."

"Copy."

The Hawkeye officer changed to a frequency used by the Soviet fighter pilots, adjusted his lip microphone, and flipped the frequency switch. "This is navy airborne controller, call sign Eight Ball. All Soviet aircraft are warned to stand clear of U.S. operations. Repeat, all Soviet aircraft remain clear of U.S. operations."

The four F-14s, breaking out of the dark clouds at 43,000 feet, continued toward the projected position of the Stealth bomber. The fighter pilots listened to the radar controller alternately warn the Soviet aircraft, then change to Guard and call the B-2. The orders to the pilot of the bomber went unanswered.

Chuck Matthews had resigned himself to the only choice he had left. He needed to create a major distraction in order for his desperate plan to work.

General Brotskharnov, staring intently through the curved windshield, saw flecks of blue sky overhead. "We must descend to stay in the clouds."

Matthews, contemplating the odds of his survival, wordlessly programmed the flight director to descend back to 40,000 feet.

SUNDOWNER LEAD

The F-14 passed over Shadow 37 a half mile off the bomber's left wing. The B-2 was visible as it descended through the wisps of clouds.

"O . . . kay," the pilot said to himself as he called the-Hawkeye and started a left 180-degree turn. "Eight Ball, Sundowner One has a tally on the B-2."

"Roger. Stand by."

"Two," the pilot radioed, "come port with me and let's start a descent."

"Two."

The fighter pilot eased the Tomcat's nose down and talked to his flight again. "Hal, you and Rich fly high cover."

"Three."

"Four."

"Sundowner lead," the Hawkeye controller said in a slow, even voice. "Make visual contact with the crew and attempt comm on Guard—call sign Shadow Three Seven. Have the aircraft turn toward Hawaii."

"Roger," the Tomcat pilot radioed. "Sundowners, come up Guard."

"Two."

"Three."

"Four."

Sundowner One looked over his shoulder. "Two, stay high behind me."

"Copy."

The lead F-14 closed rapidly on the B-2, then deployed his speed brakes and radioed the bomber on 243.0. "Shadow Three Seven, Sundowner lead on Guard. Come port one-five-zero . . . acknowledge."

Matthews, startled by the unexpected radio call, looked out of his side window as the Tomcat slid into view. The pilot raised his visor and waved. Brotskharnov swore loudly and grabbed the flight controls, shoving the nose down.

"Jesus Christ," Matthews said, feeling the negative g load as loose objects floated up in the cockpit.

Simmons, almost dropping his revolver, gripped his seat tightly.

"Shadow Three Seven," the F-14 pilot said as he countered the violent maneuver. "We have been ordered to shoot you down. Do you copy?"

Matthews decided to make his move. "Let me have the controls!"

Brotskharnov appeared suspicious, then released the stick.

"I know the aircraft better," Matthews shouted, clutching the control stick. "I can evade them!"

The B-2 was between cloud layers when Matthews snapped the bomber into a tight left turn. "Check out the right," Matthews ordered. "See anyone?"

Brotskharnov and Simmons leaned closer to the right side window, gazing out over the wing. Matthews, seizing the opportunity, reached up and pulled his red-flagged ejection seat pin. The rocket-powered seat was now armed to fire.

Matthews quickly stuffed the bright cloth and metal pin under his left thigh as Brotskharnov turned to him. "I do not see fighters."

"Keep checking," Matthews replied, then trimmed the B-2's nose full up, fighting the stick to keep the bomber from climbing.

"Shadow Three Seven," the F-14 pilot radioed in a strained voice. "I am going to fire a missile in thirty seconds. Turn to one-five-zero . . . your last warning."

The Tomcat dropped back 200 yards as the pilot selected master arm on and heard the lock-on tone. "Ten seconds," the pilot radioed, watching the bomber turn again. "Five seconds."

Matthews quickly moved his hand toward the alternate ejection handle. The bomber was nearing a thick wall of clouds when the F-14 pilot fired a Sidewinder at Shadow 37.

"Fox Two!"

Matthews jinked the bomber up. Brotskharnov and Simmons braced themselves as the B-2 plunged into the cloud bank. The missile, fired too close to track properly, flashed under the bomber's left wing.

The Hawkeye controller watched the Sidewinder continue toward the horizon, then noticed something alarming. "The MIGs fired!" the radar controller shouted over Guard. "They detected your shot! Two missiles . . . the MiGs have two missiles away.''

''Sundowners,'' the flight leader ordered, ''unload—let's go for the deck! Take it down!''

''Oh, Jesus!'' a voice shouted as Matthews grasped his ejection handle. ''Lead is on fire! Lead is hit!''

''All aircraft,'' the Hawkeye controller shouted, ''go Weapons Hold . . . Weapons Hold.''

Matthews gripped the handle firmly, focusing on the next three seconds. His mind raced as he fought to hold the nose in level flight.

Adrenaline pumping, Matthews paused a fraction of a second, then yanked on the ejection handle.

The explosive blast hurled the American pilot more than 150 feet above the B-2. Matthews tumbled through the sky, separated from his seat, then went into free-fall to a lower altitude, where his parachute would automatically open.

The Stealth, trimmed full nose up, pitched violently upward into the clouds. Brotskharnov, blinded and burned by the rocket blast, slumped semiconscious in his seat. The Russian pilot groaned in agony as Simmons unstrapped, then staggered to grab Matthews's control stick. The entire front and left side of the technician's body was blackened by the explosive ejection.

Simmons grasped the stick with his burned hands, shoving forward to lower the nose. He could barely see as he forced the B-2's nose toward level flight. Unaware that the trim was full nose up, the technician kept pressure on the stick. His mind, desperate in his pain and panic, searched for a way to remain alive.

Simmons horsed the bomber around, forcing the nose down. Feeling the howling wind increase, Simmons pulled the three throttles back to idle and raised the nose.

Brotskharnov, now unconscious, was hanging over the left side of his ejection seat. His limp body was impeding Simmons's efforts to control the B-2. The technician shoved the Russian back and to the right. Brotskharnov's head flopped over onto his right shoulder, pulling his upper torso over the right side of the seat.

The gravely injured technician, on his knees in the cavity left by the pilot's seat, felt the bomber tremble at the verge of a stall. The B-2, pointed skyward, was losing speed rapidly. As the airspeed decayed, the nose dropped dangerously low.

Simmons, recognizing that the Stealth was becoming unmaneuverable, shoved the throttles forward and pulled savagely on the control stick. Shadow 37 stalled, rolled off on the right wing, then spun out of control toward the cold, windswept sea.

The bomber, spinning inverted, fell seven miles through the dark clouds as Simmons tried to recover control of the aircraft. He cried out in anguish as the image of Irina Rykhov flashed through his mind. He was rolling the B-2 when it emerged from the low rain clouds. As he screamed in terror, Shadow 37 slammed into the water and exploded in a thunderous fireball.

EPILOGUE

Lieutenant Colonel Charles Matthews was the only witness to the crash of Shadow 37.

He was hanging from his parachute, descending in the cold rain, when the Stealth bomber exploded three miles away. The flash and low, rolling rumble startled the B-2 pilot as he prepared his life raft for entry into the storm-tossed ocean. Matthews plunged into the ice-cold water, gasping for air as his windswept parachute dragged him over 200 yards through the towering waves. He swallowed two gulps of seawater before he could release the parachute risers.

Freeing himself from the parachute canopy, he struggled into the one-man raft, shivering uncontrollably until he was able to zip the raft's rubber and nylon cover closed around his neck.

Sundowner One, hit by the Soviet air-to-air missile, trailed flames from its starboard side until the pilot secured the right engine. The blazing fire went out after the engine fuel and hydraulic systems were stopcocked.

The F-14 limped back to the USS *Carl Vinson* where the

crew discovered the right main landing gear was jammed in the up position. After repeated attempts to deploy the landing gear the crew faced the inevitable; they would have to abandon the wounded Tomcat.

The pilot, who was the operations officer of VF-111, conferred with the Air Boss, briefed his radar intercept officer, then flew by the carrier and made a controlled ejection 300 yards to the left of the bridge.

Both men arced through the freezing rain, separated from their seats, then stopped in midair as their parachutes opened. They watched the F-14, nose down, dive into the mountainous waves and disappear.

The radar intercept officer, followed by the pilot, splashed down. Quickly releasing their parachutes, they fought to keep their heads above water as the giant waves washed over them.

Overhead, an SH-3 Sea King plane-guard helicopter pitched and rolled as the pilot wrestled the controls. Seconds later, a rescue harness was lowered to the F-14 crew.

The RIO grabbed the sling in a death-grip, placed it over his head and slipped the collar under his armpits. The hoist operator immediately raised the officer to the helicopter's open hatch, helped him in, then lowered the harness to the other crewman.

The pilot, freezing and exhausted, tried in vain to don the collar as it skipped across the swells. The hoist operator, seeing that the pilot was in jeopardy, ordered the swimmer into the water.

The rescue specialist, wearing a thick wetsuit, leaped from the Sea King and assisted the fatigued pilot into the elusive harness. The hoist operator quickly plucked the pilot from the water and again lowered the sling. The swimmer was then winched up to the hatch while the Sea King headed for the *Carl Vinson*.

Both Tomcat crewmen were returned to flight status forty-eight hours later.

• • •

American and Soviet carrier aircraft separated without further escalations in hostilities, but tensions remained high as both sides evaluated the situation.

The message traffic increased threefold during the two hours after the air-to-air missile attack. Both governments voiced cautious apologies and encouraged open discussions to prevent further incidents.

Aircraft from *Carl Vinson*, supplemented by a variety of airplanes from Alaska, continued the search for the Stealth bomber.

Three hours after Shadow 37 had actually crashed, with the weather worsening and darkness approaching, the search was cancelled. By that time, if it had not crashed, the commanders agreed, it would have already landed on Russian soil.

Twenty-five minutes after the search was terminated, a White House message was sent to the task force commander who was on the *Carl Vinson*. The message stated that the president of the Soviet Union had guaranteed the safe and expeditious return of the crew and the aircraft if the bomber was found to have landed anywhere in Russia.

Chuck Matthews, after spending a chilly night in his life raft, heard a jet early the next morning. He fired four flares, then shouted with joy as the jet turned toward him.

Matthews was surprised when the Sukhoi Su-27 pilot circled the raft twice and rocked his wings. The Russian fighter pilot, flying a regular maritime patrol, radioed the coordinates to the *Tbilisi* and then returned to the carrier.

Fifty minutes later, Matthews was hoisted aboard a Soviet helicopter and flown to the USS *Carl Vinson*.

After Matthews had undergone a quick debrief, the White House was immediately notified of the fate of Shadow 37 and Major Paul Evans.

Matthews remained on board the carrier for twenty-four hours before being transported to Elmendorf Air Force Base. From there, he was flown to Washington, D.C., in an Air

Force KC-135, and was thoroughly debriefed at the White House and the Pentagon. After a thirty-day leave, Matthews returned to Whiteman Air Force Base where he was promoted to squadron commanding officer.

Aerial photographs of San Julian after the air attack indicated that the Stealth hangar had been gutted by fire. The Joint Chiefs assessed the damage and concluded that the tapes that Matthews had mentioned must have been destroyed. The Stealth was gone, but the secrets of its technology remained documented only in the United States. Nevertheless, the president of the Soviet Union publicly apologized for the B 2 affair, and pledged to prosecute the chief of the KGB. The promise was fulfilled when Vladimir Golodnikov was sentenced to spend the rest of his life in the Borisovka Prison. Only a few individuals close to the Soviet president knew that Golodnikov had never reached the prison. His body, accompanied by papers with a false identification, had been buried in a shallow grave at a cemetery on the outskirts of Moscow.

Gennadi Levchenko and Natanoly Obukhov, relieved to learn that Vladimir Golodnikov had confessed to directing the rogue Stealth operation, had been returned to Moscow after the former KGB chief had been sentenced.

Levchenko was reassigned to duty in the United States and continued to work with Irina Rykhov and Aleksey Pankyev. The threesome would be responsible for gleaning critical information about the Navy's A-12 Avenger II advanced tactical aircraft.

Gennadi Levchenko, coordinating the efforts of Rykhov and Pankyev, had later established a residence close to Holloman Air Force Base, New Mexico. He had been pleased when security guidelines had been relaxed, allowing the F-117A Stealth attack aircraft to transition from Tonapah to Holloman.

His next assignment involved finding a knowledgeable F-

117A crewmember to join the fold. The Kremlin had given the operation a high priority.

Relations with Cuba remained extremely volatile. Moscow, embarrassed and bewildered by the fiery strong man, in agreement with the United States, penalized Castro for his country's participation in the hijacking by cutting off further subsidies unless Cuba could compensate in some measure for the loss of the B-2 bomber.

However, in weekly broadcasts Castro continually threatened to sink the American aircraft carriers if the United States should provoke him again. The threat was not taken too seriously though President Jarrett kept two carrier groups in the Gulf of Mexico. The carrier air wings had remained on five-minute alert, with an airborne two-fighter BARCAP, for three weeks. At that point, having had only one uneventful MiG encounter, the president had elected to stand down from the alert five status and operate at normal tempo.

Fidel Castro stubbornly refused to agree to any restitution agreement. He renewed his pledge to perfect a single Leninist party in the Western hemisphere based on the principles of centralism. The last chapter in his reign of terror was only pages away.